Jezebel

Jezebel

❁

Gordon A. Kessler

For information address: Gordon A. Kessler, P.O. Box 1101,
Newton, Kansas 67114-1101 or www.jezebelthenovel.com
Fax: 1-800-567-6797
Comments welcome

This book was printed in the United States of America.

To order additional copies of this book, contact:
Gordon A. Kessler
P.O. Box 1101
Newton, Kansas 67114
or on the Internet at: www.Jezebelthenovel.com

Dedication

To those who kept the faith:

Audrey and Dustin, Mom and Gary, Karen, Rhonda, Carol, Roxy, Bonnie, Hazel, Colleen, Gayle, Mike, Mark, Steve, Wynn, Vickie and the rest of the critique group and the KWA

Thank you, the reader, for forgiving some creative warps in time as this novel was written in 1992 and since revised, and thank you Wichita and Sedgwick County, for allowing a little artistic license and a few liberties with our fair city including the merger of certain city and county offices.

Special thanks to Dr. Deborah Briggs,
Department of Veterinary Diagnosis
Kansas State University
Thanks for the tour
and
Mike McQuay, whose talent as a writer was only surpassed by his ability and enthusiasm to teach others. Thanks, Mike, and rest in peace.

Dedicated to Gervase Arwood Michael Kessler

PREFACE

One day, during a hard winter, a deer crossed our snowed-up garden fence and was torn to pieces by my three dogs. As I stood horror-stricken by the mutilated corpse I became conscious of the unconditional faith which I placed in the social inhibition of these blood-thirsty beasts, for my children were at that time smaller and more (defenseless) than the deer whose gory remains lay before me in the snow. I was myself astonished at the absolute fearlessness with which I daily entrusted the fragile limbs of my children to the wolflike jaws.

—Konrad Lorenz, *Man Meets Dog*

Lying beside me is a predator weighing about 35 kilograms, baring in his sleep a set of recurved teeth designed specifically to rend the flesh and crack the bones of large animals. Along comes my daughter, Ariana, four years of age and weighing about 20 kilograms, looking for trouble as must all healthy children of her age. Aha! Here sleeps the big hairy beast, almost twice her weight and countless times her equal in strength and swiftness-but, in sleep, defenseless. Ariana hurls herself onto the sleeping form, her weight driving a grunt from the animal's lungs and he awakens, nosing her face affectionately before rolling clumsily onto his back, paws in the air, eager at once for such abuse as the child can dish out.

—John C. Mcloughlin, *The Canine Clan*

PROLOGUE

The firefighters were the first victims. As they responded to the call of a downtown high-rise fire, in their minds they pictured an inferno.

The windshield of the blood red hook-and-ladder truck, like a storefront window, made it easy to see the three of them in the front seat. The enormous fire engine was the pride of the Wichita Fire Department, the newest member of its fleet. When it came lumbering down the street, bystanders would dispense with all other distractions and watch. On this day, with its red lights pulsing, air horn blasting and siren keening through the brittle morning air, the citizens stopped and stared. Although the high horsepower Detroit Diesel motor pushed them at over fifty miles per hour, the shear massiveness of the twenty-ton fire truck made it appear to be cruising along only half that fast.

Kellogg Avenue during morning rush hour in Wichita, Kansas, was not a pleasant place to drive on an ice-sheeted day in February. Though confident, Fire Captain Jill Sawyer was tense at the wheel, every muscle taut. She concentrated on some of the less attentive traffic in front of them and the corner they must make a mile ahead at Broadway.

Lieutenant George Chambers rode shotgun. His eyes scanned the roadway as he gave out cautions like, "To the right" and "Watch that blue Chevy."

The firehouse mascot, a seven-year-old Dalmatian named Burney, took his earned place on the seat in between. Even the dog was on edge, his neck rigid and eyes alert. He whined at unaware drivers who cut them off, sometimes letting out sharp *yips* in complaint.

Four more of the squad's firefighters were in the separate crew cab behind.

They were all heroes.

Although the last of a dying tradition of fire station mascots, even Burney had been honored three times for bravery. Most recently he'd vaulted through the window of a fire-engulfed mobile home and sniffed out a three-year-old hiding in a clothes hamper.

Burney was wired. He took his job seriously.

Jill glanced at him.

The Dalmatian's lips stretched in what looked like a smile. He growled at a white van getting a little close to their right front fender.

George Chambers said, "Tell 'im, Burney."

"Good boy, Burney," Jill said and just before she looked back to the road she saw the dog give her a quick glance and slap his tail once on the seat in acknowledgement.

Jill edged the truck to the left side of their lane to pass the van safely, knowing she'd have to get around the guy and back into the right turning lane soon.

The van matched their speed as if racing them.

"Dumb bastard," George Chambers said.

"What's he trying to do?" Jill said grimacing as she guided the big engine by a car on the left.

Burney barked and put his paws on the dash.

"Jeez," George said, "the guy's nuts."

"I'll have to slow down and let him have the road," Jill said.

"No, wait, *he's* slowing down," George said and began rolling down his window. "I think the asshole wants to talk."

"Don't bother, we'll shoot on by."

"It's that guy—that foamer," George said. "I'm going to tell him to get the hell out of the way."

Burney shifted over to George's lap and looked down through the window.

"What, foamer?" Jill asked.

There were always guys hanging around the fire station. The firefighters called them foamers because they seemed to nearly foam at the mouth with enthusiasm at even the mention or sight of a fire truck. They were like little boys who always wanted to be firemen when they grew up—turn on the siren, brave the fires—but they'd never made it. Many of them were doctors and lawyers, but the majority of them were average Joes. To Jill, they were all nuts but harmless except when their fanaticism got in the way.

Burney growled.

Jill glanced over once more and saw the dog's toothy grin and thought it was for the guy in the white van.

A car changed lanes in front of them and Jill had to tap the brake to avoid it. When she looked back, she could see through the side-view mirror that the van had stayed constant alongside.

"What the hell, Burney?" George said.

Burney was showing *George* his teeth, the dog's eyes intense.

Jill raised her voice. "Burney! Sit, boy!" She was trading glances now between the busy roadway and the dog.

"Jesus, Burney. Wadid I do?" George said.

Jill demanded, "I said sit, Burney! No!"

It was a sudden move, like a trap being sprung. Burney swung around and grabbed Jill by her throat.

The pain was overwhelming. Jill tried to pull away. She inadvertently turned the wheel. The huge mass of steel responded violently, careening toward the median. She attempted to correct her mistake. The slick road was unforgiving.

She stomped for the brake. Disoriented, she punched the accelerator.

They crested the overpass above I-35 and crashed through two concrete barricades, leaping an eight-foot gap separating the opposing lanes. They fishtailed into the oncoming lane of traffic on the other side.

Warm blood streamed down Jill's chest—hot rivulets down her back and shoulder. Burney had ripped into her jugular.

"God, Burney," she cried, her right hand around the dog's blood-soaked snout. She slapped at the dog's face. No response. Clamped on like a bulldog.

"Damn it!" George said reaching for the dog. Centrifugal force pushed him back into the door on his side before he could grab a hold.

Whipping to the right, the sixty-foot fire engine swatted a sand-spreader truck from the glazed pavement. The orange dump truck crashed onto its side on the shoulder.

For the next twenty yards, the fire truck skidded sideways on the eight-lane thoroughfare until its big tires found a small patch of dry roadway. Delicately balanced on the driver's side wheels, it skated for another fifty feet like a daredevil stunt act. When the tires blew out, the bottom side panel grated into the boulevard's surface with a tremendous screeching that could be heard throughout the downtown area.

Like an empty drum, it began a cumbersome roll.

Ladders broke away from the truck's sides and skittered across the lanes.

Four hoses slung out from the thing like tentacles of a tormented squid. Their heavy nozzles smacked the concrete in loud cracks as they bounced down the roadway. One found the windshield of a group of carpoolers in a Toyota SUV. It smashed through, crushing the driver's chest and hooked into the steering column. The SUV suddenly became a pull toy behind the tumbling apparatus, yanked and jerked along as it was forced to follow.

The ninety-five foot aerial-platform arm tore away from its turret on the back, telescoped out to its full length and flipped end over end, stabbing the highway and automobiles like a child sticking at toads.

The cars and pickup trucks in front of the debacle slid on the frosted pavement, smashing into one another as they attempted to avoid the melee.

The fire engine rolled on, demolishing the vehicles in its path, crushing them like bugs into flattened hunks of iron. It was as if a maniacal auto-smashing machine had been set loose on the city.

Finally slapping down the guardrail, the behemoth tumbled over the edge of the highway and fell nose first. It slammed into the middle of Interstate 35's southbound lane forty feet below.

The conflagration that followed would burn beyond recognition the bodies of the three in the front seat. In the aftermath, five civilians would be found dead in their cars along with twenty-three other citizens that were seriously injured.

The four firefighters in the back compartment would make it through the devastation with only minor concussions and burns along with a few cuts and scrapes. Sawyer and Chambers would never know the terrible irony: that they had been summoned to a false alarm—a prank.

Investigators would be unable to determine an obvious reason for the driver to lose control of Engine No. 97. They interviewed the witnesses. Some, in the opposing lanes, could see inside the cab as the fire engine highballed toward them. One man had seen something in a glance. From a distance of twenty-five yards during that brief moment just prior to the crash, he said it looked as though the dog had only reached over to give the driver a lick—a gesture of affection for his longtime friend and master. Still, that man's wife, sitting next to him on the passenger's side at the time, would recount the incredible fear and surprise she saw in the *rider's* face as he gaped over at the driver and the dog. The investigators thought nothing of it. How could the woman be sure of what she had seen at that speed and distance?

During the autopsy, the medical examiner would not find the jagged opening Burney had torn into Jill Sawyer's throat among the charred tissue. No one would consider linking this catastrophe to the ensuing slaughter six months later—except Tony Parker.

But, he'd never talk.

Wichita, Kansas, is a thriving oasis of commerce and technology located in the middle of the golden wheat fields and fertile plains of America's breadbasket. More than 300,000 people of every nationality and origin call the city home and flourish there. Known affectionately as "River City" by its citizens, it is the "Air Capital" to the rest of the world. Many of the premier influences in aviation history began in this town: pioneers such as Cessna, Beech, Stearman and Lear. It still hosts Boeing, Raytheon, Cessna, and Bombardier-Learjet and leads the world in the production of private aircraft.

In contrast, Wichita is no less proud of its "Old West" reputation for being a hub for rugged cowboys and gunslingers and is especially proud of its Native American heritage.

On a Friday morning, late in August, this letter appeared in the editorial section of the *Wichita Post* newspaper:

Dear Editor,

I am amazed at the outcry of so many Wichita citizens concerned with the recent pit-bull attacks. Their ignorance is unimaginable. Pit bulls are not the problem in this city. It is those few pit-bull owners who have trained their dogs to be potential problems. Now, it seems that it is not only pit pulls that some groups are against but all dogs in general. It is my opinion, from experience, that few dogs are naturally bad or vicious. It takes abuse and unnecessary attack training to exacerbate a dog's pre-domesticated, natural aggression and make the dog dangerous. It's those people who teach these dogs to be harmful that should be put away, banned from our city.

For more than fifteen thousand years, man and dog have cohabited. Dogs have been trained to be our companions, our best friends, and they have done a very good job of it. They have helped to provide for our families, protected us, saved our lives, and some even have died defending us, their masters. Let's not blame the dog for the evil that is in man.

Tony Parker,
Animal Control Director
Sedgwick County

CHAPTER 1

R inging. . . .
The morning sunlight blasted through a big picture window, looking out onto a freshly cut, but browning, front yard. Inside, the living-room furniture was modern but not the least bit extravagant. Near the window, the blaring television was tuned to the usual *Tom and Jerry* show, and from another room, an infant screamed as loudly as its sixteen-month-old lungs would allow. A typical Friday morning.

Just as a bulldog bit Tom in the cartoon, the phone rang for the second time, and six-year-old Nicholas Parker raced into the room. He dropped to his knees and crawled behind a chair in a nearby corner. There he sat, motionless—waiting. Motionless except for his heaving chest and flaring nostrils, as he tried to quiet his oxygen-starved lungs. Grape juice from this morning's breakfast stained his otherwise bright white T-shirt. His blue jeans, just bought the week before at the local Wal Mart, already showed torturous wear on the knees.

Ringing. . . .

With his bare feet tucked under his buttocks, he hunched over. A huge flurry of white and brown St. Bernard charged into the doorway and stopped and stood as a statue. The boy checked his breathing, and his lungs held tight to the last breath, capturing every molecule of oxygen. A drop of sweat rolled from underneath the boy's blond hair, overhanging his forehead. It trickled down to his brow, paused there for a moment and then seeped into his wide-open left eye. It burned. The youngster winced and blinked to wash out the salt.

Ringing. . . .

The massive dog stomped farther into the room, its keen ears perked, ready to detect even the slightest disturbance. The Saint's large paws jolted its frame with every lumbering step, and its hide shifted loosely on its body like a large furry parka several sizes too big. The huge animal stopped sideways to the chair, close enough for the boy to reach out and touch it. It lifted its large head and sniffed the air. Its sensitive nose seemed to tell it the human child had been there recently, and probably was still. It moved its head around the room, sniffing, searching for any sign, any movement, any part of the boy.

The phone rang for the fifth time. Nicholas Parker's eyes shifted around the temporary refuge. His lungs pleaded for air. He had to breathe, his body insisted on it. He knew when he did the predator would hear him, yet he had to. He released the air in his lungs slowly from his bottom lip. His hot breath warmed his upper lip but cooled the sweat-covered skin above it. No sound came out, yet the dog snapped its head with ear cocked in reaction. Perhaps it'd heard it. Perhaps it'd smelled the boy's breath, saturated with grape juice.

"Raptor! Help, raptor attack!" the boy yelled frantically, gasping for air.

He shoved the chair out of the way with his forearm and scampered out from behind it, opposite the dog.

Running across the sofa, he leaped between the sofa back and a lamp on a stand beside it. The St. Bernard bolted across the room, barking in the excitement of the chase. It also bounded onto the sofa and brushed by the lamp, knocking it to the floor with a shattering crash.

*_*_*

"All right, you two, no more late night horror shows for you," Tony Parker said sternly.

He walked through the living room doorway from the kitchen with a newspaper in his hand. After yanking the cord from the wall outlet, he picked the broken lamp up from the floor and wondered if there might still be enough Super Glue left in the kitchen drawer to fix the thing for a third time.

He set the lamp on a nearby chair then reached to the end table and picked up the phone. His wavy, dark-brown hair and tanned skin contrasted with the white T-shirt he also wore, minus the grape juice. His broad shoulders and muscular biceps stretched the tight knit fabric, and it hung loosely only at the waist, although, a bit of a paunch showed around his middle.

"Hello, hello—? I'm sorry, I can't hear you. Can you hold on just a minute?"

Parker tucked the newspaper under his arm and cupped one hand over the phone.

"Honey, can you do something about all this noise? I'm on the phone!" he yelled out, hoping his wife Julie would come to his rescue.

With no answer, he quickly set the phone and paper down and took the matter into his own hands as the two primary offenders ran by. He snatched up his son and swung him gently to his knees. Grabbing the collar of the St. Bernard at full locomotion proved a much more difficult task, but he managed with a strained grunt.

"That's enough, Nick! Settle down, I'm on the phone!"

Nicholas glanced up solemnly, head bowed. The dog mimicked him with a similar, but much sadder, look. Parker released the two culprits and scanned the room for the TV remote. As usual, it was nowhere in sight. He picked up the phone, put a finger in one ear and raised the receiver to the other.

"Come on, Yankee," Nicholas yelled, escaping through the doorway with the dog close behind. "Now, you can be *Alien!*"

"I'm sorry, go ahead." Parker shook his head.

"Yeah, Mr. Parker?"

"Hi Chin." Parker recognized the voice of Tommy Chin, a twenty-five-year-old Vietnamese immigrant and his second in command. "Excuse the noise. What's up?"

"We just received a call from a woman out in Sand Creek. Skunk. I thought you might want to go since it's closest to your end of town," Chin said.

"Yeah sure, I'll run out there first. I was just getting ready to hit the door. Got a name?"

"The caller is a Mrs. Bumfield, second house, south end of town."

"Since there're only about a dozen houses in that entire town, she shouldn't be hard to find. I'll take care of it and be in soon." Parker hung up.

"Julie! Jooolee!" he called, looking up the stairs to the second floor bedrooms.

He turned to check the kitchen and bumped into her, the baby in her arms. Julie's beauty showed through her lightly wrinkled face, distressed dishwater-blonde hair, and food-splattered blouse. Laugh lines accentuated her polished-brown eyes.

"Whoa, I'm sorry, sweetheart. I've got to go," he said with his hands on her arms. "Hey, my letter to the editor made this morning's paper."

Julie's eyes rolled. "Oh boy, are you ready for the flak?"

"I wouldn't have sent it in if I wasn't."

"By the way," Julie said in a reprimanding tone, "you left the seat up on the toilet again this morning."

Parker chuckled. "Uh-oh, was the water cold? You didn't get stuck, did you?"

Julie frowned. "It's not funny, Tony Parker. I'll get even someday."

"Oooh, I'm shakin'." He kissed little Audrey on her baby food-smeared face and then his unprepared wife on the lips with a smack. "Mmm, bananas, my favorite."

Parker broke away and scooped up his truck keys along with a seldom-used pager from the kitchen counter. He hated pagers. To him, being tied down with telephones and radios was bad enough. After stepping into the adjoining laundry room, he picked a black name badge off a shelf over the dryer and then grabbed a freshly ironed, light blue uniform shirt from a hanger on a closet rod to the side. He put the shirt on quickly and pinned on the badge as he passed Julie and headed for the front door. The badge read *T. PARKER* in big white letters.

"You oughta be shaking," Julie scolded as he walked by. She kicked him in the butt softly. "Now get out of here."

"Tell Nick 'bye for me, will you?" he said, walking by the stairs.

"*Graaa!* I'm going to eat you!" Nicholas yelled, jumping onto his father's back, his arms wrapping around his neck.

"Why, you little booger." Parker pulled his son around to his chest. "Where'd you come from?"

"I'm not a booger. I'm a *ill-a-jitmut alien*," Nicholas exclaimed, "and I'm going to eat you!"

"Not if I eat you first!" Parker snarled back. He put his lips on his son's neck and blew, making a loud, flatulent sound.

Nicholas erupted in ecstatic giggles.

"Besides, I think you mean an *illegal* alien, and they don't eat people, you poor confused child."

"Yeah, but *ill-a-jitmut* aliens do!"

"We'll have to discuss this later. I've got to go, you vicious alien." Parker flipped his son upside down and then set him gently on his feet. "I'll finish eating you tonight."

"Okay, Daddy," Nicholas said cheerfully. "Then we can play a game. I know, *Dweebs, Geeks, and Weird-oooos!*"

"I can't wait." Tony looked at Julie with a reluctant smile.

Julie returned an understanding grin. "Have a good day—and be careful, darling. Oh, and remind everyone at work about our anniversary picnic on Sunday. Find out how many might show up."

Tony gave her his most charming smile, pursed his lips and then ducked out the door. He hustled out to the white, four-wheel-drive GMC Jimmy truck with a big *Sedgwick County Animal Control* sign on the side, and he drove off.

*_*_*

Julie Parker carried Audrey up the stairs to the master bathroom. She set her daughter on a fluffy, sky-blue bath mat and began drawing water in the tub.

"Time for your bath, young lady." She started pulling the little girl's pajamas off. Audrey gurgled a happy reply.

Julie's mind drifted back to the many trying times she and Tony had seen. Things would be better soon. They had to be. They'd been through so much. Now their luck would change. They finally had control of their lives, and they seemed headed in the right direction.

Tony and Julie had been sweethearts since high school, with a long, four-year intermission when he joined the Marines. They'd decided a commitment during that time wouldn't be fair to either of them. When he came home, they realized they had been miserable the whole time, and they married two years later. Nicholas came along just after Tony finished college and was working for Sedgwick County as an animal control officer. Julie was teaching third grade at a local public school. When Nick was not quite a year old, Tony went back to school at Kansas State, a hundred and forty miles away, to get his doctor's degree in veterinary medicine. It was a three-year, post-graduate program, and he could only come home on the weekends. It had been tough on both of them, but they hoped the sacrifice would be worthwhile someday.

Then, just two years ago, Julie found out she was pregnant, and there were complications. Tony quit school to be with the family and was fortunate enough to hook the Sedgwick County Animal Control Director's job. He only had a year left of vet school, but they hoped he'd be able to go back within a couple of years.

They had spent many sleepless nights watching over little, three-pound Audrey, struggling for life in the terrible contraption that confined her. Julie remembered the many tears they'd shed. A clear-plastic-covered incubator seemed an awful place for an innocent, fragile baby girl.

Having a *preemie*, teetering on the edge of life and death, had been a terrible, anxious time. Not having adequate insurance to cover the huge medical expenses only added to the stress. Now, at sixteen months, Audrey grew strong and healthy and had been out of the hospital for nearly a year, but her parents were still overly protective. A sniffle, a cough, a slight fever, and they rushed to the emergency room in a race for life.

Tony landing the Director's job was the one lucky break they'd had for some time. Being the chief dogcatcher wasn't a terribly dangerous job. He'd been bitten a couple of times: once, by an overexcited Chihuahua, and another time by a frightened Siamese cat. Nothing even close to life threatening had happened, but still, Julie worried.

CHAPTER 2

"AC One to dispatch," Tony Parker called over the microphone as he picked up speed and switched on his emergency lights.

"Dispatcher," a female voice answered. "Go ahead, Mr. Parker."

"Good morning, Janet. Just checking in. I'm proceeding to the call in Sand Creek."

"Ten-four, AC One. Be advised AC Four is also proceeding to the scene and has requested you meet at Fifty-third and Meridian to ride together."

Sarah! What's that little vixen going to do to try to fluster me this time?

Parker grinned. "All right, Janet. Thanks. AC One out."

Sarah Hill had become Tony Parker's right hand over the last year and a half since she'd come on board as one of Sedgwick County's fourteen animal control officers. Just out of college with a zoology degree, she was sharp and great with animals. She didn't need to be told what to do. She and Tony worked well together and shared some sort of chemistry.

He loved Julie deeply and had since high school. He needed her. She was a solid place to go when he needed strength. He depended upon her to be there *always* to listen to his complaints about the world and to defend him blindly when he found himself against the odds. But the passion seemed to be growing stale, withering. Their sex life had become too predictable, ordinary, expected, like the old weekly bath, taken every Saturday night whether needed or not.

Sarah was fresh and different, exciting and youthful. She made Parker feel young when she teased and flirted with him. To imagine he could have her at the snap of a finger excited him. Yet, he knew nothing would ever happen. It gave him a sense of security in his married life, a feeling he could never have if he were to have an affair. After all, he spent all of his off time with his family, and the only occasions he was with Sarah, they were busy working.

Sarah Hill sat parked and waiting in her baby blue Ford van at the convenience store on the corner of Fifty-third and Meridian Streets. Parker pulled in alongside, and Hill hopped out of her animal-control van, purse in hand, and trotted over to the Jimmy's passenger side.

Parker watched as she passed by the front of the Jimmy. He stared at her features: the long, soft, light-blonde hair tucked under the dark-blue Sedgwick County Animal Control cap; the tanned face, pudding smooth with delicate features; the large, vibrant-blue eyes; the generous breasts jiggling under the light-blue blouse as she trotted; the slim but nicely rounded butt poured into dark-blue slacks—the perfect definition of *tight ass*. She had a body that looked great, even hidden in the two-tone blue uniform that must have been tailor fit—none of the other women officers modeled theirs so well.

She jumped in.

"Hi, handsome," Sarah Hill said in her perky voice. "How about giving a girl a ride?"

"Morning, Sarah," he said, as he thought, *You're as unbelievably beautiful as always.*

Parker pulled onto the gravel road and headed north toward Sand Creek.

"Skunk, huh?" Hill wrinkled her nose. "I'd rather take on a bear. It takes forever to get rid of that nasty smell."

"Yeah, and they've really been bad this season. Still better than dealing with the average human, though. Ninety-nine percent are assholes. But animals are different. They aren't naturally corrupt like people. They're kind of innocent."

"Well, you're in a warm and fuzzy mood this morning. But, that's what I like about you, Tone." Sarah Hill smiled. "You and I think a lot alike. We have the same passion for animals. Not so much of a passion for our *fellow man* though."

Parker nodded. "It's the masters who are the problem, not the pets. Most people don't understand that about us *heartless* dogcatch-ers. They think we enjoy chasing and putting down their beloved but neglected pets. They let them run loose only to get run over or poi-soned. They abandon them to become a nuisance and eventually starve. They train them to be vicious, causing people to misunder-stand and fear them. They don't get them the proper vaccinations, so their animals get infections and diseases. They don't spay or neuter them, so their pets give birth to more deprived and unwanted ani-mals. The average animal owner is as irresponsible with their pets as they are with themselves."

Hill chuckled. "Wow, we're getting deep. It's too early in the morning to think this serious. But, by the way, I liked your letter to the editor."

"Oh, you saw it? Thanks." *At least someone appreciated it.*

Sarah Hill's attention went to her hands. "Ah man! My hands look like hell." She opened her purse and took out a tube of lotion. "The damned apartment manager still hasn't gotten anybody to fix my frickin' dishwasher." She popped the lid back, squirted out a gener-ous amount and began rubbing her hands together.

She glanced over at Parker's hands on the steering wheel. "Damn, Tone, talk about lobster hands."

"What?" Parker said. "They're not so bad."

"Let me see." Hill pried his right hand from the wheel. "Relax, loosen up. I'm not going to bite you—yet."

Parker frowned at her.

"What you need is some of this organic hand lotion. It has aloe in it. Great stuff."

She began rubbing the lotion into his hand. It smelled sweet, like fresh, sliced peaches. It felt nice, sensual somehow. He liked it, but he shouldn't. He was a married man. Having his hand rubbed by a beautiful young woman seemed a little adulterous—maybe.

Hill grinned. "Nothing like a good, old fashion hand job, huh Tone?"

"Sarah!" Parker said in the same tone he used to tell Nicholas not to be naughty.

She paid no attention. "You have such big, strong hands. Big—long fingers." Sarah rubbed firmly. She rubbed and massaged his hand. Each finger, one at a time. Rubbing the slick warm lotion into his skin. Each finger, rubbing, massaging, squeezing. Rubbing back and forth, up and down, massaging, squeezing, milking each finger with both hands.

"Okay, I think that one's done." She helped to put his now limp hand back on the wheel as if it had become disabled.

"Sarah," Parker started again, "I don't think you ought to do this."

"Sheesh, Tone, lighten up," Hill said in her playful voice. "Does Julie have that short a leash on you? I mean, it's not like you're banging me on the hood of the truck or something."

What an idea! Parker thought.

"Come on, hand it over," She insisted. "You can't go around with one soft hand and one like an armadillo paw."

That was reasonable. Besides, it did feel very good. Parker frowned but brought his left hand across slowly. Hill squirted out more lotion and massaged it in.

"Mmmm," she said. "Now tell the truth. Doesn't that feel good?"

Parker shrugged. Admitting it would make him responsible for what was happening.

"This lotion is all natural, you know. You can use it on other parts of your body, too—anywhere. And it's edible." She smiled up at Parker, scooting closer while putting everything into rubbing the slick lotion into his hand.

"Sarah, I'm a happily married man," Parker objected. "A wife and two kids. Hell, I'm old enough to be your father. Well, almost."

Massaging, rubbing, squeezing. "Relax, sweetheart. All I'm doing is putting lotion on your hand," she said softly. "You act like I'm getting to you. Like I'm trying to talk you into something you *want* to do."

Parker sighed, frustrated for words.

"All right, Tony, I'll confess. I am after you. But, if you didn't like it, you could have stopped me a long time ago—months ago, couldn't you? Come on now, tell the truth." She grinned again.

"Why me, Sarah?"

"Like I said, we have the same passion for the underdog. Besides, I'm attracted to you. You aren't a bad lookin' man, Tony Parker. And that little bit of gray sprinkled on your sideburns doesn't say 'old man' to me. It says 'experienced.'"

Gray? Is it that noticeable? Old man?

She massaged, rubbed, squeezed, milked—masturbated every finger. Her touch was firm, yet tender, and she was very good with it.

"Such big, strong hands." She smiled up at Parker and then drew her face near his hand with lips parted.

Parker's jaw dropped and he stared. *No! She's not going to . . . !*

Hill kissed the end of Parker's middle finger. She licked it slowly up and down.

He couldn't speak.

She took his finger into her warm, moist mouth, drawing it slowly up past the second knuckle. She began sucking and moving her tongue around it.

Lord! Can a man have an orgasm from having his finger sucked?

An air horn blasted.

Parker looked up to see the front grill of a Mack cement mixer. He'd crossed over into its path.

"Damn!" He slammed on the brakes and jerked the wheel to the right as far as he could with his free but slick right hand.

Hill was thrown forward, and he felt a sharp pain on the end of his middle finger as he pulled his hand back to gain control of the steering wheel. The Jimmy swerved and started down into the ditch as the big cement truck raced by. He pulled it back onto the road, and it bounced and slid to a stop sideways to the roadway, gravel flying.

Parker sat staring out blankly. Hill did the same momentarily but broke the silence with a giggle.

"Damn, Tone, was it good for you?"

"Please, don't ever do that again while I'm driving."

"Hmmm, maybe later then—at my apartment?"

"Sarah, you know what I mean."

"Uh-huh, and you know what I mean."

It took a moment for Parker to regain his composure and resume driving. Within a couple of minutes, they could see the small grain elevator that was the landmark for Sand Creek.

"All right," he said, "you get the net, and I'll get the gunny sack. If I can, I'll try to put the little critter in the sack first thing and avoid getting us sprayed too much."

"Okay, Tone. You don't want me to bring the rifle, just in case?"

"No, I doubt if we'll need it."

"Are you like *afraid* of guns or something? I mean, you keep one in the truck—I'm guessing because it's mandatory—but I never see you get it out, no matter what's going on. Like last week on that cougar call. I've never seen you even look at a gun."

Parker was slow to answer. "I had a bad experience once. Vietnam. I shot someone."

"You mean the enemy?"

"That's what they told us."

"That was war, Tony. From what I heard, there was a lot of shooting going on."

"War? They told us it was a *police action*."

"Did you kill him?"

Parker gazed out the windshield. "Yeah."

CHAPTER 3

"Over here, over here!" An excited man in overalls did jumping jacks sideways around the corner of the white, two-story farmhouse. His left cheek bulged, full of chewing tobacco. His bare, meaty shoulders and back were bronzed from the sun, and they shone with perspiration.

"Oh, relax Eldon, that varmint ain't goin' nowhere," a tall, big boned woman in blue jeans and a crisp, white short-sleeved blouse said, waving him down. "You always get so darned excited." She turned to Parker and Hill as they parked. "We're the Bumfields—the ones that called. That's Eldon," she said nodding to the animated man. "I'm Pearl."

Parker jogged around to the back of the truck, grinned at Pearl Bumfield and yanked open the back window and tailgate. "Tony Parker, ma'am. That's Sarah Hill." He pulled out the five-foot-long aluminum-handled net and tossed it to Hill.

"Don't get too close, Mr. Bumfield," Parker said, trotting over to the man. He carried a gunnysack in his left hand and wore a thick, padded-leather glove on the other. Hill followed two steps back, holding the net with both hands.

"He's in the garage," Bumfield said, hanging onto his straw hat with a green visor built into the brim. "I trapped him in there when he came at me. Scared the hell out of me. He's the biggest, meanest one I ever seen!"

"You folks stay back," Parker said, approaching the weathered-gray, single-car garage. His blue, short-sleeved uniform shirt showed evidence of the already sizzling morning temperature by the large dark spots under each arm. His brown leather cowboy boots kicked up a gray dust as he hustled up the dirt driveway, and the gusty wind blew the dust cloud away as soon as it rose.

Parker stepped to the double, side-hinged doors, taking care not to make any noise that might alert the animal. Hill stayed just behind and to his side, watching close for signals. The old wood frame creaked in the gusty north wind that had already forced it to lean precariously after decades of resisting its constant attack. Parker tried to peek into the unlit garage through the crack between the doors but could see nothing. He turned his head to the side and tried to hear the thing he stalked, but still there was nothing.

Parker fumbled with the large bolt fit tightly into the rusty hasp on the doors. His gloved right hand made it doubly difficult, but the bolt finally pulled free, rasping loudly against the steel latch. He let it drop to the ground and slowly pulled the left door open by the hasp.

The cool air was welcome on his face as he looked over the dark room. A greasy, dusty smell filled the dilapidated shack. Then a different scent hit him, a rank odor invading his nostrils, pungent and strong. Parker held his breath and gulped.

The garage was small and had an earth floor. Buckets full of rusted metal pieces cluttered the ground. Broken shelves hung along the walls, laden with fruit jars filled with nuts and bolts and other miscellaneous parts. A half-assembled, antique tractor engine sat in the far corner.

"Are you sure he didn't get away?" Parker asked, with some disappointment.

"Naw, he's in there," Bumfield answered and then spat out some of the brown juice.

"*Grak-ak-ak-ak!*" came a strange snarl from behind the tractor engine, and suddenly, a gym-bag-sized blur of black and white torpe-doed toward the doorway.

Hill stepped up and swatted the net down on the angry creature, catching it ineffectively by its hindquarters. She attempted to pin it, but it slipped loose and darted to Parker.

He reached down with his leather glove and snatched it up be-fore it had a chance to do harm. The skunk struggled frantically, clawing and biting at the glove, drooling saliva as he held it by its neck.

"It's okay, I got him," Parker called out, holding the skunk up high with the gunnysack underneath.

"Get him in the bag!" Hill said, dropping the net and grabbing the gunnysack with both hands.

Loud, vicious barking erupted, and a large yellow and gray dog appeared from nowhere and jumped at the skunk.

Parker stepped back, startled. His grip loosened, and the skunk took advantage of the opportunity. It struggled free and dropped to Parker's side then scampered like a squirrel up his chest to the side of his throat. Its sharp, omnivorous teeth punctured deep into the base of his neck just under his collar, and it shook its head savagely, setting a firm grip.

"Jeez-huss!" Parker cried out.

"Dawg, get back!" Bumfield yelled, running at the dog with a gar-den rake raised above his head. "Damn fool dog, get out of here!"

Parker pulled the skunk loose, its teeth tearing away from deep into his flesh, leaving a half-inch hole. Blood immediately leaked from his neck and under his shirt, seeping through the fabric. He dropped the furious beast into the sack, and Hill hurried to tie it shut as Parker applied pressure to the wound with his gloved hand.

"Oh, for goodness sake! Are you all right?" Mrs. Bumfield cried, running to Parker.

"Yeah, I'm okay," he said, still wincing.

"Damn Dawg! Sometimes, I just think we oughta get rid of him,"

she said. "Come on in the house, and we'll get that cleaned up."
Then, insistently, she said, "Come on, now."

"All right, sure," Tony said and began to follow the woman, who
was scurrying in front of him. Eldon Bumfield threw his rake down,
missing the big dog by a couple of feet. He kicked at the air in front of
the animal's snout. Dawg briefly romped as if in play and then trotted
around the corner of the house as Bumfield took Parker by the arm to
assist him.

Sarah Hill sprinted across the yard and yelled back, "I'll put this
little bastard in the truck and be right in, Tony."

Oh, great, Parker thought. *Now there'll be an ER visit and lots of paper-work.*

Tony Parker sat in an overstuffed, forest-green corduroy chair in
the Bumfields' living room with a wet washcloth pressed against his
neck. He leaned over a wash pan half full of pink water on the coffee
table in front of him. Sarah Hill stooped at his right side with her
hands on her knees and concern in her face.

Parker looked around the room. It reminded him of his long
deceased grandmother's house from when he used to visit her as a
young boy. Garage-sale-type items, cookie jars, colored glass and pot-
tery pieces filled the lamp stands and shelves along the walls. News-
papers and magazines cluttered the corners in loose stacks. A tapestry depicting a bunch of dogs playing poker hung crooked on the far
wall. One dog was passing an ace to another under the table with his
toes.

Mrs. Bumfield reached over and gently pulled the washcloth and
Parker's hand away from the wound.

"I think it's quit bleeding enough to put the bandage on now,"
she said. "You'd better go straight to the emergency room. Just send
us the bill."

"Oh, it's all right. Don't worry about it," Parker assured her.

"Don't worry about it?" Mr. Bumfield blurted. "Son, that critter was mad as a hatter."

"No, I'm okay. The state requires all the animal control officers to be vaccinated for just about everything. But *you* need to be careful. Keep a good eye out for any animals acting strange—that's including your dog. If the skunk was diseased, it could have infected others."

As Mrs. Bumfield applied a gauze patch with white tape to Parker's neck, a girl about four years old peeked around the doorway. She clutched a small, homemade Raggedy Ann-type doll. The little girl's large dark eyes gazed up from her bowed face. Stubby pigtails made from dark brown hair stuck out high on her head, and she wore a brick-red dress noticeably similar to that of the doll's. Her wide smile stretched her lips thin and caused deep dimples on her chubby, freckled cheeks as she twisted her body back and forth nervously.

"Well, hi there, cutie," Tony Parker said, smiling back.

"Tony, this is our granddaughter, Tricia," Mr. Bumfield said. "She's staying with us until her mama gets settled in with a new job out in Denver. Her mama's just divorced—you know how it is. But—ain't she a doll?"

Tricia leaned back against her grandfather and took forced, choppy steps as he coaxed her closer.

"Hi, Tricia. I'm Tony."

Her thin-lipped smile stayed as she squeaked, "Did the skunk bite you?"

Parker grinned. "Just a little scratch, sweetheart."

Hill chuckled. "I think you've got yourself a girlfriend, Tone."

"You've got a pretty doll, Tricia," Parker said.

Tricia raised the doll up under her chin. "Grammy made it for me. Her name's Raggedy A-yun."

Mrs. Bumfield smoothed down a last strip of white tape. She finished up the dressing by kissing her hand and patting it lightly on the bandage. "There, good as new, Tony."

Parker took one of the doll's small hands and shook it. "Glad to meet you, Raggedy Ann. And it's been a real privilege meeting you,

Tricia." He gently brushed her pretty little cheek with the back of his index finger and then looked up at her grandmother. "Thanks, Mrs. Bumfield. You're good folks."

He stood and pulled a business card from his pocket. He placed it next to the phone on a small table.

"Be sure to call me if you need anything. My home number's written on the card below the office number."

The Bumfields accompanied Parker and Hill out the door and down the porch steps.

"Oh no, not again," Mrs. Bumfield said, as they walked to the truck.

Parker and Hill turned and Parker feared the worst.

"Can I ask you to help with one more thing, Tony?" she said, looking up into a large elm tree in the front yard.

"Sure, if I can," Parker said, stepping back, trying to trace her sight.

"Little Pussy's stuck up in the tree—poor little thing. Dawg probably scared her up there again. This time, she's way high."

Parker looked up to a branch more than twenty feet above. He saw the little gray kitten looking down at them with big, round eyes.

It pleaded, mewing softly.

Mrs. Bumfield stood looking into the elm with her hands on her hips. "I can't climb trees none too good, and Eldon, he's too darned fat."

Mr. Bumfield chuckled. "Hey, watch it there, woman."

"Shush, Eldon. This is serious. Tricia's grown real attached to that kitten."

"No problem, Mrs. Bumfield. I'll get her."

Parker hadn't climbed a tree in years but managed without incident. As they left Sand Creek, a report came in of a buck dear trapped in an east Wichita backyard. They responded, and it took more than two hours to deal with the animal, sedate it and haul it back out to the county to be released. The rest of the day was a jumble of paperwork, stray cats and the rescue of a squirrel that had fallen down a sewer vent pipe and then climbed out of a newlywed couple's toilet. There seemed no time to visit the emergency room about a simple little bite. Besides, he was confident in his inoculation, and he'd hardly noticed the injury since the morning.

Completely exhausted, Parker got ready for bed early that night with something Sarah Hill had asked on his mind. "Have you had your serum level checked lately?" she'd asked during the drive back to town. He had, three months ago. It was good. Rabies antibody count had been high, as it was supposed to be.

Parker looked over to Julie as he walked into the bedroom from the bath. She lay in the king-sized waterbed, studying a *Good Housekeeping* magazine. She'd probably found a new dessert recipe she would try out soon, or maybe she was reading some clever gardening tips. *God, she's a great wife.* He sighed and nodded in affirmation of his thoughts. Julie glanced to him with a grin, but soon a look of concern came over her face.

She asked, "How's the bite, sweetheart?"

"Except for the bandage," he said, touching the wound lightly, "I wouldn't even know it was there."

"The ER doctor didn't think you'd have any problems—didn't give you a prescription?"

Parker lied. "Nope. Said it'd be as good as new in a couple of days." Julie worried way too much. He wouldn't tell her he hadn't gone to the emergency room. Why have her bothered by such a little thing, now?

"You go to Via Christi? Who was the doctor? Maybe I know him."

"Uh, new guy," he said. "Some kid, really. But he seemed sharp. I can't even remember his name."

"Hmm," Julie said.

Parker couldn't tell if she was acknowledging what he'd said or she was skeptical. She went back to her magazine.

Parker went to a roll-top desk opposite the bed. He shuffled through various manila folders in the file drawer, pulled out a jacketed, typed report and rolled into bed beside her.

Rabies in Humans was typed on the cover. He opened the old thesis he'd written in his veterinary school days and began leafing through. One sentence stuck out. *Only around forty percent of those bitten by rabid animals actually develop rabies when left untreated, if they were not previously inoculated.* Sure, there was a risk, but he'd had the pre-exposure vaccine, even though it was thought to be only eighty percent effective. Figuring it in his head, he came up with the probability: he had a eight in one hundred chance of getting rabies even if the animal was rabid. It was so slim, minute, extremely unlikely. Those were like lottery odds. He'd never won the lottery. He wouldn't get rabies.

Parker read on silently.

> *Rabies in humans is considered one hundred percent fatal, since once symptoms appear, there is no known cure and death is inevitable. Even treatment administered after exposure and before the onset of symptoms is not completely reliable and neither is pre-exposure inoculation. However, there has been one known survivor in hundreds of thousands of confirmed cases. A twelve-year-old boy in Indiana, bitten on the hand by a rabid bat, survived after months of intensive hospital treatment.*
>
> *Transmission of the virus to humans may occur from any warm-blooded animal, including birds, cattle, and horses, but especially from raccoons, skunks, wolves, coyotes, bats, wildcats, domestic cats, dogs and even other humans. The virus may enter the body from any open wound or scratch or mucous membrane, from the bite or even the lick of an infected animal. In one instance, the virus was transmitted to a couple of spelunkers in aerosol fashion from bat urine in a cave.*
>
> *Human rabies symptoms usually appear within five to fifteen days. However, in unconfirmed cases, the onset of symptoms has been reported to have occurred in as much as a year after infection or in as little as four days.*

In a few rare and questionable cases, the onset of symptoms was claimed to have occurred within twenty-four hours. It is thought the amount of infection and the proximity of the bite to the brain of the patient are the biggest factors determining the length of time before symptoms occur.

Parker frowned, thinking of his neck wound.

Symptoms generally occur in three stages, but they are not always clearly defined. Initially, there may be fever and swelling around the wound. Soon after, there may be times of body fever, headaches, and nausea. A loud and irritating ringing of the ears may occur. The patient may attack others and tear clothing in fits of anger. The male patient sometimes experiences a painful erection. All human patients seem to have a fear of water, or hydrophobia, and experience excruciatingly painful convulsions of the throat at the sight or even the thought of it (unlike popular belief, this symptom is rare in canines). The tongue might swell, and the body's joints are likely to become extremely stiff and achy. Paralysis is followed shortly by death in the final stage.

Julie set her magazine on the nightstand on her side of the bed, switched off the light and rolled over to Parker. She snuggled her head on his shoulder. Her hair was soft and smelled fresh and clean. Her hand moved slowly and gently from his stomach to just underneath the waistband of the boxer shorts he wore like pajamas. "How about putting that down and holding me instead?"

Parker smiled, dropped the thesis to the floor and turned off his light. After much tenderness and considerate love making, they fell asleep.

*_*_*

The dark figure crouched close to the five-foot chain-link fence that surrounded the Parkers' backyard. He looked up at the unlit, second-story master bedroom window with his right eye, a black patch covering his left. Deep, jagged scars disfigured that side of the small oriental man's face. He was dressed all in black.

"Patience, my friend," he whispered, his fingers squeezing the heavy wire fence.

Yankee stood, tail wagging, nuzzling the man's fingers. He whined, chimpanzee-like, begging for a scratch behind the ear.

The man looked at the dog and smiled. He pushed away from the fence and trotted down the street, head and shoulders hunched over.

*_*_*

Tony Parker's eyelids rolled back to brightness. White, white, everything was white. A sheet covered his face. *It must be morning.*

His neck throbbed, painful and deep. He felt of it gently without disturbing the sheet. The wound had swollen to enormous proportions. It throbbed hard, and he could feel it in his fingers. It was hot, burning.

Parker grimaced. His frown began to exaggerate over his face, wrinkling his nose and curling his lips, exposing large, inhuman teeth—carnivorous, long fangs. He could feel his face distorting, bones expanding, nose growing. It stretched out from his face into a snout. Thick dark hair began to sprout over his face and hands. His eyes yellowed. His ears grew pointed. His fingernails curled into large dark claws.

He tried to speak but growled instead, confused, scared.

He felt mad, enraged, but didn't understand why. He had an overwhelming hunger. He wanted meat; fresh, raw meat—a fresh kill, bloody and raw.

Someone entered the room. They rustled beside the bed.

He could see shapes through the thin sheet. A woman stood holding a baby in one arm, smiling with her finger to her lips while looking at a young boy. They were familiar, yet he couldn't remember them. He was confused, disoriented. Julie, he remembered. Her name was Julie, his wife. His children, Audrey and Nicholas, were with her. It meant nothing.

"*Shhh,*" she whispered. "Let's surprise Daddy. We'll scare him."

Parker's lip twitched as it curled. He licked his snout.

They moved closer to the bed. Nicholas giggled with excitement. They leaned their heads close to Parker's sheet-covered face.

He growled low without wanting to. *Come no closer. Get back. Run!*

Nicholas giggled again and reached for the top of the sheet.

Parker growled once more.

Nicholas yanked the sheet back, and the horrible monster that Tony Parker had become leapt out. It tore into the woman's throat, blood spraying, then ran the boy down at the doorway, tearing into his neck as the child cried, "No, Daddy, no!"

The boy lay lifeless on the floor, and the terrible thing returned for the infant.

--*

Parker's body jolted as he gasped and his eyes snapped wide. He lay on his stomach, heaving through his open mouth. The bright-red eyes of the clock radio next to the bed looked back at him with an evil stare. It was eleven thirty. The bedroom was dark.

"Tony, are you all right? What's wrong?" Julie asked, lying with her back to him, still half asleep.

She rolled over slowly as he rose to his elbows and he looked to her. She was okay, alive. His beautiful wife, Julie, was all right. But it was so real—too damned real to be a dream.

He pushed out of bed and strode to the medicine cabinet mirror in the master bathroom, flipping on the light as he went in. He saw *himself.* The same face looked back as did any other time. Nothing different—no werewolf. It was a dream, so terrifying, yet so real. He peeled back the bandage on his neck and looked underneath. The wound wasn't swollen. It wasn't warm. It didn't throb.

He returned to the bedroom, going to the window. The street below was dark. It *was* the middle of the night.

A chill shot up his spine as he looked out. Something was wrong. He couldn't figure it for sure, but something was wrong out there. He looked down the dimly lit street. A car, a light-colored truck or van maybe, started its engine, turned on its lights and drove away. Tony watched the crimson glow of the taillights until they disappeared into the night.

"Sweetheart, you all right?" Julie asked, her voice groggy. She rubbed her eyes.

"Yeah, I'm sorry. Just a bad dream."

"Come on back to bed," she coaxed and patted the place beside her.

Parker didn't answer but obeyed. He sat down on the side of the bed and scratched his head.

"Come on and lie down," Julie said and reached over and touched his side. "What was the dream about?"

"Nothing."

Parker lay down. Julie rolled back over, and he moved in behind her. He put his arms around hers and pulled as close as he could without hurting her. Julie stroked his forearm and snuggled the back of her head underneath his chin and her hips against his groin.

"Nothing," he whispered.

CHAPTER 4

S ilent darkness. Light filtered through a tear in Alvin
MacGreggor's living room window shade from a bright, blue-
white full moon. It cast eerie shadows and dark shapes throughout
the room. The sheer curtains on the window flowed airily from the
gentle breeze of a large box fan.

It was one of those hot, sticky, Kansas nights with both the temperature and the humidity more than ninety. It would be almost
unsurvivable without a fan to cool the sweat-dampened skin, still nearly
unbearable without air conditioning.

Eighty-five-year-old MacGreggor slept peacefully in his worn out
La-Z-Boy. Overdressed for the heat, he wore light-blue pajamas, a red-
plaid robe, brown slippers and had covered himself up to his chest
with a tattered quilt—evidence of poor circulation.

Fluctuating lights from the graphic equalizers of a compact disc
player in the corner made an intermittent soft green glow. After a lull
between songs, Enya began singing *China Roses*, melodically, soft and
inviting—of a *new world—heaven....*

Slowly, deliberately, a huge, jet-black form moved past the dining
room table and into the living room directly toward the old man. The
huge shape advanced fluidly, its back and hackles, sleek and stealthy,
like that of a jungle cat.

It eased to a stop mere inches from the old man's face. A low, rumbling growl slowly erupted from the enormous animal's throat as it revealed tremendous, white fangs.

Enya's ethereal voice sings of China Roses....

"Jezebel? Is that you, Jezebel?" The old man wrenched his face to focus on the black image looming in front of him in the darkness.

The Great Dane gazed at him, motionless. A terrible battle raged inside her head as she remembered a human's voice say, *Man—enemy. Kill!*

MacGreggor reached out as if to a friend who had come to his sick bed. He stroked the shadow's neck just below her pointed ear with the back of his hand.

The dark animal bowed her head and licked her chops. With large dark eyes, she watched the arm extending out beside her.

Enya sings of following a new moon....

She looked over to a well-chewed, red-rubber dog bone near the door, glanced toward her water and food bowls in the kitchen and then looked back at MacGreggor's face. She whined softly, but then another low growl came involuntarily. *Man enemy. Kill—kill—kill!*

"Jazbo?"

The huge Great Dane's reply came swiftly as her fangs pierced deep into the old man's neck, tearing the right jugular vein and then struck again in a death grip over his throat.

Vertebrae crunched like cracking knuckles.

MacGreggor's face contorted with a frightened and frantic look as if searching into the darkness for help that would not come, salvation that would pass him by. The old man gurgled with deep red bubbles growing in his open mouth. He convulsed spastically, his life pumping from his body, gushing and squirting out into the mouth of the huge canine, overflowing and streaming down her neck. Blood, splashing off the old man's chin, splattered into the merciless animal's already red eyes as she held her grip until the old man convulsed and shook and shuddered no more.

Enya sings about seeing the sun...the stars.

CHAPTER 5

L t. Jack Simpson parked the brown, unmarked Chevy police car in front of Thelma's Diner and gave a deep sigh. The bright, already steamy morning caused sweat beads on his dark-chocolate forehead, and his eyes were bloodshot. It had been a long night on the job.

The diner was small and made from concrete block, painted white, but neat and clean both outside and in. It was a local hangout for the city police and in the white gravel parking lot, Simpson noticed a patrol car along with an old green Ford pickup and a blue Volkswagen bug. He pushed out of the car and took slow, tired steps to the door of the diner. The smell of bacon lured strong and tempting, but he would settle for a cup of coffee. He'd unwind a bit in Thelma's and then have a bowl of Cheerios with his three young daughters when he got home. After that, he'd get a few hours sleep. He looked forward to a much-needed rest this weekend. The only thing going on was Tony and Julie Parker's picnic on Sunday. A nice peaceful weekend.

Simpson swung the door in without looking.

A young uniformed cop caught it with a Styrofoam cup, and coffee dumped down his front.

"Oh, damn. Sorry!" Simpson said.

The lanky, baby-faced cop said nothing but gaped down at his stained uniform.

"What do you think you're doing to my partner, Simpson?" an officer of about fifty boomed.

"Well, *Big Jim* Morowsky. How the hell are you?" Simpson held his hand out with a big smile on his face. Morowsky was a tall man, well over six feet, with a belly that had been forced too many beers and late-night leftovers.

"I'm doing great," Morowsky said, taking his hand, "but I can see you're still causing trouble."

"Yeah." Simpson looked at the young cop. "Sorry about that, my man."

"Cox, this is the orneriest detective you'll ever care to meet, Jack Simpson. Simpson, meet Farley Cox, first day on the job."

"You're shittin' me," Simpson said. "Hope you're good at baby-sitting."

"Aw, he's not going to be so bad," Morowsky replied. "He's John Cox's son."

"Hell, Morowsky, I meant he was baby sitting you!"

They both laughed.

"Watch it Simpson. I've still got pull downtown. One call, and I could have you back in a squad car, right alongside me."

"You know, that wouldn't be so bad." Simpson grinned. He and Morowsky had been teamed together twenty years earlier when it wasn't so cool to have an African American as a partner. Simpson said to Cox, "So you're John *The Man's* son, huh? You've got some big shoes to fill, kid."

The shy young officer smiled and nodded.

"Hey, we've got to go," Morowsky said. "Have to check on an elderly resident that doesn't answer his door. I'll chew the fat with you later, Simpson."

"From the looks of it, there'll be plenty to chew." Simpson patted Morowsky's gut. "Take care of old man Morowsky, Cox. He's kind of feeble without his cane."

"Bite me, Simpson!" Morowsky said with his back turned and then exited.

Jack Simpson smiled and swung around to the first empty booth.

"The usual, Jack?" a heavyset, graying redhead in a white dress asked.

"Yeah, thanks, Thelma."

Within a minute, she brought a cup of steaming coffee to his table along with a spoon and a glass of ice water.

"Rough night, Jack?"

"Uh-huh...." Simpson took a tentative sip of the scalding coffee, then winced as he set it down and spooned in two teaspoons of ice. "Dead kids and drugs."

Thelma frowned and shook her head. She put her hand on his shoulder. "Well, you just sit here and relax. The coffee's on the house."

Simpson gave a thankful smile, and Thelma walked away.

He was halfway finished, taking small tastes, when a static squawk came from the seat across from him. Simpson rose to see a police walkie-talkie.

"Damn." Simpson got up, reached over and picked up the radio. "Can you put my coffee in a take-out cup, Thelma?"

Thelma glanced over. "Sure, Jack."

She poured fresh coffee into a Styrofoam cup, put a plastic lid on it and handed it to Simpson when he met her across the counter.

"Thanks, Thelma. You're a sweetheart."

Thelma winked, and Simpson went through the doorway.

"Six Adam Three to Sergeant Jim Morowsky. You read me Morowsky?" Simpson asked, sitting in his parked car.

"Five Adam Seven. Morowsky. Go ahead, Six Adam Three."

Jack Simpson thought for a second. He didn't want the dispatcher, or any of the other officers, to know about them leaving a radio. They could get written up for it.

"Uh, this is Simpson. I think I've got something you might want. If you give me your location, I'll meet you there."

*_*_*

Morowsky looked at Cox as they pulled up to the curb in their patrol car. Cox grabbed for the empty radio pouch on his belt. He was in deep shit now. Morowsky had given him the responsibility of carrying their only hand-held radio, and Cox had left it at the diner. He remembered getting all excited when their first call came in. Morowsky let him answer it. When he was done stuttering to the dispatcher, he'd laid it on the seat as he got out of the booth.

"Our twenty is eleven thirty-seven Whiteside," Morowsky said into the microphone. "Appreciate it Jack." He returned the mike to its hook.

Cox looked out his side window, away from Morowsky's frown. This was it, Cox's first call as a Wichita police officer. Now was his chance to prove to his father and the rest of the world he was a real man, that he could be a good cop, but he certainly started the day off wrong.

He'd had a lucky break, drawing Morowsky as a partner. When the shit hit the fan, Morowsky was known to be the guy to have at your back. He was a lot like Cox's father. John *the Man* Cox had retired just last year as one of the most decorated cops in Wichita history.

Although Big Jim's actions didn't always show it, he didn't appear to mind baby-sitting a rookie, especially a rookie whose father was a local hero.

Officer Cox looked at the small, white house as he opened the passenger's side door. It seemed out of place on the big corner lot. Paint was peeling, and a number of the old shake shingles were missing, unlike the other well-kept homes in the neighborhood. The lawn was a surprise, nice and neatly cut by a caring neighbor, no doubt, but looking close, it was only trimmed crab grass and dandelions.

An elderly woman came scurrying toward the two uniformed cops as they stepped onto the lawn. Deeply wrinkled, tired flesh hung from her cheekbones and sagged in jowls, adding to the worried look that filled her face. The skin of her arms drooped on her slight frame creating the look of a bony skeleton slipped into a body too big.

"Are you Mrs. Crane?" Sergeant Morowsky asked, while adjusting his baton and pulling up his pistol belt.

"Yes. I'm sorry to trouble you officers. It's just that Mr. MacGreggor always answers the door when I stop in on my morning walk. If I'd had a key, I would of went on in to see if he was okay, but he isn't a very trusting soul," the elderly woman said. "I check on him every morning. Then, every afternoon I bring him his mail and read it to him. And then I feed his...."

"All right, ma'am, no trouble at all," the sergeant interrupted. "We'll check it out. I'm sure he's all right. Are you sure he's even home?"

"The old fool had better be. I told him not to go anywhere without letting me know. He doesn't get around that well anymore."

The sergeant strode up and onto the wood porch. Cox followed directly behind, adjusting his baton and pulling up his pistol belt, mimicking the sergeant.

Officer Cox's tan uniform was crisp and neatly pressed except for the wet coffee spot darkening a large area on his right side. It extended from just below his gun belt down to his knee.

The old woman eyed the spot then glanced up at the rookie's face and back at the spot with a questioning look. The rookie rubbed it, hoping, somehow, that would make it vanish. His attention was too much on the coffee stain and not enough on the first step of the porch.

"Oh-ooph!" Cox grunted as his left toe kicked the first riser and his right toe followed, sprawling him out on the steps.

The sergeant looked over his shoulder at the embarrassed rookie. "Get on your feet, junior. We got work to do." He rolled his eyes and pushed out an extended sigh.

Cox lifted himself and brushed off, wondering how he was going to make a good cop if he couldn't even climb simple steps. He wanted to make it real bad. He may not become a great cop like his father, but he was going to try his hardest to be a good one.

Mrs. Crane hung back in the front yard, fretting. "Oh, I hope he's all right. He *is* a pain in the butt most of the time, but I do hope he hasn't passed. I wouldn't know how to fill my days without taking care of the old crank."

Cox's eyes widened when he heard the word *passed*. He didn't know if he could take seeing a corpse, a *dead man*, yet. He knew it would happen someday, but he prayed it would not be today.

The sergeant gave a few taps on the door and then called out, "Mr. MacGreggor. Mr. MacGreggor, are you in there?"

Not hearing a response, the sergeant stepped to the left and peered through the living-room window with his hands to the pane. Cox looked in over the sergeant's shoulder, but with the bright sun shining from behind, no lights on inside, all shades drawn and only a narrow space between the shade and the window frame, it was difficult to make out anything in the dark house. All he could see was his partner's strained face in the reflection of the glass.

"What the . . . ?" The sergeant seemed stunned, his brows pulling to the middle of his forehead in a frown. He sidestepped back to the door, grabbed the doorknob and shook it.

"What's wrong, Sarge?" Cox demanded.

The sergeant didn't answer as he shouldered the door twice, finally breaking in. The junior man rushed in behind with his hand on the handle of his gun and heart racing.

Mr. MacGreggor lay in his La-Z-Boy as peaceful as could be—with his jugular vein ripped open. Dried blood stained the side of the chair. It made a dark spot the size of a couch cushion on the light green carpet beneath it.

"Ho-lee shit!" Cox exclaimed.

The two approached the dead man slowly, Cox taking care to keep Morowsky in between. This sight hadn't set too well with the jelly doughnut he'd had at Thelma's half an hour earlier. The pastry tasted sour the second time around as he tried to keep it down.

"Somebody cut his throat!" Cox blurted.

"No, this ain't no cut," Morowsky said, inspecting the gash. "This looks like—teeth marks. Some kind of animal." His eyes widened, and he seized the grip of his holstered .40 caliber Glock 22 and scanned the room. "Get out! Get out and call for back up!" he shouted. "I don't know what the hell did this!"

Cox bolted out the doorway and hurdled the porch steps. He held onto his hat with one hand and, in nervous confusion, pulled out his Glock semi-automatic with the other.

Mrs. Crane sidestepped out of his way and ran toward her porch steps next door.

As he landed on the sidewalk, Cox fumbled his gun. It flipped up, spinning. He slapped it to the concrete, trying to snatch it from midair. The gun bounced once. He met it with the toe of his right foot, kicking it across the yard and under the patrol car.

He went to his hands and knees and groped frantically under the car for the gun.

Hysterical screams came from inside the house. Then a plea, "Help!"

Cox jumped up, his search brief and unsuccessful. "Sarge?" he answered, his high-pitched voice cracking.

He ran toward the house to help his partner, nervously grabbed his empty holster, then ran back to the squad car to radio for help. The young man's hands trembled out of control as he made the call. His face dripped sweat, and his uniform shirt, crisp and dry moments before, was dark and spotted from perspiration.

"F-f-five Adam Seven to dispatch."

"This is dispatch," a voice squawked the calm reply. "Go ahead, Five Adam Seven."

"Uh, uh. . . . " Cox knew there must be a number designation for what had happened here, but he couldn't remember. "We've got a, uh, two-eleven, uh, no a five, uh—shit! There's a dead man. Eleven thirty-seven Whiteside. His throat's all tore up. We need help, backup, right away!"

Cox threw the microphone back into the car. He needed a gun. He had to find *his* gun. He stammered like a chicken surrounded by coyotes, jockeying back and forth around the car in indecision.

The rookie took a last, brief look under the car. No luck. He must help his partner. He approached the house in slow stumbling steps. Perspiration spilled from Cox's pores, running from the sweatband of his cap, down his forehead and into his eyes. His jaw and lip trembled and he breathed from his open mouth. And then he froze. He froze like a statue out on MacGreggor's lawn, so solidly that he wasn't sure he'd be able to move even when backup arrived. They'd find him standing there, waiting for pigeons to crap on his shoulders with his partner in some sort of horrifying fix inside the house only thirty feet away. He couldn't move. Every joint was locked. He tried to force himself but it was like when his father held him down when he was little, covering young Farley's mouth, forcing him to stop crying. His father's hand had remained clamped over his mouth no matter how much Farley had gasped, blew mucous out his nose, struggled for air. *There aren't any damn monsters in your damn closet!*

Finally, something snapped inside his head, and once again, it was like his father's fingers, snapping in front of his face, trying to get Farley to move when his dad coached his little-league ball team, *Trying to get you to do something—anything, wakeup—Good gawd!* his father would say. Cox burst forward and with two leaping strides, he mounted the porch and flung himself flat against the front wall, just left of the door. The old wood-lap siding gave slightly, and the wall shuddered. His lungs coughed out air from the force. He swallowed hard. It hurt, like swallowing a bone chip with sharp edges.

He shifted his eyes toward the door and slowly inched his head to the doorway. He peeked in, wide-eyed. The big sergeant lay motionless on his stomach, feet toward Cox in a narrow hallway leading to the kitchen.

"Sarge," he whispered, cautious not to alert the sergeant's attacker. No response. He must have been knocked unconscious.

He had to help his partner; he just had to. Lt. Simpson was on the way, and backup would be there soon. But would it be soon enough for the sergeant? What would they say when they found out Cox had

lost his gun? The guidebook hadn't covered this. His classroom training left this out. He was alone, now, and unarmed.

Sergeant Morowsky's gun lay a few inches from the Sarge's extended hand. The time had come. This was Farley Cox's chance to
prove himself to his father. What he would do next, how he would
handle this situation, would either make his father proud or kick the
old man square in the balls with shame.

Cox scanned the room. The sergeant's assailant wasn't in view. If
he could get to Morowsky's gun, he'd be okay. Maybe it—whatever it
was—had gone.

The young officer edged into the house, hands on both sides of
the open doorway ready to push start a run in any direction necessary.

A long, crimson line of blood trailed from the sergeant's body.
He'd been dragged. Something like a rope ran along the length of
the blood trail. No, it wasn't a rope—it was a section of the sergeant's
intestines.

The jelly doughnut that had remained at the ready after the last
time filled his mouth with the sour taste again, but he choked it back
once more.

Cox dropped to all fours and scampered beside a couch opposite
the old man in the recliner. He bumped hard into the CD player on
a stand nearby. It jacked back and forth briefly. He held his panting to
listen for any sounds from his adversary.

Seconds passed. No sound or movement. From his angle, he could
only see the big sergeant's legs in the hallway. Morowsky's neatly
pressed, light brown trousers soaked up the vermilion puddle they
lay in. His black, spit-shined shoes were splattered in blood.

The CD player startled the young officer with Enya's rhythmic
Orinoco Flow. She sings of sailing...."

Again he thought of the gun. He had to go for the gun. Gathering
his courage, he crawled slowly out into the open toward the hallway
and his partner's motionless body. The hall was six feet long. On the
left side was a closed door—probably a closet—a dark open basement
doorway on the right. The sergeant's legs and lower body lay only

fifteen feet away, but he couldn't see his face, or head for that matter, to determine if there might be a sign of life.

"Sarge. Sarge, can you hear me?" Cox whispered. "It's okay, Sarge. I'm going to get you out of here. Hold on."

He crawled to the sergeant's feet and stopped, straining to see down the dark open stairway to the basement.

Enya wants to reach—and beach on Tripoli shores....

No movement, nothing, only darkness.

He looked back.

The gun was six feet in front of him. Then, he saw the reason he couldn't see the sergeant's head. It wasn't there.

His eyes bugged as he held himself back from making any noise. The jelly doughnut came up in full force, filled his cheeks, and flushed through his sinuses, causing them to burn. He gulped the sour cud back, but some escaped through his nose and dripped onto Sergeant Morowsky's right calf.

Unimaginable. He couldn't fathom the kind of beast that could have done this. It was the thing of nightmares and ghost stories.

Cox again recalled his father yelling at him when he'd had a nightmare as a young boy. *There's no such thing as monsters!* he'd shouted as he brutally tossed little Farley back into bed.

The gun.

He inched forward.

Another trail of blood. Smeared. Large paw prints—very large. They led from the sergeant's upper torso, around the doorway, into the kitchen and under a metal table. He glanced to his right side and down the basement stairway once again and then back to the sergeant's gun.

He moved closer. His eyes followed the trail of blood around the corner. Surely, this thing was in the kitchen or already gone. He'd soon be able to reach the gun and use it if he needed—he guessed the need would come very quickly.

He inched more, close enough to see where the trail ended.

The sergeant's head looked back at Cox with a terror-stricken face in the middle of the floor.

"Oh, shit, shit, shit!" he said, unable to hold it back.

He lurched for the gun. He surprised himself by not fumbling it. He held it in his trembling right hand, pointing into the kitchen. His knees straddled the sergeant's body, and he leaned on his left hand for support.

The Sergeant's still warm blood soaked into the knees of Cox's trousers, and he felt its stickiness on his hand near the sergeant's shoulder. The sweet, salty smell of gore filled his lungs. His stomach churned.

Still no movement, no sound. He looked at the blood trail and noticed again how it was smeared. *Why is it so smeared, and why does it only go out to Sarge's head, then stop?*

The answer came to him. It came fast and hit him like a bucket of ice water. The paw prints didn't smear going into the kitchen, they smeared coming out. The prints led back to the right side of the body.

Too late.

A cool breeze pushed up the basement steps, wrapped around his neck and signaled a needling tingle to start from his tailbone and race up his spine. It widened as it raced and slammed into his brain, making his head shudder. Something had come up the basement steps beside him.

A low growl.

Enya wants to crash on your shores....

He rolled his eyes to the dark basement doorway.

The thing was two feet from his face.

Cox didn't dare move.

It was a dog but not just any dog. Huge and black. Spindly legs. Terrifying dark eyes. Pointed, demon-like ears. Tremendous ivory fangs protruding from a hideous, curled and snarling snout.

John *the Man* Cox had been wrong. *There truly are monsters!*

The large black animal opened its mouth and growled again. Cox felt its hot breath on his face and smelled the rancid odor. Strings of saliva stretched from its lower to upper enormous, white fangs. One of the thing's lower fangs had been broken off. A small, bloody piece of flesh hung from the jagged edge.

Officer Farley Cox knew he'd have to move fast. He'd sit back quickly and shoot.

In the next half second, time slowed in his mind, almost to a stop. His body had no time to react, but his mind saw his doom in slow motion. At the first indication of movement, his first flinch, the incredible canine responded in a blur. Its head lunged forward like a rattlesnake's and engulfed Cox's face. One of the monstrous fangs pierced his right temple, and it stung.

For a fraction of a second he was seven again, reaching out to pet a stray dog that wagged its tail in apparent friendship. He had patted its head. It had suddenly snarled and snapped his hand. It had startled him and caused a bitter taste on his tongue. The same bitter taste as now.

Enya finishes, singing of sailing away.

*_*_*

Outside, Lt. Jack Simpson's unmarked police car screeched to a halt behind the patrol car. He had been nine blocks away when he heard Cox's radio distress call.

Simpson leaped out and ran into the yard toward the small house with his tie swung over his shoulder and his open, gray sports jacket flapping behind him like a cape.

The patrol car was vacant. The twelve-gage shotgun loaded with double-ought buckshot was in easy view, sticking up from the console, still probably locked in its bracket. An elderly neighbor lady peeked from her slightly opened screen door and he waved her back inside as he pulled out his Smith and Wesson .357.

He dropped behind some lilac bushes in front of the house and sat with his back against them as he checked to make sure there were bullets in his gun. Taking a deep breath, he knelt and peered around the edge of the bushes, over the porch and into the house. Squinting to see past the living room and dining room, he could make out a dark shape in the dim hallway.

A huge shadow stood holding the rookie's limp body by the face. Dark drool dripped from the thing's chin. The sergeant's body lay under the rookie with what looked like blood splattered and puddled all around.

"Oh, no! Jeez, what the hell?" Simpson said under his trembling breath. He squinted in an attempt to make out this awful thing he had found.

The shadow shifted its eyes in his direction and acknowledged him with a growl.

Without hesitation, Jack Simpson quickly raised his revolver with both hands, aimed and fired.

CHAPTER 6

At eight thirty in the morning, Tony Parker leaned to the medicine-cabinet mirror, face freshly lathered with shaving cream. He stood shirtless, still in the Batman boxer shorts that Nicholas had given him last Christmas.

He turned his head, placed his index finger on his sideburn and raised the blue Bic safety razor into place underneath, then took a long, slow swipe at his cheek. Taking his finger away, he noticed the gray hairs starting to infiltrate up the side of his head, getting fewer, but still evident all the way up to his temples. He turned and looked at the other side. It was the same.

He thought about what Sarah had said yesterday—the "gray sprinkled" on his side burns. *I can't be getting gray this young. I'm still a kid, a teenager in an overly used, middle-aged body.* It didn't mean "old man," she'd said. That was the kind of thing someone said to make another feel better and was always a lie.

"Experienced," he scoffed. "Experienced old man!"

Parker heard the phone ring as he rinsed the razor and banged it on the side of the sink. Julie's soft voice answered it in the adjoining master bedroom. He took another swipe with the razor, this time at the other side of his face, wishing he could start at his temple and remove all the gray hair.

Julie's head peeked around the edge of the half-open door.

"Sweetheart, it's the dispatcher." There was a hint of dread in her voice. "I hope they don't want you to go in today."

Parker grabbed a towel and wiped off the shaving cream as he hurried to the phone next to the bed.

"This is Parker."

"Mr. Parker, sorry to bother you at home on a Saturday morning, but Lt. Jack Simpson of the Wichita PD requested we call you," the voice said.

Something bad was happening. Jack wouldn't have the dispatcher call otherwise. "That's okay, Janet. What's up?"

"There's been a wild-animal attack at Eleven thirty-seven Whiteside. I don't have any other information yet."

"Injuries? What kind of animal?"

"Sorry, Mr. Parker, that's all I have. He did request an ambulance. I will keep you advised, as soon as I find out anymore."

"All right, Janet. I'm on my way. I'll call you from the truck." Parker hung up and turned to see Julie standing just five feet away with arms crossed. She said nothing.

"I'm sorry, Julie. Jack called in a wild-animal attack and especially requested me."

"But today we were going to do the shopping for the picnic tomorrow. Remember, our fifteenth anniversary picnic?" She frowned.

Of course, he remembered. She was trying to make him feel guilty if he went.

"Look, Julie, Jack wouldn't have asked for me unless there was something terribly wrong. There must be somebody hurt. I just hope it wasn't another pit-bull attack. That'd be perfect timing with my letter to the editor yesterday. I've got to go, babe."

"Oh, I know. I was just hoping we'd have the whole day to ourselves. You won't be gone all day, will you?"

Parker smiled and caressed her chin gently. "No, I promise. I won't be long."

*_*_*

"AC One to dispatcher," Parker called as he backed out of the driveway.

"Dispatcher. Go ahead, Mr. Parker."

"Yeah, Janet, call Officer Sarah Hill at her apartment and see if she won't meet me out in front, will you?" Sarah was really concerned about this sort of thing. She'd want to be involved, even on her day off. Besides, he'd enjoy her company.

"Sure, Mr. Parker, hold on."

"Hey, Top Dog, you read me?" a male voice said over the speaker.

"Yeah, hey, I know that ain't Janet. Tyrone, what it be, brutha'?"

"Betta watch it, Top Dog. I got your brutha hangin' right here," Tyrone answered back with a chuckle. It was incredible what the man got away with on the radio. He'd been reprimanded numerous times. Besides being a damned good dispatcher, Parker figured he had some sort of leverage that kept him on the job and as free as he cared to be with his language. "Lt. Simpson just called in. Looks bad, Tony. The good thing is, it's all over. The animal is dead. The bad is, Simpson requested the coroner, and there're three dead bodies."

"What the hell was it?"

"Don't know, man. That's all he said. Oh, and Sarah's line is busy. Must be rappin' to one of her boy friends. You want us to keep trying?"

"No, that's all right, Tyrone. I'm only a couple of blocks away now. I'll swing by and pick her up. Sounds like the emergency is over."

*_*_*

Parker pulled to a screeching stop behind some parked cars in the parking lot on one end of Sarah Hill's three-story apartment building. He left the truck running with emergency flashers blinking and sprinted to the stairway.

"Third floor," he complained under his breath as he passed the second level. "Why does she have to have an apartment on the third floor?"

Panting hard as he made the third landing, he noticed Hill's door ajar six inches. It was a little unnerving, especially considering this morning's event. He walked slowly to the door, almost expecting to see something wrong. He peeked in at the front room.

The living room lay in shambles.

The coffee table had been thrown on its side. Two of the three cushions from the couch were on the floor beside it. Two wineglasses and an empty bottle lay there also, along with a pizza box trapped under the coffee table. He eased the door open enough to step inside. Parker's heart already pounded into his throat from the run up the stairs. Now it raced like a top-fuel dragster.

He stepped, cautiously into the room. What had happened here, he could not imagine. He'd been there only a couple of times before to pick her up when her car was in the shop. From those couple of times, it had been obvious that Hill was a meticulous housekeeper. This wasn't like her. Something was amiss.

On one side of the living room was the doorway to the bedroom, on the other side was the bathroom. The kitchen/dining room was in the middle, separated by a half-wall with a countertop.

Parker moved vigilantly toward the bedroom, fearing what he might find. Again the door was partway open. The bed was in every bit as much a mess as the living room. Pillows and covers were strewn across the floor. A large crimson spot blotted the bed sheet. Parker squinted as if that would help him figure it out. He shoved the door open and walked in. His heart trampolined into his throat. Several dark red spots were on the bed beside the large one in the middle.

Blood!

Movement.

Something moved under the blanket that was lying to the side of the bed. His head snapped in that direction. The right eye and snout of a large white chow emerged from the blanket, and it started a low, extended growl.

It was Hill's dog, Sheik. But why was he growling at him? Parker had been around the dog a few times and the animal had always been friendly. He hoped Sheik's aggressive behavior was because he hadn't recognized Parker yet.

His pulse rate shifted even higher. He panted. The dog was sure to see his pounding heart through his open mouth.

Behind him, the front door slammed shut, and Parker spun around.

Sarah Hill screamed.

The dog barked and sprang out from under the blanket.

Parker was caught completely off guard. He didn't expect to see Sarah unharmed, especially completely nude and unharmed.

"Tony! Well, what do you know? What more could a naked girl ask for, but a big, strong, handsome man panting in her bedroom doorway?" she asked, still a little nervousness in her voice.

Evidently, Sheik now recognized Parker. The dog ran to his hand and nuzzled it for a customary scratch behind the ear.

Parker stared, still dumbfounded. Hill hadn't moved since screaming. Fifteen feet away, she just stood there holding a large white bath towel, a hand on her hip, one knee bent slightly, still very naked. *Playboy* would have been proud of such a pose.

He surveyed her body. He had imagined what it must look like, firm and curvy. A dogcatcher's uniform did little to enhance a woman's figure, but it could not hide certain things. Her bare body was even more impressive than what he had imagined. With her almost platinum blonde hair flowing down onto her lightly tanned, smooth shoulders and her sanguineous, full lips and nipples, she was a rich dessert, long fantasized. A luscious strawberry shortcake. Her tan lines emphasized her breasts that were ample for her five-foot-three-inch frame, but firm and round like honeydew melons ripe and ready for a lusty feast. Her waist was trim, almost small enough for him to be able to put his hands all the way around. A small triangular tuft of blonde cotton was in place between her shapely thighs, and her nicely tanned, trim legs finished her perfectly created body.

"So, Tone, did you break into my home just to pant at me?" she asked now with a more relaxed, devilish grin.

She strolled toward him. With each step, she moved dangerously closer to a fantasy he had enjoyed before though only in his mind. As she came closer and closer, Parker fell deeper and deeper into her spell. She finally stopped, toe to shoe tip and looked up at him with beckoning blue eyes and a suggestive teasing smile on her face. He smelled the freshness of her recently bathed, powdered and perfumed body. His nostrils flared.

She leaned against him, pushing her breasts firmly against his shirt and stomach. It felt as though her hard nipples were burning holes through his shirt and into his skin. A tempestuous heat radiated from the wounds and slowly enveloped his body. His hands longed for the pleasure this less sensitive part of his body enjoyed. His fingers stretched out from his hands, still down at his sides, like a child thinking of sneaking a forbidden cookie as soon as no one was looking.

She flipped her long blonde hair over her shoulder, exposing one side of her creamy, smooth neck and she wet her lips, moving her tongue slowly from side to side, causing them to glisten.

In a brief daydream, he reached out and grabbed her baby soft, but firm hips and lifted them to his middle and then fell passionately onto her bed. In reality, his hands clenched tightly into fists.

She brought her hands up to both sides of his neck and slowly moved them to his shoulders, pressing firmly, feeling his solid build. She watched her hands while she rubbed them down his biceps and over to his pectorals.

She seemed to study for a moment, then gazed back up into Parker's anxious eyes, cocked her head and gave a long, jagged sigh. Her warm breath blew against his throat and the chest hair protruding slightly from the neck of his shirt. It made a hot flash ignite from within and caused his flesh to burn. An uncomfortable tightness grew in the crotch of Parker's trousers.

Hill's grin widened. She must have noticed it also. "So are you going to bring me to the height of ecstasy with that throbbing love muscle bulging in your pants?"

Parker's throat constricted. His lips were dry, but saliva built up in his mouth, and he had an insuppressible urge to swallow. What would it hurt? No one would know. How could anyone find out? This was his chance. His chance to have Sarah. Beautiful, sexy, sassy young Sarah.

He swallowed hard. Licked his lips. "Swiss Army knife," Parker said with a forced grin, still under the spell Sarah's body cast over him, "fifteen blades."

"Ewww! Scissors, fork, knife, spoon, and French tickler, I'll bet." Hill stared into his eyes, still holding a wide grin.

Why had he said fifteen? Fifteen as in fifteen-year anniversary, with Julie. His beautiful, loving wife, Julie. Mother of his cherished children. Trusting, faithful, always there, Julie.

"I need you...," Parker blurted out, finally breaking from the trance, words easily misunderstood under the circumstances.

Hill brought one hand up and ran her finger down his nose to his top lip, rolling the bottom lip out slightly.

"You need me, huh? I didn't think I was ever going to hear that from you."

"Wild animal—attack."

Hill pulled Parker's bottom lip down nearly to his chin with her finger. It finally snapped back with a *plip*.

"I shoulda figured. Last time you showed up here on a Saturday you wanted to take me to a dog fight," she said in a disappointed tone. She sidestepped around him and pulled a pink blouse out of an open closet and draped it on a chair beside the bed. "Tony Parker, you really know how to show a girl a good time."

The danger passed; the spell was broken. Still, he could not take his eyes away from of her. He gaped, eyes wide, lips parted, questioning God for creating such a beautiful woman, laying her on a platter before him, then giving him a conscience.

"Jack called it in and asked for me. The animal is dead, whatever it was, and so are three people," he said in a monotone, still staring.

"Good lord, they don't know what it is?" She pulled a pair of faded Levi's from a dresser drawer.

"They haven't told the dispatcher yet. It's just down the street. I thought you might like to come along."

"Oh sure, there's nothing I'd rather do on a Saturday morning. What about the guys on duty?"

"I thought that—we'd handle it."

"Uh-huh."

Parker looked away while Hill stood, pulling on her jeans. "So what the hell happened here?"

"Kind of a personal question, isn't it, coming from a guy who's just broken into my apartment?"

"Yeah, I'm sorry about that. The door was open and the living room all messed up. Then, the blo...."

"Oh, Ken must have left the door open when he left."

"Ken?"

"Yeah, Ken Hardessy. You're not jealous are you?"

"Oh gee, Lt. Hardessy? You've got to be kidding. That asshole has been married four times. He's just a womanizer. He's using you."

"That he may be, but he isn't married right now. And I can't have you." She winked at Parker as she slipped on her white and pink Nikes. "Besides, I know he's using me. And I'm using him. It's just for sex."

Parker moaned, frowning and shaking his head. Lt. Hardessy was a vice officer and a K-9 unit dog handler. Everyone that worked for the city or county knew him and his reputation as a playboy and a back stabber.

By now Hill had given her long blonde hair a couple of quick brushes, patted some powder on her face and grabbed her purse, ready to go.

"What about the blood?" Parker asked, timidly.

"Blood?" Hill followed Parker's eyes over to the bed. "Oh that. That's cherry-flavored body lotion. You know, the kind that gets hot when you blow on it." She stood on her toe tips and puffed into his ear as she walked by. "I guess ol' 'Hard-assy' got a little carried away."

Parker moaned again, preceding her out the door.

"Mama will be right back, Sheik," Hill said and closed the door behind.

The drive to the scene was quiet. Parker had little time to consider what had happened in Hill's apartment or what it meant, if anything, between Sarah and him. If he weren't married, there was no doubt in his mind, the two of them would be lovers, perhaps even more. Parker did feel jealous.

He drove with both hands on the wheel, looking straight ahead. He cleared his throat several times, wanting to say something but never did. He wanted to say *something*, anything, so his jealousy wouldn't be quite so apparent. To show that his mind was clear of it. He couldn't. The casualness of her sex life bothered him, especially when she was involved with someone as unsuitable as Lt. Hardessy, as if anyone would be suitable for her in his mind.

Evidently Hill felt the upper hand in their relationship now and wanted to punish Parker for not giving in to her many previous advances. She sat on the inside half of her bucket seat, against the console, as close as she could get without being too obvious—not blatant, but obvious enough to make him uncomfortable. She held the smile of a cat with a belly full of canaries, glancing at him sleepy-eyed. Her hand rested on Parker's side of the console. She leaned on it, drumming her fingers ticklishly close to his right thigh.

It was working. Tony Parker, a happily married man, felt punished for not having an affair.

CHAPTER 7

B y the time Parker and Hill pulled up to within half a block of
the little corner house in the peaceful old neighborhood,
the street was jammed with ambulances and cop cars. Police had
already taped off the yard with the *Police Line, Do Not Cross* yellow crime-
scene tape. One policeman stood up after being down on all fours
beside a patrol car. He held a Glock pistol carefully with a pencil
through its trigger guard.

Parker trotted up to the porch of the old house with Hill carrying
the tranquilizer gun behind him. The tall black detective stepped
out the door, wearing white plastic gloves.

"Damn, Jack, what happened?" Parker asked.

"You tell me, Tony. You tell me," Simpson said, putting his hand
on Parker's shoulder.

Parker and Hill started to go around Simpson to the open door
when Simpson stopped them, putting his arm across the doorway.

"Wait a minute, Sarah. It's pretty gruesome in there."

"Don't worry about me," she said, pushing past Parker. "I can
handle gruesome."

Simpson looked at Parker and shrugged his shoulders. He glanced
back at Hill and turned sideways, allowing her to look in.

She raised her hand to her mouth, appearing nearly overwhelmed.

Parker looked in over her shoulder, eyes wide, without comment.

The bodies hadn't been removed. The coroner, a short, obese man with a cue-ball head, was kneeling as he inspected the sergeant's torso. A couple of uniformed officers stood nearby with their Latex-gloved hands on their hips and expressionless faces. Another man flashed pictures of the bodies from different angles in the room.

There, on top of the sergeant's body, lay the young rookie with the monster's mouth still stretched across his face. One of the beast's fangs had pierced his right temple. A single trail of nearly dried blood made a line down the side of his head, in front of his right ear and down the back of his neck.

"Who?" Parker asked.

"Jim Morowsky and a rookie, John Cox's son," Jack answered.

Parker cringed. He knew Morowsky was a good friend of Jack's. He didn't know the kid, but he'd met his father.

"Great Dane," Parker observed.

"Damn big one, too," Hill added.

They entered the room slowly. One of the officers raised his hand to stop them, but he dropped it when Simpson followed them in.

"It's okay guys. You know Tony Parker, Animal Control Director. And this is one of his men," Simpson said. After the officers smirked, Simpson corrected himself with, "Uh, one of his women—ah, shit, Officer Sarah Hill."

Parker narrowed his eyes at Jack. He knew Jack was aware there was more than just the usual working relationship between the two. This was probably a Freudian slip. Parker had known Jack Simpson since the last football game of their senior year in high school. They had been best friends ever since. They'd joined the Marines together under the buddy system and served in Vietnam at the same time, Simpson in an infantry 'grunt' unit, and Parker as a dog handler, sniffing out booby traps and VC. Now, once in a great while, they got to work together when bad things happened between animal and man.

"What's his name?" Parker asked, looking down at the old man, wincing from the rank carrion.

"Alvin MacGreggor," Simpson answered.

"The throat the only wound?"

Simpson nodded. "Apparently."

Hill gagged. "Looks like it was enough."

"Has anybody touched or moved anything?" Parker asked.

"We turned the CD player off," Simpson said. "It was blasting out some kind of Irish folksy gibberish when we came in. The old man must have been nearly deaf."

"Can we turn on some lights and raise the shades?" Parker asked.

Simpson nodded to the officers, and they responded.

Dark red blood was splattered on the walls and woodwork—blood from arteries squirting out life as if from giant squirt guns. It had struck the walls in streams and then dripped down, as in an abstract painting that the artist had really put his heart into.

"I can't figure some people out," Parker said, with one corner of his mouth curled. "A three thousand dollar sound system, a thousand dollars worth of Enya, Sinead O'Connor, the Chieftains, RiverDance and...." Parker looked in surprise at the CD case. "...Slim Whitman, hmm—definitely not my mug of beer—and living in a dump like this." He glanced around the room. "Look at the stuffing coming out of his chair and those ratty window shades."

The three walked over to the two officers lying on the floor.

"Looks like the Dane dragged the big guy," Parker said, noting the blood and guts trail. "That was one strong dog. What do you figure Morowsky weighs?"

"With or without his head?" the coroner questioned.

"Shit, Doctor Walker," Simpson scolded, "I worked with these guys, this ain't no time to joke around."

"Sorry Simpson. In my line of work, you can't take these things too serious—it'll get to you. I'd say he'd go about two sixty."

"I'd like a time of death on the old man when you have it pinpointed, Doctor," Parker said.

"You going to take the dog's head for rabies tests?" Walker asked.

"Might not be rabies," Hill said, staring at the dog.

"Maybe not," Parker said, "but we'd better do it anyway."

"Not rabies? What the hell you mean, not rabies?" Simpson asked. "A dog does all this because of an attitude? What else could it be?"

"I don't know," Parker said. "A dog'd need one hell of a good reason to do something like this. Could be abuse, maybe a brain tumor. I'd hate to speculate."

He bent down and observed the bullet wound in the dog's side. A lump blocked his throat as he stroked the dog's flank. He blinked and exhaled long. "Good shooting, Jack," he said blankly, "right through the heart." He patted the dog's shoulder, then looked up at Simpson.

Simpson smiled back proudly, then took a more serious face. "This is one damn big son-of-a-bitch, Tony," he said. "I didn't know they got this big."

"Oh yeah, he's big all right," Parker answered, looking back at the dog. "Got a tape, Doctor Walker?"

Within a few seconds, the doctor shoved his hand in front of Parker with a small, metal tape measure in it. Parker took it and pulled out the tape. He laid it along the dog's front leg to its hackles.

"Not all that unusual, though," he said. "He's probably around thirty-eight or nine inches at the shoulders. You don't see a lot of them this big, but he's a couple of inches shy of any kind of a record."

Parker checked the dog's ID tags. They were typical dog tags, telling the dog's name, owner's name, address, vet's name, and rabies vaccination date. Typical, except for the separate nametag that appeared to be gold, pure twenty-four-carat gold, with a two or three-carat diamond dead center.

"Whoa, look at this," Parker said amazed. "This thing's worth more than all the jewelry I've bought Julie over the last fifteen years."

Simpson read the nametag, "Beelzebub. Hell of a name for a dog."

"Rabies booster just two days ago," Parker said. "Hey, Dr. White Cloud's the vet. Cantankerous old coot."

"Then it really isn't rabies?" Simpson asked.

Parker inspected the dog's carcass in admiration. "Can't be sure," he said. "Sometimes the vaccination doesn't take. But even if it doesn't, only twenty-five percent of all rabies cases in dogs are the furious kind. Most are what's called 'dumb rabies.' Usually, even with furious rabies, the dog only attacks briefly, just bites and runs. And it'll rarely attack its master. Of course, with a dog this big, that bite is one damn big chomp." He looked to the dead sergeant's headless neck, then back to the Great Dane. "The dog looks in pretty good shape for rabies, too. A lot of times they're noticeably injured from biting themselves. Not a lot of slobber, either. Usually, you would expect more than this. Still, you never know for sure about rabies." He looked down the dark stairway. "What about down there?"

"Nobody's been down there yet," Simpson said. "The light's burned out."

Parker frowned.

"Well, shit, Tony. You know I hate dogs. There might be another one down there."

"That's it," the coroner said, looking up from the bodies. "Simpson might be right."

"What do you mean?" Parker asked.

"Well, look at the dog's lower left canine," the coroner said, pointing to its mouth with an ink pen. "It's broken off. Been that way for a considerable amount of time. A year or better." He stood up and walked over to MacGreggor's body. "Now look at the deep grooves in the old man's neck made by the canine teeth—all four of them."

"Are you saying there's another one of these monsters around here?" Simpson asked, looking over his shoulder to the dark basement.

"Well, that would explain the different bite pattern," the coroner said.

"The pattern is different, too?" Parker asked.

"Yes. You see, it appears the animal that tore into the old man's throat had a bigger mouth than the dog that took the head off the sergeant, the one that is lying dead at your feet," he said, pointing back with his ink pen to the big, dead Great Dane.

"What I figure happened is: late last night around midnight, the old man was sleeping in his chair. The larger animal attacked him with little or no warning. He died quickly, almost mercifully compared to the sergeant over there. The old man couldn't have lasted more than a few seconds according to the way the carotid artery was torn open.

"When the sergeant was killed this morning, there was a struggle. He probably lived for a full fifteen seconds after being gutted and before the dog we have here finally snapped his head off. It'd probably been hiding down in the basement. When it heard the sergeant break in, it came up quickly and attacked immediately without giving the sergeant any warning. Not even time to draw his gun, at first.

"Sergeant Morowsky, standing here," the coroner noted, standing in the middle of the living room sideways to the basement doorway, "saw the dog coming at him and had just enough time to block its head down, like this." He motioned with his right arm. "The dog's large fangs caught the sergeant's over-extended stomach and dug in. It ripped into his intestines with the sergeant still standing erect. Then, it attacked again, without pause.

"This time, the sergeant went for his gun, and the dog was free to go for his throat. Morowsky tried to push the dog off—remember the dog was standing on its hind legs, toe-to-toe and eye-to-eye with the sergeant—and couldn't fire his revolver. He was probably nearly unconscious.

"The dog dragged him over to the doorway, here. The sergeant dropped the gun. Then, after two, maybe three bites, and with a little more pressure, his head came rolling off. The gun the younger officer has in his hand is the sergeant's. The neighbor said he'd kicked his under the patrol car and couldn't find it. He came in unarmed to assist his partner.

"Officer Cox came over to the sergeant's body and got the gun. The smaller dog had gone into hiding again, down in the basement. As Cox knelt over the sergeant, the dog came up the stairs and grabbed him by the head. One of the two-inch-long fangs pierced his temple and entered his brain. He died immediately. Then, Lt. Simpson arrived.

"This is all speculation, of course. We'll know for sure, later, after running some tests. Why the bigger dog didn't attack the officers, and where it is now, I can't tell you."

All eyes in the room focused on the basement doorway.

"'Bigger,' you keep saying," Simpson said. "That can't be, can it, Tony?"

"I guess anything's possible," Parker said. "If I remember right, the biggest, or should I say the tallest, dog on record was a Great Dane. I think he was supposed to be a little over forty-one inches at the shoulders." He looked to the officer standing nearby. "Give me your flashlight."

The officer handed it to him, and Parker stepped over the two bodies and straddled the dog, whose hind legs hung over the top step. He descended the stairway slowly. Hill came behind with the tranquilizer gun, and Simpson cautiously brought up the rear with his .357 drawn and held head-high. The dark steps creaked as they proceeded.

The basement reeked of dog, mixed with the usual damp, musty cellar smell. It was small, fifteen feet by fifteen, with an open crawlspace under the rest of the house.

Parker's light found a wicker dog bed in the corner as he neared the foot of the steps. A brass nameplate hung three feet above the huge, silk-cushioned bed.

"Beelzebub," he read aloud.

A shiver clawed its way up his spine as his light searched the small basement for another dog. The light caught something in the adjacent corner, twelve feet away. Another dog bed. Another nameplate, this one smeared with blood.

"Jezebel!" Parker said, stunned. "There is another one."

He froze in place on the bottom step, still searching the darkness. A noise could be heard over the slowly creaking steps from the cautious feet behind him. It sent another shiver up Parker's backbone.

"Shhh!" he said and held his hand behind him, touching Hill's ankle.

The other two stopped and stood motionless. As Parker listened, he wondered how he could run back up the steps without running over his two companions.

A steady, low, rumbling growl.

Parker directed the light around warily. A creaking, breaking noise came from under Parker's feet.

A loud crack.

The step he stood on gave way with a crash.

The flashlight banged against the handrail and went out.

Parker slipped the eight inches to the floor and fell back against Hill. She dropped her gun and held onto him with both arms, trembling. Simpson had already reached the top of the steps and was poised with both hands on his revolver, aiming down while yelling out for backup.

Parker and Hill sat statuesque for a long moment. Parker rapped the light on the wall twice and it blinked back on. He began searching the darkness once more.

Still, a low, steady growl.

His eyes were adjusting to the darkness. Another faint light came from the far corner. He shone the light there quickly.

The sound wasn't a growl. An old gas water heater, burner roaring, kept the old man's bath water warm.

After an analytical pause, Parker and Hill laughed in relief.

Simpson sounded frantic. "You guys all right? What the hell's going on down there?"

Their laughter diminished until they looked up to respond to Simpson and burst out laughing again. Simpson's concern seemed less sincere, standing safe at the top of the steps with his pistol aimed.

"Well, shit, bust a gut, why don't you?" Simpson said. He holstered the revolver. "I told you, I don't like dogs."

"Nothing here," Parker said, dusting himself off. "Nothing but two dog beds that're worth more than most of the furniture in the house."

Parker glanced around and noticed the lid of a shoebox lying in the crawl space at the top of the wall between the two dog beds. He picked it up and noted streaks of dust on it as if it had been wiped off recently.

He tossed the lid back where he'd found it and followed Hill back up the stairs.

Parker stepped over the bodies once more. "Let's take a look at the rest of the house."

In the kitchen he found an electric clock on the floor. It was unplugged, the prongs bent, and the plastic outlet cover on the wall it leaned against was cracked, looking like it had been yanked out of the receptacle. A light spot in the shape of a square clock showed on the old, yellowed wallpaper six feet up. The plug-in was near the hall doorway. The clock pointed to twelve thirty.

"What about the clock?" Parker asked, looking down at it.

"Probably been that way for months. The one on the CD player wasn't correct, either," Simpson answered. "Look at all the dust on that thing."

Beside the clock sat two huge Tupperware bowls. One bowl contained a few pieces of dry dog food, the other, a half inch of water.

Parker looked around the room. The back door had a three-foot-tall dog port in the middle of it.

"That's big enough for a Shetland pony to walk through," he said. "I'll bet it let in one hell of a draft in the winter. You might have someone check the back yard." He opened the door gingerly and looked out to insure another dog wasn't there. "Look for blood and dog hair on the privacy fence. That's probably how the dog left. And you might put some strap iron on the inside of this dog-port door to keep it from opening out. If we're not able to catch the dog by tonight, maybe the thing'll come back and we can set a trap inside the house."

"Will do, Tony. That's it except for the old man's bedroom,"

Simpson said. "The door was closed tight, and nothing looked disturbed when we got here."

Parker looked in anyway. Nothing seemed disturbed, just like Simpson had said. The bed had been made, and everything seemed clean and neatly arranged.

"Are all the window screens in place and locked?"

"Yeah, I think so," Simpson said. "Check it out, Smith. Hey, what is this anyway? You Sherlock Holmes or something? This is a dog attack we're talking about—isn't it?"

"Uh-huh, it's just odd. I've got a funny feeling about it."

"Me, too," Hill said.

"I don't get it," Parker said. "Why would a dog—even a rabid dog—attack its master, especially a harmless old man sleeping in a recliner? And did you notice the blood on the nameplate on the basement wall downstairs? It looks as if the bigger dog beat its own head against the wall, like it was trying to make itself stop or even kill itself."

"Bullshit, Tony! Now you're going to tell me this crazy, murdering dog was sorry for what it did and became suicidal?" Simpson asked.

"Just the same, have them check it out. I want to know what time the blood was put there, and whose it was."

As they stepped out of the room, the body bags and gurneys were being brought in.

Two emergency medical technicians lifted the old man from his recliner to place him in a heavy, rubberized canvas bag on a gurney. A piece of paper tumbled over the arm of the chair and fell lightly to the floor.

"What's that?" Parker asked, pointing.

Simpson walked over and picked it up carefully by its corner with the tips of his thumb and forefinger.

"A page from a *Bible*. There's a passage highlighted. *Do not give dogs what is sacred: do not throw your pearls to pigs. If you do, they may trample them under their feet, and then turn and tear you to pieces.*" Simpson's eyes shifted to Parker. "I think he should have followed Jesus' advice."

"Maybe it's from his pastor," Parker said.

"No pastor would tear a page from the Good Book. That'd be sacrilegious," Simpson answered. "There're initials printed up at the top. *TP.* Hmm, *TP, TP....* " Simpson's eyes lit up as if he had made a remarkable discovery. "Tony Parker," Simpson speculated. "Maybe it's for you."

"Yeah, right," Parker said with a half smile.

"Well, *TP* are your initials, and it's about dogs, and you're the head dog catcher."

"Yeah, and it's also about pigs and you're a pig," Parker came back.

Sarah Hill had been quiet. "Maybe someone else left it after his death. Maybe someone is trying to tell you something."

"Oh, come on, Sarah," Simpson said, "or should I call you Dr. Watson—now you're going back to Parker's conspiracy theory? The damned dog killed the old man on his own."

Parker turned and looked at Hill, unintentionally staring, thinking, wondering if it were possible. The *Bible* verse could be a clue, a hint to what was going on, why the dogs attacked. Perhaps it was a piece to a puzzle not yet assembled. All the meaningful pieces not found, it represented only blank blue sky to a very frightening picture.

Simpson looked to one of the uniformed officers. "Smith, check to see if the old man has a *Bible* and if it's missing page 991."

The cop nodded and started searching the shelves.

Simpson looked through the living room window. "It's that asshole reporter from Channel Two, Haskins."

Parker looked to see the reporter streak across the lawn with his cameraman tailing him.

Simpson slipped the *Bible* page inside his jacket.

Before Parker had time to prepare himself, Haskins stood in the front door with the bright camera lights blazing through from behind. Parker, Simpson and Hill blocked the reporter's view of the bodies. He was a slim man with sharp features and sandy blond hair.

"Well, Officer Parker, another one of your beloved pit bulls attack a harmless citizen again?" he asked into the microphone and then shoved it into Parker's face for his comment.

Haskins had obviously not yet been informed of the gravity of the incident, only that it was an animal attack.

"Not this time, Asskiss—I mean Haskins."

Parker had known Haskins since returning from Vietnam, years ago, when Julie was in college. Julie had been dating Haskins, but upon his arrival, Parker found it easy to talk Julie into coming back to him and breaking up with Haskins. Now, after all those years and a couple of recent serious pit-bull attacks, Haskins finally found a way to get back at Parker by making him sound like he was defending the dogs and not doing his job properly.

"But it was a dog attack, wasn't it, Parker?" Haskins asked, sarcastically. Spying a red rubber dog bone on the floor, he picked it up and pointed it into Parker's face. "So, did the attacker use a bone to beat its victim?"

Parker didn't answer. He knew what Haskins was trying to do. He'd get Parker riled up on camera and edit out his own idiotic comments. Parker stepped to the side and squeezed between the cameraman and the doorway. Hill followed him out. Sheer horror showed on Haskins' face as the camera light shone across the scene of torn up bodies being placed into body bags. His chin dropped, and his tongue snaked around inside his open mouth. He was obviously trying to suppress the urge to vomit.

Parker stuck his head back in the doorway and, seeing the dog bone still in Haskins' hand, said with a wink, "Oh, and Jack, make sure that everybody without gloves that's touched anything the dogs might have come in contact with gets rabies shots. Poor bastards!" He turned and walked away, shaking his head. "Twenty-one hellacious shots in the stomach." When he reached the porch steps, he looked back and watched Haskins.

The reporter stood aghast as Simpson squeezed past, taking care not to brush against him. The coroner was next to walk by. He had a black plastic bag hanging heavily from one hand.

There was a sound like plastic wrap being ripped from the roll and a thump on the floor. Sergeant Morowsky's head had slipped from a tear in the bag and rolled up against the reporter's left foot.

"Damn!" the coroner said, "I keep telling 'em we need Hefty bags, but the bastards just go on giving us these shitty, no frills, generic ones." He scooped the head up and wrapped it with the plastic. "Next time, I guess I should just put all the parts together inside the body bag."

Haskins choked and dropped the bone. He ran outside and lost his breakfast while leaning over the porch railing. The cameraman followed him out and got some nice footage of the entire event while Haskins, between regurgitations, tried to wave him off. Parker, Simpson and Hill all watched, grinning morbidly.

Officer Smith came out the door and was careful to avoid the spewing reporter. He stepped up to Simpson, holding a small white *Bible*.

"This was the only one I found," Smith said. "Too small. That page isn't missing, anyway."

Simpson grunted and gave a nod.

"Did anyone see anything?" Parker asked.

"Just the neighbor, Mrs. Crane," Simpson said, looking to the old woman standing at her screen next door.

CHAPTER 8

M rs. Crane wavered in her doorway. With one hand on the inside handle of the screen door and one over her forehead, Tony Parker knew it would only be seconds before she was on the floor. He sprinted across her yard and onto her porch with Jack Simpson following. Reaching through the doorway, Parker caught the old woman by the upper arm just in time.

"I think you'd better sit down, Mrs. Crane," Parker said, leading her to a large overstuffed chair in her living room.

"Yes—yes, I think you're right," she said frailly. "But who are you?"

"Tony Parker, Animal Control Director."

"Who?"

"I'm the dog catcher, ma'am."

"Oh."

"Are you okay, Mrs. Crane?" Simpson asked, coming into the room from her kitchen with a glass of water.

"Oh, yes. I'll be fine now, I think," she said, taking the glass.

"Can you answer a few questions for us, Mrs. Crane?" Parker asked and patted her hand gently.

She nodded and set the glass down on a lamp table after a sip.

"Did you see any of what happened this morning?"

"Yes, I called the police when Mr. MacGreggor wouldn't come to the door, at about eight. I always check on him first thing in the morning when I go on my walk. Then I go over every afternoon and help him read his mail, make his bed, do some light housekeeping and feed the dogs. His eyesight isn't, or wasn't . . . " She choked and twisted a handkerchief she had pulled out of a pocket in her skirt. " . . . very good."

She dabbed at her eyes and wiped the cloth under her nose before continuing. "I couldn't hear anything in his house except for that weird Irish music, and that wasn't like him to have it on first thing in the morning like that. He usually played it at night before he went to bed. Didn't have a television. He didn't have much at all, except for that high falootin hi-fi and all those DC's or what ever they call 'em. He belonged to some kind of a record club. Then there were his dogs. I guess I shoulda told those poor officers about those dogs." She stared at the wall.

Parker and Simpson glanced at each other.

"I doubt if that would have made any difference, ma'am," Parker said. "What happened after the police arrived?"

"They had to break the door in to get inside. Then I heard some yellin', and the young man came running out and kicked his gun clear under their car. I guess he didn't mean to 'cause he ran over and started to look for it, but I don't think he ever did find it. He must not of remembered the shotgun sticking up inside their car. Then the man inside started screaming. I was a little scared, so I got inside. I couldn't see anything except the young man standing outside his car, talking on the radio. He was so young. Not much more than a boy.

"Then, he went inside the house, and I didn't see or hear a thing until this nice young black man drove up." She looked at Simpson and smiled.

Simpson smiled back.

"What can you tell us about Mr. MacGreggor and his dogs?" Parker asked.

"He got the dogs about five years ago. They were just cute little— well, big puppies. He had them sent over from Great Britain. Mr. MacGreggor had an old army buddy that married an English girl and lived there. He was a big breeder of prize winning Great Danes, and the two old fools kept in touch through the mail. Mr. MacGreggor was pretty lonely in that old house by himself. I couldn't be all things to him, you know. And his friend kept sending him pictures of his prize-winning dogs and kept telling him how gooda companions they made 'cause they were so loyal and loving and such.

"One day he finally gave in and asked him to send him a couple. They came from champion bloodlines, both of them. They were the only things he loved more than his music. He made sure they always had the best—the best dog food, silk cushions to lay on, a diamond on each of their dog tags big enough to choke a horse. . . . "

"Diamond dog tags," Simpson said, shaking his head.

"Yes, three carats. Both of them."

"Where'd he get his money?" Simpson asked. "I mean, his house is a run down shack."

"You know, I never really found out. Whenever he needed anything, he'd pay for it in cash, usually hundred dollar bills. Once a month, I'd go buy money orders for him to pay the few bills he had."

Parker asked, "Did he get a pension check or Social Security? Money from a relative?"

"No, I never saw a dime. And I opened all of his mail—with that letter opener that has a diamond at the base of its blade. It's three carats, too. They gave it to him when he retired from that insurance company he used to work for. It was the only thing he owned that was worth much besides that record player. He thought the diamond was so pretty that he got one for each of the dogs when they finally showed up."

Parker said to Simpson. "Did you find a letter opener?"

"No, and believe me, I'd remember one like that. We'll check it out."

Mrs. Crane continued, "He didn't have any relatives that I ever heard of, let alone rich ones. His wife died twelve years ago, and he didn't have any children. He had one brother, but he and his wife were killed in a car accident about ten years ago. Now, they did have a son. That would be Mr. MacGreggor's nephew. But they were poorer than church mice, and he hadn't heard anything out of the boy since about four years ago. That was when the boy asked to borrow some money from him. Mr. MacGreggor was a real tight wad. He told him to go straight to hell!" she said, leaning into Parker's face. "Never saw him again.

"The only thing I can figure is the old man collected a whole mess of money on his wife's insurance and rat holed it, and whatever else he'd saved over the years, somewhere in the house. I saw him take some money out of a shoebox once."

Simpson shook his head. "Didn't find anything."

Parker raised his eyebrows. "I saw a shoebox lid in the crawl space when we were in the basement. The dust had been wiped from it. I didn't find the box, though."

Parker looked back to the old woman. "What about the dogs, Mrs. Crane?" he asked. "Were they out of control over there?"

"Oh, no! Why, they were the nicest, most even-tempered animals I've ever seen. That's what was so surprising about all this. They were always very obedient, and Mr. MacGreggor just loved them to pieces," she said with a hint of jealously. She paused. "Especially that Jezebel, or 'Jazbo,' as he'd call her. She was the sweetest and smartest dog I've ever seen, and biggest, too."

"You mean, next to Beelzebub," Parker said, hoping the coroner was wrong.

"Oh, no!" she said. "She was nearly a hand taller than him."

"Holy . . . ," Simpson said, looking at Parker.

"That'd put her at about forty two or three inches at the shoulder," Parker said. "A record height, by as much as an inch."

"But she was as gentle as a kitten," Mrs. Crane said. "She'd always greet me with her long ol' tail just a whippin' back and forth. Now that thing would hurt if she hit you with it. She'd be wagging it around and knocking things off the table when she got real excited. But she'd never hurt anyone on purpose. Now, I couldn't vouch for

Beelzebub so much, although he seemed friendly enough. It was just that he was kind of shy, maybe a little sneaky."

Parker handed Mrs. Crane his card. It had his home number hand printed at the bottom. "We won't trouble you any longer, Mrs. Crane. But be sure to call me if you think of anything else that might be important. You'll be all right?"

"Oh, yes—yes, I'm fine."

"And, Mrs. Crane," Parker said, as he rose from the chair.

She looked up at him, innocently. "Yes?"

"Beelzebub is dead, but Jezebel seems to have gotten away. There'll be officers patrolling the neighborhood night and day until we find her, right, Jack?" Parker glanced over his shoulder at Simpson.

Jack nodded to the old woman.

Tony continued, "But if you see Jezebel, don't go near her. Stay inside and call me right away, okay?"

Mrs. Crane looked down at her handkerchief. "Yes, I understand."

Parker and Simpson turned and walked out the door. Haskins and his cameraman had left, but there was still a flurry of activity.

"Damn it, Tony, what is this, anyway?" Simpson asked as they walked down the porch steps. "I'm getting the impression you think this is more than a dog attack. You think the damn dog ripped off his master and ran off to the Bahamas or something?"

"Her."

"What?"

"Her master. Jezebel is a she. You guys gonna make it to the picnic tomorrow?" he asked with his back turned, not responding to Simpson's question as he walked to the truck.

"Uh, yeah. Wouldn't miss it for the world. You know that."

"You'll take care of the press for me, won't you? Downplay it some. We don't want a panic. But we do want to let people know she's out there and to be on the lookout so we can catch her before anyone else gets hurt."

"Sure, Tony. Where are you going to be?"

"I'm going to run ol' Beelzebub out to Doc's and have him

examined. Maybe he can give us a little more insight on this. After that, I'll be out with the posse."

Hill stood at the back of the Jimmy truck with the coroner and Tommy Chin, who had just arrived. She broke away and hopped into the passenger's side when she saw Parker heading that way.

"Chin, did Sarah fill you in?"

"Yeah, boss. Incredible."

"Will you handle things for a bit?" Parker asked.

"Sure, boss."

"Get everyone down here that's working today and everybody that's on call. Have them go door to door to warn the neighbors within a mile of here and see if anyone's seen this monster," Parker said. He turned toward the truck.

"You got it, boss."

Parker stopped and glanced back at Chin with a considered look. "Hey, Tommy. Call me if anything turns up. And be careful. If you can't reach me by radio, I'll be at Doc White Cloud's."

"Sure thing, boss. Wish I could be at the picnic tomorrow. Tell Julie happy fifteenth for me, will you?"

"There might not be a picnic if we don't find this thing."

Parker looked in his side mirror as they drove away and saw Simpson standing on the lawn looking over the scene. He appeared somewhat awestruck.

CHAPTER 9

Tony Parker was eager to see his old friend Dr. Johnny White Cloud, and for more than social reasons. He dropped Sarah Hill off at her apartment. Since she'd be on call, she'd need her rest if Jezebel wasn't found by second shift.

Doc White Cloud and his wife Patsy were more than friends to Tony Parker. When Parker was a freshman in high school, his father died from a heart attack. He didn't have any brothers or sisters, and the White Clouds became a part of his family. He worked at Doc's clinic after school, on Saturdays, and a regular forty hours per week during the summer. He cleaned out cages, groomed and fed animals, and did other odd jobs.

Parker's interest in veterinary medicine was born there. The White Clouds treated him like a son, not having children of their own, and after Parker's mother died of cancer while he was overseas, the relationship seemed to help them all fill the parent/child gap.

Dog days of summer, Parker thought as he pulled away from Hill's apartment building. Doc had told him about the "days of the dog" when he was a teenager, working at the clinic. It was the period during the summer that the earth passed closest to Sirius, the Dog Star. According to Doc, the combined heat of it and the sun made those few weeks the hottest of the year. The "dog days" was the time dogs and humans go mad and bad things happened. It was the end of

August now, and it seemed the dog days were hanging on a little longer than usual.

Parker pulled down the tall hedge-lined, gravel drive and then into the parking lot. He wasn't the only customer of the morning. In front of the white house converted into a clinic was a well-kept black, sixty-three Chevy pickup parked between Doc's turquoise Lincoln Continental and the white clinic van. An outside phone bell rang twice as Parker stepped out of the truck.

"Tony Parker, fancy seeing you again so soon," Mrs. Bumfield said. She opened the driver's side door of the old truck, and her big ugly Heinz fifty-seven whined from the back. "How ya doin'?" She held out her hand for a shake and looked over her shoulder at Eldon Bumfield as he came out of the office door. "Look who's here, Eldon. Tony Parker, the man that saved the town of Sand Creek, Kansas, and my kitten."

"Tony, how the devil are you?" Bumfield asked. Brown tobacco juice seeped from the corner of his overloaded cheek, and he wore what looked like the same overalls and beat-up straw hat with green plastic sun visor.

"Just fine. Good to see you, Mr. and Mrs. Bumfield. No more ferocious skunks, I hope?"

"No, sir," Bumfield answered. "You got the last and only one, thank the good Lord. How's that bite?"

Tony flipped his hand. "Hasn't given me any problems."

"I sure want to thank you again for getting my kitten out of that tree," the woman said. "I don't know what I woulda done. 'Course, she wouldn't have been up there if Dawg hadn't been in one of his bad moods. Seems like he gets that way about once a month. 'Think it's some kind of male dog menopause or somethun. Lucky we had you out there for that skunk when we did."

Mr. Bumfield looked at his wife and frowned. She caught the clue.

"Oh, me, here I am carrying on so. You know, I do that sometimes, when I'm excited about seeing somebody. Anyway, Tony, thanks for saving my Little Pussy," she said.

Bumfield looked at her and shook his head. "Watch how you say that. Dawg might get the wrong idea."

Mrs. Bumfield hit the man with a swipe of her homemade patchwork purse, and they all chuckled.

"So, isn't Dawg feeling well?" Parker asked, reaching over to pet him.

"Oh, yeah," Eldon Bumfield answered. "We just brought him in to be treated for mange. Every dog in Sand Creek has had to be treated. All thirty-five or so have had it to some extent. We were gettin' concerned that the thirty-one human beins might get it if we didn't nip it in the bud."

Parker stopped petting Dawg and wiped his hand on his trousers.

Bumfield reached over the side of the pickup bed and took Dawg by the collar.

"Come on, Dawg," he said. "Now don't you give me a hard time."

He assisted the big beast over the side and to the ground in a clumsy skirmish, then trotted him to the office door and inside. Within fifteen seconds he had deposited Dawg and jogged back out, hustling to the pickup. His meaty upper body jiggled like Jell-O slapped with a spoon.

"Well, better go," Bumfield said, getting into the passenger side of the truck. "Come and visit us sometime, Tony. I know Tricia would like to see you again. All she's been talking about since yesterday is how you climbed up in that tree and rescued the kitten."

Parker smiled, thinking of cute little Tricia and her doll and of the Bumfield's down-home hospitality. He remembered the tapestry on their living room wall depicting a group of dogs playing poker and thought how appropriately it fit in. He waved as they pulled away.

Dr. White Cloud stepped out the office door. He was a short and stocky man with long, coarse, salt-and-pepper hair, braided into a ponytail. His darkly tanned skin was like leather, covering his large-featured face, and he wore turquoise and silver jewelry on his fingers, wrists and neck.

"Thanks again for saving my Little Pussy," Mrs. Bumfield yelled as they drove away waving.

Doc grinned wide. "Tony, how wonderful you've come to visit." He also waved to the Bumfields as the left. "And I can see you're still proudly serving, or should I say servicing, the community."

"Hey Doc, give me a break," Parker said, grinning back. "How've you been?"

They shook hands and patted shoulders, then turned toward the door.

"Real good, Tony. Yankee over those ear mites?" Doc asked.

"Oh yeah, he's fine. How's that big, ugly, slobbering mutt of yours?"

"Patsy's all right. I just try to stay out of her way."

Parker laughed and softly backhanded the old vet on the shoulder. "I meant Red, your dog, not your wife."

On queue, a short Native-American woman nearly as wide as she was tall came through the doorway, smiling. She wore a long white dress with large pink and blue flowers.

"Look, Patsy, honey," Doc said, showing the woman a quick smile. "Tony's here."

"Tony, oh, Tony!" She ran up to Parker with her two long, braided pigtails slapping her back and gave him a two-hundred-and-fifty-pound bear hug.

The old vet stepped back. "Damn, Tony, next thing you know, you'll be saving her pussy, too."

Patsy didn't hear, or maybe didn't care to hear, Doc's foolishness. "Oh, Tony, it's so good to see you. How you been? When are you and the family coming over for supper like you used to?"

"How about after we come back from vacation, week after next? Would that work?"

"You bet, Tony. We'll have a nice roast. I'll fix it up just the way you like."

Doc patted Tony on the back. "So, you must be here to finally make me an offer on my practice and let me retire."

"No, not yet. I have decided to quit my job and go back to school full time starting the second semester. I've got a year left, you know. Julie's going to go back to teaching while I'm up at K-State. When I'm finished, then I'll be able to make you an offer."

"Julie mentioned you were going back to school when she brought Yankee in. Sounds good, Tony. Happy to hear it," Doc said with a big smile. "Make sure that offer's one I can't refuse, okay?"

"Sure thing, Doc. You folks are going to make it to the picnic tomorrow, aren't you?"

"I'm sorry to say, we're not. Just got word Patsy's uncle down in Ponca City passed away yesterday. He was ninety-three. Have to go to one of those family powwows, tomorrow. You know what I mean," Doc said. "They put him in the ground on Monday, and we'll be back that night.

"I'm sorry to hear about that, Patsy," Tony said. He turned back to Doc. "A real powwow, huh?"

"Not really. This'll be a white man's wake. Patsy's mother's family. It'll be the same as when Uncle Arlo died. The men sat around on the porch, talking about how they were going to miss poor old Uncle Arlo. We watched baseball on a little black and white TV while passing bottles of wine around, Ripple, I think. The women were inside doing God knows what. Whew, I had a headache from that wine for two days. It won't be anything like your powwow last New Year's Eve. Remember? You and Jack were juggling those antique depression glasses, and I ended up wearing Julie's bra. Hope she's not still mad at me for getting into her underwear drawer."

"Naw, I'm sure she isn't. She laughs every time she thinks about it."

"Now that was a powwow any red man could appreciate."

"But Doc, I'm a white man."

"You just think you are, Tony. Deep down inside, I know you've got some Native American blood in you. There was an Indian in the wood pile some where down the road; I'll just bet my reputation on it."

"Your reputation as what, Doc, a Native American or a veterinarian?"

The old vet paused for a moment. He motioned as if he was putting on Julie's bra again. "As a transvestite!"

The two men laughed, and Patsy shook her head.

Doc said, "Damn it, Tony, we just don't get together as much as we used to."

"I know, Doc. Hey, maybe I can talk Jack into a poker party this next Friday night over at his place, like old times."

"Sure, Tony. Just let me know. I promise I won't miss it. I don't care who dies."

"I'll hold you to it."

Doc nodded. "I sense, though, this time is no social visit. So if your dog isn't sick, and you aren't ready to buy me out, what's up?"

Parker's face grew solemn. "There's been a very serious dog attack. One of your customers."

"Oh, no! Was someone hurt bad?" Patsy asked.

"Yeah, three people were killed."

"Oh, Lord!" Doc exclaimed. "What...? Who?"

"Alvin MacGreggor and two police officers were killed by MacGreggor's two Great Danes."

"No, that can't be." Doc frowned. "I never would have thought those dogs could hurt a flea."

"Well, they did, but I can't figure it out, either. The only thing that would make even a little sense would be that they had rabies. But I'm skeptical. The male's tag shows you gave him his rabies booster the day before yesterday."

"That's right," Doc confirmed. "I gave them both rabies boosters."

"The male took a bullet through the heart. He's in the truck. I was hoping you might be able to help figure this thing out."

"Sure, Tony, I'll do what I can," Doc said, changing directions and heading toward the Jimmy. "What about the female, Jezebel?"

"She's loose."

Doc stopped with his hand on the tailgate of the truck. He turned to look at Parker. "Loose?"

Parker nodded and opened the back.

"When a dog howls, a man will die," Doc said with a blank stare.

"Huh?"

"Red was barking a lot late last night, and I went outside to calm him down before the neighbors complained. I heard a strange howl. Kind of hoarse, way off in the distance. It's an old wives tale, but the howl was so strange it made me think of it."

Parker took the dog's front end and pulled it out far enough for Doc to take the hindquarters, and they walked sideways with it to the clinic.

"We'll examine him and send his head in for rabies tests," Doc said as Patsy opened the door. She followed them in and then took her place behind the reception desk.

White Cloud and Parker walked through the waiting room and into the examination room. They laid the cumbersome beast onto a stainless-steel table on casters in the middle of the room. Dawg sat in a huge wire cage in the far corner and already rested comfortably but remained alert to the commotion they made with the body of the Great Dane. A short oriental man stood next to the sink, drying off some mirror-finished surgeon's tools and large hypodermic needles. He wore a black T-shirt and black work pants and shoes, and had coal black hair and dark skin. He was noticeably disfigured and scarred on the left side of his face and hand and had a black eye patch over his left eye. Something about him made Tony feel uneasy.

"Oh, Tony, you haven't met Truong yet, have you?"

An unexplainable chill in the warm morning air made Parker shiver as Doc made the introduction.

"No." He thrust out his hand. "Glad to meet you, Truong. I'm Tony Parker."

Truong flinched at Parker's hand, appearing surprised, but shook it anyway and bowed, face down, never meeting Tony eye to eye.

"Truong's kind of shy, but he's a damn good worker. And he's cheap," the old vet said. "Him and old Yankee really hit it off when Julie brought him in a couple of weeks ago."

"Nothing against you, Truong, but Yankee would hit it off with anybody, even a burglar if the big sissy didn't run and hide first," Parker said.

"You be surprised," Truong said, with a heavy oriental accent, head still bowed. "Yankee might be gallant warrior, when need be."

"Truong, go get the Alvin MacGreggor file, will you?" Doc said, looking down at the large dog's body. Truong quickly folded the white towel, draped it on a towel rack and left the room.

When Parker was sure Truong couldn't hear, he asked in a whisper, "What's the story with him?"

"He came here about six months ago," Doc said in a low tone. "Said he was good with animals and would work for room and board. So I snatched him up. I guess he was in some sort of traffic accident years ago that kind of messed his left side up, put out one eye. But he gets around fine. He emigrated from Thailand just a few months back. He *is* damn good with dogs. Even sleeps with them. Of course, I can relate to him there." Doc smiled.

Truong came back into the room and handed Doc a manila folder. Doc pulled out a set of small-lensed reading glasses and put them on.

"I'll let you work," Parker said, taking a step back. "Call me if you need anything."

Dr. White Cloud glanced over his reading glasses and gave a look unusually sober for the old vet. "Tony, be careful. This dog that's loose, Jezebel, she's a beauty. Biggest damn dog I've ever seen. Forty-two inches at the shoulders and fangs as long as your little finger."

Parker nodded. "That'd be a record, wouldn't it? Especially for a female. Is she a freak?"

"Yeah, probably would be a record if anybody troubled to have it recorded. But she's no freak. Beautiful animal. Black and sleek and intelligent, too. That's the scary part. She's also the smartest dog I've ever seen. A lot smarter than most humans that walk through these doors. She was real even tempered, too. She liked to play. But she'd get homesick and start howling if we'd keep her here for more than a couple of hours. She had a real strange howl, kind of hoarse. I didn't think Great Danes howled, but this one...." Doc paused, and

Parker wondered if he was thinking about the howl he'd heard last night.

"I'd believe she spoke seven languages and was running for governor from the way people talk about her," Parker said.

"Yeah, she's something all right. But, Tony—Tony, if she's gone mad—well, I just hate to think. Be careful, Tony."

CHAPTER 10

The day's heat carried over into the still twilight. The air clung thick with low foggy patches and had the fresh, clean smell of an imminent rain. Storm clouds in the west caused dark to come early, and distant flashes of lightning promised the needed moisture, though that promise had been broken for several weeks in a row.

The little Lutheran church down by the river let out, and half a dozen voices broke the evening's silence. Pastor Carl Santini's bright white collar seemed luminescent in contrast to his black shirt and pants. He stood on the short stoop in front of the large double doors and bade good evening to each of the parishioners with a cheerful smile and friendly handshake as they stepped out. The old preacher's hands were wracked with arthritis, twisted from years of torture from the disease, but the large smile on the little man's face didn't give away the pain shocking his frail body as some of the more enthusiastic handshakers proved their sincerity with firm grips.

It hadn't been a scheduled service but a meeting of the church council that caused them to stay late. The church budget was the issue. After some debate, it seemed every aspect had been handled in a satisfactory manner to all.

Pastor Carl waved as the last of them walked away. He rubbed his hands together, attempting to alleviate at least some of the pain and noted the unusual darkness. He flipped the light switch just inside the door for the outside light but without results. How odd that both the street light in front of the church and the light over the door would be burned out at the same time. He'd have to make sure the janitor knew to replace the bulb over the door and report the streetlight to the city.

The night grew silent after the last of the church council members drove off into the peaceful evening. He raised his wire-framed glasses to his forehead and rubbed the bridge of his nose with his thumb and index finger. After adjusting the glasses back into place, he took a second to look up at the few stars peeking through scattered clouds.

Pastor Carl thought about the insignificance he felt. As thousands of times before, he gazed at the twinkling pinholes in the blackening sky. He could see them well due to the darker-than-usual street.

He hadn't made a big difference in the little world in which he had survived his sixty-eight years. But he was happy to think he had made the lives of many of his fellow worshipers just a little more bearable, special, maybe more meaningful. He wished he could have done more. He wished he could have saved more souls, perhaps as a missionary to cannibals in New Zealand or as an evangelist with millions of television supporters. He drew a long breath while he looked up and reached into his trouser pocket to find the key to the door.

A growl-like noise broke the stillness.

At first, Pastor Carl thought he had imagined it. He looked, straining into the darkness of the street. A park with lots of bushes and trees was across the street, but nothing, or no one, could be seen to make such a noise. Small homes lined the deserted street going the other way. Only a few had their lights on. But the strange noise wasn't one he would associate with them. Perhaps it came from a hopped up car with loud mufflers, driven by an untamed youth several blocks away.

Now a howl. A distant howl but no less alarming. It keened long, sad and hoarse, unlike any he'd heard before.

That dog, that huge killer dog, was still out there. He'd heard about it on the radio. Everyone talked about it at the council meeting. Pastor Carl had even asked God to help them find it before it had a chance to hurt anyone else. Could this be that dog? The MacGreggor house wasn't but half a dozen blocks down the street. No, it couldn't be. A neighbor kid was trying to frighten an old man. Surely that was all it was.

He pulled out a set of keys attached to a small ring with a white luminous cross on it. His eyes shifted around the darkness. He fumbled with the keys with fingers that might as well have been toes. They slipped from his hands and dropped to the ground striking the concrete with a clatter.

The odd sound came again.

Pastor Carl looked up from a bent position as he reached for the keys. The noise came louder, this time closer, much closer, and definitely a growl, not a noisy muffler. He gazed into the darkness, still reaching. Nothing in sight. He finally grabbed up the keys and with shaking, gnarled hands found the correct one and locked the door quickly.

He turned, looked out at his car parked across the street and stepped toward it.

Something moving over there. Something dark and big. He stopped halfway down the walk. The thing shifted back and forth behind his car. *It must be a prankster, a juvenile trying to scare a poor old man out of his wits.*

"All right now," Pastor Carl said in a reprimanding tone, "I see you over there. The joke's over. You've had your fun."

No reply. Still the shadowy figure moved back and forth behind the car.

"I said enough!" Pastor Carl was more insistent this time. "I know who you are, and I'll tell your parents. Now go on home."

The shadow stopped. Pastor Carl's skin crawled. This was no prankster. He sensed an evil presence, something diabolical.

"Oh, Lord Jesus," he prayed. His trembling hand rose with the keys, and again he searched for the one to the church door.

The shadow came around the car.

It advanced into the street. It came for him. He would be unable to get to the car. The thing approached in between. No place to run, his aged body wouldn't last. He must get back to the church. Inside, he would be safe.

Once again, as he bungled with the keys, his fluttering hands fumbled them, and they fell fifteen feet in front of the door. Without looking to see how close the thing was, he bent down as quickly as he could and groped for the keys. As he did, his wire framed glasses slipped from his face and also fell to the ground.

"Damn it!" he exclaimed, then considered his slip briefly. "Forgive me, Lord."

The world became a dark haze. He felt the shadow's presence as his hand finally made contact with the keys. He looked. Now within ten feet, his elderly eyes saw only a dark blur moving slowly, steadily toward him.

No time to feel for the glasses. He stood upright.

"Have mercy on me, Father!" Pastor Carl prayed as he turned and scurried toward the door while searching among the half-dozen keys for the elusive door key.

He found the correct one and shoved it at the door lock. The key glanced off, scratching the brown painted steel.

Pastor Carl screamed. He was thrown against the entryway. The thing had him. He raised the luminous cross in front of his face.

"Away with you, Satan!" he cried out.

The key chain was batted from his hand, and he could feel his fingers, wet with blood.

A flash of light shot in his eyes. A sort of sparkle like from a precious stone, a diamond perhaps, reflected what little light it had captured from the house lights down the street. He tried to focus, but his old, tired eyes showed him nothing but a large fuzzy shape, hulking in the darkness in front of him.

Again, the thing came at him. He felt pain in his throat, and warm blood drenched his shirt as he thought of how his bright white collar would be ruined.

*_*_*

They had seen neither *hide nor hair* of Jezebel. To Tony Parker it was as if she hadn't been at all. He'd never actually seen her. She was only a rumor, or, more accurately, a legend.

Parker looked forward to this night. It was nine thirty, and he and Julie got ready for bed early. Everything seemed perfect. He had saved the peace with Julie. Frustrated from the unsuccessful attempt to find even a trace of Jezebel, he went home around six p.m. Although the long day and relentless heat had taken its toll on his not-as-young-as-it-used-to-be body, he took the family out for pizza, then to the mall. The pizza, now haunting him, seemed to be burning a good-sized hole in his stomach.

They had gotten all of their shopping done in preparation for the picnic tomorrow that Julie had been insistent they have, no matter what this Jezebel did. They had picked up some last minute items for Nick for school. He'd be a big first grader on Monday. It didn't seem possible.

At Sears, Tony told Julie to pick out a new outfit and shoes. That would be her anniversary present, even though she'd said she was willing to settle on a vacation to Missouri the week after next to see her folks. She had a whole hundred dollars to blow. That wouldn't have seemed like much before Audrey came along, but now, it was a fortune.

Julie showed her child-like enthusiasm as she danced down the aisles and through the multitude of clothes racks. Tony had seen the guilt flush Julie's face as he laid down the hundred-dollar bill at the register. He felt it himself as the clerk asked for another five fifty and, looking into his wallet at a lonesome ten-dollar bill, realized they had burned up a whopping two hundred and fifty dollars that night.

Lying naked under the covers of the king-sized waterbed, Tony watched as Julie came out of the bathroom drying off from her shower. The only light in the room came from the television, in which he had lost all interest.

The years hadn't hurt Julie a bit in Tony's mind. There was no thought of comparing this morning's view of Sarah Hill with her. He couldn't see the few extra dimples in her cute, but slightly wider-than-twenty-years-ago, butt. He didn't notice that her breasts suspended just a bit lower on her chest. He didn't see the lines in her face that stayed, even after smiling. He was still every bit as much in love with her as ever before.

Tonight, he felt an old spark. It amused him and he was reminded of the days gone by when he and Julie were first married. They would make love tonight. He knew they would. He could tell she wanted to by the way she had smiled at him. The way she'd held onto his arm in the shopping mall. The way she touched him lightly as they talked in the Pizza Hut during supper.

The lovemaking would be as it had been many times before. It might not be as wild a session as when they were younger, but the years hadn't eaten away all of the passion. They would make love once, maybe twice, before they collapsed into each other's arms on sweat dampened sheets, their steamy, sex-heated bodies writhing and heaving from their frenzied rapture.

Tony showed a small grin as he watched her from across the room. Julie looked over and grinned back.

"What?" she asked.

"Oh, nothin'," he said, grinning wider with his hands clasped behind his head and covers pulled up to his navel.

"Come on, what?" she insisted, with a chuckle.

"You."

"Me, what?"

"You're still my beautiful prom queen," he said in a dramatic tone.

She fired her towel like a fastball, and it hit Tony in the face. "And you're the same silver-tongued devil, too!" She jumped onto the bed, straddling him and pinning him down by the wrists.

Tony heard the Ten O'clock News come on the TV. Julie's senses seemed closed to the television and everything else as she stared down into Tony's eyes, still smiling.

"And with tonight's top story, Henry Haskins," the anchorwoman said.

Julie bent down and kissed Tony, open mouthed, and Tony received her with eyes wide, listening.

Haskins' voice came on the TV. "Thank you, Sally. The citizens of Wichita are in grave danger tonight as a huge, black, monstrous Great Dane roams our streets, unchallenged, and three men are dead."

"Oh, shit!" Tony said, pulling away, frowning.

"Now what?" Julie asked, jerking her head back.

Tony didn't answer. He looked around Julie to see the newscast. Julie bent down again and began planting small kisses methodically, starting on his forehead and slowly working down the side of his face.

"At around midnight last night, a man was savagely murdered by this beast in his home in the eleven-hundred block on Whiteside. This morning, two officers, responding to a call from a neighbor, were also killed at that home. Here is my report, taken shortly after the officers were killed."

The first five seconds of the report showed Haskins puking over the railing. The picture went back to a frowning Haskins. He looked off camera. "I told you to edit that!" he yelled.

The picture returned to the report, showing Haskins standing in front of the MacGreggor house.

"Citizens of Wichita, beware! Roaming our streets is a giant, killer Great Dane that could be, at this very moment, stalking your neighborhood for its next victims. The demonic animal is as black as a hell bound night, has two-inch, razor-sharp, flesh-ripping fangs, and is nearly big enough to look a man eye to eye while standing on all fours. This animal, reportedly named Jezebel, is extremely dangerous and will likely kill at random with no provocation. After three gory deaths, it is apparent that the dog goes for its victims' throats with tremendous jaws capable of popping a man's head off, effortlessly."

The picture went back to Haskins and the aghast anchorwoman behind their desk.

The reported continued, live, "Details are sketchy at present, but it appears there were two Great Danes that did the killing. One of them, the largest, is still at large. The officers killed were Sergeant James Morowsky, a nineteen-year veteran of the Wichita Police Department, and Officer Farley Cox, who had just began his career in law enforcement, ironically enough, this morning. The name of the other victim, who was also the owner of the dogs, is being withheld, pending notification of next of kin.

"And, Sally, this real life monster is still on the loose. It's quite possibly rabid, and the Sedgwick County Animal Control office seems to be relatively impotent in this type of emergency, unable to turn up even the slightest clue as to the whereabouts of the animal. We are still very vulnerable and unprotected. It is strongly recommended that Wichita citizens, especially those living near the eleven-hundred block on Whiteside, stay in their homes, doors and windows closed."

Sally the anchorwoman faced Haskins for a long moment with her eyes clenched and mouth open.

By now Julie had worked her way down to Tony's stomach. She looked up to his face as she toyed with the hair on his chest with her forefinger.

"Twenty years with the same man," Julie said, still smiling, seemingly oblivious to the television.

"Except for the little fling with that asshole!" Tony said without thinking, still looking around Julie.

Julie frowned and pushed off of Tony. She stood to the side of the bed and looked at the TV.

"You're the asshole!" she said, walking over to her closet and getting out a long, pink, terry-cloth robe. She walked to the bed and yanked the pillow out from underneath Tony's head.

"Oh, shit, I'm sorry. I didn't mean it. He just rubbed me the wrong way today. Come back to bed."

"Well don't expect me to rub you the right way after that!" she said, as she stormed out of the room. "Go screw yourself!"

The door slammed shut.

Ten seconds later it swung open as quickly. Parker could see by the look on his wife's face there wasn't going to be a second-thought apology.

"No—no, I'm not going to let you off that easy!" she said in as loud a whisper as she could get away with, obviously trying not to wake the kids.

She stared for a moment with her knuckles on her hips. Her glare punished like a switch on an unprotected backside. He knew what was coming.

"You have the—the...."

If she says balls, she's really pissed.

"... nerve to talk about something that happened over sixteen years ago and was completely innocent. He *was* the only one. You hadn't asked me to marry you, or even to wait for you, while you were in the service. Remember? You said it would be better if we were free to see others. You said it, not me."

"And you agreed and did it, didn't you?" *Why did I say that?*

"Yes, I did. He was nice to me, and I was lonely. I don't suppose that ever happened to you in Vietnam, or Japan, or anywhere else you were, did it?"

Parker didn't answer. He wasn't going to lie, and he certainly wasn't going to tell the truth. Julie wouldn't really want to know.

"Now...," Julie began.

Oh boy, here it comes!

"...you actually have the—balls...."

That's it, she's really pissed.

"...to bring something like that up when you and darling little Sarah are out playing grab ass all day, every day?"

"Oh, come on, Julie. You know that isn't true. We work together, that's all. Yeah, I like her. She's a nice girl. Hell, she's just a kid."

"Don't give me that, Tony Parker. I've seen the way you look at her. And I don't mind that. I'll admit she is something for a man to look at. But it's the way she looks at you that bothers me. I know the way you are to a cute face and a little smile. You're a marshmallow. She'll take you to bed, and before you even know it, it'll be too late if it isn't already."

This wasn't a statement. It was a question, and by her expression, she was expecting an answer.

"Well?" she demanded.

"Well what? Have we been to bed together? No. Hell no. We haven't been to bed, the kitchen sink, or the hood of the truck!" *That was a mistake!*

Julie looked at him. Tony could tell she was wondering why he would say something like "the hood of the truck."

"Come on, Julie, get real."

"All I can say to you, Tony, is that I trust you as much as a man can be trusted. I've seen girls like Sarah before, and I've seen what they can do to marriages."

"And what do you suggest I do, fire her?"

"I don't care. Fire her, transfer her, or at the least, give her the idea you're not interested!"

"I have, and you have nothing to worry about, believe me."

"You're the one that had better be worried. Sarah Hill is the type that doesn't give up until she gets what she wants. And guess what, you'll end up with nothing—nothing Tony. We've been together too long for me to just give you up, and I won't, as long as I know you're mine and only mine. But as soon as you cross the line, you can count on me not sticking around. I'll be gone so fast it'll leave your head spinning, and the only thing you'll have is Sarah for as long as she doesn't get bored of you.

"I shouldn't have to compete for my husband at this stage in our lives. I've stuck by you through thick and thin, and there's been a lot of thin. Don't get me wrong; I'm not complaining. It's just that I've got a lot of time and tears invested in you, in us. I've dreamed your dreams, cried your tears when you were hurt and too dumb to admit it, and I've given birth to your children. In twenty-five years I know where I want to be—it's my one and only dream, now. I want to be with you, not rich but out of debt, and enjoying grandchildren. Sarah threatens that dream, and it's not right. I'm entitled to that one dream in my life, Tony, and the only way that little bitch is going to steal it away from me is if you let her. You think about that!"

Julie walked out and closed the door, this time a little softer.

This thing with Sarah wasn't just a fun little game. It was serious. The wrong move and he could lose everything. His wife, his family, everything.

Parker blew out, frustrated. He turned the TV off with the remote and rolled to his side. He finally slipped off to sleep after tossing and turning for nearly an hour. He slept just as restlessly. His mind was fuzzy and blurred, and he dreamed of fog—a wispy, yet thick, fog, hanging low on a street. A light mist gave haloes to the streetlights, and small pools of water spotted the pavement. He heard no sound in this dream, but the stillness was loud and tangible.

In the grayish soup, a dark vision appeared. Floating down the middle of the street, it slowly formed into a recognizable shape.

An animal. A large black animal. A huge Great Dane. It walked with confidence. Long, thin legs. Mouth closed, head and eyes fixed straight ahead. Occasionally, its feet splashed one of the pools. Light from the streetlights caused a sparkle from underneath its neck with every step of its left forefoot. A large diamond, set on a gold tag, captured the light and shot it out like a laser. The dog maintained its pace for what seemed like minutes.

Finally, it stopped. With its body still pointing down the street, it slowly turned its head to the right and looked up a sidewalk leading to the front door of a house. It stared, still emotionless, at the door. At Tony Parker's door.

CHAPTER 11

Parker woke with sweat covering his face in beads. Morning light invaded the room. He felt next to him on the bed. Alone. And then, he remembered the volleys of sharp words the night before. Julie had spent the night in the guest bedroom. He heard the master bath shower and hoped when she came out he could somehow smooth things over.

He called in to the animal control office first thing. There had still been no sign of Jezebel. If she was rabid, she was probably dying somewhere if not already dead—*If* she was rabid. As he hung up, Julie walked swiftly through the room in her bathrobe and out the door. There were no words exchanged. Parker really hadn't had the chance. Julie obviously didn't have the inclination. She would be going to get the kids up and ready.

There would be church to go to this morning—the little Lutheran Church down by the river. Tony had promised he'd go. He'd take his pager. After that, there was the picnic at one o'clock in the park five miles away. A picnic when people were being killed. It wasn't right. It didn't make sense. But it was important to Julie, real important. She wouldn't care if he had to work twenty-four hours a day until they found this incredible beast, as long as he went to church and the picnic. That is, until next weekend when their vacation started and they were to go to Missouri to visit Julie's folks. Surely they'd find Jezebel by then.

At a quarter till nine, Parker stepped out of the shower and the phone rang. Jack Simpson was calling from the Friendship Lutheran Church, down by the river.

"You'd better get down here, right away. But don't dress for church and don't bring the family," was all Simpson had said.

When Parker arrived, the ambulance was already leaving. It pulled away from the front of the church quickly with red lights and siren. A crowd had gathered. Most of them were church members that had arrived early, unaware, until then, of the terrible thing that had happened. He looked at their faces, all familiar, some friends. They all knew Tony Parker—what he was. They knew about the monster he searched for—that huge murderous beast he was responsible for finding.

A commotion of loud voices, prayerful words and crying came from the crowd. It quieted to whispers, and the group parted as Parker came up the walk. He saw Simpson kneeling just on the other side of the yellow crime scene tape. White chalk made an outline on the bottom of the door. Large letters had been painted on the door in some kind of a dark paint, almost black—reddish black.

Parker heard the crowd's sibilant whispers and saw their accusing faces as he stepped through. "He's the one . . . ," "He's supposed to . . . ," ". . . not doing his job," "It's up to him to...."

As he stepped closer, he could read some of the letters on the entryway from between the people. *Z—E—B.*

A few steps closer and he could read it all. The letters spelled out a frightening thing. A terrible meaning of horrendous proportions. *JEZEBEL T P,* it spelled. It wasn't written in paint. No, this was blood. More, much more, stained the sidewalk. It was a lake of blood, all around and inside the white chalk outline of a man lying against the door.

Simpson turned to look at him as he approached. A serious, strained look covered his face. There would be no service this morning.

"Pastor Santini," Simpson confirmed Parker's suspicion. "The janitor found him this morning when he came down to open the church and get it ready for morning services. Looks like he was attacked late last night as he locked up after a council meeting. Judging by the blood's coagulation, probably ten to twelve hours ago."

Parker stared at the outline. "He's dead?"

"Not yet. The old guy surprised us. We couldn't feel a pulse. His body was cold. We chalked him and waited for the ambulance. Turned out he was still, by some miracle, alive. Can't see how he's gonna make it though." Simpson glanced at the blood around him. "He lost so much blood."

Parker gritted his teeth and looked at the door. "Jezebel?"

"That's what it says." Jack lowered his voice, glancing around at the people standing against the yellow tape. "And there's that *TP* again. He was really torn up, hardly recognizable. Looks like the old man wrote this during the final seconds of consciousness as the blood pumped from his body—that's what it *looks* like."

A deep voice came from the crowd. "So what are you doing about it, Parker?"

He didn't acknowledge it. "Any other clues, Jack?"

"No, not really," Simpson said, coming to his feet. "I've got men inside looking through all the *Bibles* to see if any have a page missing that would match up to the one we found at MacGreggor's. We don't really have anything else to go on."

Another voice came from the crowd. "Hey, Parker, when are you going to catch this dog from Hell?"

Parker ignored it.

"It's quite a coincidence," Jack said. "I mean the *Bible* page and the *TP* and all. They both must have known what *TP* was, and it looks like they both knew Jezebel, one way or the other. Did old man MacGreggor ever come to this church?"

"No," Tony answered, "I don't think so. I don't have perfect attendance here, but I'm pretty sure he didn't."

"Well, they have some other connection, then. And it has to do with this *TP*," Simpson said, looking at the letters on the door.

Parker stared also.

"You sure you aren't the connection?" Jack asked, still looking expressionless at the door.

"Damn it, Jack!" Parker roared. He glared at the side of Simpson's face briefly, turned and ducked back under the yellow tape and stormed through the crowd. Their sneers and jeers followed him like a gauntlet. These people usually greeted him with smiles and good words. None now.

"You sure you aren't the connection?" Jack says. Of course he wasn't connected. How could he be? Parker knew that Jack didn't mean any offense by the question. He didn't mean he thought Parker had any-thing to do with the two men's deaths. Parker knew that. He knew what Simpson asked and why. There might be some connection he'd overlooked. *TP* could be Tony Parker, for some strange, unknown reason. Somehow, there could be some kind of connection, but how? *TP* could mean anything; toilet paper, top priority, they could be books of the *Bible*: Thessalonians, Psalms, disciples: Thomas, Peter. *TP* could mean anything.

He'd seen something else in Simpson's eyes that the detective had not verbalized. He could tell Simpson was skeptical about the pastor writing with his own blood. He'd said it "looks" like the pastor had written the name of his attacker. There was, somehow, something much more to this thing than was apparent. Parker knew that. Simpson probably didn't want to cause any undue alarm or suspicion, but Parker could tell that his friend was now convinced also.

Nearly twelve hours had passed since Pastor Carl had been at-tacked. Jezebel's trail was cold. Parker checked in with the shelter by radio. His people still searched diligently, working double shifts. The police searched. There didn't seem to be much more to do. Jezebel had attacked two nights in a row. If she still lived, she might not come out to be found until tonight.

He would wear his pager and take two hours off for the picnic, max. Afterward, he'd rejoin the search. A damn silly picnic, but he dared not cancel. He needed Julie. He needed her on his side as an ally. He knew the news of Pastor Carl's attack would affect her. If the pastor should die, she would be devastated. But at the same time, this attack might bring this terrible mess more to home so she could better understand what he was having to deal with. She would have her picnic, even if he had to talk her into it. After all, several of the invited came from out of town. It would be too late to stop them.

CHAPTER 12

"There they are!" Julie called out, waving as Jack Simpson pulled into the parking lot in his old brown Chevy. His wife, Sadie, and family pulled in behind in their new green Olds Bravada. "Tony, whistle to the kids, and we'll start eating."

Parker was glad Julie had taken Pastor Santini's attack so well. They had called the hospital before they had left for the park. He was still in surgery in critical condition, just hanging on. They would check on his condition after the picnic.

The park overflowed with people enjoying the bright Sunday afternoon. The Parkers were lucky enough to find a couple of empty picnic tables sparsely surrounded by evergreen trees. Two tables weren't nearly enough for all twenty-four adults and sixteen kids that had come, But in anticipation, most had brought blankets or lawn chairs or both.

The tables were laden with food: covered dishes, pies, and even a couple of buckets of the Colonel's fried chicken. The women gathered around the picnic tables, chitchatting and sorting out the food, mostly chitchatting, while the men, some sitting in lawn chairs, some standing, shot the breeze.

The clear afternoon was a little cooler than it had been but was still in the upper nineties. The wind, inescapable as the typical Kansas wind was, came steady and light. Instead of blowing like a blast furnace and adding to the tormenting temperature, it contained a hint of the cool front promised and rumored for days.

The majority of the children played touch football in a clearing nearby. Yankee watched the children longingly as he lay beneath a large pine he was tied to. Occasionally, his head rose as a breeze brought the smell of fried chicken or roast beef or ham to his sensitive nose, and he licked his snout in anticipation of the half-eaten sandwiches and wasted helpings of roast beef from the children's plates. Parker's shrill whistle made Yankee sit up and pay attention. He anxiously watched as the children ran by laughing and giggling. The dog snapped his head, apparently picking up a familiar scent as Nick sprinted past. Yankee's tongue slipped around his muzzle like a writhing snake. The boy was sure to sneak an extra slice of ham for his best friend.

Everyone gathered around the tables as Simpson sat down his picnic basket and unfolded two lawn chairs. Parker grabbed up Sadie like a rag doll and kissed her long and hard on the lips. Her limbs hung limp, and she didn't fight, not even in play. They'd been friends since Jack and she started dating fourteen years ago. She had a slight build and was barely five feet tall. She had large, sensitive eyes and smooth, dark chocolate-brown skin, a bubbly sense of humor and always looked neat and fresh as if she were getting her picture taken.

"I can't do without my little Hershey's Kiss," Tony said, setting her back down to her feet gently.

"Wow!" Sadie said, fanning herself with a paper plate.

"Hey, would you two knock it off?" Simpson said, with a forced smile. "You do that exact same thing every time we get together."

Parker got the desired reaction out of him. He knew he would be the only one who could get away with it.

"Not the exact same thing, Jack," Parker said with a slap to Simpson's shoulder. "This time she damn near gagged me with her tongue!"

Sadie looked at Parker with an embarrassed smirk as she passed out the plates and plastic forks to Jack and their three girls.

Parker didn't have to worry about Julie's reaction. She always put up with this display anytime the four of them were together. She never seemed to mind. There didn't seem to be any jealousy. The Simpsons were good friends and were always there when the Parkers needed anything. They had even sat up at the hospital with little Audrey when she was in intensive care and Julie and Tony needed a break.

"We were about ready to give up on you guys!" Julie said.

"Duty called, and, of course, Jack had to go," Sadie said, frowning.

Julie looked back with an understanding grin and a shake of the head.

"Tell you about it later," Simpson said to Parker.

Parker was curious. It must be about Jezebel. Maybe some new information. Maybe they'd found her—but no, such good news wouldn't have been harmful to bring up. It must be bad. Maybe she'd killed again. This wasn't the right time to talk shop, not with Sadie and Julie right there. He'd ask Simpson about it the first chance he had when they were alone. Still, the curiosity gnawed on him like an itch that he couldn't scratch.

Something else chewed on Parker. He felt eyes, beautiful eyes, stealing glances at him—Sarah's eyes. Occasionally he'd look over to her and give her a slight grin. Unfailingly, he'd look to Julie and see she had seen the exchange every time it took place.

The usual teasing came as they ate their meals, "same man, same woman" sorts of things, "how could you put up with him/her." Most of the kids rushed through their main courses and, with fists full of brownies and cookies, ran back to where they were playing before. Yankee had his expected feast when one out of every four children who passed threw him something. He swallowed whole slices of ham. Some of the things he ate couldn't have had time to be identified by his taste buds before being gulped down.

Simpson's oldest daughter, thirteen-year-old Clarisse, fed Audrey a mixture of the softer foods at the table, and Julie and Sadie were assuring the teenager that someday she would make an excellent mother. Sarah Hill sat at the picnic table nearby with some of the other city and county workers.

"That was some letter to the editor in Saturday's paper, Tony. Looks like you feel pretty strongly about it," Parker's retired neighbor, George Mates, said. "You really think it's not the dog's fault if it attacks somebody?"

"That's right," Parker answered. "Any animal that has been domesticated or taken out of the wild isn't responsible for its actions, George. It's the master who's responsible for knowing how to keep the animal happy and out of a position where someone could be harmed by it. Some animals are like weapons. They won't hurt anyone if they're left alone. Don't get me wrong, I'm not saying these animals aren't dangerous."

"You know," Simpson said, "some people might think that's what you were trying to say. They might think you were defending the animals' right to be kept in the city."

"And that's not the point at all," Parker said. "The point is that they aren't the problem. If we'd get tough with these jerks and fine every owner that has an animal involved in an incident a couple thousand bucks, maybe they'd get the idea and either find out how to keep them away from people or not have them at all."

"What about this big Great Dane, Jezebel, I think they call her?" Dot Chambers, Julie's sister-in-law from Kansas City asked. "What about her?"

"You've heard about her clear up in Kansas City?" Parker asked.

"Sure, the whole country has by now," she said. "It was on cable, *Headline News.*"

"Damn. It's all because of that asshole TV reporter, Haskins!" Parker said.

Parker glanced at Julie and met her scowl. He looked around the table and noticed a few young ears.

"All right, enough talking shop. We're all here to have a good time," Julie said.

Parker realized it was time to change subjects. He picked a football up from the ground as he got up from the table. "Hey, Jack, how about a little football?" he said, shoving the ball into Simpson's stomach as he sat at the table.

"Oooff! Not again. We do this every time, Tony," Simpson said, "and you always try some bull to make a fool out of me. When are you going to realize, I ain't your Charlie Brown?"

There were a few chuckles from the full mouths around the table.

"Ah, come on Simpson. Not this time. Go on out there, and I'll kick it to you, and you can run it back. Go on. And Sadie, you can hold it for me."

"In your dreams, Tony," Sadie countered, catching Parker off guard. Sadie was generally shy, but once in a while, she'd show her wit.

"And sweet dreams they'd be." Parker grinned back. "Go way out there, *ol' buddy!*"

"I'm not going to do it this time. You're not going to make a fool out of me," Simpson said and took another bite of fried chicken.

"What's the matter, scare-d-cat? You afraid when you run it back I'll hurt you? Come on, big, tough guy. Let's see what you got!" Parker said.

"Well, all right. But no tricks this time—*old buddy.*" Simpson stood up and pushed away from the table and threw the chicken bone he'd been chomping on into a nearby trashcan. He began jogging out toward a clearing.

Parker knew he'd get Simpson to play. Jack had always had a passion for the sport, just not quite enough talent to get him a scholarship for college. Parker set the ball down and motioned for Sadie to hold it. A leery Simpson turned occasionally as he trotted.

"Keep going, keep going."

Trouble brewed nearby as Parker stepped back into kicking position. He saw Julie and Sarah standing together—alone, talking—trouble. Sarah leaned against a tree in a get-out-of-my-face sort of stance. Julie did all the talking.

Parker noticed Simpson slowing down and looking back, so he

waved him on. His attention went back to the girls. He couldn't make
out what was being said, but he heard words—harshly spoken words
with sharp barbs that come out when lips contort for emphasis.

Simpson looked back again, getting noticeably winded.

"Come on, Parker, you can't kick this far!" he puffed.

"Keep going, keep going!" Parker yelled.

Parker remembered the night he first met Simpson. It had been
the last game of the high school football season, and Simpson's team
was playing Parker's for top honors in the city. The score was twenty-
one to twenty in favor of Simpson's team. Parker's team had the ball,
fourth and fifteen, at the twenty-five yard line with twelve seconds left
on the clock. Parker was the team's star field-goal kicker and hadn't
missed a field goal all season. Simpson was playing defensive tackle,
and with his height and speed, he'd sacked many a quarterback and
field goal kicker. The ball had been snapped and set, and Parker sent
it sailing with a solid kick. He could feel that it was a good kick from
the start. Suddenly, Simpson's long arms reached out from nowhere
and tipped the ball, sending it wobbling. Simpson's momentum carried him onto Parker, and they lay in a pile as Parker watched the ball
soar. When it finally reached its distance, it struck the inside of the
right goal post and bounced out in front of the goal.

The crowd went insane, and Simpson started laughing uncontrollably. Parker's anger simmered, as Simpson looked back at him,
he-hawing like a jackass. The game had meant a lot to Parker, maybe
even a scholarship, and tension built as he watched this large black
man, who he didn't know, laugh in his face while sprawled on top of
him.

"You stupid, bastard nigger!" Parker had lashed out as he took a
swing at Simpson's helmet protected face.

"Ignorant, white-trash asshole!" Simpson had yelled and swung
back.

They had rolled together, swinging back and forth until the offi-
cials pried them apart.

Later that night, they had run into each other at a party and without helmets were mutually unrecognized. They began talking and, after a few minutes, started discussing the game. When they realized who they were talking with, they both had a laugh and had been friends ever since. Parker was ashamed of what he had called Simpson and that part of the evening was never brought up again.

Parker saw Simpson slow down and stop seventy-five yards out. Simpson panted with his hands on his knees, still facing away. He knew this was as far as Simpson would go. He walked over to Sadie and motioned her to get up. She looked surprised but grinned and went along.

"Jack's going to be ma-ad," Sadie said.

"That's all right, he expects it," Parker assured her. "Actually, I think he likes it."

He put his arm around her shoulders, and they began walking toward the picnic table. Julie and Sarah still *talked*.

Parker released Sadie and picked up his paper plate from his place at the table. He piled on a large helping of potato salad and looked over at the girls. Sarah's body language had softened somewhat from a don't-tell-me-what-to-do posture. It relieved him. Now, maybe Sarah wouldn't tempt him with what he couldn't have, and Julie would vent some anger and be a little easier to get along with.

Parker sighed and sidestepped in front of the baked beans. He paused for a moment when he heard an odd *thud, thud, thud* and a steam-engine-like puffing.

"*AAAAAAAH*!" Simpson screamed as he reached for Parker's plate and shoved it into his face.

The paper plate stuck momentarily then fell away. Large chunks of potato salad clung to Parker's nose, cheeks, and forehead, some of it falling down the front of his shirt. Everyone around the tables laughed, including Sadie and Jack.

"Shit!" Parker said, fingering off his face.

"No, you're lucky," Simpson said, doubled over in hysterics. "Its just potato salad."

An unattended banana lay on the edge of the picnic table, and Parker grabbed it.

"Ah, now, Tony!" Simpson said. He picked up a carrot stick and pointed it in his direction. "Slowly put the banana on the table, raise your hands above your head, and back away from it."

"Hu-hu," Parker chuckled at Simpson.

"No, Tony, don't do it!" Simpson exclaimed as he turned and tried to make an escape.

Parker was right behind, attempting to shove the banana up Simpson's pants.

"No, Tony, no!" Simpson pleaded. "I thought you were learning to be a vet, not a proctologist! Ouw!"

A near miss and a clever maneuver and Simpson smashed the banana in Parker's hand. Parker tossed what was left at Simpson and caught him on the cheek with a small piece that Simpson quickly wiped away with his forearm. After a couple of playful shoves, they both laughed it off and decided that was enough. Parker cleaned himself off with a paper towel and took a new paper plate behind Simpson's lead. The potato salad didn't seem appealing this time, and he looked over the table, undecided. In all the excitement, he hadn't noticed Julie and Sarah had finished their *talk* and Julie was on her way back to the group. She walked with her head up and a slight smile in a kind of pleased, victorious stride.

Julie arrived as Parker reached for the baked beans. She beat him to the serving spoon, and he submitted, expecting her to serve him like she had many times in the past. He smiled at her. She smiled at him.

"Would you like some baked beans with your potato salad?" she asked, holding the spoon over his plate.

He just smiled until he realized what she meant. The spoon slapped against his chest, direct center, just above the neckline of his shirt. The beans and juice rolled both underneath and over the front of his shirt. Laughter again broke out. His smile still curled the corners of his mouth but lost its sincerity.

CHAPTER 13

"Hey, everybody, how about some volleyball?" Simpson said in an obvious attempt to take the attention away from what was becoming a tense moment. "Come on, Tony, help me get the equipment out of the trunk."

Parker grabbed a handful of napkins and followed Simpson to the parking lot.

"What's up with you two?" Simpson asked, as soon as they were out of earshot.

"I think Julie's a little jealous of Sarah."

"Does she have reason to be?"

"No! Not really. I mean nothing's going on between us. We haven't done anything. She's just a friend—a damn good worker, and we work well together. I guess she's jealous of that."

"Uh-huh," Simpson said, sounding unconvinced.

Parker looked around the park, searching for a better explanation as they walked. The wind rustled through the trees, and he could hear children playing and laughing.

"There's been another dog attack," Simpson said, opening the trunk. "That's the reason I was late."

"Jack, why didn't you call me?"

"Are you kiddin', and have Julie pissed at me? No thanks. Besides, we took care of everything like the last time. You can read the report and go to the scene later. They just removed the bodies. No one touched anything else."

"Bodies?" Parker asked, as he watched a child running a couple of hundred feet away.

"Yeah, a blind man in his late twenties living alone."

A large, dark image ran through the trees in the same direction as the boy.

Tony stared as he asked, "Was it Jezebel?"

"No, it was the guy's own sight dog. A German shepherd. The man had been dead for a couple of days. Since before MacGreggor. The officer first on the scene found the dog lying on top of the man like he was protecting him or something."

"You said bodies. You mean the dog was killed?"

"Yeah. The officer had no choice. The dog wasn't letting anyone come near his master's body. Tommy Chin took it to Doc's and left it with his assistant."

Parker turned to Simpson. "Why didn't Chin call me?"

"You can give me credit for that. I told him not to bother you since I was going to see you here. You woulda really been in hot water if you'd showed up late, too."

Parker nodded with a crooked grin and looked back at the running boy. "If this happens again, we need to catch the dog alive."

"You think it's going to happen again?"

"I don't know," Parker said, becoming preoccupied with the boy. Through the trees, he could barely make out that the dark image chasing the kid was a dog. The boy seemed to be running frantically—running from the dog. He wasn't laughing. He was screaming.

"Jack, look at that!" Parker pointed.

It took a second for Simpson to see it, but when he did, he acted.

He moved around Parker, dug the car keys from his pocket, reached through the open window of his car and unlocked the glove compartment.

Screams came from behind a large group of trees the boy ran

towards. The boy, and then the dog, disappeared behind the trees as Parker stared. A dozen or more children screamed.

Now a Frisbee. The running boy came out of the trees with a Frisbee. He held it up in front of the large black lab, and the dog jumped at it. The children laughed along with their screams. They were playing. No danger. Just a group of kids having fun in the park and a dog playing Frisbee with a boy. A birthday party. Four or five adults sat watching from lawn chairs nearby.

Simpson tossed his .357 back into the glove compartment and slammed it shut.

"Damn!" he said. "We're too jumpy."

He went back to the trunk, and Parker joined him. They raised their heads and took notice when Sarah walked toward her car fifty yards away. She opened her car door and pulled out a large-brimmed white hat with a pink scarf tied around it as a band. It looked good on her. Anything would.

Parker smiled when Sarah glanced over. She smiled back and gave a little wave. He nodded and gave back the wave.

"I hope the *nothing* that happened between you two was worth it," Simpson said, watching her as she turned away and continued her walk back to the picnic tables. "She does have a nice tail."

"Yeah," Parker said, noticing her tight jeans. Then he saw that Julie had caught him looking again. He looked down quickly and pulled out a volleyball from the trunk.

"Your vacation's coming up a week from tomorrow, isn't it?" Simpson asked.

"Yeah, I guess we're going to the Ozarks. Gonna spend some time with Julie's folks. Probably do some bass fishing with her dad."

"Sounds relaxing. You and the father-in-law getting along these days?"

"Oh, yeah. Haven't seen him in about six months. Been getting along just fine."

"Hey, how about having a poker game like we used to this Friday night? We'll invite the old regulars. See if Doc White Cloud can come."

Parker smiled. "That's a coincidence. Doc and I were just talking about that. Sounds good. But it'll have to be at your place."

"All right, no problem," Simpson said, "It'll give Sadie a chance to go shopping. You might give Julie a couple of bucks to go along with her. You know, they say women shop to relieve stress. It might get you off the hook and make Julie a happy camper."

"I'm afraid it'll take a lot more than a couple of bucks to make Julie a happy camper. So, what about this blind man?" Parker asked.

"His name was Steven Johnson. In some sort of industrial accident and lost sight in both eyes a couple of years back. Just moved to town from Omaha two months ago. His neighbors didn't know much about him. I guess he kind of kept to himself."

"What about the dog?"

"German shepherd. Had a rabies shot just last week. The vet was Dr. White Cloud."

Parker cringed.

"You think it's more than coincidence?"

"I don't know; I can't figure it out. I'll pay Doc a visit on Tuesday. Patsy's uncle's funeral is tomorrow, and they're out of town. What did the blind man's house look like?"

"West side, in a new addition off of Central. Nothing was disturbed in the house. The victim's only apparent wound was his left jugular vein. It was ripped open."

They stood, gazing out at their families and friends back at the picnic tables.

"There's more, Tony," Simpson said.

Parker winced. "What?"

"There was another page torn from a *Bible*. This time it was clothes pinned to the mailbox next to the front door."

"Did it have initials again?"

"Yeah, *T P.*"

Parker's eyes widened. "Same scripture?"

"No, this time it was, 'eye for eye, tooth for tooth.'"

"Eye for eye—blind man, tooth for tooth—dog?" Parker speculated.

"Yeah, maybe, but that doesn't make any sense. Maybe it means something else."

"One thing's for sure, now. It isn't just the dogs. There *is* someone else involved somehow."

"But how?"

"Hell, I don't know; you're the detective."

"And you're *TP.*"

Parker frowned. "Anything new on the MacGreggor case?"

Simpson recited as if reading from a note pad. "Doc's assistant is driving both of the dogs' heads up to Kansas State University first thing tomorrow. The only wound on the dead dog was the one my bullet made, so we're guessing the blood on the wall—being dog blood—came from the other dog, Jezebel. Looked like she'd been ramming her head against the wall in some sort of rabies fit. Probably right after the old man was killed. Dr. Walker was good enough to examine the bodies before he went on vacation, otherwise they would have been dissected by some recent med-school grad. The cadavers have really been stacking up down there, what with all the OD's and suicides lately. People are just going nuts this summer—must be the heat. And, with everyone taking summer vacations, the coroner's office is operating on half-staff. They're having to put a lot of stiffs on ice.

"Anyway, Jezebel's the one that killed the old man at around midnight, maybe a little before. Both officers were killed by the male. No fingerprints besides the old man's and the neighbor lady's, and no sign of Jezebel. Except, we did find a trace of blood on the cedar fence in the back yard. It looked like she'd left right after banging her head on the wall. Oh, and we made contact with the nephew, uh—Daryl Bailey. He's flying in from Des Moines tomorrow. Seemed kind of anxious to see the house."

"Hmm, let me know when he gets here, will you? I'd like to talk to him."

"Okay, now, tell me what's going on in that little BB brain of yours."

"If you want to know the truth, I'm not sure. Things just don't add up. I am convinced these dogs don't have rabies, yet they attack. Attack their own masters and kill anyone else that comes along for apparently no reason. Somehow, there's more going on that we don't know about. Something is setting these dogs off, and I think they're only unwilling participants."

"Sounds nuts to me."

"Three dogs, in two separate houses, kill four people. A pastor is nearly killed at his church. All within a couple of days in Wichita, Kansas? These *Bible* verses and the initials. You give me your theory." Parker said as they began walking to the picnic tables with the volleyball equipment. He frowned when he saw that someone, probably Nick, had unhooked Yankee's leash, and the dog now trotted toward them.

"Coincidence. That's all it can be. We're just jumping to conclusions," Simpson said, petting Yankee as they walked.

Parker smiled briefly, watching Jack stroke the big Saint Bernard. He knew Yankee was the only dog Simpson trusted enough to touch since he was a kid, and it had taken a couple of years of being around his docile pet to do that.

When Simpson was five, a neighbor kept a huge black mastiff in his front yard behind a too short, four-foot picket fence. The ugly old dog would reach its head over the fence and bark and growl continuously at anyone in sight. One day, Simpson and his older brother were riding their bikes home from school, and the dog leaped the fence effortlessly. It chased his brother down and knocked him off his bike. Simpson's brother was badly mauled before a passing motorist intervened with a tire iron and beat the dog to death.

Simpson's brother still carried the scars, mostly on his arms and legs, and Simpson still carried the mental scars from watching the attack.

"I'm on call this afternoon," Simpson said. "You want to do a little patrolling after the picnic? Maybe go by the blind man's house.

"Yeah, sure, I'll ride with you. But there's more to it, Jack," Parker said. "I know there is. It's not just coincidence."

"Hey, easy boy!" Simpson said, yanking his hand back from the dog.

"What's wrong?" Parker asked and looked down at Yankee.

Yankee growled, and the fur rose on his back. He glared toward the picnic tables.

A commotion. Startled voices.

Everyone looked toward a spruce tree with low boughs. A huge black and brown rottweiler stepped out from behind the tree with its teeth bared. It stared at the picnickers as it took slow guarded steps toward them, drooling in long strings that glistened in the sunlight.

Parker grabbed Yankee by the collar and walked swiftly with Simpson at his side.

"All right now," he called out. "Everyone, stay calm. It's okay. Just don't make any sudden moves." There was no reason for this animal to be aggressive unless he was sick or had rabies. Maybe he'd killed a rabbit in the trees and was trying to guard it.

Ted Baker, the Parkers' divorced neighbor, took the initiative and stood up from the table. He picked up a three-foot stick and approached the dog.

"Careful Ted," Parker said, now at a trot. "Don't get too close."

Baker didn't seem to hear as he stepped even closer, now within six feet of the rottweiler. The dog advanced cautiously, its growls vicious like that of a wolf in a bear trap.

"Damn it, Ted," Parker yelled as he sprinted, "don't get so damn close. Get back!"

Baker brought the stick to waist level and began swinging it aggressively.

"Get out of...," Baker began but didn't have time to finish as the rottweiler sprang like a leopard and took him by the right wrist. The man wailed and twisted his arm away and the blood streamed. The dog stood its ground while Baker fell back on his seat and scooted backwards to the group.

Sadie Simpson snatched up a tea towel that was covering a pan of rolls, knelt beside Baker and aided him in wrapping his blood-gushing wrist.

The children who had been playing in the clearing nearby came running and screaming back to the group. A large collie and a German shepherd followed, giving angry barks and snarls. A frightened young boy, one of the Thortons' kids who lived down the street from the Parkers, stopped and tried to retrieve the ball cap he'd dropped. The large collie blocked his way. It headed him off. When the boy went left, the dog followed. The boy went right; the dog was there. The boy went left again, and the dog jogged back into his way, this time growling viciously. The boy finally got the message and ran to the others.

Jack asked, "What's going on here?"

Parker saw Simpson looking behind them. Two more dogs, a golden retriever and another German shepherd, this one with mixed blood, advanced from behind. Another two dogs, an Irish setter and a large Heinz fifty-seven cur ran up, one on each side, and stopped within fifteen feet of the group.

Parker scanned 360 degrees, looking at each of the dogs. Yankee danced around, eyeing each of them also.

"We're being herded," Parker said. "We're being herded together, like a bunch of sheep."

"What for?" Simpson asked. "Why would they?"

Parker and Simpson were now up to the rest of the group. They stood around the tables with the dogs encircling them. Two more dogs, a Siberian husky and another large mixed breed, appeared and joined in. Some of the younger children cried in scared, nervous sobs.

"Tony, do something!" Julie begged.

"All right, everyone, just stay calm. Don't show fear. No sudden moves, and for God's sake, no one run."

The dogs closed in.

"Now what?" Simpson asked.

"Don't look directly into their eyes. Men, get to the outside of the circle and stand with one side out. No sudden moves, but everyone get a weapon, a knife or a fork or something. And don't show it; keep it hidden."

The dogs advanced several steps closer, their snarls increasing in intensity.

"It's not working, Tony!" Julie cried.

"God, Tony, what's going on?" Sarah exclaimed.

"If I can get back to the car, I can get my gun," Simpson said.

"A gun might make things worse," Parker said. "You couldn't get all of them. They might attack after the first shot."

"Or they might all run," Simpson said back.

"Getting to the cars is the thing we've got to do, but when you get your gun, don't shoot unless they attack," Parker insisted. He raised his voice so all could hear. "We're going to ease our way to the cars. Jack and I will lead. Everyone stay together and take it very slow."

They started, inching down the gradual slope to the parking lot. The dogs followed, closing in at the same time. They still snarled savagely, now within an arm's length of the group.

Ted Baker's fifteen-year-old son, Paul, lost his senses and broke from the bunch, running desperately toward the cars. The mixed shepherd and the collie pursued him. Within twenty feet the shepherd nailed him by the heel, and the collie followed with a leaping tackle. The other dogs held fast to their positions as if mystically linked together. They were like well-trained soldiers from an elite army.

"Damn it, Jack, this is it!" Parker yelled and let go of Yankee's collar. He ran to the boy's aid with Simpson running after him.

Parker grabbed the collie by the neck and jerked him off the boy, who was on his back with arms up, trying to defend himself. The boy's arms and face already showed several bleeding gashes.

Simpson grabbed the shepherd around the middle and hurled it into a nearby cedar tree. Yankee quickly overpowered the collie and was on top of it.

Parker looked up at the other dogs. He was surprised that an incredible melee hadn't begun. Instead, all of them stood motionless with perked ears. Yankee and the collie both stopped battling, and Yankee stood with head raised and ears cocked. The marauding dogs, as suddenly as they'd appeared, retreated, sprinting back into the trees as if a shot, inaudible to human ears, had been fired.

Everyone stood in silence, dumbfounded. A moment later, they all seemed to realize they were out of immediate danger and stampeded to their cars. Paul Baker's father ran over and helped his son up and to their car. Sadie and the kids were already getting into their Olds. Julie had scrambled, with Audrey in her arms and with Nick in tow, to the minivan, jumped in and rolled up the windows. Sarah Hill raced to her car. Parker, Simpson and Yankee stood and watched as everyone made it to safety.

Jack trotted over to the passenger's side of his Chevy and opened the door and leaned across the seat. He took out his .357 and held it in his lap as he called in on his radio. Parker stood next to the door, holding Yankee by the collar.

"Six Adam Three to Dispatch," Simpson called, his words rushed.

"Dispatcher, go ahead, Six Adam Three," the radio squawked back.

"Code 30," Simpson barked into the microphone. "Officer needs assistance. We have multiple vicious dogs at Tabor Park. There are at least two injuries. Get an ambulance and all available officers Code 3.

"Ten Four, Six Adam Three."

"I want all officers to shoot to kill, I repeat, shoot to kill any dogs appearing vicious and running loose in this area," Simpson said.

"Jack, you can't do that," Parker said. "Think about it."

Simpson paused. "10-23, dispatch, hold on."

Parker said, "Have them call Animal Control for me. Let's work together. If you go shooting every loose dog, you're going to end up killing a lot of innocent animals, and someone's going to get hurt."

"Dispatch, cancel that shoot to kill," Simpson said somewhat calmer. "Call in all available animal control officers. Have all officers proceed with caution and identify and restrain any dogs appearing to be a threat. Shoot to kill as last resort only."

"Ten Four, Six Adam Three."

They heard sirens within two minutes. Soon, the entire park seemed overrun by police and animal control officers. Not a trace of the vicious animals was found.

CHAPTER 14

At a quarter till three, Donna and Bart Hartwell and their two-and-a-half-year-old son Joshua arrived on the riverbank of the Little Arkansas River within a stone's throw of the Douglas street bridge. The Sunday afternoon traffic roared above as hundreds of other citizens rushed about, enjoying the beautiful day.

It didn't matter that it was a lousy place to fish. They probably wouldn't catch anything, but they were together. Donna would be going to work at five at the downtown McDonald's, and Bart worked the graveyard shift at Boeing. They were together. They were young. This was a rare moment they could relax and share.

"Okay, Josh, now you stay back from the water while Daddy baits your hook," Bart said.

Donna stood well up the bank, her tongue sticking out the corner of her mouth as she struggled with a fat, juicy earthworm. Joshua toddled back and forth impatiently behind his parents.

A grasshopper flipped down the path, and the boy waddled after it. He reached to capture his flighty little prey but fell forward when his toes hit a rock just off the path. He caught himself with his hands and looked down into a dry drainage ditch. A large drainage culvert was set in the gradual-sloping bank beside the bike path. He seemed distracted by the dark hole. The grasshopper made a getaway, and Josh descended toward the black gap on his hands and knees.

Inside the concrete tunnel, a shadow lay low, back a few feet from the opening, wary of her increasingly noisy surroundings. She had sought relief from the coming day's heat as the sun rose this morning, and the cool cement seemed to be ideal in the quiet of the pre-dawn. Now, she felt trapped. The onrush of traffic and continuous parade of people captured her in the storm drain with no escape. The people were after her. She must stay hidden.

Jezebel lay with her head on her paws. With wide eyes and perked ears, she studied the animal stumbling toward her and recognized it as a human pup. She had seen only a couple before. The last time was when the old female human brought two over to her master's den. They were harmless and innocent little creatures that liked to play and whine. Her nostrils flared, and her glistening black nose twitched. She remembered their smell, fresh and sweet, yet with a slight uriny scent. The same odor came from this one.

Jezebel had never had pups of her own. Her instincts told her she should, she needed to, but the pups never came. She had enjoyed playing with the human pups before and wished they could have stayed so she could have licked and cleaned them and lain down with them to protect and keep them warm. They weren't her pups, but she needed to have them. She was supposed to have pups.

"Be careful, now, Joshua," Donna cautioned. "Don't you go too far."

"Dog-gee?" Joshua said and stopped halfway to his goal.

Human pup. Lick, sniff, play!

Jezebel voiced a light whine. She darted her tongue, and her tail slapped the concrete twice.

The human woman looked back at the culvert apparently hearing the sound. Jezebel's eyes shifted to her. Confusion once again stirred her brain. *Man—enemy, kill. Kill!*

"No, I don't think there's a doggie in there, honey," Donna said. She went back to struggling with the worm. "Why don't you come up and help me catch a big old fish?" Donna looked back at Joshua. "Now, don't get down there too far and get all dirty.

"Oh, Donna," Bart said, "he's a boy. He was born to get dirty. What's a little dirt when there's adventure to be had? Maybe there is a dog in there." Bart looked over his shoulder and craned his neck as he pushed a large, meaty night crawler on a second fishhook. He squinted, but the bright sun would not allow him to see into the darkened crotch of the ditch.

"Mamma, doggie!" the boy yelled out in excitement, as he stumbled closer, within five feet of the dark gap under the path.

"All right, it's time to fish, and I don't think your silly doggie's going to want to fish with us," Donna said, starting toward the boy. "Come on, come on up." She began stepping down with arms stretched.

Kill! Kill! Kill!

--*

Parker drove his family home in an unusually quiet minivan. There hadn't been a word said during the entire fifteen-minute drive.

Without speaking, Parker changed and left in his truck. As he drove, he tried to think of anyone who could be trying to get back at him for something he had done. Someone seeking revenge, maybe even someone trying to frame him. He could think of no one. Haskins had always tried to be a thorn in his side, but that was all he'd tried to do. This was much more serious than that. Haskins was stupid, but he wasn't entirely insane. Whoever was involved in these horrible attacks was definitely one hundred percent wacko.

He wondered if he wouldn't be one of the suspects in this confusing case if it weren't for Jack Simpson being his best friend.

Parker picked Simpson up at his house, and they joined in the search.

--*

"Joshua, I said come on," Donna Hartwell said, reaching. All week long, Joshua had asked his mother, "Fishy? Go fishy, Mama?" Now, the little devil wasn't interested and was looking for imaginary dogs in holes.

"Doggie, Mamma, doggie!" the boy said again, even more excited as he reached into the dark hole. "Doggie, Daddy!"

"There's no doggie in here, sweetie," Donna said with a quick glance, beginning to lift the boy.

Joshua began to cry, still reaching to the culvert opening. "Doggie! Doggie!"

Donna looked back to the darkness. Something glistened. Two objects, round and black. Liquid black. Eyes. Her own eyes adjusted to the darkness, and she saw a dark shape three feet in front of her, a foot from Joshua's outstretched arms. A large shape, very large. The eyes blinked. Donna froze. She'd heard of this beast, this murdering monster, and, now, it stared at her eye to eye. It had killed without reason with its tremendous, vicious fangs.

Donna's jaw locked and trembled as she tried to shape words. The huge beast blinked again. Speech seemed impossible; the words would not come. She raked in a deep breath.

Finally she screamed, "Jezebel!" With two hastened steps, she stumbled up the embankment with Joshua gripped tightly in her arms.

Bart looked over his shoulder, eyes wide.

Long, black legs began flinging out of the dark hole like a huge tarantula trying to get a foothold. In a split second she was up, out of the hole, and standing with legs cocked, showing her murderous fangs. She stood for scant seconds, then became a black blur streaking out from the ditch and into nearby bushes.

--*

Parker and Simpson received the call as they pulled away from Simpson's house. Jezebel had been spotted downtown near the river. They searched relentlessly for the rest of the afternoon without results. Due to the intensity of the search, Parker hadn't had a chance to go to the blind man's house. He'd do that tomorrow. Maybe he'd find a clue there to help make some sense of the mess.

They checked in on Pastor Santini. He was out of surgery and in the ICU, still unconscious and in serious condition.

When Parker returned home after eleven that evening, Julie was already in bed and either sleeping or pretending to be. He didn't try to wake her. Instead, he said nothing and got into bed as quietly as possible.

Sometime in the middle of the night, Jezebel returned to Parker's foggy dreams. The same dream as before. Once again, she moved through the mist. Quietly, resolutely. Once again, she stopped. Once again she looked up the sidewalk, to the door of the house—Parker's house. But this time, she slowly approached the door. She walked with purpose, head in a guarded position, not showing her deadly weapons, the ivory stilettos. She walked to the door and stopped short of the first step to the porch. Her muscles tightened.

--*

Several miles away in a dark room, a big Heinz fifty-seven stood motionless, watching in anticipation from a large cage. "DAWG" it said in prominent letters on his dog tags.

His tail wagged. He buffed softly and whined. His feet pranced in excitement.

A chrome-plated, wire gate opened with a *nitch* and *clank*. It slowly creaked as it swung wide.

A man's hand with a doctor's rubber glove patted Dawg on the head. It moved down his back to his rump. The other hand revealed a hypodermic needle. Pressure from the thumb made a small amount of clear liquid squirt out, and the hand quickly pushed the needle into the animal's hip.

Dawg acknowledged the needle with a short yelp but continued wagging his tail, looking up at the dark man who had a patch over one eye.

The needle withdrew, and Truong gazed back and smiled. He raised the black eye patch covering his left eye.

Dawg whined and continued to stand, wagging his tail, as Truong patted him. For a moment, there was no reaction. But soon Dawg began bobbing his head. He staggered, stumbled, and loosing his balance, he collapsed, eyes wide, trying to focus, rocking his head back and forth. His tail thumped against the floor. In the dog's mind, the walls of the cage became a blur. They melted, and everything around him distorted. Truong's face appeared directly in front of his nose. Dawg saw an eye, a very dark eye. Dark and deep like a well.

Dawg heard a blowing noise. Two long puffs, two short, a long. But it wasn't just blowing. A whistle was masked in the noise, high pitched and inaudible to human ears but not to Dawg's. He heard it with piercing clarity.

The eye Dawg stared into seemed to widen and grow even deeper as it came closer and closer. Dawg was caught up in it. He couldn't fight it. He didn't want to. There was something seductive about it. It drew him closer until, at last, he fell in, tumbling end over end. He passed fangs and claws and walls of blood as he fell and fell and fell.

Suddenly, he no longer tumbled. He heard the beating of hooves and paws on damp earth, and he was running. A pack of large, wolf-like dogs raced down a dried up creek bed, and Dawg sprinted amongst them. He was excited as all the dogs seemed to be. They were in chase. A large bull elk ran in front, and they closed in. The stag jogged from side to side of the creek bed, avoiding tree limbs and roots and other brush-like debris, gracefully jumping over much of it. Still the dogs drew nearer.

Without warning, a large, dark dog leaped from one side of the creek bank, onto the stag's back and tore into its throat. The huge stag stumbled and fell, and the entire pack stormed in and ripped at the ill-fated animal. Dawg joined the frenzy. He also attacked the big buck savagely, tugging and slashing. He saw the big, dark dog. He sensed he was the undisputed pack leader, far superior to all the others. He saw one of the dark leader's eyes. It was dark and deep like a well.

Now, several human-like creatures appeared, wearing furs made from animal hides, some made from other dogs. Their spears and rocks flew. Clubs bashed the dogs. The pack fought back, but many of the dogs fell dead to the primitive weapons. The dark pack leader looked at Dawg with his dark, deep eye. A sort of whine came from the leader's throat. It turned into a piercing whistle that seemed to envelope Dawg. Dawg sensed a command.

Attack, attack the man-animals! Kill! Tear open their throats!

Dawg obeyed, easily overcoming one of the adversaries and knocking him to the ground. He tore at his foe's neck, and soon, the man-enemy quit fighting and lay motionless on the ground. Dawg smelled the blood. It smelled good, and he licked it from his snout. The taste made his excitement soar even higher. More dogs appeared, and within seconds, four of the man-enemies lay dead on the ground, being ripped apart by the vicious dogs. The remaining half dozen of their enemies fled with two of the dogs still in pursuit as the rest of the pack began feeding on its new kills.

Dawg saw the eye of the dark one once again. He seemed pleased with Dawg. Dawg was pleased also, and the meat of the man-enemy tasted sweet.

Dawg continued his hallucination. He lay on his side with all four paws twitching, fur raised on his neck and hackles, lip curled, revealing his deadly weapons.

Buff, Buff! he sounded in a dream-muffled bark.

CHAPTER 15

Tony Parker woke with the previous night's dream still fresh in his mind. Again, Julie's place beside him was empty and cold. The clock radio next to the bed told why. It was seven thirty. Normally, he was in his office by eight. Usually, he woke on his own by six thirty and took his time showering and getting ready for work while Julie fixed him a nice breakfast. He smelled coffee, and bacon and eggs. Maybe Julie wasn't upset anymore. Maybe all was forgotten, and they'd be back to their old, happy selves again.

"Come on, Nicholas!" Julie's voice rang out. It was a pleasant sound. "You don't want to be late for the first day of school, do you? Your breakfast is getting cold."

"Coming, Mama!" Nick yelled back from his room down the hall.

When Nick's feet hit the stairway, it sounded as though a centipede were descending the steps rather than a small boy.

Parker rose from bed and took a quick shower. By the time he dressed and went downstairs, Julie was preparing to leave with Audrey in her arms, and Nick waited at the front door, eager to get to school.

Parker caught them on the way out. He kissed Nick on the forehead.

"Have a good day in school, big guy!" he said.

"I will. Bye," Nick said and ran out the door.

Parker reached and caught Julie on the cheek with a kiss. Julie's expressionless face made it obvious the cold shoulder was still solidly frozen. He pecked Audrey on the nose.

"There are eggs in the refrigerator if you want to make yourself breakfast," Julie said and walked out the door.

--*

Parker and Hill checked out the blind man's house first thing. They looked through the house carefully. For exactly what, they did not know. Nothing seemed out of the ordinary—nice, middle-class house, new furniture. Several windows were unlocked, but all with untampered screens. No signs of a struggle. The victim had been found beside his bed, carotid artery ripped, with the dog lying on top.

A picture of the man and his dog sat on the fireplace mantle in the living room. Hill took it down and gazed at it.

"Good looking pair. Too bad," she said, wiping a thin layer of dust off with her hand.

"Yeah. Got any ideas?" Parker asked, looking over her shoulder.

"I know it isn't rabies."

"Now, how do you know that? Women's intuition?"

"Come on. You don't think its rabies, either."

"What the hell is it, then?" Parker asked, taking the picture from Hill's hands. He slammed it back onto the mantle. "It's the same MO as with MacGreggor—no motive." He went to a window and stared out with his hands on his hips. "The dog attacks, unprovoked, and kills its master. Then, it looks to me like it shows remorse. Something's setting them off, causing them to do things they don't want to do. But what—and how?"

Hill walked over to Parker. She reached out and gently straightened his collar, then patted it down.

"You got me," Hill said with a familiar, impish grin. Apparently, her little talk with Julie had done little, if any, good.

Parker felt a strange rush of adrenaline go through his body. A tingling sensation tickled his spine, and goose bumps grew on his arms. His senses seemed heightened. He could smell Sarah's perfume and it excited him. He gazed into her wanton eyes and watched as she moistened her lips, and noticed the dimple in her half-smiling cheek. Parker could feel his face fill with an excited grin. It was an eager, self-serving, hungry grin. It wasn't the broad smile a person gives back in kindness; it was a lustful grin with only himself in mind. The look she returned showed incredible surprise.

This was it. Now was the time. He would have cute, little teasing Sarah. He would have her hot, firm young body. He would take her and feast on her, no holds barred, until *he* was satisfied. No more teasing. He would take control and have *his* way. No one else would know. No one else would find out, and if they did, it didn't matter. Right now, it *really* didn't matter because, *right now*, he would have sex with Sarah with no one to please or account to except himself.

Parker reached around her and pulled her body up firmly into his arms, lifting her off her feet, and kissed her long and passionately on the lips. He felt Sarah's backbone go limp as her body melted in his arms in complete submission. She wrapped her legs tightly around his middle. He pressed his lips increasingly harder against Sarah's, and she pulled her mouth away with an uncomfortable frown.

"Oh, Tony, I knew there was an animal inside you somewhere," she said, gasping.

Parker began kissing her hard down the side of the neck, nipping and biting her soft, smooth skin. The scent of her, the fragrance of her perfume mixed with the natural smell of her body, excited him even more. He was a fiery rocket, out of control, burning hotter every second while building speed.

Without looking up, he carried her through the doorway into the dining room and over to the small, round dining table. He dropped her with a thud, not taking care to be gentle, her legs still clenching tightly to his body. He grabbed with both hands and with one tremendous yank, ripped her uniform shirt and bra open, exposing her large, firm breasts.

Hill's eyes widened with shock. He leaned down and locked mouths with her again, clutching both breasts. He slowly moved his lips back down her neck and rubbed a strong erection up and down in jerks against her crotch. She responded, moving her hips in a slow fluid motion.

"Tony, I never imagined," she gasped, stroking his thick hair. "I wouldn't have dreamed!"

He worked down to her breast, still kissing, firmly caressing, nipping, and biting. He put his lips around her nipple and suckled.

"Oh, Tony, yes. This is what I've been waiting for. Oh, yes! Give it to me now. I want you inside of me!"

He continued mouthing her nipple. His nips and bites increased in strength, harder and harder, until he began to taste blood.

"Ewww! Easy, Tony," she said. "That's just a bit too hard, baby. I don't like that."

I don't care. I like it! He didn't respond but continued, biting harder.

"Tony, I said easy!" she said, this time pleading. "Tony!"

Still, he wouldn't respond. He didn't care.

She hit him on the side of the head with the heel of her hand. Parker felt a dull pain in his temple that jarred his head, and he raised, furious his pleasure was interrupted. He looked at her angrily. A string of saliva dripped from the corner of his wet mouth.

Hill glared back. "That's enough, Tony!"

A noise came from outside the open front door. Footsteps. Parker could hear them, but didn't care.

"Tony, someone's coming," Hill said as she pulled her blouse back together, searching for any buttons still attached.

She grimaced up at Parker, fear covering her face. He stood over her, staring down, panting and eager to resume. He wanted more. He couldn't stop himself. He yearned to finish what had started. That was all that mattered.

"I said someone's coming, Tony," Hill said. She raised her right foot to his stomach and gave him a firm push. "Now, get away!"

"Everything all right in here?" a frowning police officer asked from just inside the front door.

Parker had stumbled back. He stared angrily at the officer from over his shoulder.

Hill peered around Parker as she slipped off the table, still holding her torn blouse. "Yeah, we were just talking."

"Are you sure about that?" the officer said with his arms folded across his chest.

This intruder agitated Parker, cop or not. If it weren't for him, he could be with Sarah, having her, humping and groping her body.

Parker spun around and blurted out in a deep, angry voice, "She said, we were just talking. Don't you understand English?" He felt his face distort in a snarl, eyes bugging. The officer flinched, seeming shocked at the response. Parker saw him look down to Parker's groin, and he glanced down at himself. His trousers tented at the top of one leg.

"See something you'd like?" Parker asked, looking up slowly with a wicked smile.

"It's okay, really," Hill pleaded with the officer. "We'll be leaving now. Please, it's okay."

The officer frowned at both of them briefly, and Parker still stared back, grinning. The cop turned and walked out the door, shaking his head.

Hill whispered urgently, "Damn, Tony, what in the hell got into you?"

There hadn't been time to answer before a call came over the radio in Parker's truck.

"Dispatcher to AC One, come in Tony."

He heard it through the open front door and broke and ran like a quarter horse out of the starting gate. He couldn't understand what had just happened. It was incredible. It didn't make sense. He wasn't like that. Sure, there had been times in his life he wished he were, when if he'd been a little more pushy, he'd have gotten his way, gotten what *he* wanted, said what *he* wanted to say. But this was just so foreign, so different from his nature, that it was unbelievable, even to himself. It was as if there was another Tony Parker, a Mr. Hyde, who exposed himself. It was frightening. Especially so, since he had enjoyed being this Mr. Hyde. Would it happen again? If so, would he be able to return to the person he really was? Would he want to?

As he bolted out the door, Parker noticed a familiar minivan driving by. He stopped instantly in the middle of the sidewalk and stood as close to at attention as he had been since the Marines.

Julie's minivan. She had seen him, most likely recognizing the truck first, then saw him fly from the house. She was probably on the way back home with a carload of groceries. Julie's window was down, and she had either forgotten her anger, and his sudden appearance hadn't given her time to remember, or she had decided she'd been mad long enough. She smiled, waved, and opened her mouth as she began to speak, driving slowly. Her cheerful look transformed abruptly into a scowl, and her mouth slammed shut. She looked past him.

Parker turned to see Sarah Hill on the porch, fumbling with the front of her blouse, lipstick smeared, hair ruffled. He imagined the same lipstick was smeared on his face, and he put the back of his hand up to his mouth and wiped it across his mug. He looked back at Julie, seeing now she also noticed his still tented pants.

Julie roared off, forcing the old white minivan to give all it had.

Parker stomped over to the driver's side of the truck and picked up the microphone. There was no way he could explain this to Julie. He didn't even understand it himself.

"Dispatch, this is Parker. Go ahead," he puffed, leaning in the driver's side door.

"Looks like another dog attack, Top Dog, but this one's in progress."

"Where, Tyrone?" he asked, opening the door.

"11503 W. Kennedy."

"Okay, we're on our way." He passed the handset around the window frame. "Is it a black Great Dane?"

"Don't know, man. The caller was just a kid, all he said was that a dog was hurting some girl named Cindy."

"All right, we're about three minutes away." Parker jumped into the Jimmy. Hill trotted up on the other side. "Call Lt. Simpson and get him out there. Remind him we'd like to take this one alive," Parker said, pulling the truck door shut.

"Gotcha, Top Dog."

"I hope it's Jezebel!" Parker said to Hill as she climbed in. He hung up the handset, started the truck and turned on the lights.

"Are you kidding?" Hill said. Her voice was strained. "I pray it isn't!"

CHAPTER 16

Sarah Hill was quiet on the way to the call. Parker took a quick glance at her as he steered out of a corner. She had fixed her blouse back to where it looked surprisingly good, considering it was missing two buttons, and she proceeded to touch up her make up and lipstick as the truck jostled and swayed down the streets. Except for her unusual silence, it was as if nothing had happened. He was glad his bite had not been bad enough to cause blood to soak through her bra and blouse. Still, he knew the damage he'd caused was more than superficial. When Parker understood, himself, what had come over him, he'd be better able to apologize.

Parker stood on the brake in front of the caller's house and jumped out, immediately running to the tailgate and opening it. Hill climbed up on one knee and grabbed the control stick, a pole with a thin rope attached to slip over an uncooperative animal's neck, and she handed it to Parker. She pulled the tranquilizer rifle off a rack on the side and hopped out.

"You back me up," Parker said, and turned to run up to the chalk white, saltbox house.

Just then, a small boy of about seven came running out from the side, screaming as if death were his shadow. His face was flushed and dirty and streaked with tears.

Parker could see the boy was apparently unharmed as he ran to him. He knelt down and grabbed him by the arms.

"Where's the dog? Is Cindy all right?"

"They're back there," the boy cried, pointing to the back yard. "He's hurting her!"

"Stay here, kid. Come on!" Parker snapped to Hill. "Get that thing ready."

Hill cocked the rifle and clicked the safety off.

There was whining as they came around the corner. Parker stopped short when he saw what was happening, and Hill ran into the back of him. Two dogs stood tail to tail, locked together: a female collie and a large male cur, who was whining in obvious discomfort. The dogs seemed startled by their intrusion and looked up at them in surprise.

"Cindy, you run-a-round bitch!" Hill said, relaxing the tension in her body and putting one hand on her hip. "Well, now that you got your man, don't let him go."

"Shit!" Parker said, lowering the stick.

"Do something, do something, he's hurting her!" the boy screamed at them, coming up from behind.

Parker cringed. "In the position they're in, I'd say he's the one being hurt."

"You better explain it to him, Tony," Hill said.

"Why don't you? You seem to know more about this kind of thing."

Parker's sharp words apparently cut deep, and he wished he could take them back, especially considering what had just happened at the blind man's house.

"Me?" she said. "What is it with you, Tony?"

Hill glared and then turned to the boy, bending down and holding his arms. "It's okay. Cindy's just playing with her boyfriend."

The boy looked at his dog, tears still rolling down his cheeks. Hill pulled out a handkerchief and wiped his tears. "Sometimes when they play like this, the girl dog has puppies a couple of months later," she added.

"Wow, really?" the boy said in glee. He ran over to hug the collie.

"You'd better leave them alone for a while, son," Parker said. "They'll be done *playing* after a bit." He turned to the male. "You got yourself into this, you get yourself out."

The male whined back.

"Hey, young man, why aren't you in school?" Parker asked.

"I missed the bus because of Cindy," the boy answered. "Mom and Dad are at work."

A blaring siren and a screech from around the front of the house indicated Simpson had arrived. Hill and Parker walked up to meet him as he ran into the yard. Parker smiled at Simpson, but Hill jumped in to comment first.

"Hey, Simpson, you heard the one about the young Indian brave that went to his father one day and asked how he and his brothers got their names?"

"Huh, what's going on?" he said, trying to get around Hill.

"The father said, '*Uhg*, when first brother born, I look out teepee and see eagle soaring in sky. I name him Soaring Eagle,'" Hill said in a deep voice, backing up with her arms blocking Simpson's advance.

"Come on, what's going on?" Simpson said, frustrated.

"'When next brother born, I look out and see elk leaping over bush. I name him Leaping Elk.'"

"Come on, Sarah, let me by! What the hell is going on?" He broke away from her and ran frantically around the corner of the house and stopped wide-eyed, mouth agape, hand on his holstered revolver.

Hill continued, "Then the old Indian looks to his son and asks, 'Why you ask....'"

"Two Dogs Screwing!" Simpson finished the punch line.

Hill raised her eyebrows. "Oh, did Doc White Cloud already tell you that one?" she asked.

It was like Hill to relieve a tense situation with humor.

"Did Doc really tell you that?" Parker asked, somewhat surprised that Doc would be so crass with a woman.

"Yeah, but I had to tell him a couple real juicy ones of my own, first."

Hill seemed to have at least temporarily forgiven Parker. She was the type that bounced back quick. Parker could imagine what kind of jokes she'd told Doc.

"I think we've had a couple too many false alarms, ol' buddy," Parker said putting his arm around Simpson's shoulders.

"You ain't a shittin'," Simpson agreed as they walked back to the curb.

"Anything new?" Parker asked.

"Nothing except ol' man MacGreggor's nephew is in town, and I'm supposed to meet him at the house in twenty minutes to let him inside."

"Let's go!" Parker said anxiously. "Sarah, have the dispatcher call the kid's mother and tell her what happened. Then take him to school, will you?" He jumped into the front seat of Simpson's car and waved without looking back.

When Simpson and Parker arrived at the MacGreggor place, MacGreggor's nephew, Daryl Bailey, was already there, waiting. He appeared around thirty years old and had a shock of red hair and ears that stuck out like cup handles. Parker couldn't help but think of how the man had an uncanny resemblance to an old television personality. He looked eager to get into the house—maybe too eager. The next-door neighbor, Mrs. Crane, had told them MacGreggor and his nephew weren't on the best of terms, and there wasn't anything in the house of any value except the stereo system.

After being warned not to touch anything because of the possibility of rabies, the man rushed inside and straight for the basement steps. Simpson and Parker waited outside the door.

Simpson waved to two cops in a patrol car across the street, then looked back in the house.

"Shit, Tony, look at that!" Simpson exclaimed, pointing to the back door thirty-five feet away.

New wood was exposed on the door of the dog port and on the sides. It had been broken. Parker and Simpson hustled inside and to the back of the house.

"Tony," Simpson said, standing beside Parker and looking around the house cautiously, "do you think she's in here?"

"Easy Jack, this was broken going out. Anyway, if she were still here, our new Howdy-Doody-looking friend would have been screaming by now."

"Probably just some kid—you think?"

"Yeah, well, don't count on it," Parker said. He pinched hair from the splintered wood and brought it up to Simpson's face. "Unless that kid has short black hair."

Simpson stared at the dog fur between Parker's fingers. "And we've had this place under surveillance the whole time."

"Well, you'd better have the port fixed. A little stronger. Maybe some bigger screws. And make sure your men have their shit together this time."

Simpson frowned back as the nephew came up the stairs with the shoebox lid in his hand and a sour look on his face.

"What happened to the box?" the man asked.

"What was in the box?" Parker asked.

"Don't play games with me. It's rightfully mine. I'm the only heir," Bailey said back.

"The box was gone when we got here," Simpson said. "Now what was in it?"

"Over five hundred thousand, last I counted. But that was more than five years ago," he said, looking down at the box lid. "I want to talk to the first bastard cop on the scene. He's probably the thieving son-of-a-bitch that took it."

"You're speaking to him," Simpson said.

"You?"

"Yeah, I was the first 'thieving son-of-a-bitch' at the scene—that lived, that is."

"Where'd the money come from?" Parker asked.

"Life insurance on Aunt Rose."

"How'd you know about it?"

"I found it one day when he told me to feed the dogs. He caught me counting it."

"Before you could take it?" Parker asked, his stare cold, his voice flat.

"What do ya mean by that?" Bailey said, throwing the lid to the floor and drawing his fingers to a fist.

Parker could feel the hair on the back of his neck raise and a breath-taking rush of adrenaline shot through his body. A nervous, broad grin forced itself across his face.

"I mean," Parker answered, his hands also balling to fists, "I don't know you, but for some reason, I already don't like you. As far as I'm concerned, you could in some way be involved in your uncle's death!"

Bailey turned to Simpson. "What in the hell is this dog catcher doing, accusing me? Is he some kind of undercover cop or something? Because if he isn't, you'd better get him the hell out of my face!"

Parker stepped closer to him, nearly nose to nose, his jaw clenched.

"Back off, Tony," Simpson said, wedging between the two and shoving them apart. "Now, let's cool down. What can you tell us about the dogs?"

Bailey backed up two steps. He took a deep breath and glanced out of the corner of his eyes at Parker before looking to Simpson. "What can you say about dogs?" he said. "I hated them. I guess they knew it, too. They growled whenever I got near them. They were like any other dogs as far as I know, just a hell of a lot bigger."

"You were afraid of them?" Simpson asked.

"No, not really. I knew they wouldn't bite me or anything. They never acted aggressive like that. They just got off growling at me, like my uncle did."

"We'll let you know if any money comes up," Simpson said.

"It'd better," Bailey said. He looked toward the back of the house. "I'm sure there's no reason for me looking through the rest of the place. You bastards probably ransacked everything. Every loose dime is most likely in some cop's pocket." He turned and walked out the door, shaking his head.

Simpson and Parker followed him out and watched until he got into his car.

"What the hell got into you?" Simpson asked.

"You saw the jerk," Parker said, as they walked to the car. "He didn't care a bit about his uncle. All he wanted was his money. Then he did everything but accuse you of stealing it. He's the most likely suspect for that."

"You know that doesn't make sense. He was hundreds of miles away. And if he had stolen it, he wouldn't have said anything about it, or even showed up here for that matter."

"Okay, you're right. But this changes everything, don't you see? Two dogs, probably not rabid, attack and kill three men for no apparent reason. One dog is missing and so is half a million dollars! Doesn't that sound a little suspicious to you?"

"Come on, Tony, don't jump to conclusions. The old man probably spent it over the past five years," Simpson said, getting into the car. "Get in. I'll take you to your office."

"Spent it on what, dog food and CDs? And now, we have another man dead and one dying. And what about that pack of dogs in the park? There's human involvement somehow. This *TP* thing means something." Parker looked at Simpson with a scowl. "Now don't start on me about it somehow meaning me. It doesn't." Parker opened the passenger's side of Simpson's car and slipped in. "Somewhere out there is a murderer and thief, and a very dangerous dog!"

CHAPTER 17

In Sand Creek, Tricia Carpenter sat on the wooden seat of an ancient homemade swing set in the backyard of her grandparent's home. Her thin smile and dimples seemed permanent on her face. She didn't mind the baking sun so much under the protective branches of the old walnut tree with a light breeze from the south.

Pearl and Eldon Bumfield were inside, trying to stay cool with open windows and seven fans of various types circulating the stale air. Every five minutes, Grammy Pearl would appear in the kitchen window and wave, and Tricia would wave back.

She sat on the swing with both arms looped around the side chains, holding her most prized possession, Raggedy Ann, by the hands. She swung back and forth, toeing the dust with well-worn, white sneakers.

She had spent hours in that same swing this past summer, discussing important issues with her little homemade friend. Grammy Pearl and Grandy Eldon were nice, and she loved them very much, but they didn't seem to understand her quite like Raggedy Ann did.

The little girl felt a belch coming on and opened her mouth wide. A burp that could have come as easily from a hamster came out. It was nothing like the window rattling one that exploded from Grandy's gullet during lunch not thirty minutes earlier.

With her best Shirley Temple, *Good Ship Lollipop*, deep voice she reported, "Not bad manners, just good beer!"

Raggedy Ann and Tricia had been talking about a lot of things today. They had talked about how well Tricia had helped Grammy fix lunch. They had talked about that silly Jimmy Lawrence, who lived next door and was always showing off. They had talked about Tony Parker, the nice man who came and got rid of the bad skunk, rescued the kitten and called her cutie and Raggedy Ann pretty. They had talked about Tricia's mama and what it would be like to live in Denver when she finally found a job and sent for her. They had talked about Tricia's father and how much fun they had when she saw him last, more than two months ago, and they went to a Kansas City Royals ball game, and how great the cotton candy was. And they had even talked about Dawg and how he acted much happier since Grandy brought him back from the Doctor's office and how he wasn't itchin' as much as he was before.

As Tricia looked up to see Grammy wave from the kitchen window for the fifth time, she noticed a white van driving into town. It wasn't an unusual occurrence to see someone drive into town but neither was it something that happened without notice in a town the size of Sand Creek. She waved back to her grandmother then broke out in song.

"Ring around the rosy," she started singing and made Raggedy Ann dance on her knees as she watched the white van drive past the first house. "Pocket full of posies. Ashes, ashes, all fall down!" The last part of the song made Tricia frown as she remembered playing ring around the rosy with Jimmy Lawrence. When they came to the *all fall down* part, Jimmy had pushed her down hard, and it had hurt. It had jarred her teeth and hurt her bottom. She'd cried and run away from him, screaming that she would never play with him again.

Tricia stopped singing. Something about the van driving down the street gave her goose bumps. She didn't know what it was, but something made her feel uneasy. But it wasn't really the van; it was the driver. He had rolled his window down and leaned his head out as he drove very slowly. He was a dark man with black hair, and he had a patch covering one eye like a pirate.

Tricia shivered. The man who looked like a pirate had something in his mouth. It was shiny, and he made his cheeks puff out as if he blew a whistle, but there was no whistle sound.

Dogs started barking.

The dogs in Sand Creek always barked. They barked during the day and in the middle of the night. They barked when they saw a rabbit or a cat. They barked when they *thought* they saw a rabbit or a cat. They barked when they *wanted* to see a rabbit or a cat. One would start barking, then they would all join in like a small church's choir where few had the talent to sing, but all had the enthusiasm.

Within a minute, there wasn't only barking, but also growling. Screams and shouts filled the air. People cried.

She began to worry. Something was wrong.

She slipped from the swing and started toward the back door of the house. The barking and yelling and growling and screaming continued, now, seeming to come from all eight of the small town's houses.

When she realized screaming even came from Grammy and Grandy's house, she stopped. They yelled and cussed. She couldn't understand what they said, but they sounded upset. She had heard similar voices when her daddy and mommy were still married. It had gotten especially bad just before she and her mommy had moved out. It had been nearly as bad as what came from Grammy and Grandy's right now.

Tricia decided not to go in the back way but, instead, go around to the front. She was curious about what the pirate in the white van was doing, anyway. She tiptoed as if someone might be able to hear tiny soft footsteps in the Bermuda grass over the commotion going on all over town. She walked between her grandparent's house and the five-foot, dog-eared cedar fence that surrounded the Lawrence's yard.

Growling came from nearby. Very loud and angry growling erupted from behind the Lawrence's fence. She stopped and watched just six feet away. The Lawrences had a dog. Its name was Butch, a big, brown bulldog. But this didn't sound like Butch. She had never heard him growl with such fervor. She clutched Raggedy Ann tight with both hands and faced the fence. Running feet. A lot of very frantic running came toward Tricia from the opposite side of the fence. She could see motion between the large, twelve-inch slats.

Something crashed against the boards. Tricia's eyes widened. She froze, too scared to move. An arm, covered in streams of red, flung over the top of the fence, directly in front of her. A face appeared, also bloody—Jimmy Lawrence's face.

"Tricia—*ugh, ugh*. Help me!" he pleaded, looking down at her. He seemed to be straining, and Tricia could see a brown shape wriggling on the other side of the fence. It growled. Butch.

Fear held Tricia's body. She could do nothing but stare. The boy winced and gasped. With a look of terror, he fell back behind the fence.

"Ashes, ashes. All fall down," Tricia whispered, without intending to.

She could see the boy and the dog struggling on the other side. A lot of red and a lot of brown. She took two steps backward, turned and ran toward the front of her grandparent's house.

CHAPTER 18

The high sun attacked the earth with fierce heat as the chil
dren at the Cooper Elementary School in Wichita finished
their lunches. The first day of school was hotter than forecasted and
almost called off due to the over-one-hundred-degree temperature
and high humidity. Hope of a cold front, moving through in the early
afternoon, still existed, but no hint of it had come yet.

The children frolicked behind the old brick schoolhouse on the
sand playground. The L-shaped school building created two sides of
a rectangle, covering half of the block. A wrought iron fence with
brick posts every fifteen feet made up the other two sides. Sidewalks
wide enough to allow a large truck to pass led out onto the street at
each end between the fence and the building, on the opposite corners. In view through the fence on the south side was a park with a
wading pool, an 1880 vintage locomotive, a cannon from the Civil War
and numerous trees, mostly pine.

Nicholas Parker stood in the middle of the playground amidst
the ruckus. Dozens of other kids ran and played, screamed and yelled,
defying the heat. Nick had his hands in his pockets and kicked at the
sand as he talked with a little girl with dark brown hair, cut in Dutch-
boy style, and a face with a generous sprinkling of freckles.

A larger boy two years older with sandy-blond hair bumped into

Nick, knocking him off balance, and he caught himself with one hand.

"Hey, Parker, I hear your dad is a chicken shit!" the bigger boy said.

Nicholas got up immediately with his fists balled and bottom lip protruding.

"He is not a chicken shit, Haskins!" Nick said.

"Yeah, he is. He's a chicken, and he isn't worth a shit! My dad says so," the older boy insisted. "And that monster, Jezebel, is going to eat him!"

"No, he's not, and there ain't no monster gonna eat him!" Nick said. "And you're father's a dweeb! And my dad says he's uh asshole, a big asshole!"

"Oh, yeah! Well, my dad can kick your dad's ass, and I can kick your ass, and the monster's gonna eat you, too!" the Haskins boy said and scuffed the ground twice. The sand sprayed against Nick's blue jeans.

The forecasted cold front came upon them suddenly and without warning. The wind gusted violently. It blew so hard the children staggered. Sand blew into the Haskins boy's face. As the rude bully rubbed his eyes, Nick saw the opportunity at hand and kicked him in the shin. With the bigger boy holding onto his own leg, Nick kicked him again, this time in the groin, and the kid fell to the ground in the swirling sand. Nick stood over him with both fists armed at his sides. The Haskins boy lay on the ground for a moment then jumped up and ran away.

"Wow!" the little girl said, revealing a large gap in her open smile where her two front teeth used to be. "You just beat up a third grader. Wow!"

Nick said nothing. He stood and watched Haskins until he lost him in the blowing sand and dust and playing schoolmates.

The little girl took a step closer and asked boldly, "You want to get married?"

He looked at her, puzzled. *Girls are so weird.* "No, I don't think so."

"Come on, it's easy. It'll be fun. Ple-ease. Then we can get divorced if you want."

"No, I don't think we should."

The chilled wind had already cooled the playground nearly twenty degrees, and Nick shivered.

"Kelly Becker and I got married, and he thought it was fun. Come on."

"Well, what do I have to do?"

"We just hold hands and walk down an aisle and then dance," she said, matter-of-factly.

"What about sex? We don't have to have sex, do we?" Nick asked and shivered again.

"Of course not, silly," the girl said with a chuckle. "Married people don't have sex."

"Yeah, well, what if someone sees? They'll laugh at me."

"Oh, no they won't. People do it all the time. Don't you watch TV?"

"Well, uh, where we gonna get married?"

"We can't do it here, there's no aisle," she said, looking around. "We'll have to do it over there." She pointed to the wide concrete sidewalk between the school building and the fence.

The wind still blew hard, and Nick squinted to see where she pointed. He looked past, into the park. Something moved on the other side of the dusty playground. The little girl saw it, too. Something black. Something big. Moving from evergreen tree to evergreen tree. Moving toward the playground.

The little girl stared blankly for a second, then her eyes widened. She screamed with a deafening shrillness, "Ahhhhhh, Jezebel! It's Jezebel!"

The entire playground of over-active children came to a stop amidst whispers of, "Jezebel. . . . Where...? Over there. . . . Jezebel. . . . Jezebel."

The children's individual screams melted together into a high-pitched siren as they ran off the playground toward the school door in a stampede. The teachers watched and craned their necks to see what caused the uproar.

Nick hadn't moved. He stood alone in the middle of the playground, eyes fixed on the black object still moving closer every second. He thought about what the Haskins boy had said. His shiver turned into a strong shudder. He lost control, and his blue jeans began to darken, starting from the crotch and continuing down his left leg. He didn't want to get eaten. He wanted to run, but all of his joints seemed locked. He could not move.

Jezebel had come for him, *to eat* him like the Haskins boy had said. He couldn't see the monster's eyes, but in his mind he could see them. They glowed angry and red, and her mouth was big and had teeth like a shark's—like the monster from *Alien*. She slobbered and growled and wanted to *eat him*.

Nick saw his teacher, Miss Berry, herding the students inside. He wanted to run to her, but still his joints were locked. She looked back to the playground. The black thing in the park still approached through the dust and blowing sand. Miss Berry sprinted out to him, the sand swirling around her. She picked him up, and he gripped her tightly as she hustled back to the building. Nick's fear would not allow him to look over her shoulder at what might be pursuing them.

Tony Parker had just arrived at the animal-control shelter when the call came in. Jack Simpson had left, and Parker pulled his truck into the garage stall to wash it down, and clean out the inside. The stall smelled medicinally clean. It did not have the antiseptic scent of a hospital but more of a heavy, pungent odor, common around livestock or a veterinary clinic.

Tommy Chin came out and grabbed him by the arm as he vacuumed out the back.

"Tony, trouble!" Chin yelled over the noise.

Parker took a couple of steps over to the wall and turned the vacuum cleaner off. "What's up?"

"They think they've spotted Jezebel."

"Where?"

"Cooper Elementary School."

"My God! That's Nick's school!" Parker exclaimed. He threw the vacuum hose down and ran to the driver's side of the truck.

Chin stepped back as Parker laid rubber on the damp concrete floor. The piercing squeal of the tires echoed through the stall, and the sweet smell of exhaust mixed with the bitter smell of burning rubber.

A gray haze now cloaked the sky, and dust and a light mist made the windshield of the truck a nearly opaque blur. The wind blew against the side of the truck making it difficult to manage, and a thin film of mud made the streets slick. Parker drove frantically with emergency lights on, yet few motorists seemed willing to concede.

"Come on, come on!" Parker yelled to an unyielding senior citizen in a large antique Buick in front of him.

He pounded the dash when the old woman came to a yellow light and stopped.

"Damn it! If you can't drive that old battleship, keep it off the road!" he yelled and pulled around into the left turn lane.

The truck slid nearly sideways when Parker shoved the accelerator to the floorboard and sped through the intersection. Two cars, coming from opposing directions on the intersecting street, slid out of control and smashed into each other, narrowly missing the back end of the Jimmy. Parker regained control, but the left rear quarter panel of the truck bumped the left front fender of a Cadillac stopped at the light in the oncoming lane.

"Ah shit! I'm gonna catch hell for this," he said aloud.

He picked up the microphone as he continued recklessly down the street. "AC One to dispatcher!"

"This is the dispatcher. Go ahead, AC One," a woman's voice that Parker didn't recognize came back. There had been a number of new people hired this summer.

"There's been an accident at the intersection of Twenty-first and Hillside. Better send an ambulance. There may be injuries."

"Roger, AC One. Stay at the scene and assist the injured until emergency personnel arrive."

"Sorry, I can't. I am proceeding to an animal control emergency at present."

"Please be advised that an injury auto accident takes priority, AC One."

Parker reached over and turned his radio off. "Not this time!"

The schoolyard was deserted when Parker finally arrived. He jumped the curb and drove across the playground to the side door and slammed on the brakes. Springing out of the truck, he slipped and nearly fell on the loose sand covering the cement slab in front of the door. He hit the door hard with both hands, and swung it wide as he hustled in.

The hallway was full of children, huddled in groups, some of them still noticeably upset and sobbing. Parker spotted Nick with Miss Berry's arm on his shoulder and ran to him. He dropped to his knees and grabbed Nick by the head with both hands. The fear still covered Nick's chalky-white face. He could smell his hot, sweaty, urine-soaked clothes.

"Are you all right, Nicholas?"

Nick nodded slowly as tears flowed.

Parker pulled Nick's head into his chest and hugged him firmly. "Thank God! Oh, thank God!"

Parker looked up at the young teacher, her face also filled with fear and uncertainty. "Is everyone okay?"

"Yes, I think so."

"Where is she?"

"In the park across the street."

"Stay with him," he instructed. "And keep everyone inside."

Parker got up and hurried outside. He went to the back of the truck and pulled out the control stick. Looking across the playground into the park, he could see nothing except trees in the midst of the blowing dust and sand. He squinted to protect his eyes and trotted toward the park.

He searched slowly from tree to tree, cautiously holding the control stick like a pugil stick, ready to defend himself. He stepped around each tree, finding nothing. Nearly ready to give up, he scanned across the park one last time.

Movement behind one of the big, bushy evergreen trees ahead alerted him. Something black. Parker approached with a deer hunter's attentiveness, moving closer to his prey. His heart pounded in his chest. He could feel it in the arteries in his neck. If it was Jezebel, the control stick would do him little good unless he caught her completely by surprise.

Parker edged to the side of the tree and paused. He swallowed. He took a deep breath. Eyes wide and teeth clenched, he leaped out, control stick at the ready.

Plastic. A black plastic tarp flirted with the wind. Most likely, it had been blown off a pickup load of tree limbs headed for the dump.

Parker whistled out the breath he'd been holding and jabbed the plastic with the stick. No, not plastic. This was rubberized canvas. It had a zipper. An empty body bag. A small piece of paper was safety-pinned to one end. *TP* was printed in big black letters.

Parker suddenly felt nauseous and feverish. He staggered, dizzy and off balance. What was wrong? It must be the flu, a summer cold. Maybe it was a little stress-induced high blood pressure. He had to regain his composure. He quickly scanned the area to ensure that he was alone.

There would be no way of telling if this had been what the children had seen. In many ways he was relieved, even though he desperately needed to catch the giant canine. If it had been Jezebel, it would have been almost as if she were stalking Parker and his family—like in the dreams. But considering the body bag and the initials again, maybe it wasn't a *dog* tracking him down.

He picked up the body bag and rolled it up as he walked toward the school. He would tell them that what they'd seen was just a plastic tarp, blown off a load of trash, on its way to the dump.

CHAPTER 19

Tricia Carpenter ran up and onto the front porch of her grandparents' house, screaming, "Grandy! Grammy! Butch is hurting Jimmy!"

She burst through the screen door and swung it wide, allowing it to bang shut behind her. She stopped in the front hallway when she saw Grandy.

Fifteen feet away, he lay on his back in the middle of the living room floor with Dawg and three other of the local mutts tearing at his guts through his wide open belly. His throat lay open. He didn't move.

Tricia stared. The dogs fed in a frenzy and hadn't noticed her or even paid attention to the slam of the screen door.

Dawg seemed to enjoy his fresh kill, but he stopped and raised his head as if thinking. Fear paralyzed Tricia. *He's thinking about me. He's wondering where me and Raggedy Ann are!*

Dawg sniffed the air and slowly turned his head. He looked back at Tricia and licked his snout. The other dogs stopped their enthusiastic feeding and raised their heads to glare at Tricia, as if in tune with Dawg's thoughts. Tricia stared back.

A bloody arm swathed across Tricia's body and swung her around toward the door.

"Run, Tricia, *run!*" came a frantic voice.

Tricia ran the two steps to the door without recognizing the blood-covered arm and desperate voice. She stopped and turned.

It was Grammy. The blood wasn't just on her arm. It covered her face and matted her hair. Large gashes crossed her cheek and forehead and arms. Ripped flesh hung in a flap on her left leg.

She looked at Tricia with teary eyes. Her arms and body shook convulsively, and her lips trembled. "Run, Tricia," she said again. This time her voice came out in a cracking whisper, and she turned to face the dogs as they attacked.

Tricia ran out the door, and it slapped shut again. She stopped at the foot of the porch steps, unsure of where to go. The mysterious white van went by slowly as she stood there, panting, shaking. The black pirate inside smiled broadly at her as he drove. He waved.

Tricia looked up and down the street. Confusion reigned everywhere she looked. People running. People screaming. People being run down by dogs. Many of the dogs had already made their kills and were feeding. Growls and barks came from far and near. She heard them coming from the Lawrence's house next door through their open living room window. She heard the dogs inside her grandparent's house, heard Grammy screaming and wailing.

Tears poured from Tricia's eyes. She wished she could help Grammy, but she didn't know what to do. She held her doll so tightly that she was nearly twisting it apart.

A sound caught Tricia's ears, different from the barks and screams and growls and yells going on around her. A *meow*. She looked up into the large elm shading the front yard and saw Little Pussy on its usual limb. She understood how it felt but realized the kitten was much safer than she was right now. But she couldn't climb the tree. The lowest branch was way over her head.

Tricia turned and ran around the side of the house once again. She ran toward the old garage where the skunk had been captured and up to the hasp on the door. She tried to push the large bolt out of the hasp, but it was fitted too tightly. She pushed and pushed, grunting desperately, but still, it would not budge.

She finally gave up and turned back to the front yard. Several dogs ran by, but none noticed her. A bark came from the front yard. It sounded like Dawg. He must have finished with Grammy. Now he would be coming for her!

Tricia raced frantically into the back yard toward the old swing set. But then, a hole caught her eye. A dark hole. A place to hide. She didn't think about what it was. She only thought about it being a place to get out of sight.

She fell to her knees, crawled in and scampered to the back. Through the opening she saw Dawg come around the corner of the house and pause, sniffing the air. Two more dogs trotted around the house and stopped behind Dawg. They all sniffed.

Tricia huddled in the dark shadow at the back of the hole, looking straight at the dogs. She tried to quiet her trembling breath, and she held Raggedy Ann up to her lips. Only then did she realize where she was. She hid in an old wooden crate. The old wooden crate used as Dawg's doghouse! She gasped.

The dogs jerked their heads in reaction.

CHAPTER 20

Parker took Nick home after the incident. Even after being assured what he had seen was just a piece of plastic and not a man-killing dog, his son still could not get over the shakes. Parker thought the best place for him would be in his own bed.

"What happened?" Julie asked. Worry filled her eyes as she stood in the front doorway watching Tony carry her six-year-old son up the walk to the steps. "Is Nick all right?" She reached out to him

"Yeah, he's all right," Parker said. "Nothing to be worried about. He just got a little scared, that's all."

"Scared? Of what? Are you sure he's not hurt?" she asked, holding the storm door back and stroking Nick's forehead as they passed.

Nick began crying uncontrollably and stretched out and latched onto his mother. "Mamma, Mamma, she's going to eat me, and she's gonna get Daddy, too!"

"Oh sweetheart, nobody's going to eat you," she told him as she rubbed his back. "It's all right."

Julie and Tony sat on the couch, staring at each other for a long moment, as Julie held Nick on her lap.

Tony knew a lot was on Julie's mind, but she held it back in consideration of her son's trauma.

"The kids were all out on the playground, and they thought they saw Jezebel in the park across the street," Tony said. "It turned out to be a piece of black plastic."

Julie looked back at Tony skeptically. She rose from the couch and started up the stairs to Nick's bedroom.

"Nothing happened with me and Sarah," Parker said to Julie's back. "At least not what you think. I'd like to explain."

He watched them go up the stairs. Julie said nothing.

Parker called his office to let them know he would be on call at home the rest of the day. He then went to the kitchen cabinets, pulled out a fifth of W. L. Weller's and poured out half a glass over a handful of ice cubes. Drinking in the middle of the afternoon wasn't a habit of his. In fact, the bottle hadn't been touched since Jack and Sadie had been over for the evening three weeks ago. Parker needed something to calm his nerves. He knew the whiskey wouldn't help, but it seemed like the thing to do. Nick's shakes had been contagious, and Parker had caught a severe case himself. He felt chilled, yet feverish, again.

Parker sat back in his easy chair and stared out the big picture window. This Jezebel thing was out of control. It was personal, now. The solution to this problem evaded him. All thirteen of his field officers worked double shifts, looking for this phantom of a hound. He was on call twenty-four hours and, except for tonight, would also be working double shifts. The police were on the watch for the beast, and every citizen in town, in the state, seemed to be aware of her. He could do nothing but wait. She would turn up soon. She had to.

This thing with Sarah had to be dealt with, too. He didn't look forward to explaining it to Julie. This time, he wouldn't lie. The truth about this fix he was in had to come out—for Julie—for himself. He wondered how she would react to any explanation, let alone the vague, confused one he had—if she'd even listen.

Parker's stomach churned. His head began to throb. This little flu bug sure didn't help any, if that was what it was. Maybe he should take some medicine. No, that wouldn't mix with the alcohol.

Parker sat, staring at nothing for the better part of half an hour before Julie came back down the stairs. She walked over to Tony's chair, sat down on the arm and gazed into his eyes, like she had many times before when she was worried or puzzled and looked to Tony for the answer. He saw her look at the drink in his hand, now empty except for a teaspoon of tainted water in the bottom.

"How's Nick?" Tony asked, turning his head away.

"I think he's all right, now. He's asleep. Now, tell me, what's going on?" she asked, taking the glass from his hand and setting it on the lamp stand nearby.

"It's pure paranoia," he answered. "The whole town is caught up in it. All because of that damned Haskins!" He knew the name *Haskins* had stuck a dagger in both of their hearts as soon as he spat it out. "Everyone is afraid of a dog that is probably lying dead somewhere by now."

"Why do you think she's dead?"

"That's the only way a dog like that could get by, loose, in this city without being discovered. If she has rabies, she's probably dead."

Tony's assumption had not convinced Julie, or himself. He got up from the chair and walked over to the window, still looking away.

"I'm working double shifts until this is over. That includes this weekend," he said.

"Surely, it will be over by the weekend, won't it? We promised Mom and Dad we'd come up. They were counting on it. We haven't seen them for a long time." Her voice lacked emotion. He was surprised she still planned on them going together after this morning.

"I don't know if it will or not."

"Well, if it isn't, we'll go anyway. You need a break. We need a break."

"No, I can't. This is my job. It's what I get paid for. When something like this comes up, I can't just leave."

"That's bullshit, Tony, and you know it! You're going to quit in a few months, anyway. Is it because you want to stay here—or because you just don't want to see Dad?"

The pause in her question consciously left out two words: *with Sarah.*

"Get real, will you? I've got a job to do, and I'm going to do it. Besides, your dad would probably rather go fishing with Haskins."

Tony didn't apologize this time, but he wished he could. He turned to see Julie's backside leave the room for the kitchen. He could hear Julie open a cabinet and then turn on the faucet, pouring herself a glass of tap water.

It surprised him she hadn't said anything about Sarah. He wouldn't have blamed her if she had thrown him out, knowing what she had seen. He knew that when she did let her feelings out there would be one hell of a confrontation. It could mean losing his family. Divorce. Maybe that was why she hadn't said anything. Maybe she knew a divorce was inevitable when she said her piece—that she wanted to hold on for as long as she could, hoping she'd discover some other explanation for what she saw but was afraid to learn the truth. Tony hoped, somehow, she could hold on forever.

"Oh, I'll be home tonight, so you can go to your aerobics class," he said loud enough for her to hear in the next room. Julie had been teaching the evening aerobics class three nights a week at a health club downtown over the summer. Tonight was the last night—a make-up night for when Julie had been down with a bad cold and no one was able to sub for her.

"I'm not going, not with Nick like this."

"Don't be ridiculous. You said he's all right. I'll be here."

"For some reason, that doesn't assure me very much," Julie sneered as she walked back through the room and up the stairs toward the children's rooms.

Tony felt a hot flash and a burning on his neck. "Now, what in the hell do you mean by that?"

"I don't know. I just said it, okay?" she said and disappeared.

"No, it's not *okay!*" Tony roared. He hated it when Julie walked away in the middle of an unresolved argument. Not that there was a resolution. Parker didn't even understand why they were arguing.

His mind was fuzzy. He felt light-headed and didn't know why. He hadn't had that much to drink. Maybe the flu. He thought of it and tried to remember what had set them off. It clouded his mind and was confusing to think about. He went back to the kitchen cabinet and took out the bottle of Weller's. This time he grabbed a large tumbler, filled it with ice and brought both glass and bottle back to his chair.

Several hours had passed, and Parker realized he was staring out at early evening shadows. He gripped the half-full, iceless tumbler, still in a daze. The bottle lay empty on the floor. Yankee had knocked it off the lamp stand when Parker let him in for some understanding companionship. Paper towels still soaked up the booze on the large spot where it had spilled.

Parker felt Julie's presence and turned to look at her, Yankee doing the same. Julie came down the stairs and stood at the foot. She had that disgusted look on her face. She wore her aerobics outfit, and he looked at her through unfocused eyes. Even through his alcohol-blurred eyes, she was a vision to behold. He liked the way her tight outfit caressed her body. The pink and green top accented her bust, and her light brown hair was back in a ponytail. It reminded him of the way she had looked in high school. The argument had long since left his fuzzy brain, and he smiled at her.

"Oh, this is just great, you—shit head!" she said with her hands on her hips, the previous confrontation, obviously, still fresh in her mind. "Now, I suppose you're drunk."

He frowned, trying to look sober and serious. "No, I'm all right. I thought you weren't going tonight."

"I changed my mind, okay?"

"Okay, sure," Tony said sheepishly. He knew he was in trouble and was having a hard time discerning for what. His best defense was to go along with everything Julie said. "You can go. I'm fine," he said as the hand he leaned on slipped, making his head bob.

"It's not you I'm worried about—shit head!"

Parker frowned again, wishing for a different nickname. Julie walked over to Tony's side, and he watched her every step. She picked up the half-full tumbler and walked swiftly to the kitchen with it. He heard the whiskey pouring down the drain.

"What happens if Audrey needs changed? Can you do it?"

"Sure, no problem."

"Okay, but you'd better not screw up. You get in here right now and drink some coffee. If you need anything, the health club's number is by the phone. I just fed and changed Audrey, and Nick is still sleeping." Julie came back through the living room and grabbed her purse off the coat-closet doorknob. "I should be home by a quarter after ten."

"It's okay, sweetheart. I've done this before," Tony said smiling.

"Yeah, but you've never done it drunk, shit head."

"I'm not drunk, and I wish you wouldn't call me that."

"It's the only name that fits, right now," she said. "You two deserve each other."

Tony blinked for a moment, thinking at first Julie meant he and Sarah. He looked at Yankee and noticed the stupid, puzzled, intoxicated look on his face—the natural look the dog had been born with.

"Now, get your butt in the kitchen and make yourself some coffee. I've got to go or I'll be late." She walked to the front door. "Oh, and darling," she said with a gentle change of voice.

"Yes, sweetheart," Tony answered back, surprised at the pleasant tone.

"Don't burn the house down—shit head!" she said and slammed the door.

The coffee seemed to help sober Parker some. After two and a half cups, he fell asleep in his chair with the TV on and Yankee by his side.

CHAPTER 21

Darkness had fallen over the Bumfields' back yard. The small burg of Sand Creek had been wiped out by the dogs. None of the residents understood the gravity of their situation until too late to call for help—too late to run to their cars and flee.

Not a single car had driven down the street of the little town since the pirate in the white van left. Tricia knew there probably wouldn't be any until Mr. Burke, the mailman, came sometime before lunch, tomorrow.

She was exhausted, worn out from holding her body taut and from crying quietly over her grandparents. She knew they were dead. She understood what death was. After all, she was a big girl. She was five years old, now, or at least would be in October. She caught herself nodding off as she huddled in the back of Dawg's doghouse.

She had been lucky earlier this afternoon. Just as Dawg and the other two dogs seemed to be picking up her scent and homing in on her, Mr. Lawrence from next door came out of his house, screaming. All three dogs had been distracted and forgot all about her. They had run off, chasing Mr. Lawrence, with the Lawrences' own dog, Butch, trailing the pack.

Tricia didn't know what to do. It had been so frightening, so traumatic. She remembered how Grammy had shown her how to dial 911 for help if there was ever an emergency. She had shown her how to call her mother in Denver and had let her punch the numbers. She remembered Tony Parker and how he came and helped out in the last emergency. He was the dogcatcher. He'd know what to do. Tony Parker's card lay with all the others next to the phone in the living room.

Tricia was tired and hungry. She didn't want to leave her safe haven but felt she must. It was unbearable to wait for help any longer. Besides, what if Dawg came back looking for her? Or what if Dawg just came back to his doghouse? He surely would, sooner or later. Probably sooner than help would come. Sooner than Mr. Burke would come to deliver *those damned bills* as Grandy would say.

She paused from her thoughts to wipe her streaming eyes and running nose on Raggedy Ann and then rubbed her soiled doll on the side of her dress. She had to get into the house. She had to get in soon and call Tony Parker.

Tricia crouched low in the opening of the doghouse, taking care to examine everything within sight. No movement. There hadn't been any barks for hours, yells and screams for even longer. Once in a while, she would hear some growls, probably from the dogs fighting over their kills.

No growls, now. The night was still. Time to move—*shit or get off the pot* as Grandy had said when driving himself and Tricia into Wichita to the grocery store one day. He'd said it to an elderly man stopped at a green light. Then, he'd caught himself and told Tricia to *excuse me, Ma'am,* and he'd tipped his hat to her. She remembered giggling at his clowning. The tears came back to her eyes but she wouldn't allow them to flow.

"Shit or get off the pot!" she said in her low Shirley Temple, *Good Ship Lollipop* voice and popped out of the doghouse. She darted for the back door of the house.

With her hand on the screen door handle, she looked in the open doorway. What if Dawg and the others were inside? *All* of them. But then again, maybe they were all gone. Maybe they all ran off. *Maybe* they saw a rabbit and all ran away, chasing it, and would never come back. She frowned thinking of it. After today, these dogs probably wouldn't much care for rabbits.

Tricia moved slowly, tiptoeing her way into the house and through the kitchen toward the living room. It was hard to see in the dark, and she wanted to turn on a light but knew she shouldn't. She tried to be quiet, as quiet as a mouse, and so far she had been.

She bumped into something. A kitchen chair. It banged into the table, and a half-full glass of milk, left over from lunch, fell over and spilled on the table. Tricia pulled Raggedy Ann up close to her face and stopped still. She stood silently in the darkness, waiting to hear anything move that might have heard her. More than a minute passed before she was sure she hadn't alerted the dogs and moved again, creeping to the living room.

She eased through the doorway and stepped toward the phone table in front of the large, wide-open living room window. The window screen was torn into strips. Light shone through from the streetlight. It gave the room an eerie, spooky feel.

She hadn't thought about this being the last place she'd seen Grandy, but she was reminded of it by the time she made the middle of the room. She had stepped on something, and she looked down. In the dark shadows on the floor, she could make out Grandy's body. She couldn't really recognize it and wouldn't have been able to even in the light, but it was in the same place as it had been earlier in the day, so it must be him. She wanted to scream. She wanted to so badly but held herself back, even though she realized her foot rested *inside* Grandy's body.

Tricia drew a deep breath. She stepped quickly over her grandfather and briskly toward the phone. When she reached out for it, her excited hand knocked the handset off, and it clattered onto the table. She pursed her lips and slowly scanned the room.

She saw eyes. A pair of eyes, glowing in the dark. They rose slightly. *Oh no! A dog, and he's seen me, and he's in the hallway!*

Every joint in Tricia's little body locked. She could do nothing but stare back at the eyes.

A small, meek mew came from the thing. The same *meow* she'd distinguished from all the other commotion when she ran out of the house earlier in the day. It was Little Pussy. He lay on a ravaged body. Tricia knew it must be Grammy's, but she couldn't see for sure.

She began crying uncontrollably, and her limbs convulsed. The kitten sprung up from its place on the chest of Grammy's half-devoured body and ran to her. It stopped at her feet and arched its back and rubbed up against the little girl's calf. Tricia saw it through blurred eyes. She whimpered.

Tony Parker's card lay on top of the phone table. She recognized it because she had picked it up and looked at it after Tony Parker and everyone else had gone outside. She could barely make it out through the sheet of tears covering her eyes. She laid Raggedy Ann down next to the phone and picked up the handset.

Tricia wiped her eyes with the back of her hand and looked at the card. Below the number printed on the card, there was another number hand printed. Tricia couldn't read words yet, but she remembered Tony Parker saying his home number was on it. At this time of night, that's where he would be, and the hand-printed number must be his home phone number.

Tricia took care in pushing the correct numbers, just as Grammy had taught her. She was excited she had done so without a hitch— knew that Grammy would be proud... *if she were alive*—and she turned away from the window and bent down and grabbed up the kitten. She waited for the phone to make the connection and start ringing as the kitten nuzzled her cheek.

She glanced over to the opposite wall at Grammy's favorite picture. She'd told Tricia she liked it so much because it reminded her of Tricia and Dawg. It depicted a young girl, who had most likely just been scolded, standing in a corner. A dog was behind her, looking as if it wished to console her. On the glass cover of the picture, Tricia could see her own reflection, standing in front of the window in the dim light. It was ghost-like and covered the little girl in the picture.

The phone rang. One, two, three rings.

Oh, please be home!

Someone picked up the phone. Tricia was surprised by what sounded like crying from the other end. *Are they there, too? Have all the dogs in the world gone crazy and they're at Tony Parker's house too?*

"Hello," Tony Parker's voice answered the phone.

Tricia raked in an excited breath, preparing to *spill her guts*, as Grandy would have said—oh, poor Grandy, who had *spilled his guts* all over the living room—about what had happened. But then she noticed Little Pussy stiffen up and spit while looking, over Tricia's shoulder. Tricia glanced to the picture on the wall again. Her own reflection was still there, but now there was a new image, imposed phantom-like over the dog in the picture. It was large and hulking, and its eyes glowed an evil amber. She turned her head slowly and looked over her shoulder. Dawg's body filled the open window. He stood with his front paws on the torn out screen frame only three feet away, glaring at Tricia with lip curled and huge teeth bared.

She gasped.

"Who is this?" Tony Parker asked.

Tricia couldn't speak. She stared into Dawg's evil, vicious eyes. He hadn't budged, still glaring as if he wanted her to make the first move.

Finally, Tricia found enough breath to whisper, "Dawg!"

CHAPTER 22

The workout helped Julie get the troubles between her and Tony off her mind, and she began to worry about Tony. He'd never acted like this. She knew Sarah was a threat, but she really never believed Tony would ever give in to the little flirt. She hated him for backing her into a corner, forcing her to make a decision. She hated him for lusting for Sarah, young desirable Sarah, instead of her. She hated him for screwing her, if he had. She hated him, yet she loved him dearly. At times she felt she was too much like her mother, who had remained married to her father for more than forty years now, all the time knowing he continuously had affairs.

It's a man's world. She shook her head.

Maybe there *was* a logical explanation for what she'd seen. She didn't know how, but maybe. But, why wouldn't he tell her if there was? Make her listen to his explanation, no matter how many times she turned away. It just wasn't like him.

She hadn't seen him drink like tonight since his wild days, before they were married. This Jezebel thing seemed to be eating him up inside. It was making him do and say things he normally wouldn't. And now it was eating on Nick and even her.

It was ten o'clock and the class was finally over. It had seemed like she'd been there all day, instead of just an hour. Julie's class was the last of the evening, and she rushed the few remaining stragglers out the door, anxious to get home to her family.

"Julie, are you going to be teaching the late class again this fall?" one of the ladies asked as she dried the sweat from her face with a towel.

"No, not this time," Julie said, holding the door open for the last three women to leave. "I have to get ready to teach third grade again. I'll be teaching at Lincoln, starting the second semester. My husband's going back to vet school."

"We'll sure miss you," another of the ladies said, walking out the door.

"And I'll miss all of you, too," she said smiling as she patted the last girl on the back.

"Bye," they all three said in unison while walking to their cars.

"Bye-bye," she said back and pulled the door shut behind her as she stepped out.

The door locked as intended. She had left her key inside in the manager's desk, since it was the last night she'd need it. She began walking to her minivan, which sat alone in the parking lot. The misty night had just a bit of a chill in the air, but it was calm, no wind. No noise except the distant sound of traffic and car horns on Douglas Avenue a couple of blocks away.

As Julie walked up to her white Ford minivan, a strange feeling came over her, and she shivered. A feeling that someone was watching her. She felt uneasy as she dug in her purse for the key to unlock the minivan door. When she brought the keys out, she noticed the window was down an inch and the lock button on the inside was up. She tried the handle, and the door came open.

"Hmmm," she said out loud, "must have forgotten to lock it."

After checking inside to insure she had no unwanted passengers, she slipped in quickly, slammed the door and shoved the lock down. She peered out as she found the ignition and turned the key. The engine turned over nicely, but it wouldn't start. She tried again and pumped the accelerator. Still, no positive response.

"Oh, damn it!" she cursed aloud. "I keep telling him to get this damned thing fixed."

Julie tried the ignition again and began pumping the accelerator frantically until she could smell gas. The engine turned ever slower. She paused for a moment and scanned the parking lot.

What would she do if it wouldn't start? She couldn't get back into the building to call Tony. He'd have to get the kids up to come get her, and he probably wasn't in any shape to drive, anyway. She could call a cab, or Jack and Sadie, if there were a phone. But there wasn't a phone for blocks. She couldn't remember one any closer than a Quick Trip several blocks away. She might as well jog home. It wasn't much more than a mile.

Something about this night, though, bothered her: the talk of this giant killer dog, the harsh words spoken, the night itself. Lonely, eerie, spooky.

She tried the switch again. This time, nothing but clicks. The battery was dead.

"Damn, damn, damn!" she said and hit the steering wheel.

She'd have to look under the hood. She didn't know why. Everyone does that when they have car trouble. She popped the hood release and reached for the door handle and began to pull it, watching diligently through the front windshield. The dismal setting made Julie feel more isolated than ever before.

Crack! Something hit her driver's side window. She turned quickly. A slobbering, dirty face pressed up against the window next to her.

She screamed.

The atrocious face looked back at her and smiled. Black and gray teeth. Scraggly beard. Long stringy hair. He clutched a wine bottle in one hand with the index finger of the same hand over the top of the narrowly opened window.

"Car trouble, lady?" the wino asked, slurring.

She could smell the wine, thick on his breath, through the opening.

"No, no, leave me alone!" Julie demanded.

"Come on Lady, I can help you. I'm good with my hands," he said, still smiling, showing only a few sparse teeth, and wiggling his nasty, filthy fingers.

"I said *no*! Leave me alone!" she demanded once more and rolled the window up on his finger.

"Ow! Damn!" the wino said and snatched his finger out, dropping the wine to the pavement with a crash. He looked down at the broken bottle with anger, holding his injured digit. "Bitch!" he yelled out and slugged the driver's side window with the side of his fist. "Stupid Bitch!" he yelled again and kicked the door.

"Get away from me! Leave me alone!" Julie yelled back nearly in tears.

The wino stood six feet away and wiped his nose. With a disgusting snort, he spat and began staggering away. Julie watched him until he had gone around a dark building almost a block down. Her hands shook and teeth chattered. She felt like a scared rabbit, drawing short breaths. She scanned the parking lot once again. Nothing else out there. The coast was clear this time. She made sure. She pushed out of the minivan cautiously, leaving the door open, and found the hood latch.

After lifting the hood, she looked down at the big greasy mass of metal and wires. It was an engine, she knew that. *The round thing in the middle. That's what they always mess with first, when they work on cars. They take it off and fool around with the—carburetor!* She proudly remembered this much. She stepped back from the minivan and gave a slow and cautious 360-degree scan. Satisfied she was alone, she looked back under the hood. She reached for the wing nut in the center of the air cleaner and tried turning it. It was tight, and when she broke it loose, her fingers slipped off, and she broke a fingernail.

"Ow!" she said, "Ewww, are you gonna' get it, Tony Parker!"

Julie stood back for a moment and looked at her vehicle.

"What's the use!" she said and slammed the hood. She went back over to the open door, reached in and got the keys and her purse. She threw the door shut and looked out determinedly in the direction of home.

It wasn't a bad jog to the house. A bike path went most of the way. A couple of blocks down to the river and onto the jogging path, then along the river and under a couple of bridges, then back up onto the sidewalk, and in a couple of more blocks, she'd be home. She'd jogged it in daylight many times before, a number of times with Tony. She wished Tony jogged it with her now, even if something had happened between him and Sarah. Even if he had been *unfaithful*, she wished he were with her *now*.

Julie drew a deep breath, tucked her purse under one arm and started running fast. Finding it impossible to maintain the sprinting pace and feeling a bit more relaxed, she slowed down within a block and began singing, "Julie, Julie, Julie, Do You Love Me?" It came to her lips almost involuntarily, and it seemed to help take her mind off her predicament. Tony would sing this song when he was in a playful mood and make her laugh. Sometimes, he'd use it to help mend an argument. Maybe he would sing it when she got home, and she'd laugh, and everything would be all right.

Julie made it to the jogging path without incident. She felt a bit more confident until she looked down at the river. The same feeling of being watched came over her. Another chill scampered like a mouse up her spine and made her shrug her shoulders. She paused, jogging in place. The river lay before her, black and still. Like death. Fog was slowly building on it.

A hoarse howl broke the stillness, echoing eerily, reverberating long and low.

Julie shook all over. The howl came from a ways off. She couldn't tell how far, but it was—a ways. It could have come from any dog. This dog, Jezebel, was surely dead by now. Tony had said it. *It was probably dead.* She would be all right. She just had to get this done and over with. She'd be home soon.

Julie shook once more, this time purposely, trying to shake off the apprehension, and started down the path.

"Julie, Julie, Julie, do you care?" she sang a little louder this time. She kept her eyes straight ahead, afraid to look around. She would just jog as fast as she could and not think about anything but getting home.

The fog became thicker. Her shoes made hollow, ricocheting echoes down the path. The thick damp fog labored her breathing, and she felt as if it closed in to suffocate her. The path was only visible thirty feet in front of her. The few lights along the path only made things worse, causing bright patches of nothingness fog. Up ahead, she could see the top of a bridge. As she neared, she strained her eyes to insure nothing lurked underneath.

Movement. Her fears came true. Something moved under the bridge. She came to a fork in the path. She could either go under the bridge on the level she was on now, or go up hill and around the bridge and cross the street.

She paused once more and jogged in place, squinting down the path. It could be a goose or a duck. Or another wino, probably harmless. Or a rapist. Or a dog.

It moved again. No shape. Dark. Black—like Jezebel.

Julie's entire body shuddered, and she shot up the path to the street above. She didn't look down the other path. She just ran. She made it to the empty street and looked back, gasping for air. Nothing had followed her.

It *was* nothing. Just the fog. Imagination. *Paranoia*, like Tony had said. The quickest way home was still down the jogging path. She crossed the street and went down the other side onto the path again. Once again she ran without looking back. Her jog had turned into a flat out run. She perked her ears to hear what her eyes were afraid to see, but could discern only the echoes of her own footsteps.

Suddenly, she came to the next bridge. It caught her off guard. She had been running much faster than usual and had never reached it this soon before. By the time she realized it, it was too late to take the high path to the street. She didn't want to run back. Julie feared what might be following her, but also what might be waiting for her under the bridge.

With all the energy she had, she flew under the bridge and

sprinted out the other side. Nothing lurked under the dark gloomy overpass, and she chuckled to herself.

Her toe kicked something and fear came over her again. She heard a telltale, *tink, tonk, tonk* of an empty bottle, probably a wine bottle, followed by a splash as it fell into the river.

"Damn winos!" she cursed, relieved.

Julie smiled as she approached the last street before the turn off to home. She could see the top of Blackbear Bosin's *Keeper Of The Plains* statue across the river. The huge statue of an Indian chief looking up to the heavens somehow comforted her. She thought of their good friends, Doc and Patsy White Cloud. She felt safe now. She had her second wind, and it didn't seem as hard to breathe. She jogged on, almost enjoying the night.

"Julie, Julie," she began singing again, then louder, with a laugh, *"Are you thinkin' of me?"*

The hoarse howl, this time not far off, ended her gaiety.

"Oh she-it!"

Something ominous about it this time. In the dense fog, Julie felt trapped. The prey waiting for the predator, without chance of survival. She sprinted once again. The haloed streetlights became glistening blurs in her tear-filled eyes, making it difficult for her to see. She strained her ears and turned back to look down the path.

Nothing but fog. But now, a noise. Something getting louder. Something coming closer. The pounding of her own heart made it difficult, but she could hear it. Getting closer. Closer. A rapid tapping sound, like sticks on a rock.

Julie turned and ran frantically, nearly out of control. Her arms flung around her without coordination, and she gasped for air between nervous, whimpering sobs.

She made it to the last bridge and ran up to the street without looking back. Only two more blocks and she'd be home, but her feet were lead weights, and her lungs were ripping apart in her chest. The tapping still approached from behind her as she cut across a yard and onto her street.

She wasn't going to make it. The thing, what ever it was, was directly behind. She could hear its panting and its footsteps on the sidewalk, closing on her. She had to do something quick. She spotted a house across the street with the front door open. A light from a television showed through the screen door. The only obstacle between her and safety was a row of four-foot tall bushes. She ran to them in a race for her survival.

Julie tried to smash through the thick branches of the bushes but something caught her by the arm. She tripped and fell into them. A piercing pain ripped across her shoulder. A sharp branch? A fang? She tumbled and rolled out, groping to regain her balance and get back to her feet. The terrible thing behind her had fallen, also. A dark shape struggled to get free of the bushes. It wasn't real. It couldn't be. This couldn't be happening to her. It was her imagination.

Julie groaned as she stumbled to her feet and realized the pain screaming from the gash on her shoulder.

She sprinted to the porch of the house with the open front door. Her pursuer was sure to tackle her at any second. She leaped over the steps, causing a loud bang when she landed, slammed against the door hard and yanked on it. It was locked.

"Let me in. Help!"

Vicious barking erupted as a large brown pit bull hit the screen door on the other side.

A man inside the house jumped up from his living room chair and threw the newspaper he read to the floor. "Holy Jerusalem!" he shouted, "What do you want?"

Julie turned away from the man and looked behind, feeling safer. The predator that chased her had vanished. She turned back, panting heavy, and saw a young woman clutching two frightened children at her side, but the man had left.

The dog barked again viciously, jumping on the screen.

"It," she said between breaths, "it's after me."

Behind the woman and children, the man reappeared with a shotgun.

"You'd better just get your crack-cocaine ass out of here before I call the police!" he shouted, advancing to the door, pointing the gun at her head. "What's wrong with you fools anymore. Get all hyped up on drugs and go and scare the shit out of people."

"Shoot her, Dad!" the oldest child, a boy Nick's age, yelled.

"Sorry, sorry," Julie said softly, holding her hands up in front of her.

She didn't feel like explaining, especially to a shotgun. She ran off the porch, looked up and down the street, and sprinted for home.

CHAPTER 23

Tony Parker's phone rang.

He awoke, startled, and pushed from his chair as Yankee sprang up. When he realized what had awakened him, he shook his head, took a deep breath and walked toward the thing. After the third ring, he picked the phone up, wondering if it might be Julie.

"*Yeeaaahh!*" Nick cried out, halfway down the stairs, holding a stuffed toy St. Bernard. The phone must have awakened him, too.

He looked at Nick to see that he was all right as he answered the phone.

"Hello."

No answer but breathing. Someone took a deep breath.

"Hello. Who is this?" he asked.

After a pause, a tiny voice whispered, "Dog." The line went dead.

"What the devil?" he asked aloud. He looked at the caller ID on the phone's LED. *Unavailable*, it said.

"Jezebel's got Mommy! Daddy, Jezebel's got Mommy!" Nicholas screamed out.

"No, Mommy's all right. You just had a bad dream," Parker said, hanging up the phone. He walked to Nick.

Nick ran down the stairs and met his father at the foot, crying hard.

"Then, where is Mommy?"

"She's teaching her aerobics class, sweetie."

He looked at the clock on the stereo. Ten forty-five. She'd never been this late before, and, considering the circumstances, she certainly would have called if she could. Maybe she had called. Maybe that was her that said "dog" on the phone, too frightened to say anything else.

"Are you sure, Daddy?" the boy asked, still sobbing in jerks.

Upstairs, Audrey began crying. Parker was uncertain of what to do. He'd have to call Jack and Sadie to see if one of them could come over to watch the kids in order for him to go out looking for his wife. Parker gathered Nick up and walked back to the phone.

Yankee suddenly barked wildly at the front door, fur raising on the back of his neck.

This was rare for Yankee. He was normally very docile. He seemed afraid.

The door burst open, and Julie ran inside. She immediately turned the lock on the knob and tried to throw the door shut, but Yankee bolted through, still barking frantically. It hit his flank as he passed and bounced wide open.

"What's wrong? What happened?" Parker demanded.

"I don't know what happened!" Julie screamed.

She took Nick away from Parker, both her and Nick bawling, and ran upstairs toward Audrey's room.

"Close the door!" she cried out.

Parker didn't know what had happened but knew the answer was somewhere outside. He went out and closed the door behind him. As he did, he heard it lock, and he cringed. His key was inside.

He walked out to the sidewalk and looked up and down the street. The fog moved up from the river now and rolled in heavy on the streets. Nothing seemed amiss out here, nothing different, nothing going on. He walked over to the garage. Maybe something was wrong in there. He looked through the window on the door of the one-car, detached garage. No minivan.

"Uh-oh!"

Julie had car trouble. On top of everything else, she was pissed because she had asked Tony to have the minivan tuned up, several times. He kept forgetting. Parker shook his head and walked back to the sidewalk.

He drew a deep breath and gave a long, shrill whistle for Yankee.

Within a few seconds, Yankee came trotting back to him, wagging his tail.

"What was it, old boy, tomcat?" He asked and patted him on the head. "Time for you to go to the back yard. Come on, boy."

Parker took Yankee out back and then went around to the front. He had no way to get in. Both the front and back doors were locked. The doorbell was the only way.

He pushed the button, and the bell announced his presence.

Parker waited patiently for Julie to answer. He tried to think up something to smooth her feathers.

An odd feeling came over him, now, as he stood waiting under the porch light. Someone, or something, watched him. He turned around and looked out into the neighborhood. Nothing but fog. Something lurked out there, just out of view, staring at him from the misty darkness. He felt sure of it. It was like the dreams.

The doorknob clicked, and the door opened to Julie's scowling face.

Parker walked in and, with a boyish grin, began singing, "Julie, Julie . . . "

Her hand flew up without warning and slapped his face hard. She turned immediately and hurried off upstairs without a word.

Parker stood dumbfounded, rubbing the red handprint on his cheek.

By the time he gained the courage to climb the stairs, Julie had already gotten into bed. He tried to slip in without disturbing her, but he knew she was awake. They lay in the big king-sized bed, back to back, for a long minute.

"Julie, what happened tonight?" Parker asked, softly. He rolled over and touched her shoulder.

"Ow," she complained.

Parker reached out and flipped on the lamp at the side of the bed. He gently pulled the shoulder of her silky nightgown down, revealing a gauze bandage. Carefully raising up one side, he saw the injury.

"Damn, Julie, how'd you get that? You might need stitches."

Julie began crying and turned toward Tony. He held her and stroked her hair.

"I scratched it on a branch. It's all right. I cleaned it up."

"Tell me what happened, sweetheart."

"First the damn minivan wouldn't start," she began between sobs, "and I couldn't call because I locked the key inside the building. Then a wino bothered me. I decided to run down the jogging path home, and I thought someone was chasing me, and I finally made it to our street. But I was scared so I ran up to someone's door, and they ran me off with a shotgun, then I made it home and you sing, *Julie, Julie* to me, you jerk!"

"I'm sorry. I didn't know that song upset you so much—a shotgun?"

"Oh, never mind. Just hold me."

"Who did you think was chasing you, the wino?"

"No—I don't know. Let's just forget it."

"No, now, tell me, please."

"Don't laugh at me."

"I won't, sweetheart. You know me better than that. Tell me."

"Jezebel. I thought it was that damned Jezebel chasing me."

"What? Did you see her?"

"No, not really, just something black. I heard a howl, and I thought I heard a dog running behind me."

Parker pushed away gently and rose from the bed.

"Tony, it was probably nothing, my imagination. You know, paranoia. Now, come back to bed, please."

"I've got to check it out. Maybe we can catch her."

"Tony, I said it was my imagination. Please, come back to bed. I'm scared. I need you to hold me. Have someone else check it out."

Parker knew he should stay with his family. Julie made sense. Besides, she needed him and, with her in this mood, he could comfort her, making it easier for her to forgive him for what had happened with Sarah.

"Chin. This is Parker," he said into the phone while looking down at Julie. "I just got a Jezebel sighting."

"So, what's new, Chief? We've been getting them all night."

"Listen, Chin, I know we're shorthanded down there, but I really need you, personally, to check it out. And do me a favor and take someone with you."

"All right, sure, boss."

"You know the Main Street Health Club downtown, where Julie teaches?"

"Yeah, I drive by it all the time."

"Start there and go down the bike path toward my house. Let me know if you find anything. Be careful."

CHAPTER 24

Tricia didn't know how she could get away from Dawg. He was so big and so fast. He'd knocked her down inadvertently many times before as they played. She knew he could snatch her up in a second without even trying.

The kitten struggled free from Tricia's hand and landed on the floor, spitting *bloody murder*. Tricia grabbed up Raggedy Ann and ran for the stairs in the hallway leading to the upstairs bedrooms, forgetting about the phone she had in her hand. The phone cord yanked the handset out of her hand and, at the same time, pulled loose from the wall. Tricia nearly tripped over Grammy as she made it to the stairs and was surprised Dawg hadn't leaped on her yet.

She looked back from the first step and saw the vicious animal's leather collar caught on a nail on the side of the window frame. He was stopped, but not for long. After a couple of yanks, the collar tore loose, and he bounded after her.

Tricia nearly reached the top of the stairs before Dawg caught up with her. He grabbed her by the toe of her, white canvas sneaker, and she felt a terrible pain as one of the dog's fangs pierced her foot. She jerked her foot out of Dawg's mouth as she fell face first on the top step.

"*Owww!*" she cried. "Quit it, quit it!"

She swung Raggedy Ann at his head and the dog snatched it out of her hand. Tricia crawled up to the landing and spied the small black souvenir bat her daddy bought her at the baseball game two months ago. It lay in the middle of the hall floor. Grammy had told her not to leave it there. Someone could get hurt. She was glad she had forgotten to put it away.

Tricia grabbed the small bat, rolled onto her back and swung it at the attacking dog, who still had the doll in his mouth.

This naughty dog had done some terrible things today. He'd hurt her. He'd killed Grandy and Grammy. Now he was eating Raggedy Ann.

With a wild, lucky swing, the thick end of the little wooden bat struck the top of Dawg's snout, making a hollow cracking noise. Dawg pulled back, stunned. He dropped the doll, took two steps back, and tumbled end over end down the steps.

"All fall *down!*" Tricia screeched.

She dropped the bat and reached for Raggedy Ann but saw Dawg was once again on his feet and another dog accompanied him back up the steps.

The last thing in the world Tricia wanted to do was to abandon Raggedy Ann, but she did in favor of her own life. She ran into her grandparents' bedroom and quickly slammed the door.

CHAPTER 25

A red, late-model Mercedes pulled into the driveway of a large, English Tudor home on Wichita's east side. The car's lights made bright, nearly solid white beams in the damp and misty night. The garage door opened, and the Mercedes parked alongside a late-model, white Cadillac.

Sylvia Taylor staggered to the backyard door in her fire-engine red, low-cut evening gown. Her husband John, a prominent, young Wichita attorney, was in Topeka on business. At least, that's what he had told her. The two weren't getting along very well, and while the jerk was away, Sylvia Taylor decided she would play and had gone out to drown her sorrows. She unlocked the door and shoved it open to two purebred greyhounds. The dogs greeted her, whining and wagging their tails frantically.

"Ah, did my babies miss me?" the woman slurred, bending down and letting the dogs lick her face.

She opened the door into the house, let the dogs inside with her, then closed the door behind her but failed to lock it, and the garage door remained open. She undressed as she walked through the kitchen and into the dining room.

"To the shower and to bed," she said, kicking off her shoes and slinging her belt to the floor as she walked.

She made her way unsteadily up the stairs, the dogs following eagerly. Her two pets trotted over to a large oval rug near the bed in the master bedroom and lay down. Sylvia slipped out of her dress, walked into the bathroom, and turned on the shower.

The water spraying her body had a reviving effect after downing a half-dozen too many martinis. She soaped herself up and began rinsing off, starting with her face. The soap ran down the curves of her well-proportioned torso in small streams of white foam. With her eyes closed tightly, she thought she heard the dogs growling. The soap burned as she turned her half-rinsed face to the frosted glass shower door and squinted. Two forms stood in the bathroom doorway.

"Hope, Luck, what's wrong?" she cried out.

The growls became louder until both dogs lunged at the shower door. The glass panel flexed from their attacks, making a loud banging.

"Stop it! Quit it! What's wrong with you two?" she screamed with her arms crossing her chest.

They stopped jumping but continued to growl. The woman grabbed a back brush hanging from a shower caddy.

"Bad dogs! Go lay down!" she insisted.

The dogs answered, assaulting the shower door again, this time trying to jump over it.

Sylvia shrieked, swinging the brush at the dogs' noses as they popped over the top of the door. The animals' sharp nails tapped and scraped as both of them leapt and clawed their way up the glass, finally topping it.

With a wild, hard swing that missed, Sylvia Taylor's legs slipped out from underneath her, and she fell hard, knocking the side of her head against the tub faucet.

* - * - *

Down the street, two teenagers stood on a brightly lit front porch. A boy and a girl said good night after a pleasant, evening date.

Claire Barnes pulled her lips away from the boy's still puckered mouth. "*Mmma*—I should go in now," she said. "I'm already an hour late." The ends of her short, walnut-brown hair curled under. Her blue jeans fit tight, yet her pink and white blouse hung loose on her thin body. "Dad will be furious if he wakes up and sees what time it is!"

"Awe, come on, Claire. Just a little more," Jason Williams pleaded. He looked at her with longing green eyes, no longer self conscious about a large, red, welt-like pimple on the end of his nose. He moved his hand down the front of the girl's blouse and locked lips with her again and closed his eyes.

The driveway lit up, and Jason pulled his head back.

"Damn," he said, "that thing scared me. I thought it was your dad."

"I told you when we drove up," Claire said. "It comes on automatically when it detects motion. It was probably a cat or something. It'll go off in a minute."

Claire grabbed the back of his head and pulled it back in place.

A rapid clicking startled the boy. He swung the girl around, still kissing her. Two dogs, bearing down at full speed, raced up the walk toward them.

With perfect timing, the front door opened wide to reveal Irvin Barnes, the girl's angry father. He was short and stocky with a completely bald head and a round face with small round features. His arms were short, and gray hair sprouted from his shoulders and back and around the edges of his sleeveless T-shirt. The T-shirt covered only the top of his large beer belly, over-hanging the drawstring top of his red and white striped pajama bottoms.

Jason swung Claire back toward the door, her eyes still closed and lips still locked. He saw Mr. Barnes look at his hand on Claire's breast. Claire opened her eyes and gaped at her father whose face twisted with anger, but went blank when he looked over their shoulders. The snarling dogs were now fifteen feet away.

The boy shoved Irvin Barnes out of the way and carried Claire inside. Barnes fell back, accidentally hitting the light switches as he groped for a handhold and flipped off the lights. He slammed onto his back on the hard tile floor, the jolt making him wince.

The dogs made the porch. Barnes kicked the door as hard as he could. It slammed shut, but not quick enough.

The first dog made it inside but gave a yelp as the door caught the middle of its tail. It lashed out at Barnes' calf and pulled its sharp fangs across his pajama-clad flesh. He struggled from the dog's reach, got to his feet, and limped away, blood streaming down to his ankle. Without showing pain, the dog still lunged at him as if it were on a leash.

Helen Barnes ran down the stairs in a sheer pink nightgown with ruffles. White streaked her brunette hair, and thick mascara smudged her face, giving her raccoon eyes. She ran to her injured husband who had picked up the phone and punched 911. The door would not hold the dog's tail for long. Blood ran down the door to the tile entryway. The skin around the tail pulled back two inches from where the door had originally caught it.

"Get to the car!" Barnes ordered frantically and motioned toward the garage, as he waited for a response on the phone. "We got a mad dog in our house at 1115 North Lake Breeze. Get here, now!"

Jason still held Claire as he scrambled behind Mrs. Barnes to the door of the attached garage. He could hear Claire's old man slam the phone, then his footsteps behind him. The dog's tail broke in half with a snap, and the greyhound now raced them for the door. Jason and Claire made it through and to the passenger's side of the Barnes' station wagon as the dog leaped onto Irvin Barnes' back, just inside the doorway. Barnes tripped on the steps, falling onto the garage floor, and rolled, sending the dog into the front fender of the car. Claire's dad looked like a *Dukes of Hazard* stuntman as he slid over the station wagon's hood and slipped into the driver's side. The greyhound shook off the impact with the car and was back on his feet in a second.

Jason reached over to the driver's side window visor and plucked off the remote. He opened the garage door as the greyhound jumped onto the hood, snarling and snapping. The vicious dog sent Helen and Claire into hysterical screams. Barnes started the car, jerked it into reverse, and stomped his foot on the accelerator.

"Bite this, you son-of-a-bitch!" he yelled, laughing crazily.

The dog slipped off the hood and tumbled onto the concrete floor. Barnes watched the dog absentmindedly, as the car continued accelerating backwards out the driveway and into Jason's new Trans Am, jostling them about like limp dolls.

Barnes gave Jason a look, causing more fear than the dogs had and said, "And that was for you, you little bastard. Keep your hands off my daughter's tits!"

He slammed the gearshift into drive and floored it again. They tore down the street with both dogs in pursuit.

For the third night in a row, Jezebel visited Tony Parker's dreams. She walked out of the fog as before. She stopped in front of Parker's house as before. She turned and looked at the front door as before. And, as before, she began walking up the sidewalk toward the house. Mouth closed, head low. She walked slowly, closer and closer. She stopped just short of the front steps. Her muscles tightened. She stood, eyes fixed on the door. It opened. An alarm went off.

Parker's body jolted as if plugged into the nearby wall socket, sweat once again covering his forehead. *The phone. It's only the damned phone.*

"Who could that be?" Julie's groggy voice asked. "It's almost two in the morning." She rolled over to Tony. "Are you okay, Tony?"

"Yeah, yeah, I'm all right. Bad dream," Parker said, as the phone rang again and he reached to answer it. "Hello."

"Tone?"

"Hi, Sarah. What's wrong?"

Parker saw Julie roll her.

"We just got a report of a mad dog loose in a house over at 1115

North Lake Breeze," Hill said, her words rushed. "Don't know what kind it is. I'm on my way out."

"All right, I'll be right there. Be careful!" Parker hung up and got out of bed. "I've got to go. There's an emergency."

"What? Did Sarah have a bad dream, too, *Tone?*" Julie asked, the jealousy simmering in her voice as she mocked Sarah's nickname for him.

"Someone reported a mad dog had gotten into their house. It could be Jezebel," Parker said.

"Damn, now I don't know which bitch to hate more, Jezebel or Sarah Hill," Julie said, dropping her arms down to her sides hard as she sat up in bed. She watched as he put on his pants. "Be careful, Tony."

CHAPTER 26

Parker pulled in across the street from Sarah Hill's animal control van. Hill wasn't in sight. Her tranquilizer gun was gone. He pulled out his control stick and looked around. The house and yard were dark, but he could see that the garage door and the door from the attached garage into the house were open. He wondered if Hill was inside the house.

As he walked around to the front of his truck, from the corner of his eye he saw something large and dark in the yard beside him. He didn't look straight at it immediately. He was afraid to. He stopped and stood still, shifted his eyes to the object and moved his head slowly in its direction. It was colorless in the dark, but he could see it was large and had four legs and a thick body.

Finally, he stood face to face with it. He stared. The shape didn't move. *Now what?*

He felt the hair on the back of his neck stand up. The goose bumps popped out on his arms. He drew quick, short breaths. His mouth went dry. If only Hill were behind him with the tranquilizer gun.

His only chance was to confront this monster with the control stick. He would move slowly, as close as he could, and hope to get the loop on the end around her neck before she attacked. After that, if she didn't prove too powerful, he could keep her at bay and work her over to Hill's van.

He moved slowly toward the dark figure. Her body appeared thicker than he had imagined it would be. Her ears stood up long and pointy but longer than they should be.

She hadn't moved. Two more short steps, and he noticed a figure standing beside her on two legs. Something big and round was on its head.

"What the . . . ?" he asked aloud, squinting to see.

The oversensitive motion detector on the garage light across the street sensed his movement, and it lit up. Now, the two-legged figure was clear. A concrete statue. A Mexican wearing a sombrero and, beside it, a concrete donkey with long pointed ears.

Parker let out a relieved sigh. He shook his head and dropped his arms, still holding the control stick in a tight grasp.

"Why do people put shit like this in their front yards?"

He looked back at the house across the street. There was something strange sticking out of the front door. It was a foot long and standing straight out from the doorjamb. He walked across the street, looking up and down at the houses, searching for any sign of Hill, or anything moving. Getting closer, he recognized the object sticking out of the door as a tail.

After stepping up to the door, he examined it. "Greyhound," he guessed, noting the color and short hair, disappointed it wasn't black.

Not knowing if a dog was still attached, he eased the door open. The tail dropped to the porch like a stick, and with a sigh of relief, Parker went in.

"Anybody home?" He yelled, still moving apprehensively through the house. "Sarah?"

He saw a spotty trail of blood leading to a phone in the hall and through the kitchen to the attached garage.

"Help!" a faraway scream came from outside.

"Sarah?" Parker called again, running through the house to the open door leading into the garage.

Absentmindedly, he ran through the door holding the control stick sideways.

With a crack, the stick snapped in half, and he threw the pieces down as he ran. At the end of the driveway, he stopped, trying to determine the direction.

"Sarah?" Parker repeated his call.

No answer. Barking and growling came from down the street. Parker ran down the sidewalk and around a corner, straining his eyes to see down the dimly lit road. Fifty yards away, Hill hung from the limb of a small tree with two dogs jumping at her.

"Tony, help!" she cried.

He saw the tranquilizer rifle lying across the sidewalk no more than twenty feet from her. He wouldn't be able to reach it before the dogs saw him. He was an equal distance between them and the other tranquilizer gun in the truck.

Hill hung on loosely. The dogs jumped very close. It didn't look like she could last much longer.

"Hang on, Sarah. I'm here!" he yelled.

The dogs looked to Parker but continued their attack on Hill.

"Ah! Hey, you sons-of-bitches. Leave her alone!" he screamed, running at the dogs with arms flying.

Now the dogs took notice and turned to him. They bolted and raced toward him as if they were on a dog track and he was the rabbit.

Parker turned and sprinted back down the street toward the corner. A small tree stood next to the stop sign. If he could climb into it, he would be safe until Hill got her gun and tranquilized the dogs.

The dogs' closed in behind him, their claws striking the sidewalk like drumming fingernails on glass. Only another twenty yards, and he'd be safe. Closer. Closer. He wasn't going to make it. He could hear the first dog only inches behind him. Then, for an instant, nothing. The dog had leaped. Parker ducked and turned, raising his arm for protection. He blocked the dog in midair, and boosted it over his head, sending it with forty-miles-per-hour momentum dead center into the stop sign.

The dog crumpled into the sign with a muffled, cymbal-like crash and fell to the ground in a pile.

The second dog with half a tail was not far behind but slowed when it saw what happened to its mate. Parker kicked the underside of its jaw hard as it attacked, sending it somersaulting backwards, head over freshly bobbed tail, to the ground. He ran to it and pinned it with one foot.

"Hurry, shoot it!" Parker said as Hill ran up.

The dog struggled to get up, and he knelt to hold it with his hands. Hill took aim at the dog's rump. At the last second, she moved the gun and shot the dog in the chest within inches of Parker's groin.

"Shit, what are you trying to do?" Parker exclaimed.

"Just trying to put a little excitement into our relationship," Hill said coolly. "Not like there hasn't been, lately."

This was the first time he'd been alone with Hill since his strange actions at the blind man's house. He hadn't had a chance to talk with her about it or to apologize.

"We don't have a relationship," Parker said.

"You could have fooled me. You mean you sink your teeth into every girl that comes along?" she said. She shrugged her shoulders. "Oh well, no big loss if I'da missed then, huh?"

Parker didn't answer. He couldn't tell if she was complaining or wearing his teeth marks like a medal.

"The keys are in my truck," he said. "Bring it over here, will you?"

"Yes, *Kimosabe*." Hill trotted down the street to their vehicles.

The dog squirmed for a moment longer and passed out. Parker lifted the male dog as Hill pulled up, and he put it in a cage in the back. The female that hit the stop sign was dead. At least now they had a live one to study.

Hill helped him lay the female on the floor of the Jimmy.

"The owner lives in the next block," Parker said, noticing the address on the dog's tags. "And this is great. He was vaccinated for rabies, just last Friday. Doc was the vet."

Hill and Parker stood for a moment, just looking at each other. All of the attacks were definitely tied together, and Doc, somehow, was the string.

They closed the tailgate and began walking to the address on the dog tag, hoping to find the owner unharmed.

"Chin said he didn't find anything on the path by the river," Hill said. "No sign of a dog, no footprints, nothing."

"Something chased Julie tonight," Parker explained. "She's okay, just shook up."

"Well, it wasn't me," Sarah said, smiling.

Parker frowned back.

"Just kidding. I'm glad she's all right."

As they walked up to the address, a police car stopped at the curb. Parker didn't know the two officers who got out.

"Everything all right? Need any help?" one of the officers asked.

"Yeah, I think everything's under control, now. But we might need you to stick around," Parker said. "There could be someone hurt." He briefly explained the situation as they all walked to the house.

No one answered the doorbell even after ringing it several times. They went around to the open garage door and sidestepped by the Mercedes and the Cadillac, noting them with raised eyebrows. The door into the house from the garage was unlocked, and they proceeded cautiously with the two cops leading.

"Hello. It's the police. Anyone home?" one of the policemen yelled.

Parker ducked around them. He saw the shoes in the middle of the floor and the belt near the first step of the stairs. He took the steps in long strides, and Hill followed. They searched the hall and a couple of bedrooms first, unsuccessfully. Then, in the master bedroom, Parker found a red dress on the floor and picked it up.

"I don't think it's your size," Hill told him.

The shower was on. The noise was a bit irritating to Parker, but he didn't know why. He felt a tickle in his throat and swallowed. It caused a raw feeling in his esophagus, like the beginning of a sore throat.

Parker and Hill went into the bathroom. Water droplets streaked the mirror behind a double vanity. A shape sat low in the shower.

"Let's pray we have a live one," he said.

Now, the two policemen stood behind them. Parker slid the shower door open slowly.

A young woman sat as far back as she could and looked up at him, shaking in near convulsions. Blood streamed from the side of her head, dark and red, then washed to pink onto her shoulders. She held her arms across her chest.

"It's all right. Everything's okay, now," Parker said softly. He reached for the knobs to turn off the now only lukewarm water. Suddenly and involuntarily he began swallowing in violent gulps until the water stopped running. He thought it strange, very odd, but there were more important concerns now. He held his hand out to help the woman up.

"Sheesh, Tony, what is it with you and naked women?" Hill said, pushing him and the gawking officers out of the room. She grabbed a towel and helped the woman out of the shower.

One of the policemen picked up the bedroom phone and called an ambulance.

"My babies, where are my greyhounds?" the woman asked, now robed, as Hill assisted her to sit on the side of the bed.

"Well, Mrs. Taylor—you are Mrs. Taylor?" Parker asked.

She nodded.

"Your dogs became violent and attacked some of your neighbors down the street. We had to—restrain them.

"Oh, no!" she said. "Are they all right?"

"We're not sure. It looks like they drove away."

"I mean my greyhounds, you idiot!" she snapped back.

Her lack of concern for her neighbors upset Parker.

"We had to tranquilize the male," Parker said, less sympathetically. "He lost most of his tail. We're taking him in for observation."

"Oh, poor Luck," she said. "What about Hope?"

"Hope's luck ran out, Mrs. Taylor," Parker said. "She's dead."

"You killed my baby?" she asked. "You bastard!"

"Look, Mrs. Taylor, these babies of yours tried to kill us and have apparently injured one of your neighbors," Parker scolded, his voice gruff and low.

"Ease up, Tony," Hill said, touching his arm.

Red lights danced across the walls of the bedroom, and one of the officers looked out the front window.

"The ambulance is here," he said, his hand parting the sheer curtain.

Now was not a good time to question the woman for either Parker or her.

"Come on," Parker told Hill. "I'd like to talk to you later about your dogs, Mrs. Taylor," he said in a somewhat calmer voice as he stood in the bedroom doorway.

"You can just do your talking to my husband, you dirty bastard. I'm sure you've heard of him. John Taylor. The attorney, John Taylor," she said snobbishly.

Parker had heard of him. He was one of those ambulance-chaser types. He was on TV commercials talking about *Know your rights.*

"I'll fax your precinct a copy of our report first thing in the morning," Parker told the officers and stepped out of the room.

Parker and Hill went to their vehicles without speaking.

"See you later," Hill said, breaking away to her van.

"Humph," Parker replied, getting into the Jimmy.

Parker found a piece of paper on the passenger's seat as he started the engine. It was something torn from a newspaper. He stared at it in the dark for a second. It hadn't been there before. He hadn't put it there. He reached over and picked it up then looked around to the outside of the truck. The street was empty and quiet except for the silent ambulance, its lights still flashing, the police cruiser and Hill's van driving away.

Parker turned on the dome light and frowned at the paper. *TP*, it read in big black, hand printed letters. He recognized the piece of paper well. It was his very own letter to the editor. A sentence was highlighted in bright yellow: "Let's not blame the dog for the evil that is in man." The word "man" was crossed out and "you" was printed above it.

CHAPTER 27

Morning came too soon for Parker. He'd gone home to catch a couple more hours of sleep. Doc White Cloud wouldn't be in his office until nearly eight. Parker left early and dropped the keys to Julie's minivan off at the local garage on his way to work and asked them to take a look at it.

The commotion was building when he arrived at the animal shelter. They were swamped with *Jezebel* sightings. As he came in, three officers were busy on phones at the reception counter. So far, all of the calls turned out to be false alarms or pranks. Jezebel had appeared as everything from a black Persian cat to a black and white Holstein cow amongst some trees. Sarah Hill looked exhausted after the previous eight-hour workout. She was scheduled to work the double shift until four, but Parker talked her into going home for a few hours rest. After a flurry of activity, Parker started for the door to pay Doc a visit.

"Mr. Parker, Bob's Garage wants to talk to you," one of the women officers yelled out, holding up the phone as Parker attempted to slip out.

He rushed back to the counter and took it.

"Yeah, did you get it tuned up already?" Parker asked, surprised.

"No, not yet. We just got your minivan in the shop. I thought you'd want to know, though," the mechanic said.

"I'd want to know what?"

"Well, after you told me someone followed your wife last night, I thought you'd want to know the reason the minivan wouldn't start. The coil wire was pulled out."

"Loose coil wire, huh?"

"No, I said, *pulled out.* Yanked. It looked deliberate. There's no way she could have driven that minivan there in the first place with the coil wire where it was. It didn't just pull itself out."

There *had been* someone after her. It was all so very puzzling. Jezebel couldn't have pulled the wire out any more than she could have been writing *TP* on the notes.

"I just thought you'd like to know."

"Yeah, thanks." Parker hung up with a lot of pieces to the puzzle floating in his head. They didn't fit together, and there were more of them every minute.

They'd left the dead female greyhound in a bag in Parker's truck. The male still rested in the cage in the back. At twenty minutes till eight, Parker finally pulled away from the animal shelter with the sun shining bright on the way to another sweltering day.

A strong, familiar odor invaded Parker's nostrils as he stepped into the exam room of Doc White Cloud's clinic. It was a kind of a salty, medicinal smell that could only come from a bar of blue antiseptic soap. He looked to the corner to see Doc pull an excited and soaked miniature schnauzer from a large sink. He set the frenzied dog on the nearby counter gently as it flopped like a carp on a riverbank. Truong stood next to him holding a large light-green bath towel, and a dumpy little woman in a navy blue pantsuit waited near the door.

"All right, Mrs. Ziebart," Doc said, drying his hands on a small white hand towel, "Truong here'll towel ol' Mandy off, and we'll be all finished."

Truong threw the towel over the dog and began drying him briskly while the woman stepped up and helped, dishing out a more than sufficient amount of incomprehensible baby talk.

Doc looked up as he rolled his sleeves down. He always wore long sleeves, even in the heat of the summer.

"Hi, Tony, how was the picnic?" Doc asked as Parker stepped into the exam room.

Parker gave half a smile. "Let's just say it was—interesting. You would have had to have been there."

The old Native American looked back a little puzzled. "Hmmm, anyway, you must be here to see if we've found out anything about those rabies tests. We haven't heard anything back from K-State. Should know something yet this morning, I'd think. Truong took the heads up first thing yesterday morning, while Patsy and I were down in Ponca."

"I've got another one for you, Doc. And there's a live one to watch," Parker said solemnly. "I hope you don't mind. We're full up at the shelter, and besides, I was thinking, with your learned eyes, you might be able to figure out what set them off—that is, if it isn't rabies."

"Anyone hurt this time?" Patsy asked, coming in from the reception area.

"No, at least nothing serious," Parker said to Patsy. He turned to White Cloud. "We were lucky. It was Sylvia Taylor's greyhounds. Can we sit down and talk?"

"Sure, come on in," White Cloud said, ushering him into a room adjoining the examination room. "We'll go in Truong's room. He won't mind. The floor in my office was just waxed, and it's still a little wet."

Parker followed Doc into the small, familiar room. It had been Parker's when he came home on leave from the Marines after his mother died. He'd stayed there for several months again after his discharge and until he and Julie married.

The room hadn't changed much. It had the same dirty, off-white walls. On the north wall was a large twenty-paned, wood-casement window. Next to it in the near corner an antique Philco refrigerator, repainted white with a coarse bristle brush, made a steady hum. A well-packed feather mattress topped an old army cot against the far wall to the west. It was made in bright white sheets and a well-used, olive drab, wool army blanket, stenciled with a big black *US*. The old metal writing table he'd used years ago with two ancient metal folding chairs and a single, dark-green wall locker were along the east wall.

Doc White Cloud quickly took one chair, and Parker sat on the edge of the writing table with one foot on the seat of the other chair.

No, the room hadn't changed much. Evidently, Truong wasn't much of a decorator. But he was obviously a neat nut. The bed had been made tight, in true military fashion, complete with turndown and hospital-fold corners. It would easily pass a drill instructor's dime-bounce test. A pair of brown work boots along with a pair of black tennis shoes lay neatly lined up under the middle of the bed. Nothing else lay on the shiny-waxed linoleum floor. The writing table was as neat. An old black rotary-dial phone sat on top of last year's Wichita phone book. Beside it were a yellow legal pad with a well-sharpened number two, yellow pencil on top, a neatly stacked pile of five or six *Time* magazines, a *Webster's Collegiate Dictionary* and a hardcover *Bible* of some version.

"I'm really puzzled, Doc. All these violent attacks, and I don't think it's rabies."

Doc nodded.

"Why are there so many of them?" Parker asked.

"Good question. Can't just be coincidences. I don't have any good answers for you, Tony. Maybe it's evil spirits. I've been proven wrong before, but I don't think it's rabies, either. Of course, if it is, I suppose they'll quarantine me. And we'll have to bring all the animals back in that we've given rabies shots to over the last few days for observation."

"I was hoping you'd be able to give me some ideas with your infinite wisdom."

"Don't have a clue, Tony. Believe me, I wish I did."

Parker rose from his chair. "You want to help me bring in the dogs?"

"Sure, and after that, I'll just give the university a call and see if they've got anything for us, yet."

Parker opened the door and almost tripped over Truong, who appeared to have been sweeping the floor in front of it.

"Excuse," Truong said and moved quickly out of the way, still sweeping with his head down.

Parker caught himself with a half step and answered, "No problem."

Patsy followed Doc and Tony outside as Mrs. Ziebart drove out of the parking lot in a black BMW. With Patsy's help, they took the cage and a very passive greyhound out from the back of the truck and carried it over to an out-building where the animals were boarded. They went back to the truck for the dead dog in the bag when Truong shuffled out the front door.

"Dr. White Cloud," he called timidly, looking at the ground as he talked.

"Yes, Truong, what is it?"

"University call. Say rabies test positive, both dogs."

Parker noticed Patsy frown before Truong had announced the test results and thought it to be curious, but forgot about it when Truong said, "positive."

"Are you sure, Truong?" Dr. White Cloud asked in a puzzled tone of voice.

"Yes, Doctor. Both dogs positive, rabies. Send paperwork three days."

"Well, there you go, Tony. I'm wrong again." The old vet was noticeably upset. "Better put a closed sign on the door. No more animals in or out of this place for a while."

"What's the deal, Doc? They both had their rabies booster from you just in the last few days, and I'd guess they were current from before. Could it be the batch of vaccine you used?"

"Gee, vaccine-induced rabies? I wouldn't think so, but it kind of points that way, doesn't it? I started on a new batch the middle of last week. We'll send it off and have it tested."

They carried the dead greyhound in and laid it on the examination table.

"If you'll give me all the names and addresses of Wichita clients who have had their dogs vaccinated from that batch of vaccine," Parker said, "I'll pay each of them personal visits and tell them to get their pets in right away. That'll just leave you the ones in the county to call."

"I appreciate the help. There isn't but a couple," Doc said, walking over to the file cabinet. "Betty Nightingale, she has three miniature poodles. Roary Rapids, six Dobermans."

He handed Parker the files.

"Roary Rapids, the rock singer?" Parker asked.

"The same," Doc said. He turned to Truong. "Truong, you take all the Sand Creek files and find the ones we've given rabies vaccinations to from the last batch. There should be only two or three. You can take them to your room and call from there." He turned back to Parker. "The Sand Creek clients have made up the majority of my business lately with this mange stuff. We've been keeping all their files together. I'll split the rest of the county up with Patsy. With all four of us on it, we'll get everyone notified in no time."

Parker left, thankful he and the rest if the animal-control officers had gotten the mandatory human rabies vaccinations from the health department and not from the batch Doc used. They used a little different vaccine on humans, anyway.

CHAPTER 28

Tony Parker had time to think on the way downtown, and he had a lot to think about. The state should have notified the health department by now, and the press would have the word out to the entire county within hours. With two verified cases of rabies and three possibles, one of them being on the loose and killing people, there was sure to be even more panic. This was especially so since all of the dogs had had their vaccinations recently. No dogs would be safe from scrutiny. Even more phone calls would pour in, reporting mad dogs. Most or all of them, as with the Jezebel sightings, would be false alarms.

"Dispatcher to AC One, come in, Top Dog," the radio squawked.

"Yeah, Tyrone, go ahead," Parker responded.

"Tony, you'd better get down to the health department director's office right away, Alvarez sounds ticked."

"I'm being called on the carpet?"

"Front and center, Vaseline in hand. Sounds like you're about to get reamed."

Parker returned the microphone to the dash without comment but clenched his teeth. He knew what was going to happen. Paul Alvarez was generally a fair and reasonable man. Normally pleasant, but always business-like, his Chicano accent was barely noticeable.

But when he got excited—when he was under the gun, the accent was thick and the fur flew.

But the welfare of the two dog owners who needed to be notified took precedence. Besides, the first was on the way.

Betty Nightingale had a cute little cottage on the river near the downtown area. She was a prominent figure in local politics and, more often than not, was mentioned in the society pages of the *Wichita Post* newspaper.

She answered the doorbell promptly.

"Hi, Mrs. Nightingale. My name is Tony Parker. I'm the animal control director."

"Yes, Mr. Parker. How can I help?"

"I'd like to speak with you about your dogs, ma'am."

"Do come in and sit down, then, Mr. Parker. Can I get you anything: iced tea, coffee, water?"

Water! Parker gagged unintentionally. He couldn't understand why. "No thanks, ma'am."

Mrs. Nightingale looked at him inquisitively. She turned and led him into the living room.

In her late sixties, she was still an attractive woman and stepped lively. The house smelled of age. Old and musty, yet with a Lysol cleanliness, mixed with poodle perfume. The awful concoction of smells was unusually nauseating to Parker. The three gray miniature poodles also greeted Parker in their hyper way, jumping up and barking. One of the tiny poodles jumped thigh high and actually nipped the side of his leg. Parker loved all animals, but there was something about annoying little poodles that put them in last place on his list—especially now.

A tremendous heat, like a ravaging forest fire, consumed his body and the wound on his neck, although healing nicely, began to burn and itch. His joints stiffened and ached. He rubbed his neck and wondered if it might be the flu virus—or maybe rabies flu.

Parker felt a sharp pain like a needle prick in his upper thigh and realized the high jumper nipped his leg again.

He looked down at it wild eyed. It looked back with head cocked. With Mrs. Nightingale's back still turned, Parker stuck the toe of his shoe under the midsection of the feisty thing and boosted it up like a soccer ball. He caught himself thinking of slapping it against the wall and thought better of it.

The dog gave a surprised yelp, which made its master turn around quickly. Parker snatched the startled dog from midair and cradled it in his arm. He stroked the feisty creature with his other hand.

"Love your dogs," Parker said with an overdone smile. He stroked the dog twice more, and then set it on the floor like it was a basket of thin-shelled bald-eagle eggs.

"And what can I do for you today, Mr. Parker?" she asked pleasantly as they sat in the living room.

"I'm afraid I have a little bit of bad news, ma'am. It seems there's been an outbreak of rabies in the city affecting recently vaccinated dogs. In particular, dogs recently vaccinated at Dr. Johnny White Cloud's clinic. It may just be a coincidence, but we're investigating the problem now and feel we need to take every precaution until we're sure of the cause." Parker began to feel lightheaded. The room turned slowly. The fever inside his body intensified, and sweat broke out on his brow.

"Oh, my word!" she said, holding her chest. She looked at her still fidgeting dogs. "What does this mean for me, Mr. Parker?"

"Well, I'm afraid . . . ," Parker began, but then forgot what he'd been saying. After a pause, he shook his head and started again. " . . . I'm afraid—you'll have to take your dogs in to Dr. White Cloud's clinic to be quarantined, right away."

"Oh, dear, will they be safe there?" Mrs. Nightingale asked apparently unaware of Parker's worsening condition.

"I think—lot safer than here, ma'am," Parker said, standing up. He stumbled slightly but caught himself on the back of the chair. Mrs. Nightingale seemed too involved with the thought of her precious dogs contracting rabies to notice him. Parker was glad. He knew he was okay. Probably just that damned flu bug. He'd go see a doctor, later, after this mess was over. He walked to the door.

Mrs. Nightingale stood holding the doorknob, noticeably shaken, as Parker stepped out the doorway. "If that's what must be done," she said as her phone rang. "Thank you, Mr. Parker. Excuse me, won't you?"

Parker nodded and turned away to walk back to the truck, noticing Mrs. Nightingale had left the door open slightly. He was just glad to get outside in the fresh air. He took a couple of deep breaths and began to feel much better.

--*

"Hello. . . . Yes, I remember you. . . . He just left. . . . Oh . . . ? That's silly. You're not serious.... Well, all right," she said as she held the phone down low to the floor. "Come here, girls. Come on."

The dogs neared the phone. Mrs. Nightingale watched through the living room window as Parker drove away.

--*

Parker called into the dispatcher's office and asked Tyrone to call Roary Rapids, since he lived on the other side of town. He'd hoped to find out if Rapids was home and then alert him about his dogs. If he was there, he'd go over and explain more. If he wasn't home, it would make little sense to drive across town for nothing. There was no answer. Parker asked Tyrone to keep trying while he ran down to the health department. Things were sure to be buzzing there, and he did have an ass chewing to get over with.

A thin, frail woman met Parker at the counter of the health department.

"Hi, Mr. Parker, what can we do for you?" she asked, smiling.

"Hi, Gladys, I'm here to see Mr. Alvarez."

Her smile faded. "Did you have an appointment? He seems very irritated this morning. You might be better off coming back another time."

"No, he asked to see me. I'm the reason he's irritated."

"Have a seat. I'll tell him you're here," Gladys said. She pushed a button on her phone and leaned to it. "Mr. Alvarez, Tony Parker is here."

"Tell him to wait," the speaker barked. Even in the short command, his accent was obvious, the words loud and stern.

Parker knew there would be trouble. He sat on the edge of a black vinyl chair with his elbows on his knees and hands clasped, contemplating his defense.

"Has K-State contacted you about the positive results on the dog rabies tests, yet?" he asked Gladys.

"We haven't heard anything of any dog rabies tests in weeks."

"That's odd, under the circumstances, I'd have thought they'd notify you first thing."

"The last positive rabies test we've had was a week ago. It was fox, out in the county. A few days before, we had three cases of bovine rabies on a farm near Whitewater. Does this have anything to do with that *Jezebel* deal?"

"Yeah, they told Dr. White Cloud over an hour ago."

Parker's lightheaded feeling returned but only spun his head for a moment. It made him think of the skunk. It made him think of rabies. Normally, it takes at least five days and sometimes as much as several months—normally. He had been bitten on Friday. Parker counted on his fingers: *Friday to Saturday, one; Sunday, two; Monday, three; today; four.* It would be sooner than usual to start developing symptoms. Besides, that was nonsense. He just had a touch of a nasty old flu bug, helped along by all the recent excitement. He wasn't concerned. He wasn't *really* worried. But he asked Gladys about the skunk anyway.

"Hmm," Gladys answered, looking onto a page of a green ledger book, "no—no, I don't show the animal control office sent in a skunk on Friday. It says here, they sent one in Monday, yesterday. It'll probably be Thursday before we hear anything on that one. They kind of take their time on the general rabies tests in favor of the ones marked *human exposure*. Those we hear back on the same day sometimes."

Parker remembered that he had thought about telling his people to tag the head of the skunk with "human exposure" but decided not to. It wasn't really necessary. No big rush. He'd been vaccinated. But, they hadn't sent it in on Friday. They sent it in on Monday, and, now, it would be Thursday before it was tested. He could call them and rush it along, but no, that wasn't necessary. After all, he had been vaccinated and had a high rabies antibody count. No big deal.

A woman working at a desk a few feet away had overheard their discussion and picked up a ringing telephone. She raised her pencil and waved it as she listened on the phone. She cupped her hand over the handset and looked at Parker. "It's a doctor from the K-State lab in Manhattan. He says we have two confirmed cases of dog rabies and the vet, Dr. Johnny White Cloud, has been notified. We'll get the paperwork within three days." She put the phone back to her mouth and said, "Okay, thank you."

"Wait a minute," Parker blurted and stood up.

Too late. The woman at the desk had hung up the phone. "I'm sorry, do you want me to call them back?"

"No, that's all right. I was just going to ask them if they were sure."

Parker sat back down slowly and began to twiddle his fingers. He was anxious to get this over with. He looked at the big, round clock on the wall. It was already ten thirty, and there was so much to be done. He glanced at the coffee table and saw the typical waiting-room magazines. He didn't care to read them. Across the room at the counter were several different pamphlets addressing health issues, like: "What Every Mother Should Know About Breast Feeding," "AIDS and Safe Sex," "The Flu and the Elderly." One brochure caught his eye, and he smirked, "RABIES: What to do in an Emergency".

Wonder if it covers getting your ass chewed?

CHAPTER 29

Not far down the street from Mrs. Nightingale's house was an old run down shack. A rusty, fifty-year-old Frigidaire leaned forward on the rotting wooden deck of the front porch. The wood-framed screen door had a gaping hole big enough for a rabbit to run through. Inside, an elderly couple, Calvin and Jane Tibbs, sat at their kitchen table, drinking coffee while watching a game show on TV.

"Put your hands higher up on the putter. That's no way to address the ball," Calvin Tibbs said, his pop-bottle-bottom-thick glasses on the end of his nose.

"Shhhhh, I can't hear Bob Barker when you raise your voice like that," Jane Tibbs said pawing the air at him.

The old woman caught a glimpse of something gray running across the living room. She watched for a second and then saw another furry gray blur run through the screen door and somewhere into the house. Her mouth dropped. The old man was still too involved in the show to notice. Another blur popped through the screen and into the living room.

"Sakes alive, what was that?" she said, standing up at the table and into the old man's line of sight.

"Move, old woman, she's putting for the little pickup truck," he said.

"Screw the truck! There's some damn thing running around in

the living room. I told you to fix that screen," Jane Tibbs said, grabbing a nearby broom.

"Oh, hell. It's just your eyes. Maybe another damned mouse. Now sit down, or you'll make me miss her putt."

Suddenly, one of the miniature poodles charged, snarling at the old woman. She sent it sprawling back into the living room, handling the broom as if it were a hockey stick and the dog a puck.

"Jiminee Crickets!" the old man exclaimed. "That damn thing was big, and it growled, too."

"Well, don't just sit there on your dead ass. Help me. There's more of 'em."

Calvin Tibbs sprang up from his metal kitchen chair and reached behind the door. He pulled out a loaded twelve-gage shotgun and raised it to his shoulder. The gun wavered dangerously in the old man's hands, his aim no longer steady. His wife looked down the opposite end of the barrel, moon eyed.

The shotgun discharged with a deafening explosion as Tibbs blasted the next attacker, along with the end of the old woman's broom.

"Shit fire!" Jane Tibbs said, backing away from the doorway. "Look out, the fool's got a gun. I swear, I don't know which one of you's gonna kill me first."

"Hot damn, just like back on Iwo Jima," Calvin Tibbs said, cocking the gun.

Another blast and another one of the gray creatures turned into a red mass of bloody fur as it splattered up against the doorway.

Tibbs tried to chamber another shell. This time it jammed outside the chamber.

"Damn! We're in deep shit now," he said, working the pump frantically to dislodge the shell.

Jane Tibbs responded with a war whoop as she grabbed a large meat cleaver hanging on the wall and the third attacker charged.

The old woman fell to her knees, bringing the big blade down hard with a merciless glare on her face. Her aim proved deadly, and the cleaver hit the linoleum floor with a loud juicy *swack*. At the end of the meat ax, a gray mop of fur lay, split mostly in two.

The old man shuffled over, and they both craned their necks to see if there were any more of the varmints. "I think we might oughta give in and call the exter-me-nader, Ma."

*_*_*

Thirty minutes passed. The anxiety was building, and Parker paced the floor. The lightheaded feeling returned, and the fever burned even more intensely than before. Finally, Gladys came out of Alvarez's office and said, cowering, "Mr. Alvarez will see you now."

"Have a seat, Parker," Alvarez said without looking up, shuffling papers at his desk.

"Good morning, Mr. Alvarez," Parker said respectfully and held out his hand. Without acknowledging the friendly gesture, Alvarez continued to study the papers. Parker saw there would be no handshake on this morning and sat down.

Alvarez was a short, stocky Mexican-American. He looked much younger than his fifty years and had thick, black hair and a very smooth dark complexion.

After a full minute, Alvarez looked up over his reading glasses.

"So what are you doing about this problem we have?" he asked, leaning back in his chair and holding onto opposite ends of a pencil with both hands.

"You mean, the dog attacks?" Parker asked innocently.

"Chit yes, man, what the hell else would I be talking about?"

Parker knew it had been a dumb question. "Well, Mr. Alvarez, we think we've found what started the problem. The rabies tests came back positive on the first two dogs, and we think it was caused by a bad batch of vaccine. We're notifying the animal owners involved and quarantining their dogs and the animal clinic that gave the shots. I've got all of our officers working double shifts, and the police have been assisting in the search for the animal that's still at large."

"Animal. That's right, it's just an animal—a dog. It doesn't matter how big the thing is, it's still just a damn dog. Look, Tony, the city manager has come down hard on me about this. The city wants this thing caught, and it's all up to chew. If chew can't do the job, then I'll have to get someone else."

Parker could do nothing but frown.

"Tony, I've got to do it this way. If chew can't put an end to this chit within twenty-four hours, I'm going to have to can chew. If I don't, then I'll get canned for not doin' my job. It's gotten political with this damn panic that idiot TV reporter started. Then, there's this letter-to-the-editor bullchit. What the hell did chew think chew were doing? To top it off, chew cause a traffic accident. Chew're just damn lucky no one was injured."

The fever glowed red hot in Parker's body. His neck stiffened. He didn't feel well, and Alvarez annoyed his condition, just like that damned little-assed poodle. There was a limit to how much he could take. He tried to swallow but couldn't.

"Sir, I'll do what I can. But I don't know what more can be done," Parker pleaded.

"Let me ask chew this," he said and watched the pencil as he tapped it on the top of his desk. "What about putting a reward on the thing? Say, five thousand dollars, dead or alive."

"I'd say that wouldn't be wise."

Alvarez looked up and smiled. "Too late. It's running on the front page of tomorrow morning's paper and the press releases are going out to TV and radio first thing in the morning."

"*Then*, I'd say, that's not only unwise, but incredibly stupid. Do you realize you're creating a much more dangerous situation? This city is already in a panic. You're giving all the kooks a reason to get out their guns."

"Well, then, chew better do something quick, Parker—before the word gets out in the morning. And any more attacks, any more screw ups, and chew're out of here." Alvarez broke his pencil in half, then signaled with his thumb. "Chew can start by making a search radius out as far as this thing could have gotten by now. Then, catch the son-of-a-bitch. 'Cause if chew don't, I'll be on chew, like stenk on chit," he said, standing at his chair, pointing the broken pencil at Parker.

The pressure loomed heavy on Parker's back and head like a ten-ton slab of concrete. He needed a steady paycheck for the next four months to help pay his tuition, or he might never get his vet's degree. But, the strange adrenaline rush he had felt with Hill at the blind man's house shot through him again. His heart pounded like it was trying to escape from his chest. This miniature poodle of a man made him very angry.

Parker jumped up from his chair. He leaned against Alvarez's desk with his face inches from the pointing, broken pencil.

"I said, I'm doing all that I can!" he said in a loud, unusually hoarse voice. "What do you think this is, just another panty-waisted, pit-bull attack? We're not looking for some Scooby-fuckin'-Doo. You want to know what we're really up against here?"

Alvarez's eyebrows raised and lips parted as Parker continued.

"First of all, this dog is bigger than any ever recorded. Because of that, I really don't know what she's capable of, but I can guess. She can run fast, probably as much as forty miles an hour, and for several minutes at a time. If she's in good health, she can run like that off and on for twenty-four hours a day, taking only brief stops to rest and feed—maybe attack and feed. She's been loose for three and a half days. That means she could be well into Oklahoma by now, or Nebraska, or Missouri, or even Colorado! She's strong, and she's powerful. Her jaws are like steel bear traps that can crush a man's head with ease, or pop it right off. She stands three and a half feet at the shoulders, while on all fours. On her hind legs, she could touch this ceiling with her ears. And she weighs nearly twice as much as your scrawny little ass!"

Parker grabbed the broken end of the pencil, and Alvarez stepped back, eyes bugging out, still holding the other end.

"The most terrifying thing about her is she's smart. She knows when to hide and when to attack. An unarmed man doesn't stand a chance against her. He'd be dead within a split second. We can only hope she screws up and is spotted by a cop before she kills again. If we're lucky, her rabies has killed her, and she's lying dead under someone's porch or in a ditch out in the county somewhere. Like I said, I'm doing all I can, and right now I'm wasting time in your office. I'm going back to work, now, and if *chew don't like it, chew can chove it!*"

Parker stormed from the office, leaving Alvarez standing open-mouthed. Parker realized what he was up against before, but somehow, coming from his own mouth made it sink in deeper. He *was* tracking a monster.

CHAPTER 30

Tricia Carpenter woke in her grandparents' queen-sized bed. Although it was nearly noon, she'd only had a few hours sleep. The screams and yells had stopped long ago, but sporadic howls and growls lasted all night. She finally fell asleep a little before daybreak, completely drained.

She saw it was daylight and hoped the terrible day before had been a nightmare. If it had been only a nightmare, then where were her grandparents, and why had she slept in their room? Where was Raggedy Ann? She never went anyplace without Raggedy Ann, especially not to bed.

She got up slowly and looked about the room. The bedroom door was still closed. Grammy and Grandy never closed it when they slept there. They had left it open just in case she needed them in the middle of the night. Many nights, she had run in to tell them of a nightmare she'd had, usually about her parents fighting. In her dreams, her parents always told her the fighting was her fault and neither of them wanted or loved her anymore. It had been so frightening: them saying they didn't love or want her. She wondered if it was true. After all, her father couldn't have her in Kansas City because he was always traveling. Her mother couldn't have her until she got settled in Denver. They both just gave excuses.

Maybe this all had been a nightmare. Maybe she had dreamed it and run into her grandparents' bedroom and climbed into bed with them and now they sat downstairs drinking coffee and everything was all right.

Tricia noticed her foot was tender, but didn't look at it as she stepped over to the open second-story window of the bedroom and looked out at the street below. She saw no movement, but that wasn't unusual for Sand Creek. No bodies in the street, no dead people. But maybe the dogs had carried them off.

Hunger pangs caused her stomach to ache. It was time for her traditional bowl of Fruit Loops cereal. Fruit Loops was her favorite— not so much for the taste or the *nutritional value*, but more for the colors, all the bright colors.

She limped to the door and stopped and stared at the doorknob. She remembered the nightmare. She remembered running through the doorway and slamming it behind her after she had slipped away from Dawg. She remembered after she slammed the door Dawg and the other mutt hit it hard and scratched at it feverishly.

She reached slowly and turned the doorknob. It made a metallic click, and the seldom-used hinges complained in an eerie whine as she pulled the door open.

The first thing she saw was Dawg. It startled her, but she didn't close the door.

Dawg looked over his shoulder from the top of the stairs where he lay. He didn't bark. He hadn't even growled.

Maybe it all had been a dream.

He looked at her and blinked his eyes.

Tricia's mouth formed a small *o* and she blinked back. She looked him over from the doorway, twelve feet away. His gray and yellow coat was matted with dark red stains. His muzzle was the same. But still, he just looked back as his old self would.

Then, Tricia saw her doll between Dawg's front paws. It also was covered with blood, with a large amount of Dawg's drool darkening its cloth body.

Dawg had been chewing on Raggedy Ann.

Tricia's emotions quickly changed from apprehension to anger. It hadn't been a nightmare, she knew now. It made her angry. She wanted to hurt the dog, to swat him like Grammy did when she caught him digging in the garden. She wanted to whack him again with the bat.

Tricia stepped out of the door.

Dawg's lip curled. The other mutt appeared behind him on the stairs. They growled. Dawg stood quickly.

Tricia hopped back to the doorway but tripped over her own feet and sat down hard on her bottom. It jarred her teeth. *All fall down!* She leaned back against the plywood panel in the old door and felt it with her hands as she tried to stand. It was rough and torn up as if someone had taken a chisel to it, making deep grooves and splinters. The dogs did this the night before when they scratched and scratched, trying to get in to get her, to eat her, like they had Grammy and Grandy.

Tears streamed from Tricia's eyes.

The dogs attacked.

--*

A neighbor had found Mrs. Nightingale's chewed carcass. She had several injuries, but the gashes in her throat were the significant ones.

The day had become cloudy when Tony Parker received word. He arrived in time to see her body brought out on a gurney. He felt responsible. Jack Simpson walked to Parker when he saw him get out of the truck.

"I was just here an hour and a half ago, Jack," Parker said, somewhat recovered from whatever took a hold of him in Alvarez's office. "She was fine then. I can still see her face, vibrant and alive. She told me good-bye and ran back to answer the phone."

"She was found with the phone still in her hand. By the bite marks on her ankles and the injury on her head, it looks like the dogs tripped her up, and she fell into a lamp table, knocking herself out.

That allowed the dogs to finish her off. An old couple down the street caught the dogs sneaking in their house and blew them away."

Parker looked down at his feet and shivered. "I could have saved her. She could still be alive. It's my fault. I should have brought the dogs in, myself."

"Come on, ol' buddy," Simpson said sympathetically, "you didn't know what you were dealing with. You can't blame yourself."

"After all that's happened and I didn't know what we were dealing with?" Parker shook his head. "Did you find anything else?"

"You mean like initials or a *Bible* passage?" Simpson asked.

Parker didn't answer, still looking at his feet.

"No, not this time. This mess is damned crazy, Tony. What in hell is going on?"

Parker shook his head again.

"Ah, shit. It's Haskins," Simpson said as the TV Two news truck arrived.

"You'd better keep him away from me, Jack, or you'll have another body on your hands," Parker said through his teeth.

Haskins stopped and spoke to what was probably a neighbor. Parker saw the woman point at him, and then Haskins turned to Parker.

Simpson blocked Haskins' advance with his arm as he came running with microphone in hand.

"Yet another death! Tell me, as animal control director, what are you doing about this plague of rabies and the human slaughter that is taking place?" Haskins asked tenaciously into his microphone. The cameraman's bright lights shone from behind giving the announcer a sort of surreal, almost angelic look.

"No comment," Parker said back, taking quick steps toward his Jimmy.

"According to neighbors, you had been here moments before the victim was killed, possibly right outside as she was being torn to pieces by rabid dogs."

"No comment," Parker said, nearing the truck.

Haskins pushed on with Simpson backing up, still holding his arm out to keep Haskins at bay.

"What is it you're doing, Tony Parker, Animal Control Director, to protect the good citizens of Wichita from these raging beasts, running rampant in our very streets?"

"No comment!"

Haskins turned back to the camera. "There you have it, people of Wichita. Three citizens and two police officers lay dead, throats torn open by ferocious, mad dogs, freely running the city streets. And our very own head dogcatcher says, 'No comment.'"

Parker roared off in his truck. He radioed Tommy Chin and told him to pick up what was left of the poodles.

Roary Rapids had to be found immediately. There could be no more attacks.

CHAPTER 31

Harold Burke had delivered mail to the folks at Sand Creek six days a week for the previous eighteen years. Aside from a two weeks' vacation now and then, and a few holidays, he could count the number of days he'd missed on one hand. He'd delivered even when the old back had flared up and when he'd caught a case of the creeping crud. He'd been through two Dodge station wagons and a Studebaker during that time. Now he was in the middle of wearing out a sixty-seven Plymouth GTX. It was cherry when he'd bought it six years ago. Besides putting over a hundred and twenty thousand extra miles on the engine, it was in the same cherry shape it was in when he bought it.

He crammed a Sears catalogue, an issue of *Playboy*, and an overdue electric bill into the mailbox out in front of Jake Lawrence's house and eased up to Eldon and Pearl Bumfield's when he heard screams, little girl screams. Burke stopped short of the mailbox and listened. It didn't sound like little-kid, *bet-you-can't-get-me*, play-type screams. Maybe it was the Bumfields' granddaughter that had been staying with them this summer. Oh, what was her name—Tricia, that was it. She must be in trouble, hurt or something. Maybe she'd fallen from the swing set in the backyard or cut herself with a butcher knife in the kitchen while she tried to make herself a sandwich for lunch.

Burke stepped out of his car and took two more steps into the yard, listening to find out exactly where the screams were coming from. They came again. This time, he heard barking, too. Angry barking and growls. The commotion came from inside the Bumfields' house.

Harold Burke angled his thin body to the direction of the front door and sprinted. He leaped the porch, flung open the screen and charged in.

"Pearl! Eldon!" he yelled frantically, not yet looking down. "Are you folks all right?"

Burke's leather-soled black work shoes made contact with Pearl Bumfield's drying gore, and he slipped, limbs flying, falling hard onto his shoulder and into the chest of her devastated corpse. It made a cracking, crunching, rotten-watermelon smashing noise as he landed. Several seconds passed before he understood what mess he lay in, gawking at the blood on his hands and arms and the rent carcass.

He sprang to his hands and knees and looked down at the carnage he'd landed in with disgust. Bile pumped into his mouth, but he held it back. He looked away and saw the body in the living room, guessing it to be Eldon Bumfield. He couldn't be sure. It was as recognizable as a Thanksgiving turkey on the Friday after.

The screams came again. They came from upstairs. This was no time to puke his guts into Pearl Bumfield's mostly bare-skull exposed face. Whatever atrocity happened to the Bumfields was happening right now to a little girl upstairs.

Burke had no idea what he would find, but, proceeding like the Korean War hero he was, he raced up the stairs with no regard for his own safety. Making the top landing, he saw Tricia swinging her arms hopelessly in the master bedroom doorway. The dogs hulked over her, and Dawg had just clamped onto her wrist.

"What in hell?" he exclaimed and ran to Tricia's aid. He yanked the first cur off and threw it back to the stairs. Dawg released his grip on her and came back around and caught Burke on the left inner thigh, just below the groin.

Burke screamed in pain and grabbed the dog by both sides of his head, trying to push him away, but the dog held on as tenaciously as an alligator snapping turtle.

"Run, little girl. Hide!"

The Epic Center pushes up three hundred and twenty-five feet above the Kansas plains and is the state's tallest building. It stands like a monumental monolith in the center of Wichita. A copper, diamond-cut roof caps off this beauty of architecture, its corners pointing north, south, east, and west, causing its walls to be oblique to the streets below. The highest point is the north corner, sloping down at angles to the other three corners, those at equal height. In the peak of the high north corner is a notch, made for a walkway to access the roof. A door opens out on one side of the inside of this notch. Each of the four corners of the building are flat, ten feet wide, to accommodate large corner windows on all floors all the way up the structure.

CHAPTER 32

The early afternoon sky, gray and brooding, framed the Epic Center as two black stretch limousines stopped at the curb. Out of the first, four young men in leather jackets, gold chains, and torn blue jeans emerged. All four men wore thick, black-framed sunglasses and had long, thoroughly teased hair of various shades. A fifth man in a suit got out of the second car with six black Dobermans on long leashes. The dogs seemed well behaved and were easily led over and handed to Roary Rapids, the most prominent member of the group. He had bright yellow hair, a long drawn face with fat puffy lips that were too full for his small mouth, and he looked to be in his late twenties to early thirties.

"Come on, guys, let's go see about this bullshit. Madonna can't sign us to open for her, then tell us to take a hike, just like that," the blond man said, leading the dogs and the other three men to the revolving-door entrance.

"That's right, Roary, you tell 'em," one of the others said.

They helped each of the dogs through and went in.

"Wait a minute, son," Gus Spillman, a middle-aged security guard said as they barged on and hit the up button for the elevators. "You can't bring those dogs in here."

"What? Hey man, we've done it before. These are seeing-eye dogs, you know!" Rapids said, staring through his sunglasses over the security guard's shoulder as if blind.

Spillman frowned and put his hands on his hips as the elevator door opened. "Now, see here...," he began as people coming off the elevator stepped to the side, making way for the pack of Dobermans. The strange bunch crowded inside.

Rapids waved to Gus Spillman with his fingers and gave a big smile, looking over his sunglasses as the door closed.

*_*_*

Tony Parker checked in at the shelter at one o'clock, and Sarah Hill showed up at two. She'd only had four hours sleep but decided to come in early after hearing of the latest attack. Parker was happy to see her.

Parker had been trying Rapids' number since he came in. But with no answer yet, he began to get concerned something might have happened. Something bad. At two thirty, he had decided to go to Rapid's home to investigate when he tried one last time and finally got a busy signal. On the next try, the housekeeper answered.

After explaining the situation, Parker was told Rapids had just left with his dogs to see his attorney in an office at the Epic Center. The housekeeper also told him that, only moments before Parker's call, someone had called anonymously asking as to Rapids' whereabouts and that of his dogs. Parker wasn't sure what this information meant in the scheme of things but sensed it to be another piece to his puzzle. A very troublesome piece.

The Epic Center was only a couple of miles away. Parker and Hill decided to drive over immediately, hopefully to catch Rapids before he went inside.

As they ran out to the truck, one of those spur-of-the-moment storm fronts began to roll in. It looked like this, the second cold front in as many days, would finally bring the needed rain. Dark thunderheads reached up to the heavens, flashes of lightning dancing in its black headdress, and claps of thunder announced its arrival. The wind had picked up and blew a chilling sixty-five degrees, compared to the late morning ninety-six only hours before. With emergency lights flickering, they left.

*_*_*

"Mr. Rapids, please, we've asked you before. Don't bring your dogs in with you when you come!" Doris Carney, a neatly dressed, professional-looking young receptionist said, as Rapids and his entourage approached.

"Sorry, babe," Rapids said. "Like I told you last time, these dogs go everywhere I go, whether on stage or to my attorney's office. So sue me. I'm here to see Spencer."

He sat on the corner of her desk, picked up a rubber band and shot it at a picture of the US President on the far wall.

"Do you have an appointment, Mr. Rapids?" she asked.

"Hell no! I don't need an appointment. This is Roary Rapids you're talking to. I suggest you get off your tight little ass and tell him I'm here."

Doris hesitated but obeyed. She picked up her phone and punched a button as Gus Spillman came in.

"Mr. Spencer, I'm sorry to bother you, sir, but Roary Rapids is here and insists on seeing you. . . . Yessir, I know he doesn't have an appointment. . . . Yessir, I know he is. . . . All right, Mr. Spencer." She put the phone down and looked up at Rapids. "Mr. Spencer asked that you allow him just a couple of minutes to finish up some very important business. Would you please have a seat?"

"Well, all right, then," Rapids said, "as long as it's no more than two minutes."

Doris Carney looked to the security guard glaring at Rapids and said, "It's all right, Gus. Mr. Rapids has promised me he wouldn't bring his dogs in again."

"Yeah, right. When monkeys fly out my butt," Rapids sneered.

The other band members chuckled at their leader's borrowed wit.

Gus Spillman frowned and shook his head. He turned back toward the elevator.

Eric Spencer, a tall, distinguished-looking bald man with thin lips and an eagle beak came out of his office. Before Rapids had a chance to say anything, Spencer began scolding.

"Mr. Rapids, I suggest you find yourself another attorney. Maybe someone out in LA or New York, more familiar with the entertainment business. Maybe your agent could recommend someone. That is, if he hasn't dumped you, too. And you might even consider moving there yourself."

"You listen here, you pompous bastard, my dad owns you. You'd better treat me with the respect I deserve," Rapids insisted.

"You're right, your father does *own* me, but I just got off the phone with him. He says he's even tired of fooling with you. You're on your own. If it weren't for the fortune he's made in oil, you wouldn't have this little hobby of yours. So, I would suggest you go crawling back to him on your hands and knees and beg him for an honest job. Of course, then he may insist on you changing your name back to Jubal Bugerman."

The phone rang, and Doris answered, "Hello. . . . Ah, yes, he is here, now. Can I say who's calling?" she said looking over at Rapids. "Well, yes he does have his dogs. . . . Yes. . . . Uh, I guess that would be all right." She laid the handset down, turned on the speakerphone and looked up at Rapids. "It's for you."

Everyone in the office waited in silence for a voice. Suddenly, all six dogs, previously well behaved and passive, became restless.

Then came the growls. All of the dogs growled. They looked at one another. At the people in the room. They paced.

Doris Carney stood up from her desk and backed to Spencer's door. The unarmed security guard watched from the open hall and began punching the down button on the elevator. Rapids and the other three men sat up and stared at the dogs. Everyone in the city

knew of the numerous dog attacks. It was the first thing to Rapids'
mind when the dogs began to growl.

"Now, what the hell's gotten into all of you?" Rapids asked of the
dogs.

The dogs growled again, this time even more enthusiastically.
Their muscles tensed. They held their jaws open, fangs exposed.
The question seemed to set them off like dynamite. Rapids threw the
leashes in the air, and the dogs attacked.

Spencer, Doris Carney and the three men pushed into Spencer's
office, slamming the door behind. Rapids climbed the back of a black
leather chair, leaped over the dogs and ran for Gus Spillman at the
elevator.

"Oh, shit!" Spillman said, turning to see Rapids racing at him with
all six dogs in pursuit.

"They've all gone mad! Quick, do something!" Rapids said, running, arms flying.

Spillman gave a few more pokes at the button and then ran to the
nearest doorway. The door led out to the stairway, leading up to the
mechanical room under the roof or down to the floors below. He
threw the door open and ran in.

"Close it behind you, dumb ass!" Spillman yelled, not bothering
to slow even long enough to see that Rapids made it.

Rapids came through with the dogs too close to shut the door
behind him. One of them caught Rapids in the doorway and ripped
into the seat of his pants. A tremendous pain shot through his hip as
the dog took a big chunk of flesh from Rapids' ass.

He trapped the dog, midway through the door, grabbed its snout
and finally managed to break away. Rapids shoved the murderous
canine back through and slammed the door quickly, but too quickly
for it to latch. He ran after Spillman.

The door popped open and the first dog came through, pushing
the door wide. Rapids followed Spillman up two flights of stairs, where
the guard yanked a key ring, laden with at least two-dozen keys, from
his pocket.

Rapids stood watching the keys, Spillman, then the keys again in horror as Spillman searched for the correct one. There was no place to go. The dogs were coming. The door was locked, and this bungling goof was going to get him killed.

Spillman selected a key, slid it into the knob and unlocked and opened the door quicker than Rapids thought possible. But now, it was every man for himself. Rapids thought nothing of running through like a linebacker, knocking Spillman to the floor in the middle of the doorway. All six dogs hit the small landing to the door as Rapids ran over Spillman.

Rapids ran into the large mechanical room. The only light came from a large corner window just below a giant, louvered vent and the high, north corner of the roof. He glanced back and saw the dogs pause, attacking Spillman as he lay prostrate on the floor screaming, flailing his arms. The dogs took slashing bites, tearing at his face, neck, hands and body until Gus Spillman no longer moved.

With the job finished, the dogs darted off one at a time. Spillman's body blocked the door open.

CHAPTER 33

Tony Parker pulled in behind the two limos in front of the Epic Center. He hoped it wasn't too late. It began raining large drops, slapping the sidewalk and street in splats. Parker carried a new control stick, and Sarah Hill, again, took the tranquilizer gun. They trotted through the revolving doors and into the lobby. Next to the elevators, they found a list of office numbers.

"Twenty-second floor," Parker said, finding the name *Spencer* and pushing the elevator button.

"You think we're too late?" Hill asked.

"Lord, I hope not. Not again."

As the elevator sped along to the top of the building, Hill backed up and leaned against the wall. "I'm not going near a window, I want you to know," she said, uneasy.

"You, afraid of heights? I can't believe it."

"It's my only fault, okay?"

Parker and Hill poised for the worst as the elevator doors opened on the twenty-second floor. They peeked around the door. No one was in sight. They could hear the annoying, *raa, raa, raa* of the speakerphone in Spencer's office and then the recorded voice of an operator, saying, "If you wish to place a call, please hang up. . . . "

They walked cautiously to a desk with a nameplate on top that read *Doris Carney*. They looked around. A chair lay toppled over.

Something had definitely happened here. Parker put his ear to the door marked E. Q. Spencer and, after hearing nothing, tapped lightly. The door opened slowly, and Parker stepped back.

"Thank God!" the young woman said. "You got here quick. We just called 911." The door opened wider, revealing four timid-looking men behind her.

"Where are the dogs?" a tall, well-dressed bald man asked. Parker guessed it was Spencer the attorney.

"Didn't see them. What's going on here?" Parker asked.

"The dogs," the woman answered, "they attacked us. We don't know where Gus and Mr. Rapids are."

Parker and Hill turned and walked back by the elevators. Smeared blood streaked the door marked, *To the Roof, North Corner, High End.* Hill cocked the rifle and nodded to Parker, apprehension in her eyes.

He eased the door open and looked. Nothing. The two entered the stairway, looked down and up the steps. Droplets of blood on the stairs leading up were smudged in paw prints.

They proceeded carefully, but Hill let the door go absentmindedly. It slammed shut, echoing through the stairwell, causing them to flinch.

She gritted her teeth, wincing at Parker. "Oops, sorry!" she whispered.

They continued slowly along the steps. At the first landing, they found nothing. No blood. Parker looked at the last flight of stairs. He saw nothing unusual until something dripped from the landing down to the top step. Something dark and red—more blood, and lots of it.

Parker moved up the steps sliding his back along the wall with the control stick out in front. Soon, he could see the door at the top of the steps was blocked open. A security guard's body lay in a lake of dark crimson.

Hill cringed, but they went on, stepping over the body and through the door to the mechanical room. It was too late to help him, and they hadn't found Rapids yet. They had to push on. They couldn't stop and wait for help even though the police would be arriving soon. The seconds might be precious to Roary Rapids' life.

Lightning flashed from the big corner window, accompanied by a deafening crack of thunder. A window washer's scaffold outside danced like a puppet on strings, and the shadows from the cables suspending it moved across the wall behind them like the legs of a giant spider. The control box on the window washer's rig sparked for a couple of seconds, then smoked, clearly the target of the lightning. Rain hammered the copper roof above. Thunder clapped more frequently and louder as if a furious artillery battle escalated outside. Shadows from boxes, ductwork, heating and air-conditioning and power-generation equipment filled the cavernous room. The only light came from the dark, stormy afternoon sky through the large window.

On the right, an open, steel stairway zigzagged up to the high point in the roof thirty feet above and to the side of the window. More equipment was on the left, and nothing showed signs of life.

"Mr. Rapids, are you up here?" Parker called, knowing full well he could be alerting the dogs, also.

He listened for a few seconds and then called out again. This time a voice came from the right, sounding high up.

"I'm here, help!"

Parker stepped farther into the room. A man hung from one of the roofing girders on the right. Below him were the dogs. All stared at Parker.

Parker angled his body sideways to the dogs. With his left hand, he motioned to Hill, not yet seen, to get back to the stairway.

The dogs began raving. They bolted simultaneously, charging.

"Run, Sarah!" Parker yelled.

The dogs would reach the stairway door before them. The open stairs to the roof provided the only possible escape. Hill raised the rifle to shoot. Parker dashed by and grabbed her arm before she had a chance, knowing that she might get the lead dog, but by the time she cocked the rifle for the second shot, the dogs would be all over her.

"Where are you taking me?" Hill yelled, as they ascended the steps with the dogs closing in. "I told you I don't like heights."

"I just guessed you don't like killer dogs, either," Parker said back. "Maybe they won't follow us up here. Some dogs don't like open steps."

Parker knew Hill didn't, either, but she had no choice. The dogs didn't slow down to scale the steps and were bounding up halfway as Parker and Hill reached the top.

"They're still coming," Parker said, looking to the door to the outside.

The door was their only hope. Parker swung it open, pushed Hill and himself outside and slammed it behind them.

The violent thunderstorm assaulted the city in full force now. The rain and wind were nearly overwhelming. They stood huddled against the door, already completely soaked. The driving wind gave teeth to each cold drop. It was a difficult adjustment after the day's broiling heat. The water, the rain, everywhere—it made Parker's throat raw and it felt as though it was twisting into a knot. It became difficult for him to swallow.

The walkway was eight feet wide, extending from the door to the door less, mirror-image side. It was twenty feet long and cluttered with numerous antennas of various shapes. The south end led out to the slope of the roof, going down to that corner at a forty-five degree angle. The north corner was eight feet in the opposite direction its walkway leading out to a three hundred-foot drop. Taut cables stretched just above the floor, going over the north end. A short, steel-pipe handrailing was attached at each end of the walkway. The two sides of the notch extended up fifteen feet at their highest points.

With a tremendous crack, a blinding flash of lightning struck a lightning rod near the high corner of the roof. Accompanying it, a simultaneous thunder explosion nearly sent the two of them to the floor of the walkway.

Hill clung tight to Parker's chest. They looked out timidly at the Wichita skyline. The city's lights were lit as if night had descended. With every thunderclap, Hill squeezed Parker tighter.

"It's all right, Sarah. We're safe, now," Parker said loudly over the driving rain and thunder. He coughed hoarsely.

"Safe? You call this safe?" she yelled back, trembling.

Parker put his ear up to the door to see if he could hear the dogs. Before, they had clawed feverishly at the doorjamb. He could still hear scratching. It sounded like only a couple of dogs. Maybe a single dog. They waited a few minutes, which seemed like hours. No one would come to help. They had no idea Hill and Parker were out here. The police might have already come and had the situation under control.

A forceful gust of chilling wind pushed them off balance and caused them to stagger.

Again, Parker put his ear to the door to listen. This time he heard nothing.

"I've got a plan," he yelled, looking down at Hill.

Hill looked up at him with desperation in her eyes. Her long blonde hair lay soaked in strings on her shoulders.

"Anything. Anything will be better than this," she yelled back.

"You stand here opposite the door. You're the bait," Parker said, moving Hill like a lobotomized mental-ward patient to the other side of the walkway.

She stared back at him as if to say, "Maybe this isn't better."

Parker stepped back to the hinged side of the door.

"I'll stand here behind the door and open it."

Hill's eyes widened. "You've gone crazy!"

"If the dogs are gone, we're okay. If they're not, I'll kick the first one that comes through off the roof and slam the door back shut."

She looked astonished but didn't reply. Her jaw seemed locked halfway open as if her lips couldn't shape words and her vocal cords wouldn't respond. She just stood there, watching the closed door.

"It's all right," he tried to assure her. "Okay, ready?"

He grabbed the doorknob and looked at Hill. She sank down to a sitting position, still staring at the door, terrified. Her legs were tucked under her left side, arms crossed over her chest.

Parker yanked the door open and stepped back. For a long few seconds, nothing happened.

Then, Hill's eyes popped. A clanking noise came from the steel stairs. Dogs' feet.

He took another step back. A flash of black dog shot from the doorway toward Hill. Parker met it with his right foot, mid-bounds, in the side of its chest with all he had. Pain shocked up from the stressed ankle joint, but, still, his foot followed through perfectly, up and over his head. The sixty-pound animal didn't soar like a football. Yet, it did soar.

It was against Parker's nature to hurt an animal, but he had no choice. It was either the dog or them, and for an instant, as he watched the dog sail, tumbling end over end as it fell into the darkness, he felt pride in his kick, like in the old high-school football days. *I'd like to have seen Jack try to block that one.*

Reality returned. Parker's left foot slipped out from underneath him. With help from his momentum and the rain-slick walkway, he slid to its edge, underneath the steel guardrail and over the side of the twenty-three-story building. He groped for a handhold and with one hand grabbed the bottom rung of the rail as he passed.

He looked up at the steel bar, his legs kicking air over three hundred feet above the ground. It was slick, too slick to hold onto, especially with only one hand. But before he could bring his other hand up, Tony Parker lost his hold.

CHAPTER 34

Sarah Hill shrank back in shock. Battered by the relentless wind and rain, her head swam like a mouse in a flushing toilet. The door to the stairway was still wide open, but all she could see was the empty top landing. The other dogs were yet to show themselves.

Tony Parker's arm had just disappeared over the side. It took a few seconds for it to sink in. He'd fallen.

"No-o-o-o! Tony! Tone-e-e!" Sarah Hill cried out in desperation.

She forced herself to her hands and knees and crawled toward the edge. Her fear of heights stopped her. Tony was gone. There was nothing she could do for him. It hit hard. She began to cry in hard, grieving gasps.

Rumbling erupted from the stairway. The rest of the dogs were coming.

She leaped to the door, slammed it shut and leaned against it with the knob in both hands as the five dogs hit it, clawing and scratching relentlessly, snarling, barking, and she cried more, this time a scared, quiet cry, shaking her head as if to erase what had just happened, shake away Tony falling to his death, shake away the deadly predators on the other side of the door, shake away this terrible tornadic storm that had twisted and torn her world apart.

"Not Tony. No," she said aloud and looked to the edge again.

The cables. Scaffolding hung somewhere over that corner of the building. Maybe, somehow, Tony had landed on the scaffold and survived.

She crept to the edge. With every inch she got closer, the cold wind's intensity grew, sending wave after wave of stinging, hard drops. Her stomach knotted. The heights made her nauseous and tense, not to mention the bitter storm and killer Dobermans. She was afraid to look. She had to. What if Tony wasn't there, his body splattered twenty-three stories below. *I'll fall, too!*

She paused a few feet from the edge and held her eyes closed tight. "Please, Lord. Please, Jesus, let him be alive!" she prayed. She looked over the edge. The scaffolding was more than twenty feet below. Parker lay across it precariously, his left arm and right leg hanging over the narrow platform, face down, motionless.

--*

Jack Simpson had just left the downtown police station two blocks away from the Epic Center when the call came over his radio about the attack. He'd had a talk with the police chief, who told him a similar talk was to happen between Parker and Alvarez. The chief had taken Simpson off of the case and put Lt. Hardessy in charge.

The windshield wipers slapped fast on Simpson's windshield but did little good against the pounding rain. From a block away, Simpson saw Parker's truck, amber lights flashing, in front of the building. The water distorted the lights and blurred them like a child's watercolor painting.

Suddenly, something large and black hit Simpson's hood with a tremendous crash denting in the steel six inches. A Doberman's open mouth sprayed blood on the windshield in front of the steering wheel, but the wipers cleared it off with the rain.

He slammed on his brakes in the middle of the street and sat for a moment, gaping out at the dog on his hood, it seemingly glaring back with it's own very *dead* stare.

"Damn, now the sons-of-bitches are flying."

He pulled the car to the curb behind a long line of parked cars, most of them police cruisers. As he got out, he looked over the dog and rounded the front of the car. His overcoat hung open and flapped in the wind.

With his hand on his forehead to shield his eyes from the rain, he looked up the Epic Center, scanning one story at a time. Reaching the top, he squinted. Scaffolding. Someone was standing on the roof and he was unable to tell whom at that distance in the weather. He glanced at the dog and then at the roof again.

"Nice kick!" he said aloud.

Simpson sprinted down the sidewalk to the front of the building. Other police cars, including a K-9 unit, had pulled up and were parked behind Parker's truck. Lt. Hardessy was there with his protective dog handling suit and Hero, his wonder dog of a German shepherd.

Hardessy looked up as Simpson ran through the lobby. "Hold it, Simpson," he yelled. "You've been reassigned. I'm in charge now. The chief needed someone who could get the job done."

Simpson didn't slow. He kept running toward the elevator.

"I said, hold it, Simpson," he demanded, stepping into the thickly padded, burlap-suit trousers. "I'll handle this."

"Kiss my ass, Hardessy," Simpson said, reaching the elevator door. It opened, and he stepped in.

*_*_*

Outside, on the roof, Sarah Hill begged Parker continuously to wake up. If he came to and wasn't aware of where he was, he would surely fall.

"Tony. Tony, come on, wake up," she pleaded.

His hand twitched then his head. He was slowly coming around.

"Lay still, Tony!" she screamed. "Don't move until you know where you are. You're on a scaffold, hundreds of feet in the air. If you're not careful, you'll fall."

Chapter 35

J ack Simpson had reached the top floor. He found a young woman and four men huddled together in a law office. They told Simpson where Parker and Hill had gone, and he told them to take the elevator down to the lobby.

With everyone safely in the elevator, Simpson pulled out his .357 and trotted to the stairway door. He carefully opened it and walked in. Pausing briefly, he strained to hear anything that might give a clue as to what was happening. Nothing. He proceeded up the stairs, his revolver out in front pointing to the ceiling.

At the top of the steps, Simpson found the cooling body of Gus Spillman and stepped over it. He took a deep breath as if preparing to dive into a pool of alligators and entered the mechanical room.

Nothing moved. Darkness. He took a second to search the wall for a light switch but could find none.

--*

The five Dobermans heard him enter. Trotted toward the doorway. Moved behind large boxes. Stood quietly. Waited. Licked their snouts. Showed their teeth. Waited.

*_*_*

Simpson saw the open stairs leading to the outside access of the roof. That was the way he had to go to find Parker.

A flash of lightning, and the crash of thunder closely following, caused Simpson to look to the window.

A figure outside on the scaffold was struggling to stand up. Parker.

Simpson rushed toward the window to see what he could do to help his friend.

Growls came from the darkness, loud and vicious.

Simpson halted. A figure appeared in the shadows between two large boxes, just to one side of his intended path. Strobing lightning revealed the dark shape as it showed its murderous fangs in a demonic grin.

Simpson raised his gun quickly, preparing to calm the beast with a .357 slug.

Another growl came from the left, interrupting his aim. The lightning illuminated yet another figure, materializing from the darkness, standing motionless, snarling. It stood on a six-foot wooden crate five feet away.

Simpson replaced the first Doberman in his sights with the closer one.

Three more growls from behind. He looked over his shoulder as three additional shadows appeared in another pulsing flash of light, all showing their deadly weapons from underneath curled and snarling snouts.

They had him surrounded. He could only stop one, with luck, maybe two, by gun. They poised to attack at any instant. If he fired his revolver, they might run—or they might attack. He would have to shoot and run. But *where* could he run?

Simpson took short breaths from between parted lips. Sweat beaded on his already wet forehead.

He'd shoot the closest target; the easiest shot—the one on the crate.

Movement from behind. A sort of clicking noise. The dogs were moving.

Simpson turned.

The three dogs that were behind him had disappeared as phantom-like as they had come.

He turned back to the front.

Lightning flashed. The other two dogs had also vanished.

Simpson moved closer to the window, his eyes searching the dark, shadowy surroundings. Another lightning flash and thunder explosion distracted him. He saw Parker trying to get to his feet outside.

"Tony, Tony! I'm here. Hold on!" Simpson cried out, now within eight feet of the window.

The storm and the thick glass prevented Parker from hearing.

Clicking from behind. A lot of clicking.

"The dogs!" he said, under his breath.

Now, a growl. Now, several. A chorus.

A scene from his childhood flashed through his mind. His brother was being mauled by the neighbor's mastiff. The bicycle crashing. The terrible struggle. His brother screaming, crying for help. Vicious fangs. Flesh ripping. Blood. Desperation. No way to help.

*_*_*

Outside on the scaffolding, things were fuzzy and hard to figure out in Parker's head. He started to get up, but his hand slipped, and his head bobbed over the edge of the scaffold. A window squeegee fell. The squeegee seemed to fall for eternity. Nearly out of sight, it bounced spastically on the ground.

His eyes blurred. He saw double. He felt nauseous. His head throbbed hard. *Concussion.* Parker struggled, finally coming to his feet. He gazed up the suspending cables to where Hill stood. The controls to raise and lower the scaffold still smoked from the lightning strike, fused together and useless.

A sudden bang on the large window made Parker hug the scaffold cables, startled. Simpson had been pushed face first into the window. His revolver had hit the glass at the same time and caused a crack to grow across it. Parker gaped at Simpson's horrified face only inches away, pressed against the glazing, distorted from the blur of the rain and the dizziness in his head.

"Tony, help!" Simpson pleaded, his muffled cry barely heard through the glass and over the raging storm.

All five dogs were on him. They ripped and tore at his body. One tried for his jugular, but he knocked it away with his forearm. Two replaced it, thrusting with their terrible incisors at his neck. He held his hands to his throat. Instead they went for his groin and legs. Their powerful jaws clamped onto his body, and their sharp fangs punctured his flesh, ripping, tearing, chewing, tugging and shaking when they had a fast grip on a mouthful of Jack Simpson.

"Oh, God, no! Jack!" Parker pleaded back, his face pressed up against the glass, opposite Simpson's. He beat on the glass as Simpson slid below the window, eyes bugging with pain. An all too familiar fever enveloped Parker's body. It excited him with overwhelming anger. His cold joints stiffened, and the wound on his neck was afire.

"No, no, no, no!" Parker demanded. "Jack!"

He watched, enraged. He could no longer see Jack in the dark room. A dog's head or back occasionally flipped into view as the dogs swarmed like sharks in a feeding frenzy.

He looked up the cables, this time grabbing one without thinking twice. With his feet against the side of the building, he tried to climb up the slippery steel cable, hand over hand and foot over foot against the side of the building. But on every attempt, he slid back after only making a few feet. On his last try, he fell back to the scaffold hard and kicked into a bucket hooked onto the side. A thin nylon rope was attached. If he could throw the bucket up to Hill and have her tie the rope off, he'd stand a much better chance of climbing up.

"Stand back!" he ordered.

He swung the bucket around like a lariat and then slung it up and over the railing to Hill. Hill's head ducked back as the bucket came over. She quickly reappeared with a questioning look.

"Tie it off!" he told her.

He gave her a few seconds to secure the line and then tugged twice to check it before trying to climb. Once again, Parker's attempts were thwarted. The rope was too thin and slippery. Parker cried out in anguish as he slipped down beside the window. All this time wasted, while inside, the dogs ripped Jack apart.

CHAPTER 36

Parker gritted his teeth and took two more steps up the side of the building, holding onto the thin rope. He started slipping again, but now, he knew what he must do. He'd seen it many times in the movies and on TV. Bruce Willis and Batman did it.

Parker wrapped the rope around one hand for a better hold and then bent his knees, squatting on the wall. He shoved off with his legs while holding tight to the rope. He swung out. Coming back hard, he hit feet first against the window. The glass shattered and Parker swung in, ready to begin a melee of dog bashing. Glass and rain poured in through the broken window. He lost his grip on the rope and fell flat on his back beside Jack Simpson.

The dogs were gone. He leaned over onto his side and looked at Simpson's blood-seeping body. There were wounds too numerous to count.

The roof door slammed and the metal steps rattled as Sarah Hill ran down. She sprinted over to Parker and Simpson.

"Get out of here, now," Parker said. "Go get help."

Hill obeyed and ran to the stairway door. Parker watched her until she made it through, making sure the dogs didn't follow her.

He knelt beside Simpson. He was surprised when Simpson feebly opened his eyes. He was mortally wounded, it was obvious. Blood ran from a multitude of wounds: neck, face, arms, stomach and sides, legs and groin. He lay with his head and shoulders against the wall below the large, broken window.

"Hey, Tony," he said faintly, "that was one hell of a kick you gave that Dobie. You know he landed on my hood? Nobody blocked that field goal."

Parker smiled what little he could muster, trying to comfort his dying friend. He couldn't hold it for long.

"Jack, come on now. This isn't any way to die."

When Simpson smiled back at him, Parker flashed back to the day they met. The big game, the field-goal attempt that Simpson blocked and robbed from him, and the fight afterward that ended in a long and very loyal friendship.

"I'm sorry, Jack!" Parker said, shaking his head.

"You're sorry? What for, ol' buddy?" Simpson asked.

"For calling you a—*nigger*."

"What? Tony, that was over twenty years ago, and if I remember right, I called you an ignorant, white-trash asshole."

They both chuckled until Simpson coughed up blood.

"Tony, do me a favor?" Simpson's face was serious.

"Sure, Jack."

"Don't mess around on Julie. She's the best thing you ever had."

Simpson's concern surprised him. "Sure, Jack, I know she is."

"And one more thing. Look after Sadie and the kids, will you?"

He patted Simpson's hand and then squeezed it. "Of course, Jack. You know you can count on me."

Simpson's gaze faded to a blank stare. For a moment, Parker thought he was gone.

Simpson's hand and arm moved underneath his side. He pulled out his gun. He'd been lying on it. He quickly aimed it over Parker's left shoulder.

A deafening explosion from the revolver made Parker flinch and his ears ring. He heard a yelp and turned to see cardboard boxes shifting fifteen feet away. He turned back to Simpson.

"Here, take this," Simpson said, placing the gun into Parker's hand. "You might need it." Simpson coughed and winced.

Parker hadn't fired a gun since Vietnam and didn't ever want to again, and he knew Simpson was well aware of it.

Parker looked deep into Simpson's eyes. The life was running out. He wanted to stop it, to put it back into his friend's body. But the life leaked from too many wounds until it emptied from his body.

Simpson was dead.

In a stupor Parker looked down at the gun in his hands. He was still dizzy from the concussion or from something much more horrifying. The fever still blazed. Hot flashes surged through his body, joints ached. His stiff neck stung with the wound afire. He looked about. The surroundings were surreal. Like a dream, a nightmare. His head became light and began to spin. He felt ready to faint. Steadying himself with one arm, he tried to maintain control of his consciousness.

A snarl came from behind.

Adrenaline shot through Parker's body. His back straightened. The pain disappeared. He had no thought of fear. This time, revenge.

He turned to see a single Doberman with a red gash parting the hide on its forehead where a bullet had glanced off. The animal that was preparing to attack Parker was instead about to be attacked. Parker eased toward the dog to get into a better position to murder his prey. The dog seemed startled by the look in Parker's eyes. It lowered its head and licked its chops, licking some of its own blood that had rolled down its head to the corners of its mouth.

Parker sprang. With one quick movement, he slammed the side of the revolver down across the top of the dog's skull.

The dog gave a short yelp.

Parker stood to his feet, picked the stunned animal up by its collar and one hind leg and raised it high in the air above him.

It was all coming to a head. The frustration, the anguish. It exploded inside him.

"*Aaaaah!*" he yelled, bringing the dog down hard, back first, across his knee.

The dog's spine gave way with a snap like Alvarez's wooden pencil. Parker raised the dog over his head once more. He faced the window and then hurled the dog's body through it. It struck some of the broken shards of glass hanging down from the aluminum window frame as it passed through.

CHAPTER 37

Sarah Hill ran down the two flights of stairs to the next floor. A noise came from the stairs below. It was the police coming to rescue them, maybe. She paused at the door into the twenty-second-floor elevator area. The sound came closer, maybe one floor below. She realized what it was. The dogs. They must have started their way down the stairs, then when they heard Hill, turned and now raced back up.

She swung the door wide and ran to the elevator controls. Fortunately, one opened quickly. She stepped in and pushed the lobby button and then frantically pushed the *door close* one. Four dogs got through the stairway door before it closed. As the snarling killers charged in and came up to within a few feet of the elevator, its door closed, and the dogs jumped against it.

On the street, the police weren't letting the media in the building. The news crews set up outside in the rain. Channel Two was on the northeast side, and Henry Haskins stood facing the camera with umbrella in hand.

"Here we are, bringing you live coverage from the Epic Center of the tense standoff between six Doberman dogs and the Wichita police and Sedgwick County animal-control officers. Thus far in this horrible drama unfolding on the city over the last four days, the police and animal-control officers have been completely impotent in their battle against these vicious beasts. Today we have six very dangerous and deadly Doberman dogs, trapped with an unknown number of officers and civilians on the top floors and roof of this, Kansas' tallest building."

Suddenly, the body of a dead Doberman crashed onto the sidewalk directly behind Haskins amidst shards of chiming window glass.

Haskins ducked. He turned to look at what had taken place.

A faint roar came from far atop the building.

Haskins turned back to the camera. "And as you can see it's raining glass and dogs out here."

The cameraman shook his head and frowned.

Parker glared out the window, panting with drool stringing from his mouth. To the side, Roary Rapids still clung to the same girder he had earlier. He stared at Parker, not saying a word. Parker wiped his sleeve across his face and then bent down to Simpson. It was a struggle, but finally, he picked up Simpson's large, limp body, cradled his beloved friend in his arms and turned and walked toward the door. He paused, glancing at Rapids, his lip curled in a sneer. *Let someone else help him.* Rapids looked back with surprise.

In the first-floor lobby, Lt. Hardessy finally had his gear on and situated. He had a 10mm, Smith and Wesson semi-automatic pistol in one hand and Hero's leash in the other as he stepped onto the elevator.

He and Hero stood ready when the elevator hit the twenty-second floor and the door slid open. The four remaining Dobermans were also ready.

They snarled and growled as they rushed in, taking a supposedly prepared Hardessy off guard. He hadn't had a chance to fire a shot. The dogs were all over Hero and him. With his pistol knocked to the floor, the only thing Hardessy could think of to do was to push the button to the first floor.

*_*_*

Parker opened the door from the stairway to the twenty-second floor elevator area. He saw the dogs rush inside and the slaughter begin before the elevator door closed. He hurried to the elevators, still carrying Simpson, and poked the button several times for another car.

*_*_*

Hill stood back in the far corner as at least two-dozen police officers milled around in the lobby on the first floor, waiting for instructions from Lt. Hardessy. Several of them stood around the elevators. One of the cars was coming down already.

Outside, a fretting woman pushed through the police line. She was a tall woman in her mid-forties, wearing a bright orange pantsuit.

"My daughter is in there. She's a receptionist on the twenty-second floor," she yelled, shoving her way to the revolving door.

A bell announced the arrival of the elevator to the lobby. The door opened to the floor full of anxious police officers.

The Dobermans bolted out with great surprise to all.

They seemed to realize they were greatly outnumbered and ran to escape. Lt. Hardessy lay in what looked like a pile of bleeding gunnysacks, trying to get to his feet. His dog lay beside him, dead and bloody.

The officers cleared a path, and the dogs ran toward the revolving door. The cops drew their guns. What followed sounded like a battle.

As the dogs ran down the gauntlet of police on both sides, the guns thundered. Shot after shot rang out.

The last three dogs were nearly ripped apart by the volley. Red spots appeared on their backs, necks, and legs as they fell separately and slid across the floor, ending their desperate run. An officer on each side of the line fell to the floor. Poorly aimed bullets had hit one in the shin and the other in the foot.

The fourth dog made it to the revolving door and was trapped opposite the lady concerned for her daughter. A tall officer with sergeant's stripes walked over and held the door in place with his foot to ensure no escape. He held his hand up to stop the frightened woman and pointed his revolver at the dog, now snarling back up through the glass panel.

The gun reported with a pop, and the tempered safety glass fractured into a million pieces but held its place in the door as blood splattered and drew into the cracks. He moved his foot out of the way and pushed the door to allow the woman in without looking over to her. She slid down to the floor, fainting.

A bell announced yet another elevator car's arrival. The officers lined up again.

The door opened. Amongst a multitude of pointing pistols, Parker staggered out lamely with Simpson in his arms. He stood cut, bruised, and bleeding. Hill rushed to him. This seemed to snap the trance, and the officers holstered their weapons.

The lobby was a mess of bodies, blood and dogs. A gurney lay by a glass door next to the revolving one, and Parker laid Simpson on it. He patted Simpson's hand and then pulled a folded sheet from under Jack's legs and placed it over his friend.

Parker found new strength and walked briskly from the building and Hill had to run to catch up.

"Well, if it isn't Tony Parker, the animal control director," Haskins said. "Care to say anything to our viewers at home about the slaughter you allowed inside?"

Hill was closer to Haskins and saved Parker the trouble. A swift kick placed squarely between Haskins' legs sent him bent over to the ground and was sure to leave him wordless for the rest of the evening.

"Did you get it?" Hill asked the cameraman.

The cameraman smiled back. "I got it!" he said, giving her a thumbs up.

"Here, Tony, I'll drive," Hill said, taking the keys from Parker's hand when she noticed him stagger. "I'll take you where you want to go, but, after that, it's straight to the hospital." She knew where Tony was going, and nothing would stop him. She drove straight to Sadie Simpson's and waited outside.

The doctor wanted to keep Parker, but as soon as Julie showed up, he told them he was leaving. The dizziness, stiffness, and hot flashes had subsided some and could have been contributed to the nasty bump on the head. It couldn't be rabies. It couldn't be.

Parker had to promise he'd not go to work for the rest of the week, though, and he would check in the next Monday. Sarah and Julie's eyes met as Tony and Julie started to leave. For the first time since they'd met, neither of them glared.

With the medication the doctor gave, Parker went right to sleep when he hit the bed, and nothing would disturb him. Nothing outside his head, that is.

CHAPTER 38

Harold Burke's heroic effort to save Tricia Carpenter had been much like a soldier jumping on a live hand grenade and produced similar results. The dogs had attacked the mailman, giving Tricia time to scamper behind the master bedroom door to temporary safety once again.

Tricia had sat up in her grandparents' big bed with the covers pulled up to her nose as she listened to the savagery on the other side of the door. Soon after Burke's blood oozed from the threshold, she heard more dogs join in. She heard their arguing growls as they fought over prime pieces. The growls seemed to diminish and she knew it was because they were dragging the mailman's body away, down the hall and then down the steps. She heard the dogs, at least two of them that stayed behind, lap up the blood on the floor. She even saw their greedy tongues as they tried for every drop of spilled blood under the inch-and-a-half gap under the door.

Several hours passed. Tricia Carpenter now found safety in the master bedroom closet. She ran there after the dogs renewed their aggressive pursuit of the only living prey left in Sand Creek. The thin plywood panel in the lower half of the door had given in to repeated scratching. As soon as Tricia could see Dawg's paw come through the panel, she streaked for the closet.

She huddled in the far corner of the closet, tired and hungry and thirsty, and needed to go to the bathroom. She had found a water glass beside Grammy's side of the bed earlier and guzzled down the meager three gulps that it held but that wasn't nearly enough.

Right now the most urgent matter was that she had to pee, real bad. After considerable thought, she crawled to the opposite corner of the closet and relieved herself. *How naughty*, she thought. *What would Grammy think?* But now, at least, she was only tired and hungry and thirsty.

A wood breaking, cracking noise came from the other side of the door. She heard the pounding paws of several excited dogs entering through the hole they had made in the bedroom door.

Tricia hugged herself, holding her knees close to her chin. She trembled with fear, but there were no tears. None were left.

The dogs sniffed and bounded around in their hunt. A dog sniffed very close to the closet door and a shadow passed underneath. Now the shadow came back and sniffed at the crack at the bottom. It pawed once. It sniffed. It pawed again. Suddenly, a lot of pawing and scratching erupted on the door. It rattled loosely in the jamb as if it were going to open.

Tricia wished she still had Raggedy Ann.

CHAPTER 39

Sarah Hill sat, parked in front of the animal shelter, taking a moment's breather. She watched as Tommy Chin pulled in beside her. It was a quarter till four, and Chin had just finished eight hours' rest after pulling a double shift and was coming back for another one.

The rain stopped and the sun shot columns of bright gold through a sieve of gray and black thunderheads. As he pulled to a stop, Hill heard a news bulletin come over Chin's car radio concerning the battle taking place at the Epic Center.

"Uh-oh!" Chin exclaimed. He bailed out of his light blue Honda Civic and ran for the office, without seeing Hill.

"Hey, Chin, what's the rush?" she called out her open window.

"There are six mad Dobermans loose inside the Epic Center," he panted.

"That's old news. Slow down."

Chin walked over to Hill as she slipped out of Parker's Truck. "What happened?"

"A lot." Hill clinched her teeth to hold back the tears. "Nothing good. Jack Simpson was killed. Tony's been hurt, but he's going to be okay. All the dogs are dead."

"Damn, what...?"

"Look, Chin, I've had a tough afternoon. I'm going to call it a day. I'll have to tell you the whole story later."

They walked to the door together.

"Are you all right?" Chin asked.

"Yeah, I'll be fine. I just need some rest."

"Tommy, a lady wants to talk to Tony. You want to take it?" one of the women officers behind the front counter asked as the two came through the door.

Chin nodded and reached for the phone.

"This is Officer Tommy Chin, ma'am. Mr. Parker is off duty right now, can I help?"

Hill turned in the Jimmy's keys, grabbed her purse and started for the door to go home. On her way back by the counter, Chin took Hill by the arm. He nodded to her, one of those "hold up" sort of nods, and turned on the speakerphone for her to hear.

"Yes, Mrs. Crane, what can I do for you?"

"Well, Mr. Parker asked me to call him if I saw Jezebel."

"You mean you saw her? When?"

"Last night. I've heard howling every night, but I never saw her. Last night I thought I saw a rabbit in my garden in the back yard, so I went outside. It was midnight. There wasn't a rabbit, but I heard a noise coming from the side of the house, next to Mr. MacGreggor's. When I looked through the fence, I saw Jezebel, and she was acting real strange."

"How do you mean, ma'am?"

"Well, it was hard to see her very well in the dark but she was running back and forth and jumping. She had a stick in her mouth, like she was playing fetch—or maybe, remembering. She always loved to play fetch with Mr. MacGreggor."

"So what happened, did she see you?"

"No, not at first. She just played for quite awhile. Then, something came over her, and she just stopped dead still and dropped the stick out of her mouth. All of a sudden, she let out the most blood-curdling howl you ever heard. It surprised me so much that I screamed right along with her. She looked over and saw me. I was scared for a minute, but she just up and jumped over the fence on the other side of the yard and ran off."

"Why didn't you report this last night?"

"It was so much like a dream. I had to ask myself if it was really her. Anyway, she would have been long gone by the time anyone got here. Besides, I felt sorry for her."

"And why did you call now?"

"I guess because I decided it was the right thing to do. I'd hate to think someone else got hurt and I could have prevented it."

"How's that, Mrs. Crane?"

"Well, you see, I think she's been here every night. I've been leaving food and water next to the fence for her. I don't think she's taken much, if any, of it. It looks like she's just nosed the dog food around. I'm thinking she climbs over the fence and goes in the house. At midnight—well, that's when I hear the howl. There's been a couple of officers in a police car out in front at night, but they come and go and probably couldn't tell if she was there or not from the street. I don't think they've heard her. Anyway, if I was a betting woman, and I'm not, I'd bet she'll be over there tonight."

"All right, Mrs. Crane. Thanks for the tip. We'll check it out. You stay inside tonight, okay?" Chin turned off the speakerphone. "Well, what do you think?"

Hill blew out an exhausted breath, making her cheeks puff and lips vibrate. "I think I'd better go get some sleep and meet you at MacGreggor's at eleven," Hill said, her eyes half open.

"No, that's okay. I'll get one of the other guys."

"No big deal, I'm pulling a double shift starting midnight, anyway. I just want to catch this big bitch and get it over with. We've rounded up all the other dogs that have had rabies shots from the bad batch. She's the last one."

Hill stepped toward the door but paused and turned back. "Hey, Tommy, how about getting a couple of people to take Tony's truck back to his house? He won't need it for a couple of days, but, that way, when he does, it'll be there for him."

"Sure, Sarah," Chin said, "I'll take care of it. You get home and get some sleep. See you tonight."

*_*_*

Sometime before darkness seeped into the crack under the closet door, the dogs quit scratching, and Tricia Carpenter fell into a deep dark hole in her mind that had been a very frightening place many times before. It had been a place of monsters and ghosts and of parents arguing. This time the deep, dark, sometimes-scary place was a comfort. This time, sleep was a much better and safer place to be than reality.

Tricia woke to the darkness, unsure of where she was. Her back rested in a corner of some kind, but it was a poor clue. She touched her eyes to make sure they were open and then stretched out both arms, feeling for more clues. Her wrist complained, throbbing where Dawg had bitten it. She remembered he'd bitten her foot also, and the pain quickly followed the memory. She whimpered, still reaching. Her left hand struck something that sounded wooden, and the door rattled in its jamb.

Shoes lay in front of her. The black pumps Grammy said she had bought and worn only once, to Tricia's baptism many years ago, were easy to recognize, smooth and soft. Grandy's old brown work boots, with rough leather and cracks and holes worn through, were evident. Her hand batted the clothes hanging over her head as she reached up. No doubt, it was Grammy and Grandy's closet.

She remembered everything now.

Tricia felt the closet door for holes to see if somehow, as she slept, the dogs might have ripped a hole in it, too, like the hole they had scratched through in the bedroom door. Maybe the dogs were in the closet with her. Maybe she would reach out and one of the dogs would bite her hand. It would be much safer to feel the door and not to blindly search the closet for intruders with her hands.

The door was fine. It was smooth and unblemished—from the inside. She put her ear up to the door to listen for sounds. It was quiet except for a hum she recognized as the old electric alarm clock Grammy kept on her side of the bed. She slipped her little fingers under the door and wriggled them, feeling the length of the crack. She didn't know what she felt for or what she would do if she happened upon something. What if she felt a dog? What if a dog chomped off her fingers? The thought made her gasp and jerk her hand back.

The dogs must have left. The hunger and thirst grew more intense, now, and her wrist and foot ached. She had to go for help. The only phone in the house was broken. She remembered the wire pulling out as she ran from Dawg. But the Lawrences had a phone. She could go there and call Tony Parker. He would come and help. He would save her and make all the bad dogs go away. She couldn't remember the number. She would have to go back through the living room to get his card. That is what she would do.

Tricia stood, but the pain in her right foot caused her to remember how deeply Dawg's fangs had penetrated, and she took the weight off of it. She reached out and felt for the doorknob, finding it with a rattle. The mechanism clicked as she turned the knob carefully, and she pushed the door open.

She leaned into the door too far and lost her balance, falling against it, and came down hands first. The door opened only two feet before striking something. Her hands landed on something large and furry.

Dawg grunted.

CHAPTER 40

D r. White Cloud saw the TV bulletin about the tragedy at the Epic Center. He saw Tony come out of the building, walking on his own two feet, and was thankful Tony would be all right. He had to chuckle and clap when Hill put the hurts on Haskins. He had sobbed when they announced the death of his friend, Jack Simpson. He turned the TV off and sat in the dark for a moment, thinking. Patsy always turned in early and had long since gone to bed, and it was quiet in his modern, Spanish stucco home.

Something bothered him—something that happened earlier in the day back at the office. Patsy had told him she did not hear the outside phone bell ring before Truong came out with the news of the rabies tests.

The old vet got up from his chair and walked out to the garage. He would ask Truong a few questions.

All the clinic lights were out as he pulled up in the parking lot in his turquoise green Continental. Truong must have gone to bed. Doc sat in his car for a moment, wondering if he should bother him about something so silly that it was probably nothing. Most likely, the bell rang, and nobody noticed it. No one had paid any attention. Maybe there was a short in the line.

He decided to get out and at least see if Truong might still be awake.

A strange hoarse howl, no more than five hundred yards away, made Doc flinch.

He stood with the car door open, considering it. "When a dog howls, a man will die," he said aloud, remembering the old superstition.

Something rustled in the bushes nearby.

"Who's there?" Doc called out, straining to see.

Hearing the noise again, he asked, "Who's there, I say?"

The bushes rustled again. Something came out.

He backed against the car door. "No, no, please. No!"

--*

At eleven p.m. Sarah Hill pulled up to the MacGreggor house behind Tommy Chin's van. She got out of her little green Geo Storm and walked to his open driver's side window. The night air was thick and foggy. Droplets of moisture already formed and beaded up on the hood of the van.

"So, what's the plan, Chin?"

"Hi, Sarah. Hey, I got us a wire from the guys in vice."

"A wire?"

"Yeah, you know, a microphone."

"How cool. What we really need is a bazooka. So what's the *wire* for?"

"I thought one of us could go inside the house with it. That way, if she gets in, we'll know it."

"Shit, are you crazy? Did you get this plan from Tony, or does insanity come from being in charge?"

"Don't worry, Sarah. I'll go inside," Chin said, seeming a little disappointed his plan wasn't better received.

Hill thought for a moment. She looked at the house and frowned.

"No, I'll do it. Give it to me," she demanded.

"Are you sure, Sarah? It could be dangerous."

"No shit, Sherlock. Tell me something I don't know. Jezebel's a female, a female with class like me. We have a lot in common. Besides, I'm the one with the zoology degree and countless hours of studying animal behavior. I've got to be the one."

Chin handed the small microphone and the earplug receiver to her.

"It's on. VOX, voice activated, so you don't have to push any buttons or anything. Just put the microphone in your shirt pocket and the receiver in your ear. First thing, when either of us sees her, we'll yell it out. And here, I brought an extra tranquilizer rifle," Chin said, passing the rifle through the open window.

"What's the range on this gadget?" Hill asked, placing the receiver in her ear.

"They said around two hundred yards, about a block and a half. But we'll test it when you get inside."

"All right, I guess I'm ready. Make sure you keep talking to me, or I'm liable to fall asleep. I'd hate to *miss* anything. And make sure you keep *your* eyes open. I want to know when this monster shows up. I don't want any surprises."

"You got it, Sarah. Here's the key to the front door," Chin said and tossed it to Hill's open hand.

Hill walked across the street and unlocked the door. She glanced back at Chin before she went in. Chin waved.

"You hear me?" Hill asked, stepping cautiously over the threshold.

"Loud and clear. Everything all right in there?" the receiver cracked in Hill's ear.

"Yeah, I'm going to check the place out before I settle down to my fox hole."

"I just had a scary thought, Sarah. What if she's already in there?"

"Uh-huh." Hill's eyes shifted around the room.

"You want me to come in with you?"

"No, that's all right. You just keep watch out there and be ready to come running in when I cry wolf."

Hill turned on the lights to every room before she entered. They had put a light bulb in the basement and she checked there, too. She was alone.

The house hadn't changed much since she saw it last, except the bodies were gone and most of the blood. The recliner and carpet still showed stains. The air hadn't lost any of its dog odor. Now, with the house being shut up for several days and cooking in the vicious August heat, it mixed with a very pungent stench. A kind of dead-animal smell. They hadn't done a very good job of cleaning up. It wasn't a pleasant job, anyway. Hill couldn't blame them.

She opened the window next to the recliner and turned on the large box fan. It whirred to a high-pitched whine and then settled down to a normal drone. The dog-bone chew toy Haskins had picked up when they were there before lay on the seat of the chair. A wad of socks, knotted up into a ball that might have been used as a fetch toy, accompanied it. She hadn't noticed it when she was there before. Maybe it had been under the chair or some of the other furniture. But she was sure it hadn't been there and neither had the bone. Maybe one of the officers threw it there. Maybe Jezebel put it there, wishing her master would have life again and play with her.

"It's like an oven in here. I'm going to get some cross ventilation in this dump," she said, walking to the other side of the room.

"Oh, damn it!" she exclaimed, pounding and tugging on the large window on the opposite side.

"What's wrong? You all right?" Chin questioned.

"Yeah, but this blasted window's been painted shut. She hit the window frame one last time without results.

She walked back through the house, turning off all the lights, and waited. The house was black. The moon hid behind thick clouds, and the nearest streetlight was burned out. The only light came from the clock on old man MacGreggor's CD player. It flashed twelve o'clock as it probably had since he got it.

Hill walked into the kitchen and stood, looking out the back door window just above the dog port.

"Okay, Jezebel, dog from hell, I'm ready. Come on in," she said, watching wide eyed out the window with her rifle clenched in both hands.

"Nothing out here," Chin said.

"All right, stay alert. Don't go to sleep on me."

Time crept slowly around the numbers on Hill's watch. She told herself it must have stopped several times and tapped it. Eleven forty, and still nothing. The long hours and stress wore on Hill, and her eyelids bounced closed and head bobbed. She jerked her head up and shook off the sleep that was slowly taking control of her weary body. The rifle was getting heavy, so she laid it down, leaning it against a kitchen cabinet near the door.

"Dispatcher to AC Two. Come in, Tommy," came a squawk over the radio that startled Hill. She could hear Chin's radio in the van clearly through her earpiece.

"This is AC Two. Go ahead," Chin replied.

"Tommy, we have a Jezebel sighting at 934 Carnival Drive. Please respond."

"Can't you get anyone else?"

"All other units are tied up. Besides it *is* just six blocks from your location."

"All right, we'll respond," Chin said. "Ah—Sarah, you'll have to come out. We've got a call to respond to six blocks away. Probably another black cat."

"I heard. Look, if it's just six blocks away, go ahead. I'll be okay."

"No, you'd better come out. It's almost midnight. She'll be here soon."

"What? You think this bitch can tell time? Go on, I'll be all right. You won't be gone all night, will you?"

"If you're sure. I'll make it quick. You be careful."

"I'll be okay. Just don't forget me."

Hill went to the front door and watched Chin's van make a U-turn at the corner and head down the street. The headlights flashed in Hill's face, momentarily blinding her. She winced. The light burned her already blood-shot, weary eyes.

A silent moment passed before a sound came from outside. The back yard. Scratching. Something was climbing over the fence.

The rifle. It was still next to the back door. Hill moved quickly toward the kitchen. As she made it to the hall, the dog port began to open. Hill stepped to the side, out of sight, before seeing what was coming through.

She trembled, backing up to the wall next to the large window that was painted shut. She could run for the door, but by the time she reached it, she'd be seen. No way out. Hide. Where? There was no place. Behind the sheer curtain, maybe. In the dark, she might not be seen if she was quiet and didn't move.

She pulled the curtain around her. She could see through it, but it made the already dim room even dimmer. The blowing fan was the only noise. Nothing moved except the oscillating shadows of the fan blades beating the stale air through the room. The green flash of the clock on the CD player caused an eerie, strobing light.

A dark shape slowly emerged from the hallway and moved into the room. Large. Huge. Black.

CHAPTER 41

Chin pulled up to the address of the caller. A balding man, wearing two days worth of whiskers and a torn up, soiled T-shirt, met him halfway up the walk.

"I saw her. I saw Jezebel. Is there a reward?"

"Where did you see her?" Chin asked skeptically.

"Right here, in the street in front of the house."

"When was this, sir?"

"Five or six minutes ago."

"What exactly did you see? How big was it?"

"Biggest damned dog I've ever seen. Her head came up to here." The man motioned with his hand to his Adam's apple.

Chin began to take the man more seriously. "Why are you so sure it was Jezebel?"

"Shit, there ain't another dog that damn big, is there? She was one of those Great Danes, all black. She had dog tags that sparkled in the streetlight. I'd just got off of second shift, and I was walking up to the door when she ran by."

"Ran by? Which way did she go?"

"Right down the middle of the street going that way," the man said, pointing up the street in the direction of the MacGreggor house.

"Oh, God, Sarah!" Chin exclaimed and ran back to the van.

"Hey, ain't there some kind of a reward? What about my reward?"

Chin turned the van around in the man's driveway, leaving black tire marks going in and coming out.

"Sarah, can you hear me?" he called into the microphone, knowing he was hopelessly out of range.

*_*_*

Hill froze to the wall with her arms down tight against her sides. The huge black shadow walked slowly into the room and over to the old recliner without noticing her. It whined and looked into the seat of the chair and sniffed at the toys.

Hill's jaw trembled. She clenched her teeth tight to keep them from chattering. The dusty curtain irritated her nose but she wasn't about to sneeze. She swallowed hard to suppress it.

The shadow stopped still. Something was wrong. It must have sensed Hill's presence. She'd been discovered.

The dark apparition's head snapped in Hill's direction. It sniffed the air, snout raised. There was no question. It looked directly to her, its dark eyes glistening in the nearly absent light. A sparkle of light flashed from its neck from the diamond in its dog tags.

"Oh, God, no!" Hill whined low.

A deep rumble came from the shadow in response.

It moved toward Hill, slowly, guardedly.

She shouldn't make another sound. She shouldn't breath any more than was absolutely necessary. Maybe if she stayed still, it wouldn't see her as a threat and wouldn't bother her. Stay still like Mr. MacGreggor did in his recliner. It bothered him. Killed him. Tore his throat open. Nearly severed his head, yet he was no threat. She could run, try to defend herself like the police officers probably did. They were killed. Didn't have a chance. No escape.

It moved to the other side of the window, eyes fixed on Hill. It was nearly as tall as she was. The shadows and the sheer curtain didn't allow Hill to see it clearly. For all she knew, maybe this huge thing wasn't a dog at all but something supernatural. A real monster. Even as a dog, this thing was a real monster.

It looked away from her for a moment, head cocked, apparently hearing or sensing something. It looked back at Hill and moved even closer, now with its muzzle inches from her face. Hill stiffened.

It turned away and walked past her, brushing against Hill's arm.

"Sarah, can you hear me?" Chin cried in desperation over the radio, finally in range.

"Chin, help! She's here!" Hill pried the words from her throat.

It growled a vicious reply.

"Oh, God, Chin, she's got me!"

"Hang on, Sarah. I'm coming. Run for the door or a window!"

"Can't, I'm blocked!"

Another ferocious growl.

"Shoot her!"

"Rifle's in other room!"

The monstrous apparition responded with a deafening growl, followed by three sharp barks.

"Oh, shit, this is it. She's saying grace. I'm a midnight snack!"

Bright lights exploded through the windows of the living room, and the sound of Chin's van jumping the curb came from outside. He'd brought the van right up to the porch.

The giant ghost-like shadow ran to the other side of the room. It turned and ran toward Hill. She cowered down into a ball with her arms over her face.

With a shattering crash, it smashed through the window beside her, and the shadow was gone.

Chin came running through with his tranquilizer rifle at the ready.

"Sarah! You all right?" he yelled and ran to her side. She still knelt in a ball.

"I want out of this shit! I've had enough. I quit!"

CHAPTER 42

It was foggy in Tony Parker's dreams again. And again, in the middle of the street, a giant, black Great Dane appeared. She marched down the street as if knowing where she was going.

This time, something white and shiny like porcelain glowed in the fog behind her. It was like a mime's face or perhaps an oriental *bugaku* mask. It was a terrible, pain-filled face with no eyes, only empty holes. It flashed in and out. The mask grew larger and larger. Its expression changed into a smile; clown like, with blood dripping down the corners of its large, grinning lips. It faded away when Jezebel reached the curb in front of Parker's house.

She paused again, looking at the door. She turned and walked toward it. Small puddles on the wet sidewalk splashed as she walked. She stopped at the porch and stared at the front door. The doorknob turned. The latch clicked. The door inched open until it was wide, but there was no one behind it. Jezebel walked in and up the steps toward the bedrooms. She passed Nick's room without looking. The same for little Audrey's room. She nosed the master bedroom door open and walked to Parker's side of the bed. Without looking to Julie, the huge animal glared down at Tony Parker's face only inches away.

*_*_*

The ringing telephone erupted inside Tony Parker's skull. His brain throbbed. It felt as if the phone had launched a high-voltage probe through his ear. He looked around the bright, sunlit room. The vacuum sweeper was on down the hall. He remembered his concussion and felt the bandage around his head. He yanked it off and threw it on the floor. The phone on the nightstand rang again. He cupped his hands over his face, remembering the night before, and wished it had been a bad dream.

A third annoying ring came. When he leaned over to answer it, he felt sick and, instead, lay straight down. Julie rushed into the room.

"I'm sorry, honey. I should have remembered to turn this phone off. How are you feeling this morning?" Julie asked and reached for the phone.

Parker nodded slowly, confirming he was alive.

"Hello. . . . Yes. . . . Hi, Patsy, how are you...? Oh...? Oh, my God, are you okay?" she said and turned away from Parker, obviously trying to shield him from the conversation. "Oh, I'm so sorry! If there is anything we can do, please let us know. . . . No, don't worry about Tony. You know him. It'll take a few days, but I'm sure he'll be fine.... Yes, thanks for calling. Again, I'm so sorry. You take care now, you hear...? Good-bye." She hung up the phone and looked at him, the tears already forming in her eyes.

Parker didn't know if he could take anymore bad news. He asked anyway, "What?"

Julie sat next to him on the bed and ran her hand down the side of his face to his shoulder.

"Honey," she said as her tears began to stream, "it's Doc. He's dead!"

Parker stared at her in a trance.

"How?" he asked, hoping his Native American friend had made a peaceful trip to meet the Great Spirit in the sky.

"They think it was that dog, Jezebel," she said.

Parker gritted his teeth. Once again the pain of a friend's death hit hard and sank like an ax blade into his heart. He lay staring up at the ceiling, Julie hugging his chest, crying.

Suddenly, he bolted up and pushed Julie to the side.

"I've got to do something! Something has to be done, now! I've got to stop this killing!" he said, standing up.

"What can you do? You're not well. Please, Tony, lie down," Julie pleaded.

Parker looked down at his feet. The carpet was wet. He walked to the bedroom door, feeling with his feet as he went. It was wet the entire way but not wet out of the pathway to the door. He thought of the dream—if it had been a dream.

"What's wrong sweetheart?" Julie asked.

"The floor's wet. Why is the floor wet?"

"I don't know."

"Come on, Julie," he demanded, loud and annoyed. "Why the hell is the floor wet?"

Julie started shaking. "I really don't know. I didn't spill anything."

Parker rushed through the hallway and down the steps to the front entryway. The carpet was wet. The tile in front of the door was wet. The door was ajar. He stared at it for a moment and then ran up the steps past Julie.

"Please, tell me what's wrong, Tony."

He ran to the baby's room and briefly watched his daughter. She was breathing. She slept peacefully in her bed. He ran to Nick's room. Nick wasn't there.

"Where's Nick?"

"I don't know."

"You don't know? What the hell do you mean, you don't know?" he said, running to her and grabbing her by the arms.

He glared at her. Fear filled her face. For the first time in their long acquaintance, he was giving her a reason to be afraid of him. Deathly afraid. He tried to calm himself.

"It's Jezebel. Don't you see? She's been here!" Parker screamed.

Parker couldn't tell if the look on Julie's face was of horror or disbelief.

"Mommy, Daddy," a small voice came from the stairway, "What are you guys doing? Kissy-huggy again?"

It was Nick. He was fine. They both ran to him and hugged him.

"It must have been Yankee," Julie said. "Nick let him in this morning. He was probably wet."

Parker said nothing.

Julie helped him back to bed. He didn't fight to stay awake. He was exhausted from the excitement. His head was spinning again. He soon fell into a deep, restful sleep that was not interrupted by either man or beast.

Tony Parker slept until early evening and got up hungry. Julie fixed him supper and turned in early, completely spent. Parker carried Nick to bed after he fell asleep in his lap watching television. Audrey hadn't made a sound for an hour, so he looked in on her to make sure she was all right. She lay in her baby bed on her stomach with thumb in mouth, fast asleep. Parker patted his daughter gently on the back and walked out of the room.

The house was a lonely place that night. Painful memories kept slipping into his head, and he did his best to fight them off. He decided to let Yankee in from the back yard to keep him company.

The two sat together in the living room. Parker sat in the middle of the couch, petting Yankee, who sat at his feet with his head on the cushion next to Parker's leg. Yankee looked up at his master, a sadness in his eyes that went beyond their droopiness as if sensing his master's pain. He gave Parker one of his patented chimpanzee whines.

They sat together quietly.

Parker's mind drifted from place to place, time-to-time. He thought of his childhood, his high-school days, his hitch in the Marines, in Nam, his good times with Julie, with the kids, and with Jack—and Doc.

There would be no poker party this Friday night. Parker

remembered Doc saying he wouldn't miss it, no matter who died. He frowned and shook his head.

Now, there would be two funerals to attend, probably on Friday or Saturday. There would be much more grief to deal with. Sadie and her girls and Patsy would be hard to console.

So much had happened in such a short period of time. Parker felt numb. It was all so unbelievable. It was a nightmare he was yet to wake up from.

He began to analyze what had taken place over the past few days. He thought of all the needless deaths. Why had all these people and these dogs died? Rabies? That's what the test results said, at least about two of them, so far. What if it wasn't rabies? What if it was something diabolical and plotted?

Parker speculated, trying to put all the pieces together. It was more of a game than anything, a serious, *what if* game that kept his mind off the reality of the deaths of two good friends.

Who would be hurt the most by this diabolical plot? The city? Yes. The police department? Yes. Who else? Himself—himself, personally.

Parker sat up straight. The initials on the notes. The *TP* did stand for Tony Parker. They must. He couldn't deny it any longer. If this was some kind of a plot, some madman's revenge, it was reasonable to believe he was dead in the center of it. All the problems, the deaths, the bad publicity. He might not have a job to go to on Monday. But, he hadn't personally been attacked, not a primary target for attack—yet.

A shiver raced up his spine. He looked down at Yankee, and Yankee looked back at him with the same sad look. Jezebel was still out there. Maybe she would be his assassin. But who would want to turn Parker's life upside down like this? Someone jealous, or seeking revenge? Hardessy, jealous of the relationship between Sarah and him? Haskins, jealous of his relationship with Julie and wanting revenge? Maybe.

The phone rang. Parker sprang up to catch it before it rang again. "Hello."

"Hi, Tony, how are you feeling?"

"Oh, Sarah. A lot better, thanks."

"I heard about Dr. White Cloud. I'm sorry. I know you two were close. Sheik loved him, too."

"You haven't had Sheik in for rabies shots in the last week have you?"

"No, he had his rabies booster five months ago, and it's been over a month since I had him in for eczema. Sheik should be okay, right?"

"Yeah—that is, I think so. At least, thus far, all of the attacks have been from animals that had been there within the last week and received their rabies shots. I heard they think it was Jezebel that got Doc," Parker said. "Have you heard why?"

"Well, I guess he was really slashed up. Had a lot of deep punctures, too. It sure wasn't any Chihuahua."

"Anything else? Other clues?"

"No, that's all I heard. Something else happened last night, Tony."

"What's that?"

"Now, don't go getting all worked up about this. You're out of commission, and there's nothing you can do."

"Sure, what's going on?"

"I saw Jezebel."

"What? You saw her? Where? When?"

"I saw her, and I blew it. I could have had her, but I laid my damn rifle down and missed my chance. Tommy Chin and I tried to spring a trap on her at MacGreggor's house. It turns out she's been there every night at around midnight. She jumped through a plate-glass window and got away."

"Damn, what time was it? When was Doc killed?"

"This must have been right after she killed him. The coroner said Doc died at about ten thirty. She was at MacGreggor's right on schedule, at midnight."

"Three miles in an hour and a half. Plenty of time. Was anyone hurt? You and Chin all right?"

"Yeah, but I was scared shitless for a while. She's big, Tony, real big.

I couldn't believe it. I couldn't see her that well. It was dark, and I was trying to hide behind a curtain, but she came right up to me and stared eye to eye. I've never been so scared."

"I can imagine. What about tonight?"

"I doubt if she'll show, tonight. She's bound to be leery about returning. Besides, Chin's going to be in the house with three armed cops. She'll smell a trap." Hill paused with a deep breath. "I've got one last thing to tell you."

Parker heard her swallow hard. He didn't ask what.

"—Good-bye," she said, her voice quavering.

"Good bye? What do you mean?"

"I quit today. I've had enough."

Parker didn't answer. He just listened, caught off guard.

"I know it's a bad time, but I've had it. I've got this degree in zoology going to waste. I've been sitting here, dusting off the old résumé. I'm gonna send it to every zoo in the country. Someone's gotta need me, somewhere."

"I need you—I mean, you're the best officer I've got."

"Yeah, well, if you really did need me, I'd stay, but I know better. It's no secret I've stuck around this long because of you. It's time for me to concede defeat. There's no future for us."

Parker couldn't comment. He had to let her go. He was married and very much in love with Julie. His feelings toward Sarah didn't matter. They were immoral. Adulterous.

"Speaking of having futures, have you had any more—symptoms?" Hill asked.

"If you mean to ask if I've gone nuts lately, no, I haven't. Really. I feel fine. It must have just been stress. But I still owe you an apology."

"Don't worry about it. Nothing damaged beyond repair. But you'd better go in and get those post-exposure shots. I found out this afternoon the Sand Creek skunk tested positive."

Parker closed his eyes. He had little doubt now. He had rabies. But it was too late for treatment. After the onset of the symptoms, the prognosis was always the same in humans. Death—a very horrible death. There was too much to do, this Jezebel thing to figure out before that happened. His last hours couldn't be wasted in a hospital.

"Yeah—all right."

"Don't you bullshit me, Tony. You go in and get those shots, or I'll report you to the city manager, and I'll tell Julie, too. It's not like they're that bad anymore, you big pussy. Hell, I started them today, just to be safe. Now, promise me you will, too. And keep in mind, I'll check and make sure you have."

"All right, Sarah, all right. I will." He was glad that, at least, she had been smart enough to start the treatment. After all, she'd been around the rabid skunk, could have gotten its saliva in a small scratch, an infinitesimal droplet into her eye, onto her lip. *Who am I kidding,* he thought. *I kissed her, drew blood. Oh, God, the kids—Julie.* They would go first thing in the morning to start treatment.

"You'd better. Ah, I won't keep you any longer. I just wanted to check and make sure my ex-boss was okay. Ain't it a bitch, I've finally got time off, and now, I can't sleep."

"Yeah, well, try anyway. Thanks for having the guys bring my truck back. And, Sarah—thanks for calling, uh, really. Thanks." This was it. He might never talk to her or see her again.

"Sure, Tony. Well, good-bye. Take care of yourself."

"Okay—good-bye, Sarah—oh, and, Sarah...."

"Yes, Tony," she answered anxiously.

"—Uh, well—take care."

"Bye, Tony."

Parker sat, watching the television without knowing what was on. He'd lost another friend; another very cherished friend. She wasn't dead, but still, he'd lost her. He knew he wouldn't see Sarah Hill again. He'd never look into her beautiful, blue eyes. Never see her teasing smile. Never feel the tingle in his body that she caused when she was near. Of course, with rabies, there would be a lot he'd never again do.

CHAPTER 43

It was eight o'clock. The television was tuned to channel two. The last program had gone to commercial before the next one came on.

Tony Parker sat back on the couch and started playing his *what if* mystery game. The common denominators: Parker's job, Dr. White Cloud's practice, and the *Bible* pages and letter to the editor left at the attacks.

"Okay, someone is out to get me and make me suffer, then probably kill me," Parker said to a bewildered Yankee.

It was someone having to do with Doc. Doc was dead. Patsy couldn't hurt a fly. Truong had no reason to. Besides, he just didn't seem the type.

Parker thought back to his recent visits to Doc's. He relived them in his mind. He remembered driving up on Saturday. Seeing the Bumfields. The outside phone bell rang.

The bell. When he was there on Tuesday, Truong came out and said the state called. Tests were positive—and the look Patsy gave Truong. *Why?* The outside bell *hadn't* rung. The university hadn't called because the outside bell hadn't rung.

Truong was supposed to take the heads up to Manhattan for the tests, but maybe he didn't. When they were in Truong's room, they decided they were going to call the university about the tests after they took care of the greyhounds. Parker tripped over Truong at the doorway. He'd been eavesdropping at the door. They all went outside, except Truong, and got the dogs out of the truck. That's when he said they called but there was no bell.

He had lied. Why? So they would think he'd taken the heads in? So they would think the dogs had rabies when they really didn't? Truong had probably been the one who called the health department, posing as a doctor from Kansas State to make sure no one would find out right away. But why was he playing such a crazy game? What would he have to gain?

He put all that aside for a moment and thought about the victims of the other attacks. Roary Rapids, nothing gained on that one. It did tear Parker's life apart. The speakerphone. It was on. Mrs. Nightingale was on the phone when she was attacked, but Mrs. Taylor was in the shower. It didn't make sense.

There were missing items: a diamond studded letter opener with sharp serrated edges, five hundred thousand in cash—and Parker's mind.

Parker sighed as the TV station went to commercial again. *Serrated-edged letter opener; that would make some deep puncture wounds and slash someone up pretty good.*

Haskins came on the TV and interrupted Parker's thoughts.

"Tonight on *First at the Scene* news, we'll look at a city under siege by rabid dogs. We'll also interview the assistant to the late Dr. White Cloud, who was killed last night by the giant killer dog, Jezebel. Now, here's a brief look at that interview."

"Dr. White Cloud, good man," Truong said, "good to animals."

The picture came back to Haskins, and by his stupid smirk, it was evident he was about to attempt some type of humorous journalism, once again at an inappropriate time.

"Mr. Truong will also have this message for your dog."

Silence. The TV showed Truong with a dog whistle. He blew into it, but nothing seemed to come out.

But, Yankee's ears perked up. Parker felt the dog's head jerk as he petted him. He looked down to see Yankee's lip start to quiver, then his snout wrinkle into a snarl. Yankee looked up at Parker out of the sides of his eyes. He had a strange look, wild and faraway. He growled a low horrible drone unlike Parker had ever heard from him before.

"Yankee?"

Another growl.

"No, Yankee, no! Bad dog!"

Yankee licked his chops. He appeared puzzled. He growled again. He attacked.

Parker tried to get up from the couch, but Yankee leaped at his throat and pushed him back. His jaws locked around Parker's wrist, as he tried to protect his throat. The dog's huge canine incisors had raked across Parker's neck, and it began to bleed. He pushed Yankee off and over the back of the couch. He was unprepared for the next attack. Yankee came over the back of the sofa, leaping again for his throat. Parker grabbed the back of the couch to steady himself, but the weight of the two of them made it topple over forward and Parker was pinned underneath. His head hit the floor hard. It sent the world spinning again. Yankee tugged at his wrist, but he couldn't feel the pain that should have been there.

Darkness. He passed out.

CHAPTER 44

The dog saw Parker wasn't moving. He heard someone coming down the stairs and dropped Parker's arm, then moved to a dark corner in the downstairs hall by the stairway.

*_*_*

Julie peeked out from the top of the steps, wearing a Kansas City Royals nightshirt that came down to about mid thigh.

"Honey?" she called. "Tony, what's going on down there, are you all right?"

Julie came down the steps slowly, cautiously looking to see what was going on. "Tony, is everything all right?"

She walked down to the bottom step and saw the over-turned couch with Tony's bloody arm sticking out.

"Tony!" she shrieked.

Julie turned quickly to see Yankee step out of the darkness. He announced his presence with a growl, moon eyed, pupils dilated and dark. Saliva drooled in strings from both sides of his mouth.

Julie ran up the stairs.

Yankee followed at full speed.

Julie screamed.

Nick stood at the top of the stairs, rubbing his eyes. "What's wrong, Mommy?"

Without answering, she grabbed him up and ran for the master bedroom door and the phone inside. Audrey's door was closed. She would be safe. Julie made it through the master bedroom door, slamming it behind, just as the big brute hit it with his front paws with a bang.

She ran to the phone and dialed 911 but misdialed.

"Oh, damn!" she exclaimed.

Nick looked confused and began crying.

The dog jumped at the door repeatedly, striking it hard.

Julie could hear the baby also begin to cry from her room. The jumping against the door stopped. She paused to hear what was going on. The only sound was Audrey's crying. It sounded miles away to her anxious heart.

The dog started up again, jumping against the door. This time it sounded different. It wasn't the master bedroom door. It was Audrey's door.

She punched 911 correctly this time and waited for a response. A strange sort of cracking came when Yankee hit the baby's door the last time. It puzzled her. Still no response. The Wichita 911 dispatchers had been overwhelmed with prank calls and false alarms concerning mad dogs, lately. This was apparently the case tonight.

The banging stopped. The house, quiet. Eyes shifting, ears straining. A crash came from Audrey's room.

"My God, the baby bed!" Julie screamed and threw the phone down. She ran Nick to the master bathroom. "Don't move. Do you hear me? Mommy will be right back," she said in her calmest possible voice to the still crying child.

She slammed the door shut and ran back to the master bedroom door, grabbing a fireplace poker from its stand on the way. After a deep breath, she swung the door open.

Julie screamed like an attacking Apache as she rounded the

doorway and charged into Audrey's open bedroom. The baby bed was overturned and the baby was gone.

"Oh, you dirty-son-of-a-bitch," she yelled. She held the fireplace poker above her head and turned to go look for them.

"Where's my baby?" she cried.

Julie stopped by the steps and listened. The baby didn't cry anymore. Only silence. Even Nick had quieted.

Had the dog killed Audrey? No, she couldn't bear to even consider it. Audrey was still alive. She was going to find her.

Julie glanced in the other upstairs bath. Nothing. She popped her head into Nick's room. Still nothing.

"Downstairs. They must be downstairs," she muttered. She descended the staircase slowly.

Still, no sound. Every few steps, she paused, listening, hoping to hear something, anything.

At the bottom of the steps she stopped. Tony's arm still stuck out from under the couch.

"Tony!" she whispered, insistently, "Tony!"

She heard the creaking of a door upstairs. She recognized it as the master bath door. Nick must have come out.

"Damn, doesn't he ever mind?"

At least he was upstairs. Yankee was down—she thought. She started back up to tell Nick to get back to the bathroom, then saw the top of the door to Audrey's room move. Yankee had been behind it. He'd been hiding. Julie heard the big dog's heavy feet tromp across the floor.

"Oh, no, Nick!" She ran up the stairs in time to see Yankee dart into the master bedroom. He no longer had Audrey. He'd hidden her, like a wolf might hide a rabbit it had caught until things were safe to devour it.

The high-pitched scream of the six-year-old boy shot through the house. "No, Yankee, we're not playing monsters."

Yankee gave a snarling bark. He pounced at the boy as Julie ran into the room.

Nick jumped on the waterbed and scampered across on hands and knees to the other side. The dog jumped onto the bed but turned, distracted by Julie.

"Hey, get back, you." She held the poker out in front of her in a threatening pose.

Julie saw Nick run into the closet and climb up the clothes to the shelf above the clothes rod. *Good boy*. He'd be safe there, for now.

Yankee stood in the middle of the bed, off balance from the motion of the water, snarling at Julie. He would lunge at any second. She lunged first, hoping to catch him off guard.

Julie pushed the poker out like a bayonet on the end of a rifle.

Yankee moved. The sharp end hit the waterbed mattress, rupturing it. He came back around and clamped onto Julie's forearm. She jerked it away. The flesh tore, horribly, and blood dripped.

"You son-of-a-bitch, where's my baby?" she yelled, hitting the dog on the back of the head with the poker. It didn't seem to faze him. With the last whack, it slipped from her hands. The dog left the bed. He squared up on her, eight feet away. Without a weapon, she didn't stand a chance.

He barked and charged.

She turned and bolted into the master bath doorway but was unable to get the door closed before he came through. It caught him at the neck.

More frantic, hoarse barking.

Julie held the door as tight as she could against his thick neck, hoping she could strangle him. He struggled. He pushed in jerks, trying to advance into the room. Frothing slobber flew from his mouth. He lunged hard and caught Julie's thigh, raking his teeth across it. She pushed and hit at his big, soft nose with the heel of her hand and finally repelled him, but his head still stuck through the door.

Julie twisted her face in agony. Blood ran down to her slipper. His hot, slobbering breath puffed on her leg. She held the door, terrified. More blood ran down her arm to her elbow, then dripped onto the side of Yankee's distorted, angry face. It made her feel nauseous, and she wanted to vomit. She couldn't hold the door for long, she knew that. But as long as she did, everyone else was safe. She would be killed as soon as she let go, no doubt. Maybe the police would come. Maybe the 911 operator had picked up and traced the call.

"Yankee! Bad dog, Yankee! Get back!" Tony's angry voice boomed from the stairs.

Julie was relieved but no less frightened.

Yankee stopped struggling. He stood motionless for a moment, his head still protruding into the bathroom. For an instant, she thought he might be back to his old self again. She eased up on the door only slightly. As soon as she did, the dog yanked his head back. Her body weight slammed the door.

Yankee barked out, even fiercer than before.

She could hear him bounding like a grizzly bear across the floor.

"Oh, no, Tony, Tony, I'm sorry," she cried.

She heard a muffled thump.

CHAPTER 45

The only light on at Doc White Cloud's clinic was in the reception area. Truong sat at Patsy's desk with the phone in his right hand and right index finger holding down the button. He put a stack of a dozen files back into the *F* section in the file drawer, then pulled out a dozen and a half more from the *G*s. He opened the first file then punched the listed telephone number.

"Hello, Mrs. Gabriel…? This Truong, at Dr. White Cloud clinic. . . . Yes, very bad about doctor. . . . Me like you watch Channel Two News with dog, uh, Tip, tonight ten o'clock. Me interviewed. Me have special treat, uh, kind of experiment for Tip. Me make Tip do trick from television. . . . Me can't say now. You and Tip watch, then you see. Thank you. Bye."

--*

Tony Parker had waited, mid-way, on the steps and let Yankee leap at him. He sidestepped at the last second and pushed him away and down the steps, then ran to the master bedroom and shut the door. Julie hurried out to greet him.

"Oh, Tony!" She hugged him.

"The kids?" he asked.

He saw Julie look to the closet. Clothes lay on the floor. She ran to the closet and found Nick up on the shelf and helped him down. Tony stood guard by the door.

"Audrey isn't here. I don't know where she is!" she cried. "He had her. The son-of-a-bitch took her and hid her somewhere!"

"Damn!" Tony exclaimed. "Call 911."

"I tried, but I couldn't get through."

"Well, try again, this time don't stop trying until you do. And whatever you do, don't open this door, no matter what happens, until I tell you or the police get here."

"What are you going to do?"

"I'm going to find Audrey."

Parker opened the bedroom door and looked out, just in time to see Yankee run by and down the steps, dragging what looked like a doll in his mouth.

He ran out the door, closing it quickly behind, then flew down the steps behind the dog. Yankee turned sharply at the bottom and faced him.

The Saint Bernard growled, wild eyed. Dilated eyes. Not Yankee's.

Audrey hung from his mouth by the back of her neck. His huge mouth covered the child's throat. Her eyes were closed. She was silent, but he could see no blood. Any movement form Parker could cause Yankee to sever poor little Audrey's head with not much more than a twitch from the dog's powerful jaws.

Parker had only one plan. If he raised his fist as if he were going to strike the dog, maybe he would drop the baby to defend himself. What would happen after that, he didn't know. Of course, instead of dropping her, he could just go ahead and chomp.

He had to take the chance. He had to get her from him, now.

"Bad dog, Yankee," he said, raising his fist "Bad dog!"

It worked. The dog dropped the baby and went for Parker's fist. Parker came around with the other hand and punched him square on top of the head, dazing the dog. He jumped on Yankee's back and got him in a strangle hold from behind with his forearm. He'd used this hold many times before in Marine basic training when the recruits learned to choke each other out. In a few seconds, Yankee would be unconscious. A few more, there would be brain damage. A few more and Yankee would die.

"Julie, come out here and get Audrey!" Parker yelled out.

She came running down the steps.

Parker kept Yankee in the death grip. The dog's eyes closed half-way and became blank.

"Damn it, Yankee. Why'd it have to happen to you?" he said softly into the dog's ear. Yankee continued to struggle for a few more seconds, then quit and lay limp.

"Is she alive?" Parker asked, looking up at Julie as she inspected Audrey.

She shook her gently. "Come on, baby, wake up. Come on, Audrey."

She paused and looked at the limp little body in her hands. Julie began crying. "Oh, Tony, I don't know. I think she's dead!"

Parker dropped the dog, got up and held onto the baby with Julie. Nick ran down and grabbed onto both of them.

"Come on, Audrey, open those pretty little eyes," he said in a soft, yet frantic, tone. Then, in anguish he cried out, "Oh, God, please don't take her from us. Please don't take her, too!"

Audrey's limp body twitched. It twitched again. Her little face wrinkled up into a frown. She began crying, beautiful crying.

Julie chuckled, a sort of nervous, relieved laugh, and they stood together, hugging and laughing and even crying a little.

* - * - *

They were too busy rejoicing to notice Yankee's body also twitching just a few feet away. His eyelids rolled open.

* - * - *

Something brushed against Parker's leg.

"Are you going to be a good dog now?" Nick asked. "No more playing monsters."

Lightning bolts shot through Parker's body. He turned quickly. Yankee stood behind.

Julie screamed. Parker handed the baby over to her, shielding them with his body.

Yankee cocked his ears and head. He stood with a curious look, pupils back to normal, wagging his tail, "*Uh-uh-uh-uh-errr,*" he said in his old way of chimpanzee talk.

"Thank God!" Parker said, "I think he's snapped out of it."

Nick began to pet him, but Parker knew he had to be sure the danger was over.

"Sorry, boy, but you're getting locked up."

He took him out the door and led him to the cage in back of the truck.

Parker came back in the house with head spinning, feeling confused and nauseous. He felt the symptoms again.

"What just happened here, Tony? What's going on?" Julie asked, still holding the baby, who'd finally settled down, and stroking Nick's hair.

He put his arms around all of them and said in a soft voice, "I don't know. It just doesn't add up."

He looked at each member of his family, thinking how fortunate he was to still have them.

CHAPTER 46

Parker phoned 911 and cancelled the emergency call. He and Julie inspected Audrey carefully before deciding not to take her to the emergency room. She seemed to be fine, except for a few red marks on her neck. Her soft, tender baby skin hadn't even been broken. What they all needed now was sleep. Tomorrow, they could have her checked out.

After Julie and Tony bandaged each other's injuries, Julie took the kids upstairs, and Parker sat down in his recliner and started to play the *what if* game again, his time running out. Now, there was a given: Yankee was set off by a dog whistle, blown by Truong on TV.

What if Truong had caused all of the recent dog attacks? What if he could do the same thing he'd done on TV over the phone? That would explain the speakerphone in Spencer's office and the phone being off the hook at Mrs. Nightingale's. It could explain the others. Maybe he'd done it from outside the houses.

If that were the case, it would explain why Truong didn't want to take the dogs' heads to the lab to be tested for rabies.

But still, the biggest piece of the puzzle was why. What could be his motive? Robbery, maybe? There was the possibility that half a million dollars had been taken from MacGreggor's, along with a diamond-studded letter opener. That one was easy to get away with. No one knew of the money for sure, and only Mrs. Crane knew of the letter opener. There was no obvious reason for the other attacks. The only thing they had in common, with the exception of Pastor Santini, was that they all had dogs and had taken them to Dr. White Cloud's.

Once again, why? It all pointed to Parker. Truong was out to get him. But he hardly knew this Truong character, let alone ever gave the man a reason to destroy Parker's world. But why make Parker suffer? Why not just kill Parker and get it over with?

Another big question was how. With a simple dog whistle?

Everything seemed such a mess. It was hard to concentrate. Parker's head throbbed, and his body ached. It must be the rabies. He didn't have much time. He had to fight it until he could put an end to this madness. He had to tell someone about Truong, but who would believe him? How could he prove it? He couldn't think clearly.

Parker grimaced, frustrated.

It was all too much. Overwhelming. He wanted to be with the ones he loved. He wanted to run away with them, away from this mess. But he could not run from the rabies.

He lifted from his seat, stiff, sore joints complaining, and went upstairs and found the family in Nick's bed. With the master bedroom's waterbed torn open, he understood why. He squeezed in and lay with them on the little twin bed until he was sure they all slept. It was a tight fit, but the need to be with them and feel their hearts beat superseded any need for comfort.

He heard Julie's breath slow, then calm to a peaceful sleeping rhythm and suddenly realized the danger he put them in. *Rabies is a very contagious disease,* he thought.

He rolled out of bed and stared back at his soundly sleeping family. He must leave. He could no longer endanger his family with the rabies or this madman Truong.

Parker walked outside and sat on the tailgate of the truck, looking in the cage at a very sad Yankee. He had to clear his head, but every minute that passed made it harder for him to think rationally.

--*

Ten blocks away, Sarah Hill fixed herself a rum and Coke after a hot shower and sat down in her bathrobe to read a romance paperback. Sheik lay next to her on the sofa, and she fondled his neck and back between sips.

She looked at the open book but didn't read the words, thinking of how the next few weeks were going to be so much of a change. She was about to leave everything she loved: the town, the friends, the job. She even loved her little apartment although the dishwasher didn't work and the manager was an asshole.

Then, there was Tony Parker.

Hill smiled, thinking of him.

She'd never wanted a man like she wanted Tony. She'd done everything she could to get him. Still, he'd gotten away even though she knew he wanted her as much. Maybe it was that kind of married-man morals that made her love him. It wasn't very common in the modern world of cheating and indiscriminate sex. He'd come close to slipping, once. But she wondered if even then he would have followed through if they hadn't been interrupted. She was sure there was something more to it than that and she hoped it wasn't rabies. After all, he had been through one hell of a lot. A lesser man could easily have had a nervous breakdown by now.

Hill took a sip from her drink and thought of how shocked Parker had been in the truck when she started sucking on his finger. She giggled. It was so much fun to tease and fluster him. She was an old movie buff, and to her, Tony Parker was as close to Gary Cooper, reincarnated, as a man could get. At times, he was also like the father she never knew. Hers was killed in SCUBA accident when she was three.

Tony Parker symbolized security although he wasn't rich. He had a confidence always evident in any situation, except when she teased him. That was another reason she was so attracted to him. She knew how to pull his strings when no one else could.

Hill took another sip and smiled again. A tear spilled from her eye and dripped into her drink.

The phone rang.

She laid the book down, a little irritated that her much needed peace had been disturbed.

"Yeah," she answered.

"Hello, this Truong from Doctor White Cloud clinic.

"Who? Oh, yeah, I remember you.

"Me have something like dog, Sheik, hear."

"You have something like dog Sheik hear?" she mocked. "Get real, what is this?"

"Please. Very important. This help Mr. Parker. Sheik there?"

"Yeah, he's here. But I don't think he's accepting phone calls."

"Please. Very important!"

"Sheesh! All right, all right!" She held the phone out. "Hey, Sheik, it's for you."

Sheik raised his head, ears perked. After several seconds, Hill hadn't heard anything so she put the phone back to her ear.

"Come on, already, Sheik's a busy dog. He can't talk on the phone all night."

Nothing but a dial tone.

"Wow, what a weirdo. Sorry, Sheik, prank call."

She looked at Sheik. He looked back from the corners of his eyes. His snout wrinkled. An unfamiliar look flared in his eyes, and his pupils dilated.

He growled, low at first, then drew a breath and made the next complaint with more enthusiasm.

"Well, shit! Don't get pissed at *me*."

He turned his head toward her and growled again, this time topping it off with two sharp barks.

"What the hell's wrong with you?"

Hill put it all together fast. The call—Sheik acting like the rest.

She threw the phone at Sheik and ran for the bedroom.

Sheik caught the phone hard in his mouth and dropped it on the floor. He leaped off the sofa and raced for Hill, jumping on her back, sending her to her knees. He went for her throat. She ducked. The first try broke the skin, and Sheik ended up with a mouthful of bathrobe collar.

"*Aah*, he-elp! Somebody help me! Sheik, get off. Bad boy!"

She stood, causing the dog to roll off, and tried once more for the safety behind the bedroom door. Sheik lunged again, this time his fangs sunk deep into her thigh.

"*Ah-waa*, Sheik, you bastard!" Hill cried, falling to the floor.

She hit the dog in the eye, then on the end of the nose, with the bottom of her fist. He let go but struck again before she could crawl more than a foot. Now, he clamped onto her right calf. She yanked it from his mouth. The pain of tearing flesh, tendons, and muscles made her body quake. She screamed out in agony.

"*Owwww*, get away!"

Hill spotted the large glass candlestick holder her mother had sent her from Florida last Christmas. She grabbed it off a small table nearby as Sheik went for her other arm. She brought the holder down hard in the middle of his thick skull as he bit.

She cried out again.

The dog didn't let go. He had set his jaws like Vise Grips on her elbow.

She drew the big glass candlestick holder back as far as she could and slammed it between his eyes.

It fractured with a pop and fragments of glass flew.

Sheik sounded with a yelp, reeling back with several thick chunks of broken glass embedded in his snout. Hill had many of the jagged, shards stuck in her hand. That didn't matter now. She had to get away while she could.

Using her good elbow and the other hand, she crawled frantically toward the bedroom while dragging her injured leg. Clearing the door, she tried to kick it shut, but it bounced off Sheik's side as he burst into the room.

He went for her throat again. Hill screamed as she blocked with a swing of her arm. The dog grabbed her shoulder, puncturing deep into her body. The pain was so piercing she thought she would pass out.

Hill used all of the strength she had left to push loose from his powerful grip and scamper under the bed. This time, he caught her by the foot before she could pull it under.

CHAPTER 47

Parker seemed to be passing in and out of some sort of a stupor, at times thinking clearly, at other times confused and frightened. For now, his mind cleared.

He glanced at his watch and saw it was a quarter after nine. The ten-o'clock news would be on soon with Truong's interview. If any of the dogs that were in Doc's clinic in the last couple of months were near a TV when the news on Channel Two came on, there would be more attacks, maybe dozens more.

Parker sprang off of the tailgate and ran into the house. He had to warn Hill first. It could be too late. She may have already seen the preview with Sheik. The line was busy.

"Damn!" he said and hung up the phone, then ran out the door to the truck. He pulled out of the driveway quietly, trying not to wake Julie, and waited to turn the lights on until he was down the street.

"AC One to dispatcher," he panted, finding it hard to breathe.

"Dispatcher. Go ahead, Top Dog. Didn't expect to hear your voice so soon."

"Good, it's you, Tyrone. Listen very carefully. We have a major—disaster about to happen." He heaved, gasping for breath.

"Uh, sure, Tony. You okay?"

Parker didn't answer Tyrone's concern.

"First thing, you need to get a hold of the police chief. Tell him that if Channel Two News shows the interview with a guy named Truong tonight—there will be more dog attacks, possibly over a hundred of them. The chief will be the one—that will have to tell them not to air it. I don't think they'd believe me—they might believe him. Have him contact all of the TV and radio stations and cable, too. I want bulletins on every channel and station—instructing people to lock their dogs up."

"Damn, Top Dog, you for real?"

"I'm very serious, Tyrone. Now stick with me. Next, call the animal-control office. Have the officer on duty—I think it's Tommy Chin—have him meet me at Dr. White Cloud's clinic. We're going to have to get a hold of all of the dog owners that could be affected *tonight*. I'm guessing that there's—around two hundred of them. We'll call you as soon as we have their names and phone numbers, and we'll split them with you. You and the other dispatchers can divide those names up—and call them all immediately while we call our share from the clinic."

"What do we tell them? Don't let your dog watch the news tonight—it might be bad for him?"

"Damn it, Tyrone, I'm serious. I need your help. Tell them anything, I don't know. Tell them that their dogs—have been exposed to rabies and their last vaccination was defective. Have them lock them in a garage—or a vacant room—or a securely fenced-in backyard on a leash—until the police come. And above all else—tell them to keep their dogs away from their TVs—because it might excite them. Then, give the addresses to the police—and have them go pick the dogs up and bring them to the shelter for now. I don't know what we'll do with all of them—but we'll figure something out."

"You're sure about this?"

"Trust me. I'm sure."

"What if the chief doesn't go along with it, or Channel Two? It'll be a miracle if we can get a hold of that many people by ten."

"Well then—we have a real problem on our hands, don't we? I'm on my way to Dr. White Cloud's now. But, I'm stopping at Sarah Hill's on the way. Tell Chin not to go in—if he gets there before I do. Tell him to wait outside. There might be a madman there. His name is Truong. He saw him before at the clinic—when he took one of the dogs in. He's to stay clear of him. Truong could be very—dangerous. You got that?"

"Tony, you don't sound too good. You sure you're okay?"

"I asked if you understood, Tyrone. Do you?"

"Yeah, I got it, Top Dog."

"All right, then. Get busy."

"Right. Ah, uh-oh, it sounds like it's already started. We've got two dispatchers taking calls about dog attacks."

"Probably saw the preview I did. No time to lose, Tyrone."

If Truong's interview aired, there would be little chance of preventing all the attacks. The sooner they got the names, the more lives would be saved. He had to get those names quick. He reached over and opened the glove compartment and pulled out Jack's .357. If he ran into Truong, he might have to use it.

The first thing was to alert Hill. Parker ran up the stairs to Hill's third-floor apartment. His wrist throbbed, and he held his arm close to his stomach to hold Simpson's gun in his belt while he ascended the steps. Blood stained the front of his pants and the side of his collar.

He rang the doorbell and worked the knob. The door was locked. He beat on it. Maybe she was asleep already, but the lights were still on.

"Come on, Sarah, open up. It's me, Tony."

Still no answer. Parker put his ear to the door. There was a muffled sound. The TV—or maybe Sheik growling.

Parker stepped back and kicked just to the side of the knob, and the door blasted open, splintering the jamb.

"Sarah! Sarah!" he yelled out, running into the room.

Phone on the floor. Spots of blood leading to the bedroom.

He drew the gun and stepped into the bedroom doorway. Sheik had Hill's foot in his mouth and he was dragging Hill's limp body out from under the bed. The dog dropped her foot and pounced, open-mouthed, at her exposed throat.

Parker aimed and fired.

The dog reeled around, a red spot between his shoulders. Blood flowed from the side of his neck where the bullet passed through.

He snarled.

Parker pulled the trigger again.

The dog collapsed like a plumber's canvas bag full of pipe wrenches across Hill's legs, a bullet hole just in front of one ear.

He ran to Hill, falling to her side and lifted her head up to his lap.

"Sarah, wake up. Sarah," he pleaded.

She moved her head, and he saw that the wounds, although deep and mutilating, weren't immediately life threatening.

"Tony?" she said, coming to, "Tony, what happened?"

She frowned up at Parker's face, then at the gun. She looked down at Sheik, lying across her legs, and broke into tears.

"Oh, Sheik!" she cried, pulling his bloody head up to her chest. His beautiful, snow white, fur coat was matted and stained with blood.

"He called, Tony. That son-of-a-bitch called."

"Truong?"

"Yeah. And he asked to speak to Sheik. Then, he didn't say anything, but Sheik started going nuts!"

Sarah buried her face into Sheik's neck, crying.

Parker got up and called for an ambulance, then went back to her. He held her, trying to quiet her.

"Will there be more? Will there be more of this *shit*?" she asked.

"Truong is taped on an interview to be aired during Channel Two's ten-o'clock news. I think he plans to set off as many as another two hundred dogs."

"You've got to do something. I don't know how he does it, but you've got to stop him," she said. "Don't worry about me. I'll be all right. The ambulance will be here soon."

Parker looked into her beautiful blue eyes, now badly bloodshot. Her platinum hair was sopped in red tangles. Blood smudged her face. One deep slash was plowed across her right cheek. Her pink bathrobe was spotted in blood and her neck was covered in red. Her lovely, silky smooth right shoulder was exposed, and blood flowed down to her breast from two large gashes raked into her throat. Her thigh was badly injured and bloody. Muscle and bone were exposed on her calf. Parker gaped at her injuries.

Hill looked at him and said, "I guess my men will have to love me for my mind, now, huh?"

Parker tried to give her a reassuring grin.

"How about you?" she asked.

"No problem, sweetheart. I'm okay."

Sirens keened in the distance. The ambulance was only seconds away. Parker bent down and kissed Hill on her forehead. She reached up and kissed him on the lips. The kiss told Parker that there would never be another chance, that they would never be lovers, and never again be alone together.

He heard the ambulance stop in front, then hasty footsteps coming up the stairs.

"Bye, Tony," Hill said and pushed against his chest.

Parker tucked a pillow under her head, then rushed out the door.

CHAPTER 48

Patsy White Cloud sat alone in her big empty house less than a mile from Doc's clinic. Loneliness had set in, and a tear rolled down one cheek as she sat on the sofa, watching the *Dances With Wolves* videotape she'd given Doc last Christmas. It was his favorite movie. He'd told her that it made him feel young and free again.

She unbraided her long ebony hair and brushed it slowly down over her shoulders. She remembered how Doc had liked her long black hair. He had liked the way it shone in the low light of their bedroom when she brushed it before going to bed. He had liked the way it felt soft and silky.

Patsy drew a ragged, sobbing breath.

Scratching and whining came from the back door. Red was feeling the lonelies also and wanted inside. Patsy put the movie on pause and got up. When she looked out the window, she could see the big half-Irish setter, half-German shepherd looking up at her with sad, begging eyes, wagging his tail.

"Poor old Red."

She opened the door and looked out at him. Red sat and looked back, still wagging his tail. He'd been well trained and knew he wasn't to come in unless invited.

"What's wrong, Red? Lonely, too?"

A strange, chilling howl pierced the night's stillness.

Patsy looked up and scanned the neighborhood but could see nothing. Red was alert and also looking around.

"Oh, come on in, Red. We'll be lonely together."

Red wasn't interested now. He'd run over to the fence and began a low growl, the fur on the back of his neck standing up.

"It's all right, Red. Come on in," she pleaded.

Red hesitated for a moment, then turned and came back to her. They went inside, and Patsy locked the door behind them. Red went straight to the front window and looked out with the same low growl. Patsy scurried to his side.

A car, parked at the curb three houses down and across the street, had just turned its headlights out. She couldn't make out the type of vehicle or who was in it. It looked like it could be a white van like the clinic's. It was too dark. They both watched for a full two minutes and didn't see anyone get out.

"Oh, come on Red. It's nothing. Come on over and watch the movie with me."

She yanked at his collar, and he obeyed. They sat together on the sofa with Red's head in Patsy's lap. She patted his brow and pushed the play button to continue the movie.

"You miss ol' Doc, don't you, Red?" she asked, seeing the big dog look to the chair Doc used to sit in.

Red responded with a sad whine.

"I know, Red. I miss him, too," she said, scratching behind his ears.

Suddenly, Red sat up. He looked at the front door, then to the back.

The low growl got a little louder.

"Red?"

He wasn't responsive this time. He jumped off the sofa and headed toward the back door and began barking, pacing back and forth.

"Stop it, Red. You're scaring me. Is there somebody out there? No, there can't be. Now, you stop that this instant."

He continued, barking frantically.

"Stop it, Red. Stop it, or you're going out."

More barking.

"All right then." Patsy opened the door. "Get out!"

He ran past her and out the door. He continued raving, running back and forth in the yard, jumping up on the roof of his dog house under the kitchen window and then running back out into the yard again. Patsy watched from the back door.

"Fool dog. Probably some cottontail."

She closed and locked the door. Now she wasn't just lonely, but frightened, too. Red still barked frantically. Maybe it wasn't a rabbit. Maybe it was something else. Maybe it was Jezebel.

"I'll call Tony. He'll know what to do," she said aloud and headed for the phone in the kitchen.

As she walked past the sink, the window over it broke with a loud, shattering crash.

It was Red.

He landed on her shoulder.

She knocked him to the floor.

"Stop it, Red! What's got into you?"

Red replied with a furious growl, looking up at her from terrifying, dark eyes.

He leaped for her again.

Patsy held him away from her throat. He'd pushed her back to the cabinet. It was all she could do to keep him from tearing at her neck. The big dog was nearly her height when standing on his hind legs, and his paws were on her shoulders. They struggled, looking as if they were dancing a strange death waltz, which only one of them could survive.

"Oh, Red, not you, too. Not you!"

He chewed on her wrist. Patsy searched the countertop behind her with her free hand and came across a butcher knife she'd been using earlier to cut up some chicken.

The dog yelped when she slung the large knife around and drove it deep into the side of her beloved companion's chest. His eyes became blank and lifeless, and his body went limp. She held him up close to her. His long tongue lay out the side of his mouth.

"Oh, Red! Red!" she cried and hugged the big dog.

The window in the back door broke through.

What was this? She couldn't imagine. Her eyes widened as she gawked around the corner. Something big, something dark, had entered the house. Patsy pulled the knife out of Red's side and let him flop to the floor. She held the cutlery over her head and crept nearer the back door.

Tommy Chin waved a patrol car down at an intersection just before Doctor White Cloud's clinic. He wasn't going to radio for help, but he thought since they were already there, he might as well have some back up. The policemen followed Chin down the long drive to the dark building. Tony Parker was yet to arrive.

"Okay, now what's this all about?" the first cop, Officer Draper, asked as he stepped out of the passenger's side of the patrol car.

Chin walked over as the second policeman, Officer Clark, got out.

"The animal-control director, Tony Parker, will be here in a minute. He'll be able to explain better," Chin began. "But essentially, there's a couple of hundred dogs in the county ticking like time bombs. They're about to go off and start attacking like all these others have over the last couple of days. The thing is, they're going to all go nuts tonight, and the only way to identify them is through Doctor White Cloud's records inside."

"Holy shit!" Clark exclaimed. "Are you bullshitting?"

"No, I'm not. . . . " Chin stopped when he heard something rustle in the bushes along the side of the building.

Draper had heard it also and turned in that direction. "Who's there?"

No answer, still more rustling.

"I said, who's there?" he insisted, putting his hand on the grip of his .45-caliber Beretta.

Still no answer, but a figure emerged fifty feet away. A small man, dressed in black with a black eye patch, walked toward the three. He walked swiftly, calmly, and not in a threatening manner.

"It's Truong. He's behind this. Stop him!" Chin demanded.

Truong continued, walking purposefully.

"Stop him for what?" Draper asked Chin. He turned to the little man in black. "Is your name Truong?"

Truong didn't answer but continued his swift advance, now fifteen feet away.

Chin could see he wasn't going to stop. It was like he was going to walk right over them.

"Stop him. Stop the son-of-a-bitch. He's the one behind all these attacks."

Both officers began to draw their guns.

Truong attacked before they were able to clear their holsters. His first punch struck quickly. His right hand blurred, smashing Clark's throat. Clark collapsed in a pile, his face contorting.

In the same second, Truong's right foot spun around in a roundhouse kick and struck Draper in the jaw, causing a loud crack. He caught Draper by the head as the officer leaned back against the patrol car. With one hand on the back of Draper's head and one on his chin, he twisted. Draper's neck snapped as his head was jerked, grotesquely, 180 degrees.

Clark lay on the ground sucking air in sibilant gasps. He was suffocating, airway closed.

Tommy Chin realized he was no match for this lunatic. The best way he could help Clark and himself was to get out of there and radio for help.

He sprinted toward his van, thirty feet away in the gravel parking lot. Halfway, he tripped and slid on the loose gravel. Truong would be right behind him. Chin didn't look back. He stumbled to his feet and ran again. Slamming against the side of the van, he grabbed the door handle.

Now, to jump inside and lock the door, then drive to safety and call for help. Armed or not, Truong was very deadly, and he now had access to the police officers' guns.

Chin yanked the door open, slipped inside, and hammered down the lock. He'd made it. He'd had his doubts, but he had actually made it. He reached for the keys in the ignition and took his first look back toward the patrol car. Both officers still lay on the ground. Truong wasn't in sight.

Chin turned the engine over and felt tremendous relief when it started immediately. He continued searching out the window into the night for Truong.

Out of the blackness, an arm appeared. Truong's fist busted through the driver's side window, shattering glass like an explosion. Tommy Chin saw stars, then darkness.

CHAPTER 49

The gravel growled and popped in the wheel wells of Tony Parker's Jimmy truck as he barreled down the driveway to Doc White Cloud's clinic. It was a quarter till ten. There wasn't much time to do what had to be done. Truong's interview would be aired sometime between ten and half past.

He wondered if Truong would be there, if there would be a confrontation. Truong may have done what he wanted to do and left by now. Parker hoped he hadn't. He wanted Truong. He wanted to feel his scrawny little neck in his hands as he wrung the life out. He'd never wanted to do such a thing to any living being before, but this time was different. He wanted Truong for what he had done to his family, to Sarah, to Doc, and to Jack.

Turning into the parking lot, the Jimmy's lights found two vehicles, parked askew, near the dark building. One was a police car, and the other was Tommy Chin's van. The clinic van was there, too.

Parker killed the engine and coasted to a stop several yards back and observed over the steering wheel.

Odd. No one in sight. No lights. It was as if they had gotten out of their vehicles and left.

With a flashlight in hand, he opened his door and stepped out. He scanned the area then walked carefully toward the fifty-foot gap between the cop car and Chin's van. His light found something on the ground by the patrol car. A body. Parker quickened his pace. Another body. He walked faster, then stopped, standing over the two cops. Both were obviously dead, eyes open, pain and fear of their fate covering their faces.

"Chin!" Parker looked over to Chin's vehicle, expecting to see his body on the ground like the officers'. It wasn't. Maybe he was okay.

Parker trotted toward the van. The window was broken on the driver's side, and the engine was running. He hit the door with both hands and looked in. Chin lay, slumped over the console, blood covering the side of his face, glass on his lap.

"Chin! Wake up, Chin!"

Truong couldn't have done this. Not little, disfigured, meek and mild Truong.

Parker jerked the door open and turned off the engine.

A sudden, sharp pain stabbed the base of his skull. Something poked, cold, hard and sharp.

"Sergeant Parker. What a pleasant surprise," said an unfamiliar voice. "Now, don't move, so I don't have to stick this into your brain."

Parker was puzzled. The voice wasn't like Truong's. There was nearly no accent.

He felt one of his captor's hands search his body. It stopped at Simpson's gun, tucked under his belt. The revolver replaced the sharp object pressed to the back of his head.

"You weren't going to shoot me again, now were you?"

Sergeant Parker? Shoot me again? It didn't make sense. He hadn't been called sergeant since the Marines, over twenty years ago, and the only person he'd ever shot was a North Vietnamese lieutenant.

He flashed back to the jungles of Vietnam. He was on patrol three clicks out from the firebase. A squad of soldiers accompanied him and his three dogs as they looked for booby traps or any signs of the VC. He was separated from the patrol when the dogs picked up a scent and went crazy. They took him by surprise and jerked their leashes out of his hand. He chased after them but soon lost sight in the thick foliage, even though they ran only a few yards away. He chased, following their barks with his military issue .45 drawn.

Finally, he broke through a clearing and heard a shot. An NVA lieutenant stood fifty feet away. He'd shot the lead dog and was bearing down on the second. Parker fired, striking the enemy soldier and knocking off his hat. His adversary went down.

He would always remember the NVA lieutenant's terror-stricken face as he looked into the business end of Parker's aimed .45 auto, knowing he only had a split second to live. The face haunted Parker for years after the incident.

The enemy soldier was able to return a single shot as he fell. The bullet broke a limb in front of Parker, ricocheting and hitting him between the left nipple and shoulder, passing scant inches from his heart. He remembered something like a lightning bolt passing through his body as he fell to the ground. The dogs leaped on the NVA officer and the last thing Parker could recall was something shiny flipping out of the enemy soldier's mouth and into the vegetation as he hit the ground. Now, he realized it was a dog whistle.

He had never been told what had happened after he'd passed out. He thought his shot had been true and if it wasn't, surely the dogs had finished the job.

Parker now realized the face was the same as the one on the *bugaku* mask in the dream. Truong's face without the scars.

He glimpsed over his shoulder and saw the man dressed in black with a black patch over his eye.

"Truong."

It was obvious now, but still preposterous.

"Sergeant Parker, you spoiled the surprise. You peeked," Truong said, grinning very unpleasantly.

That grin, that terrible grin, from a monster who had caused so much pain and snuffed out so many precious lives was too much for Parker to bear. He brought the flashlight around with a backhand that knocked the pistol out of Truong's right fist and bounced it off the front fender of the van. He'd caught Truong completely off guard.

Next, he came around with his left and sent it smashing upward into Truong's nose, immediately causing blood to splatter. Truong fell back and rolled onto his stomach.

Parker bent down, reaching for the gun but was surprised when Truong gave a mule kick to his temple, forcing his head into the wheel of the van. The flashlight flew.

Truong came to his feet.

No time to go for the gun. Parker stood and faced him. Truong obviously knew what he was doing. He was well schooled in the martial arts, probably *kung fu*. Parker had taken *tae kwon do* lessons while in the Marines but that was so long ago. The hand-to-hand combat training they had drilled into his brain in boot camp hadn't been put to the test in a fight to the death and was long forgotten. It was evident Truong was well practiced, seeing the bodies he'd left in the parking lot.

He came at Parker. A scissors kick hit Parker in the jaw, but he stepped back and avoided more damage.

Blood streamed from Truong's nose.

Blood rolled down both sides of Parker's face.

He came at Parker again with a sidekick, but instead of backing away, Parker stepped into his attack. He caught Truong's leg, drove his fist into Truong's groin, then yanked the little man's leg up, sending him to the ground. Truong fell onto his back but flipped over again and kicked Parker in the gut with devastating force. Parker doubled up and fell to the ground. Truong leaped on top of him, but his slight build was no match for Parker's body weight. Parker rolled on top.

It was a terrible surprise to see that Truong had somehow come up with Jack's gun. Truong slammed it into the side of Parker's face, then sent another blow to his temple. Lights flashed inside Parker's head. He felt as though he were falling. Another strike to the back of the head, and things went black.

CHAPTER 50

"Now, bring both of your hands behind your back, slowly, very slowly."

Parker came to, face down in the gravel. His arms were being pulled to his back. He heard chains and recognized the type by their feel. Truong had taken two separate choker chains and put one around each of his wrists.

"Oh, what ugly injuries," Truong said, laughing. "Looks like dog bites. You must have a doctor look at them. Now, over here."

He pulled Parker to his feet, then pushed him toward the door of the clinic. Parker had no way to fight back. He stumbled into the wall, hitting it with the side of his face. Truong opened the door and shoved him inside. He flipped a light switch, and the bright lights exploded in Parker's eyes, causing them to burn.

Parker felt the fever returning, the throbbing in his neck, the stiffness in his joints. The flu symptoms returned. Rabies flu.

Truong walked Parker into the examination room, then went to the middle of the floor. He rolled the examination table to the far side, revealing a steel restraining ring in the floor. Parker knew what was next. The ring hinged out of a recess in the concrete. It was used specifically to tie up large animals for examination and minor surgery.

"Now sit, and make yourself comfortable, Sergeant Parker."

"Give it up, Truong. The war was over years ago."

Truong thrust the gun barrel against Parker's neck. It caused him to recoil with pain.

"Sit, I said!" Truong yelled and shoved Parker to the floor.

Truong pulled the chains through the loop from both sides until Parker's wrists were against it tight, then tied the chains together several times. Parker struggled to get free. It was impossible.

Truong stepped across the room and sat on a stool, next to the sink. Parker looked at Truong's right eye. It was dark and dilated, like Yankee's eyes had been earlier.

"You are probably wondering about my good English," Truong said. "I've studied and practiced it for years. I was taught during the war to interrogate the American prisoners. Then, I refined my knowledge of it along the way. You see, it was of benefit to carry out my plan. Knowing your language well has helped me to get around in your country, and most importantly, it allows me to explain what you have done to me and what I have, now, done to you.

"Why are you doing this, Truong?" Parker asked, "Why didn't you just kill me?"

"Oh, that would have been much too easy. I want you to suffer."

"Why? That was years ago. It was war."

"War? Whose war? Not yours. You invaded my country, my home, and because you did, hundreds of thousands of my people died. It wasn't your place to come to my home and do that."

"I didn't want to be there, either. My country's leaders thought we should be. So I was there, doing what I was told to do."

"And with what results? Prolonging the inevitable? Now we are at peace, free from war, finally. And guess when that happened? Right after you filthy Americans left."

"At peace? I don't know, but free, you're not."

"Would you like to discuss Vietnamese politics now, Sergeant? Why do you insist on talking about something you know nothing about and will never understand? The fact is, you invaded my home and bombed and sprayed and shot and burned and raped my people, my friends, my family, *me*!" Truong clinched his jaw and raised the gun.

Parker bowed his head, waiting for the bullet.

CHAPTER 51

Truong rubbed the gun barrel against the disfiguring scars on his face.

"Oh no, Sergeant Parker, I'm not finished with you yet. You see, I want you to hear the whole story. I want you to be sorry for what you've done. I want you to beg for forgiveness and plead for you life. Then, I may feel sorry for you and let you live."

Parker looked up at Truong. "Give it up, Truong. No more killing, no more blood."

"What about the killing and the blood when you dropped your bombs on my country—on my children? I had three of them, all beautiful and happy. They loved their father. They expected their father to keep them safe and to protect them. But while I was away in one of *your* prison camps, the bombs fell. They fell on my house, on my mother and my children."

"I'm sorry. But, that was years ago."

"You're sorry? I believe you are. But you are not forgiven. Are you also sorry for my father and two brothers, who were killed trying to repel your invasion? Sorry for killing my uncle and three cousins? And how about my wife and my best friend? They were killed after the war, but you killed them just the same."

Truong turned away and looked out the window over the sink.

"You see, because you killed me, I killed them."

Parker looked at Truong almost sympathetically. He'd been responsible for Jack's death and Doc's. He'd been responsible for at least a half-dozen other deaths and the serious mutilation of Sarah. He hated him. But, at the same time, he felt sorry for him.

"When you and your dogs attacked me, I was unable to defend myself. I lost my gun and your dogs nearly devoured me," he said and turned back to face Parker. "You trained them well. They ripped and tore at my leg until there was little left but bone." He emphasized, making clawing motions with his badly scarred left hand. "They devoured my testicles and left me with a tiny stump of a penis." He indicated with his thumb and forefinger. "They chewed on my hand and arm, and then, they ripped at my face and punctured my left eye," he said, pushing the gun barrel against his eye patch.

Parker stared at him and swallowed hard. What he was describing was not at all unlike what he had seen over the last few days.

"Don't you think I'm pretty? Don't you think I would be sexually desirable to the opposite sex, to my wife?" Truong smiled with his right eye bulging. He chuckled briefly. "Well, when I got home, after I'd spent three years in a prison camp and your doctors had 'done all they could', my wife wasn't real happy to see me. She didn't think I was pretty or sexually desirable—as if that were even an issue with what your dogs had left me. She had found someone else who was. You see, I can't really blame them. My wife was a very attractive woman, and she needed a man, a real, whole man. So I waited until I knew they were together and walked into the bedroom—my bedroom by the way—and shoved my gun *right up my best friend's ass*—and killed them both with one bullet. They died slowly. I think they bled to death. I sat down on the bed beside them and watched." He stared at the wall behind Parker.

"I felt empty after that. You see, the only thing left in me, the only emotion I possessed was hate. Hatred for you and what you had done to me and my family. You'd killed us all, and you were alive and well and living in the wealthy and all-powerful United States of America!"

He glared down at Parker with a hideous grin and pointed the gun again.

Parker stared back, now defiantly.

"Oh, now, what's that righteous look for?" Truong asked. "For your friends that I killed? Don't you see? You killed *them*, too. This is all *your* fault."

"You're out of your mind," Parker said back.

Truong chuckled. "Yes, of course I am. How else do you think I could have lasted this long. You see, when I was being attended by your corpsman, after you'd been well taken care of, of course, I overheard them say your name and that you'd be going back to Kansas. They said you'd survived my bullet—that you'd recover without any problems. I was mad at first that I hadn't been able to kill you. But later, after *you* killed my wife, I realized it was better that you hadn't died so quickly, so easily. I had the opportunity to cause you almost as much pain and grief as you caused me." He smiled again at Parker.

Parker looked around the room. He knew when Truong finished talking he would be killed. The clock on the wall showed ten minutes till ten. The interview would, most likely, be aired around half past. There wasn't much time left, either way he looked at it. He had to get to those files quickly, or many more people would die horrible deaths. Maybe he could talk him out of it, at least talk him out of all the other killings to come.

"What's wrong, Sergeant Parker? Uncomfortable? There's no way out. You are going to die—tonight."

"I radioed for more police when I drove in. They should be here any minute now."

Truong laughed. "And you expect me to believe that? Well, if more police do come, I hope I have time to finish my little story because I'd hate to kill you before I'm done. You see, when I kill you, I will be finished. My spirit will be free, and I won't need this body. Then, I can die, too."

"I don't believe you. You don't want to die anymore than I do."

"Now, where on earth did you get that idea?"

"The money. The money you stole from MacGreggor."

Truong looked surprised. "Sergeant Parker, you are a smart man."

"If you have to kill me, go ahead, but please, not all the others. Shoot me but stop the TV station from airing the interview. Call all the dog owners and warn them."

"Shoot you? Shoot you? Sergeant Parker, I'm not going to shoot you—that is, unless the police come and make me finish my adventure prematurely. And call the people about their dogs? Why, I've already called them once. I've been calling them all evening to tell them to be sure their dogs watch the news with them tonight. I've told them I have something special for them, a surprise. You know, I think most of them will do it, too. A lot of them thought I was crazy, but I'll just bet when the interview comes on, their faithful companions will be watching right along side them."

Truong looked up at the clock.

"It won't be long now," he said. "Soon I'll finish my story, my dog friends will attack, and it will be time for you to die a very horrible death.

"Now where was I? Mmmm, oh yes. When you met me in the jungle that day, I was hoping to kill your dogs." He brought out a shiny silver dog whistle and rolled it between his fingers.

Parker now understood the way he was to be killed.

"Your dogs had been finding our booby traps and our tunnels, and I had a plan to kill them. I would call them, and they would lead you and your squad toward me. When I was sure they were on my trail, I would bring them, and you, into an ambush of claymore mines a few yards away. Then, I would disappear into the bush. My plan would have worked fine, but I underestimated the speed of your dogs. But then, I didn't expect you to turn them loose. I hadn't had time to reach my little ambush before your dogs appeared."

Truong grinned. "Then you popped out and shot me."

He paused before continuing, his eye staring at Parker with the intensity of a jaguar's at a rabbit. "I also underestimated the incredible fighting strength of the dogs. I was very impressed. But, I would have killed them, anyway, if it weren't for you. When I discovered first hand what dogs could do to a man, I became very interested. You see, that would be the way I would get even with you—eye for eye, tooth for tooth."

A strange hoarse howl came from outside. It sent shivers down Tony Parker's spine.

Truong turned and craned his neck to see out the window.

"Intriguing howl. Probably a farmer's dog or a coyote. I've heard one just like it every night. It's almost as if it were following me. Hmmm," Truong said, then turned back to Parker. "In the North Vietnamese Army, I had been an intelligence officer, specializing in interrogation and brainwashing techniques. Are you familiar with thiopental, or maybe Sodium Pentothal, Sergeant Parker?"

"Truth serum," Parker responded.

"Exactly. It's a barbiturate sometimes used to aid in hypnosis. Well, I discovered that if thiopental is used in conjunction with certain very potent mind-altering drugs, the mind becomes very pliable.

"It took many experiments, many lives both dog and human, to find the right combination of drugs that would produce the results I was seeking. But then, there were a plenty of drugs floating around at that time to choose from.

"The human mind seemed too difficult to control, however. Too complex. But certain lower animals, dogs for instance, were easily controlled with the use of my very own designer drug, accompanied by hypnosis. I'll bet you didn't know a dog could be hypnotized. It's a talent my grief has helped me develop along with the gift of a hypnotic eye. The animals seem to look into my left eye and see the pain I carry in my soul."

Truong pointed to the patch with the muzzle of the gun. "I am able to unlock the more primitive part of their brain: the part they used when they were untamed and vicious wolves and wild dogs, before being domesticated by man. It makes them very aggressive, and they attack anything living, except members of their own pack.

That makes it safe for me, you see, for they look at me as their pack leader.

"The next thing I discovered was after hypnosis, even when the drugs wore off, I could induce them to use that part of their brain again at any time, at my whim." He looked at the dog whistle. "With just a simple signal, planted during hypnosis, I can turn them on—and off."

Parker looked at the clock. It was five minutes till ten. He felt helpless.

Truong went on. "So, after years of research and experimentation, I was ready to visit you. I checked *information* for several Kansas cities and finally found you in Wichita. Then, I called around and found out you were the animal-control director. You can just imagine my delight! My plan would work even better than I had anticipated. I bought my identification and my passport to the United States on the black market and flew into Wichita and looked you up, just as simple as that.

"I had been here nearly six months, working out the fine details of my plan. I visited your house often, especially at night. I heard the music you liked to listen to on your stereo—that old-time rock-n-roll. I smelled the supper cooking on your stove. I even heard the arguments you and your wife had, about not having enough money and spending too much time at work—with Sarah Hill." He grinned again. "Just one year away from getting your veterinarian's degree, huh?

"But I was there in the daytime, also. To see Nick go to school and Julie take your baby, Audrey, grocery shopping with her. I went through your trash and found the discarded mail, the bills that you paid, the reminders and past due notices. There were some broken toys, some of Nick's outgrown clothes. I even became friends with your dog. Tell me, does that make you feel betrayed?" He looked at Parker with another of his hideous smiles.

For months Parker and his family had been watched by a ruthless killer, and he hadn't had a clue. He felt violated, raped. Truong knew everything about his family, had even called them by their names.

"From Yankee's dog tags, I found your vet, and, of course, he hired me instantly as an assistant once he found out I would work for room and board. I posed as an ignorant Thai immigrant, who was good with animals.

"My real name is Ming. I used Truong so as to help make my getaway good if there were any complications. The old man never asked to see my papers. He believed everything I said. I soon gained the old fool's trust and had plenty of time to treat many dogs. Every dog that was left here for more than a couple of hours became a soldier in my little army.

"Then, at night, I did some moonlighting and enlightened dozens more. I had picked up the drugs in San Francisco from some black market connections I have there, and I had enough to use on a lot of dogs.

"My first experiment in your country was right after I arrived. I ran across a firehouse mascot—a Dalmatian—and considered how much fun I could have. The firemen treated me like a friend—their favorite foamer, they called me—and they let me *play* with their dog."

Parker couldn't help gaping at Truong, thinking of the firefighters and their dog killed the winter before.

"I can see you remember that little *accident* they had. I wish I would have had a camera." Truong sighed. "When I used up the last of the drugs, it was time to play with *you*. I started with the blind man. I stood outside his house and blew my whistle."

He put the whistle up to his mouth and began to blow. No shrill whistle noise came out, only wind. He puffed two longs, two shorts and a long. "That was the signal. No other combination of sounds would work."

Out in the truck, Yankee began to go crazy, barking and snarling.

Truong looked through the doorway with surprise. "Well, it sounds like you brought my old friend Yankee along with you. This *is* a pleasant surprise." He looked back at Parker. "Now you won't have to die at a stranger's hands, or should I say fangs."

Parker squirmed.

"So anyway, MacGreggor was just a bonus. When I took his dogs back to him after their rabies shots, he paid the fee with a hundred-dollar bill. Dr. White Cloud said he always did and that there was a rumor he had a fortune hidden away in his house. I had seen MacGreggor come up from the basement with the money when he paid me, so I knew pretty much where it was. That night, I sat in the clinic's van outside his house and blew my little whistle. After twenty minutes or so, there hadn't been any signs of problems, so I climbed his fence and entered the house through the big dog port in the back door."

"At twelve thirty," Parker interrupted.

"How'd you . . . ," Truong began. "The clock. I pulled it off the wall as I searched in the dark for the doorway. Very good. You should be a detective. I hear there's an opening."

Parker glared as Truong continued.

"The male dog greeted me as one of his own and I went directly to the basement and got the old man's money. Then, on my way out, I laid the scripture on his lap. Something to make it more interesting, to give you something to sweat over, knowing you were somehow involved. You see, a chaplain gave me a *Bible* when I was in your American hospital. You know, I felt a little sad when I choked him to death with his own rosary beads.

"Anyway, at MacGreggor's I saw a letter opener that appealed to me and I took it along. Funny thing, the female, Jezebel, had run away. She was the most remarkable creature I had ever seen. Beautiful animal, and the smartest dog I've ever known. And she was so big. When we stood facing each other, we looked eye to eye. If there had been a way, I would have kept her for myself. She certainly served me well, though. The thought of a dog like her being loose and rabid made all of Wichita stay in at night and lock their doors and wonder why their incompetent animal-control director couldn't catch her.

"Oh, and I must thank you for your humorous antics during my fun. Sunday, in the park. The potato salad and the baked beans. I thought I would die laughing. And the way you played with my dogs was very amusing. I only wish I could have been closer to hear better." He chuckled. "There have been other amusing times: Nick in the playground and Julie on the jogging path. Your wife doesn't know how lucky she was. But that *is* only temporary.

"You lousy son-of-a-bitch!" Parker exclaimed.

"I almost forgot about your Pastor Carl. He was too easy to be much fun. MacGreggor's letter opener sliced through his old throat like butter. He is tougher than I thought, though, hanging on so long.

"Let's see. Oh yes, you'll love this about your friends in Sand Creek—but no, I think I'll save that for the very last. Give you something to think about while your life is pulsing from your body, shooting out of your ripped-open carotid artery.

"Mrs. Taylor was next with her prize greyhounds. Unfortunate they didn't kill her. But by then they made you look pretty bad. And her male dog has come in useful since then and was going to again tonight, but I'll get to that in a minute.

"Then, there was Mrs. Nightingale. I got to her a little late, but it worked out for the better from what I heard from your dear friend Henry Haskins on Channel Two News.

"Roary Rapids' dogs were the most enjoyable of all. It was perfect timing. I had hoped to set them off at a rock concert, but the way they tore through the Epic Center made up for that. Especially since they got Jack Simpson."

Parker bolted hard enough to pop the joints in his wrist, but it was to no avail.

"You bastard!"

"Oh, but wait, there's more. Then, when Dr. White Cloud came out late last night, I knew he was getting suspicious of me. I sneaked up to him and had the personal honor to slash his throat with my pretty, new letter opener. Then, I let the greyhound you brought in have him for a while. I put the dog back in his cage, and they blamed it on the only known loose dog, Jezebel. It worked so perfectly."

This bastard killed Doc! Parker's face strained. The fever came back full strength. His joints stiffened and ached tremendously. He could feel the veins bulging on his temples. His wrists bled badly from trying to work out of the chains.

Truong went on. "Then, of course, we have this evening. I hadn't planned on the interview, but again, it fit in perfectly. The preview nearly fouled things up, but it looks like everything is going to work out just fine. I've been listening to all the fun on the police scanner I keep in my locker.

"It was unfortunate that more damage wasn't done at your house, however. Although—I do have some time before my midnight flight—I've chartered a private plane. I may have a little time—to kill.

"I hadn't planned on Yankee attacking so early. As a matter of fact, I was just on my way over to visit you, to help you better understand the pain I suffered when my friends and loved ones were being killed. I was going to bring the greyhound and let him and Yankee play with you and your family.

"Oh, you son-of-a-bitch! Let me go! I'll kill you!" Parker said, jerking and pulling at the chains.

"Sarah was a necessity," Truong continued, unfazed. "I didn't like the little bitch. She was snobby and always so sure of herself, and I knew you found her very attractive. I do hope Sheik did a good job."

Parker wasn't about to tell Truong that Hill had survived. He was insane enough to go after her and try again.

Truong said, "Oh, yes, in case you were wondering about the rabies tests...."

Truong stepped into his room and pulled out an ice chest. He dumped it, ice and all, on Parker's lap. A German-shepherd head and the head of Beelzebub, Jezebel's mate, rolled out wrapped in plastic. Parker looked down and bared his teeth.

Truong finished, "I never seemed to find the time to take these in. Oh, and I almost forgot, my most recent trophy. I know you'll appreciate it." He went into the next room again.

He came out a few seconds later, holding a blood-soaked pillow-case.

"I have someone here that would like to say good-bye to you,"

Truong said, and dumped the contents of the pillowcase out on Parker's lap, also.

The thing landed between his knees. It was large and round and seemed covered in long black hair matted with fresh-smelling blood. Nauseatingly fresh.

Parker looked at it, frowning, trying to make out what it was. A head? Whose?

"Say good-bye, Patsy. 'Tony, oh, Tony,'" Truong mimicked.

Parker was overcome with an explosion of grief and pain.

He cried out, tears streaming down his face, "Ah, you dirty bastard!" Tears and saliva spat out as he yelled, voice cracking.

"Well, I've said all I would like to say, and I don't see you apologizing or pleading, so it's time for the grand finale," Truong said very calmly. "I had planned on giving you to the greyhound, but I believe this occasion calls for something special. Yankee. Oh, and don't worry. You won't be alone. I'll stay and watch."

He took a step toward the door, but stopped and stared out.

"Oh, well, come in. We were just talking about you," he said, with a big grin.

Parker was petrified with fear. He was going to die. It would be a horrible death. Now this, a visitor. The police, maybe? No. He dismissed the thought quickly. Truong would have reacted much differently. Yankee still barked in the truck. What sounded like the greyhound barked from the kennel outside. Who could it be, but—Jezebel.

CHAPTER 52

Parker saw a black muzzle appear well over halfway up in the doorway. It wasn't growling nor did it even show a snarl. The giant dog continued to walk into the room, slowly, fluidly. Parker was in awe. The beautiful dog stood with the points of her ears at the same level as Truong's. She was as black as a moonless night without a single hair of white. Nearly five feet tall from floor to ear tip. She looked a little thin and had dried scabs on her head, but otherwise, she was nature in perfection. Around her neck were her tags, the large diamond, sparkling.

She looked at Truong without blinking. He smiled back at her.

"This is indeed a great honor. How very good to see you." Truong glanced at Parker, smiling. Jezebel looked, also. "Isn't she a beauty?" Truong asked. To Jezebel, he said, "So it's been you following and howling to me over the last few days. You've been wanting to join in the fun, haven't you?"

"Maybe not, Truong," Parker said. "Maybe she's been tracking you down. Maybe she's been trying to warn your victims and stop you."

"Don't be ridiculous, Sergeant Parker. Jezebel is no longer leashed by any allegiance to man. She's free and wild. And, I might add, she looks hungry. It does appear, however she's lost her spark for killing. Probably due to that nasty injury on her head. I'm sure this will get her going again," Truong said, raising the whistle to his lips, then bringing it down slightly. "Oh, and good-bye, Sergeant Parker. I do hope you've enjoyed this as much as I."

He blew into the whistle. Two longs, two shorts and a long.

Parker braced himself for death. He was furious. He was petrified. He was in pain. Sweat rolled down his forehead. His wrists bled profusely.

Jezebel's ferocity roared from her huge throat, starting as a rumbling growl and ending in four vicious, thundering barks.

Parker flinched.

She stepped to him and had to bend her big neck down to look at him face to face. She glanced to the plastic-covered head of her mate, Beelzebub, laying two feet from Parker's leg. She sniffed at it briefly, then turned back to Parker.

She growled, showing her enormous canine incisors.

Parker leaned back as far as he could without falling backward. He held his eyes closed tight. Her warm saliva dripped on his chest. She licked her chops. She growled again, her hot breath blowing on his face.

"Don't play with him too long, Jezebel," Truong said. "We really must hurry."

Parker knew within a few seconds he would be dead. The next growl was sure to end with her enormous mouth clamping onto his throat.

His head began spinning again. He shook convulsively. He thought of what Mrs. Crane had said about Jezebel. How big and beautiful she was and yet how gentle.

Parker opened his eyes and looked down her cavernous throat.

"No, Jezebel, no," Parker said.

She responded with a less enthusiastic growl.

He remembered the most prominent comment about her, besides her size, was her intelligence. He remembered the nickname Mrs. Crane said MacGreggor called her.

"Jazbo, no. No, Jazbo!"

Jezebel closed her mouth. She looked into Parker's eyes as if searching for something familiar. She blinked.

Truong became impatient and angered with Jezebel's hesitation. He blew the whistle again. Two longs. . . .

Jezebel's roaring bark interrupted, her head twisted back at Truong. "No. Not me!" he cried.

Jezebel swung around and leaped at Truong.

He fired a wild shot and didn't have time for another.

The huge dog's enormous mouth grabbed Truong's gun hand and tore the pistol, three fingers and the major portion of his hand away. He was left with only his thumb and forefinger and the two hand bones that joined them to his wrist, exposed and white. Blood immediately gushed from the ripped flesh. Truong stared at his devastated member in wide-eyed disbelief. It seemed the pain was yet to explode in his brain. He gaped at Jezebel. She dropped the gun to the floor then tongued the reluctant fingers from her mouth as if they were lodged chicken bones, and they fell beside the gun. Truong looked at the fingers, then gawked at his hand.

"*Uuuh, hu-uh-uh-uh,*" Truong whimpered, then wrenched his face at the huge monster before him.

Jezebel lunged again. This time she caught him by the neck and yanked him from his feet. She shook him like so many dirty rags.

Truong slipped from her mouth, tossed, arms flailing, across Parker's lap. He started to get up, miraculously still alive, but Jezebel hulked over him again. She pushed him face to face against Parker, and Parker fell backward, flat on his back.

Truong's eye patch had fallen off in the scuffle, and his left eye was open wide. No life existed in the eye. Just the opposite. Death. Evil. The pupil was dilated to the size of a dime and only a thin ring of an iris showed. It was wilted like a deflated balloon. The white of the eye was dark yellow and blood-shot. It was emotionless and fixed, unlike his right eye that was filled with terror. The left eye, the dead one, was dark, very dark and deep like a well. Parker knew the eye wasn't human. It was a dog's eye.

For a moment, he thought he could see a sparkle, or flashing, or maybe explosions, in the deep dark eye. Mortar rounds exploding. Napalm incinerating. Rifles shooting. Bayonets slashing. People running. People screaming and crying. People dying. Blood flowing.

They lay nose to nose, but Parker felt neither vengeance nor pity, only fear. Truong looked at him as if begging for help. Jezebel bit again. This time, one of her lower fangs grazed Parker's throat before embedding itself into Truong's.

"*Auh, glau-huuu!*" Truong's scream muffled down to a hiss, then silenced.

There was an overshoe, mud-sucking-like sound as Truong's throat crushed, and Parker felt the small man's hot blood running down onto his neck. Something warm spilled onto his stomach and lower body. Truong had lost all muscle control and urinated.

The struggle lasted only a few brief seconds. Parker wondered if he would wet his pants when Jezebel finished him. Even if he didn't, when they found him they'd think he had because of the water from the ice chest and because of Truong. It made him angry. A trivial thing to be concerned with at a time like this. Still, it made him angry.

With all his strength, he shoved with his shoulder and sat up. He'd managed to push Truong's body back down to his legs.

Jezebel stood silently, still gripping Truong's throat, ensuring his death. She glanced at Parker out of the corner of her eye. She looked back at Truong's face then bent her head down, Truong's neck still between her jaws, and looked over his body. Satisfied he was dead, she dropped him across Parker's legs like a hunting dog obediently dropping a duck it had just retrieved at its master's feet.

Parker sat watching her and she returned what seemed to be an anxious glare.

She moved closer.

He felt the fear come back full strength. It was now his turn to die.

"No, Jezebel," he said softly.

No response.

"Jazbo, no!"

She roared as viciously as before.

The nickname seemed to make her angry. She was no longer under Truong's spell. It was as if she were saying that Parker was not her master. Only her master called her that. No one else. She wouldn't allow it. Her master was dead. No one would call her that again.

"Whoa, sorry," Parker said softly. "Nice, Jezebel, good girl."

She growled, sounding more like a loud purr, as she put her snout within three inches of Parker's nose. She made the sound again.

They stared into each other's eyes. Jezebel seemed to sense his pain. Parker understood hers and spoke easy.

"It's okay now, Jezebel. It's all over. There'll be no more pain. No more hurting. No more death. It's all over."

Parker thought of Jack and Doc and Patsy and Sarah. He thought of his family: Audrey, Nick and Julie, and how much he loved them and wished he could hug them all right this minute. Tears came to his eyes.

Jezebel gave a long, sad whine and cocked her head to the side.

Parker smiled at her and chuckled lightly.

She brought her head closer and licked his face sympathetically.

Suddenly, from behind, a rifle.

"No! Don't!" Parker yelled.

A shot rang out.

Jezebel staggered for a moment, looked at Parker, rolled her eyes and then collapsed.

Parker looked up. Tommy Chin stood in the doorway with a tranquilizer gun to his shoulder.

CHAPTER 53

As Tommy Chin helped Tony Parker get loose from the chains, headlights came up the drive. It was Julie in the minivan with a police car behind.

"Are you okay, Tony?" she cried, running to him.

They embraced. It was good to see Julie. Good to touch her. Good to hold her.

Two police officers ran in after her with their guns drawn.

"Yeah, I'm fine. What are you doing here?"

"The kids are at Bill and Barbara's. Sarah had a nurse call from the hospital. She said you needed me and to call the police. She said it was women's intuition."

Parker took Julie by the arms and led her away from the mess on the floor of the examination room before she had a chance to see. While explaining the situation to the officers, they covered the bodies and heads with blankets and stowed Jezebel safely away in Chin's van.

It was now a few minutes after ten o'clock. There was little time left. They found the necessary files on Patsy's desk and called in most of them to the dispatcher's office. Tyrone told Parker that the police chief wasn't too convinced by the story and only discussed it with the

TV station. Channel Two wasn't convinced either and decided to go ahead and air the interview. Now, maybe after what had happened, they could be convinced. But was there enough time? Tyrone would try.

Parker kept three dozen of the names, and he, Chin and Julie called them from the phones in Doc's office, the examination room and Patsy's desk in the front.

They viewed the Channel Two News on a small black-and-white TV that Patsy had kept in the reception area as Chin had the last dog owner on the phone.

--*

At the Channel Two News Center, producer Mike Stilton had taken the call from Police Chief Baker but refused to kill the interview, influenced by Henry Haskins' begging. The chief seemed confused and skeptical about the warning he'd received and wasn't very persuasive.

Colleen Jones, the preppy-looking anchorwoman, introduced Haskins. She frowned as she looked to him, then looked off camera toward Stilton. The camera zoomed in. Haskins sat behind the anchor desk with his basset hound sitting on the desk beside him and did the intro for the interview.

"Earlier today, this reporter had the opportunity to interview Mr. Ho Truong, assistant to the well respected veterinarian Dr. Johnny White Cloud who was murdered outside his practice by the killer dog Jezebel, late last night. Mr. Truong had some things to say about the doctor, along with some training tips for your dog. I know Sirius, here, my *Dog Star*, is anxious to hear him."

The interview began.

Stilton looked to the cameraman, scowling. "What does he think he's doing?" Stilton asked. "Who told him he could bring his damn dog on the set, let alone on live TV? I'm the frickin' producer here. He didn't frickin' ask me!"

The cameraman shrugged his shoulders as a young woman scurried up to Stilton.

"There's a call from the Sedgwick County dispatcher for you. It's urgent."

Stilton started toward the front office, his eyes narrowed, glaring at Haskins.

The interview continued.

Haskins' basset hound went nuts. He growled and grabbed Haskins by the throat. Haskins fell over backward, and they both disappeared behind the desk.

Stilton reached for the doorknob as the attack began. He stopped and watched, amazed.

"Aw, shit!" he exclaimed. He shook his head. "I'm firing the son-of-a-bitch this time—if he lives."

Colleen Jones stood up at the desk and began stomping. After half a dozen frantic kicks she quit, reached down, and pulled the basset hound up by the tail with both hands, holding it like a giant, dead mouse. She stepped back and slung it over the desk as if it were a hammer throw. Haskins' ex best friend tumbled limply, then slid across the floor and into the base of the camera.

Anchorwoman Jones took two more enthusiastic stomps behind the desk, slapped her palms and walked away.

*_*_*

Chin insisted into the phone, "Yes sir, I said you must lock the dog in a vacant room or in the garage, now!" Chin looked at Parker and said to him with concern. "Uh-oh, there's growling. It might be too late."

A crack loud enough for all to hear came from the phone and Chin flinched. He jerked the phone back, and Parker could hear the man's voice on the other end.

"Damn, Barney, what the hell's the matter with you?" the man said away from the phone. Now, he spoke into it. "I had to hit the damn dog with the phone. Aw, shit, I think I killed him!"

Chin and Parker exchanged relieved smirk s, and Chin hung up the phone.

There were a total of five other attacks in Wichita that night, only one being serious, but not fatal. The police had done a good job of rounding up all of the animals, and the situation seemed under control.

Parker and Chin sedated Yankee and the greyhound, hoping that when they woke up, they would be all right again. Next, would come the problem of deprogramming all of the estimated two hundred dogs affected.

After checking on Hill's condition, which was good, Parker went home and climbed into Nick's bed with Julie and the kids.

His body ached. His head spun. He felt hot and feverish. Rabies symptoms, maybe, but just as likely from his numerous injuries. Parker convinced himself that it was only normal to feel like he did, considering what he'd been through. He doubted he'd had actual rabies symptoms. If he did have the disease, he'd surely feel much worse by now, possibly even comatose or dead. Just in case, he would not kiss them, not let his blood touch their skin, not breath into their faces.

It was good to be home. It was good to hold Julie. Julie held him back tightly. He knew it was okay, now. The terrible crisis was over.

CHAPTER 54

Dawg scratched at the door again. The thin plywood panel in the middle flexed as he dug his terrible black claws relentlessly into the wood. It had been a long, long night and day since Tricia had attempted to leave her haven in the closet and stumbled into Dawg's sleeping body. She had been lucky he was sleeping and not prepared for her. She had been lucky and bounced off his chest after falling onto him. She had been able to get back into the closet and slam the door before he'd realized what happened.

Dawg had scratched at the door off and on ever since. Tricia was scared. Not scared like before when she knew she must do something but didn't know what. Now she was scared without hope. There was *nothing* she could do. No one would come to save her.

She was so very tired and hungry. She felt weak. Her mouth was dry. Her entire body trembled.

Soon Dawg would break through and get her. He would eat what he wanted of her and leave the rest to rot, and she would not be able to stop him.

Tricia stared into the darkness toward the door with her body drawn up against the corner. The time had come. A dim light showed through the door as one of Dawg's claws poked through and was hung up there for a moment. The scratching stopped for an instant as Dawg yanked on his leg to free up the snared claw. He broke free and resumed pawing, this time even more feverishly.

It wouldn't be long now. Tricia hugged herself, rubbing her arms. Her jaw trembled out of control. Suddenly, a large piece of the door panel ripped away, and Dawg's snout came through.

Tricia shrieked and put her hands down to her sides to shove herself into the corner even more. Something sharp jabbed her hand and it hurt. She thought of what Grammy had told her as she ran through the yard with a sharp stick. "Don't run with that stick in your hand. You might fall and poke your eye out," she'd yelled.

That's it! She could take this stick she had just discovered, and when Dawg shoved his head all the way through, she'd poke *him* in the eye with it. She'd poke him in *both* eyes with it. Then, maybe he'd leave her alone.

Tricia picked the thing up as Dawg chewed viciously on the panel. It wasn't a stick, but a wire coat hanger. That wouldn't work. She couldn't poke him in the eye with the curved wire end. She had to bend it straight, but she didn't have the strength. She strained, pushing the end of the wire with one thumb on top of the other. Her skin was thin and soft, and it hurt to push so hard on the stiff, blunt end. But she had to straighten it. It *was* her only hope.

Dawg had his head halfway in now. He sniffed briefly, then looked to Tricia with a snarl that reminded her of a grin—a big grin like the wolf had before he ate Granny in her *Little Red Riding Hood* storybook.

Dawg jerked his head back and resumed chewing and scratching.

The wire hanger's curved end wouldn't budge, and when Tricia took her thumb off the end, she felt the deep indentation it caused on her tender flesh. She shook her hand and blew on it. Dawg saw the movement and gave a few snarling barks that startled Tricia. It made her mad, and she hit the door with the hanger twice. Dawg was undaunted. He continued frantically and broke loose another large chunk of door. He'd be through and at her throat within seconds.

The hanger was impossible for Tricia to bend with her fingers. How could she do it? She thought of Grandy and how he used to fix things. She remembered once when she helped him repair some rotten steps on the front porch, he bent a nail as he hammered it into a board. After scolding the nail with a few *grown up* words, he put the end of the *fricker-fracker* as he called it in the crack between two of the porch's deck boards and bent it straight with his fingers. That would work, but where was a crack?

Dawg tore yet another large chunk out of the door panel and now lunged through the opening, coming in with his head and left fore-leg. The opening was still not large enough to allow his entire body to pass, and he struggled to force himself in. Now Tricia could feel his hot rancid breath and see his savage amber eyes up close, real close. Those eyes, those terrible hungry eyes, glared at her. Soon she would poke them out with the wire hanger.

There was a crack that would work right in front of her, in the door. It was only inches from Dawg's snarling snout, but it was her only hope. She forced the end of the hanger into the crack. A large string of Dawg's drool flung from his angry mouth and slapped across Tricia's hand, some of it splattering on Tricia's cheek. Dawg bit at one end of the hanger and clamped down. Tricia jerked it and pulled the curved end straight, or straight enough. She pulled the hanger back, hold-ing it in the middle, with the straightened end sticking out from between her index and middle finger. She jabbed it at Dawg's eye.

"Take that, you *fricker-fracker*!" she yelled.

Dawg defended the attack opening his fierce jaws wide. Tricia missed and drove the wire into Dawg's open mouth, stabbing his tongue. Dawg snapped down in reaction and had a firm and painful grip on Tricia's hand.

Tricia screamed and hit Dawg on the end of his snout with the side of her other fist. After three punches, Dawg released his grip and reeled back, shaking his head. He seemed lodged in the hole in the door, unable to come in further or to back out.

Tricia didn't take the time to look at the new injuries on her hand. She brought the hanger back, then again lunged at Dawg's eye, put-ting all of her weight behind it. She missed again, but this time she buried it all the way to her knuckles in the beast's right nostril. Blood spurted onto Tricia's hand, and Dawg bolted backwards through the hole in the door.

*_*_*

Once more, Jezebel came to Tony Parker in his dreams. She marched down the street the same as before. She stopped in front of the Parker house as before. She walked up to the steps, just as before, only this time, she stepped over a shattered white porcelain *bugaku* mask. Once again, the door opened, and she walked in and up the stairs.

She entered Nick's room and stood face to face with Tony.

Again, he could feel her hot breath blowing on his face. He tried to open his eyes but couldn't. He trembled again. She licked his face, making it wet.

He felt her big front paws push down on the bed, and he felt her full weight leap up on it near the foot. He felt her body, warm and heavy, lay across his legs. She gave a deep, long sigh.

Parker finally pried his eyes open and woke up. He jerked his head up and looked down at his feet. Nick slept curled up across his legs. He'd disturbed Julie, and she yawned and sighed, her warm breath blowing on his wet face. His entire face was drenched with perspiration.

The clock on Nick's dresser read two thirty a.m. He gazed down at Audrey, sleeping between him and Julie, and stroked her little back, chuckled to himself and went back to sleep.

CHAPTER 55

There was a party going on. Lots of laughing and talking—and barking. The TV blared, and *Lassie* was on. Voices commented on the show.

"I wouldn't take no shit from that boy if I was her," one deep, gruff voice said.

"And I'll tell you what, if I would've pulled that stupid cat from the river, I would've had its ass," a higher pitched voice said.

A tapestry hung crooked on the wall, depicting several *people* sitting around a card table, playing poker. It resembled the one Parker had seen at the Bumfields', only theirs was of dogs.

Looking closer at the tapestry, the people all had familiar faces. On one side sat Alvin MacGreggor. Next to him were Sergeant Big Jim Morowsky and Officer Farley Cox, the two cops killed at MacGreggor's house.

On the other side were Mrs. Nightingale and Gus Spillman, the guard at the Epic Center. Steven Johnson, the young blind man killed by his own sight dog, sat beside them wearing sunglasses. In the middle, Jack sat, smiling. Steven Johnson had just passed an ace of spades to him under the table with his toes. Pastor Carl Santini watched from the window, looking as if he wanted to come in and join the game.

Doc tended bar in the background of the tapestry, a couple of uniformed firefighters were sitting at the bar, and Patsy was stepping over a rug as she walked toward the table with drinks. The rug was like one of those bearskin kind, only this one wasn't a bear. The head of Ho Truong, alias Ming—eye patch in place—stuck up from it. His body, lying deflated and clothed in black, made up the rug.

There was more laughter and loud talking and barking and even howling. The room was full of dogs, a couple dozen of them. They sat up on a sofa like people would, drinking beer out of cans. Some sat on the arms of the couch and in a couple of chairs. Two leaned against the sofa back. They all watched television. Laughing and "carrying on so," as Mrs. Bumfield would have said.

On the floor, two naked people lay, curled up in balls like sleeping dogs.

A dog wearing a skirt and an apron, stepped into the room on her hind legs, carrying an hors d'oeuvre tray. The greedy TV watchers quickly snatched up the goodies. They snacked on the fingers and eyeballs and ears and noses from the tray. A large yellow and gray paw reached over to the middle and scooped up a pair of testicles. The tray was cleaned, except for a small, homemade Raggedy Ann doll that, although nearly shredded, seemed to be there just for decoration.

The dog in the dress turned and walked back out of the room to go get more.

A closer look at the people on the floor revealed that they had familiar faces, also. It was the Bumfields of Sand Creek, Kansas. They did not sleep. They were dead, throats torn.

In the middle of the couch, Dawg, the Bumfield's big Heinz fifty-seven mutt, pulled a cigar from his mouth, got up, and walked on his hind legs to the large picture window. He looked out at a tree. On a limb in the tree clung the Bumfield's kitten.

It pleaded with an insistent mew.

The big mutt burst out laughing, a loud vulgar guffaw, "*Ha, ha, ha, ha, ha!*"

Parker's eyes snapped open once again. Of all the nightmares he'd had over the past few days, this had been the strangest, but no less frightening. It was three thirty a.m.

"What's wrong sweetheart?" Julie asked.

"Nothing. I can't sleep. It's all right," he said remembering the Sand Creek files Doc had kept separate. The folks in Sand Creek had been overlooked.

Parker rolled out of the bed carefully, gently picking up arms and legs entangled around him and laying them back down with the love and care they deserved.

"Do you want some company? Do you want me to get up with you?"

"No, it's all right, Julie. Go back to sleep. I'll be back in a few minutes," he said, walking out quietly, then closing the door behind.

He grabbed some clothes from the master bedroom closet, took Jack's .357 from a locked nightstand and walked quietly down the steps. He picked up the phone as he put on his shirt.

Truong had started to tell him about what he had done to the people in Sand Creek but never finished. Where had his head been? How could he have forgotten them?

"Tyrone. . . . Busy night, huh...? Double shift...? You poor bastard! Well, it's about to get busier. . . . I need you to get a hold of the sheriff.... Yeah, the sheriff. . . . Tell him to go out and set up roadblocks in every direction from Sand Creek. . . . Tell him to not let anybody in or anything out. Next, I want you to call the highway patrol and tell them what we've got, and see if the city police won't cooperate, too. . . . If they won't, see if the sheriff won't get a hold of the National Guard. . . . Yeah, it's happening again, we missed some of the dogs. . . . Thirty or so. Their files were in another room. Have ambulances standing by. I'll contact you from the truck."

Parker hung up and tucked his shirt into his pants. He turned and saw Julie step out at the top of the stairs. He hid Jack's gun under his belt, behind his back.

"What's going on?" she asked impatiently.

"Nothing, sweetheart," he said as he hurried to the door. "Go back to bed."

"Tony!"

"Just a kitten stuck in a tree. Now, please, go back to bed. I'll be right back. I promise." He went through the door and closed it without looking back to Julie or giving her a chance for rebuttal.

CHAPTER 56

The achy stiffness was returning to Parker's traumatized body. He felt it in his shoulders and elbows as he guided the Jimmy recklessly down the quiet, early morning streets. His joints felt like cold, rusted steel, and his neck was rigid and painful to move. A fire raged inside his skull, and a dull throbbing hurt his temples with every beat of his racing heart. He felt a tremendous thirst, but with even the thought of water, his throat jerked and twisted in painful convulsions. He did his best to think of other things. He thought about the Bumfields and little Tricia. He wondered what he might find when he arrived in Sand Creek.

"AC base to AC One, you copy, Mr. Parker?" Tommy Chin's voice pierced Parker's eardrums like needles. He flinched, acknowledging the pain.

"Yeah," he panted, his voice now hoarse and low.

"I just thought you'd like to know. When I came back from the emergency room at two thirty I checked in on Jezebel."

Parker waited for Chin to continue. He felt there was going to be bad news. Jezebel wasn't just a dog to Parker. She was more human to him than most people he knew. She had been wronged. It was human greed and vengeance that had turned her world upside down.

"I was watching her sleeping, and all of a sudden she gave a deep sigh and just stopped breathing. I checked her for a pulse and couldn't feel anything. Her pupils were dilated. I put her in a body bag and dragged her out by the incinerator to be cremated tomorrow."

Parker hung up the microphone and turned off the radio without comment. He didn't care to hear any more. A shiver worked its way up his stiff backbone. Jezebel had died at about the same time he'd dreamed of her climbing onto the bed and laying at his feet.

Chapter 57

K eening sirens and flashing lights suddenly shocked the still night as every available law-enforcement vehicle in Sedgwick County raced toward Sand Creek, the tiny town seven miles northwest of Wichita.

Pulsing lights could be seen for miles across the flat Kansas plains. Officers were setting up roadblocks in a perimeter around the town as Tony Parker had requested. He drove down the gravel road to within sight of Sand Creek's grain elevator, illuminated by several mercury vapor lights that surrounded it.

Two highway patrol cars blocked the road ahead with one officer standing in front, resting a shotgun butt on his side. A vacant sheriff's patrol car was parked on the roadside nearby. Parker pulled up to the officer and stopped as a highway patrol helicopter droned loudly overhead.

"Are there any . . . ?" Parker paused, finding it difficult to finish.

"Looks like we're too late," the young patrolman answered, tipping his Smoky-the-Bear hat back and shaking his head. "No sign of the dogs. The dispatchers have been trying to get through to the residents by phone. There hasn't been even one to answer. Looks like they even got their mailman and a lady from the postal service who went out looking for him. Found both their cars." He glanced back toward the town. "Nothing's moving down there."

Parker felt nauseous as the officer spoke—a burning on his neck. His body ached, every joint hurting. His head and every thought inside it had been shaken up, mixed to where nothing was clear. He saw himself in the side mirror of the Jimmy as he leaned out, listening to the cop. Mucous came from his nose. His eyes were swollen and bloodshot. Now his entire body and senses numbed. His thoughts tumbled. *Rabies.... Bumfields.... Tricia.... Dawg.... Death.... Blood.... Death.... Rabies....*

He screamed, beating the steering wheel and the dash hard in a tantrum, "Damn, damn, damn!"

The officer looked shocked, holding out his hand as if trying to stop a speeding car.

"Hey, hey, easy now! You okay?" the officer asked.

Parker answered with a sort of growl.

"Jeez, man, control yourself. Now, if you'll back your truck up and park over there to the side." The officer pointed to the side of the road, still giving an amazed look.

Parker slammed the truck into reverse, then floored the accelerator. The tires roared and threw gravel on the officer. Parker backed up into the shallow ditch, then jammed the shifter into first gear and the Jimmy bolted out, and he pulled it to the side. He sat in the truck, squeezing the steering wheel, trying to understand the hurt in his head as several more law-enforcement vehicles drove past.

Parker popped the glove compartment open and pulled out Jack's gun. The pain intensified. Dull throbbing all over his body. A feverish burning. Joints grating and aching. His neck was stiffening, and he held his head cocked to one side. He looked at himself in the rearview mirror and yanked the bandage from his neck, exposing a large, dark red, pus-filled sore.

Parker raked in a deep breath and stepped out of the truck, then wiped the snot from his top lip with the shoulder of his short-sleeved shirt. He held his forearm up to block the numerous vehicles' blinding lights that irritated and burned deep into his eyes. Moving in unstable, stiff steps, he approached the crowd of a dozen or more law-enforcement officers and stopped beside the sheriff.

A tall, lanky man in his fifties with a belt that hung low on his hips turned to him. He wore a brown cowboy hat and a sheriff's badge.

"You Parker?" Sheriff Warren asked around his cigar.

Parker gave a slow nod.

"The chopper pilot says there's a pack of dogs, gathering on the other end of town and heading this way."

Parker looked at him through half-open eyes. His nose was beginning to run again, eyes watering, saliva rolling down his chin, lips parted showing the tip of his tongue.

The sheriff looked him over carefully, his gaze pausing at the pistol in his right hand.

"You okay, son?" he asked, looking back up into Parker's eyes. He squinted and leaned forward, seeing the large infected sore on his neck. "Damn, what happened to you?"

"Rabid skunk," Parker said in a gruff whisper.

The tall lawman continued eyeing him carefully.

"Sheriff, here they come!" one of the officers called out. Sheriff Warren looked over the cars toward the tiny town, glancing back once to Parker.

"All right, everybody, get behind the vehicles. And no noise! We don't want to scare 'em," Sheriff Warren commanded, throwing his cigar to the dirt.

Parker snickered. "Scare 'em," he mocked with a crooked sort of intoxicated smile.

The sheriff leaned against the front fender of the car in front of him. "Do not, I repeat, do not fire until I tell you to."

Parker moved to a clear gap between vehicles. He could see the pack of angry dogs coming up the road with Dawg in the lead. Parker stood, stooped at the shoulders, and checked the revolver's cylinder for bullets. There were two left.

A tingling heat consumed him suddenly. He looked down the road and then at the numerous officers, their guns pointed at the large group of shadows moving in their direction. He couldn't remember why he was there. It didn't make sense. The pain overwhelmed him, and convulsions erupted throughout his body, nearly sending him to his knees. He looked down the road again and saw the dogs. They were trusting, innocent creatures, betrayed and corrupted by human greed and self-pity. Over a dozen guns were trained at them.

Parker flicked the cylinder shut and spun it, then pointed it at the back of the head of an officer standing behind him. He pulled the trigger and the hammer snapped an empty chamber. One cop, who had just trotted up, heard it and looked to him. Parker pulled the trigger again. Another snap.

"Damn, what the hell are you doing?" the newcomer exclaimed.

"Screw you!" Parker barked out, now pointing the gun at the new officer. Again, he fingered the trigger. Another vacant chamber.

By now the Sheriff and several other officers turned to him and watched as he squeezed the trigger for the fourth time. Yet another snap.

"Shit!" Sheriff Warren yelled. "Grab the son-of-a-bitch!"

Parker raised the gun to his own temple. No more empty chambers. This would stop the pain. This would stop the killing.

CHAPTER 58

Tony Parker jerked the trigger of Jack's .357 with the muzzle pointed to his own temple.

The gun blasted as Sheriff Warren grabbed his hand. Everyone's attention turned to Parker.

It felt as though a machete had split his skull and nails had been driven into his eardrums. He felt blood roll down his nose.

Four of the officers wrestled him down to the ground, and Jack's .357 bounced on the gravel and landed in the nearby ditch.

"The dogs!" another cop yelled.

Suddenly, the vicious dogs leaped onto and over the car hoods, their flesh-ripping fangs revealed.

Several officers screamed, as the dogs' teeth punctured their skin.

The dogs answered with furious growls.

Pistols and shotguns discharged with loud explosions.

The dogs attacked savagely but were no match for the many guns. Fangs tore into flesh, and blood spurted from arteries and flowed from terrible red gashes. Guns fired from close range—many at point blank.

Several dogs attacked the officers holding Parker down, and he struggled free. He shook his head, smeared the blood across his face with his hand as he stood just out of the melee.

In and out, back and forth, the pain and his thoughts teetered.

He saw Dawg on top of the sheriff, ripping into his forearm. He remembered now what these terrible beasts had done.

Parker gave a guttural roar and grabbed the dog by the throat, lifting him off of the sheriff. Several other dogs saw the struggle and came to Dawg's rescue. Parker threw Dawg to the gravel and fell on top of him, again grabbing his throat and squeezing. Dawg's rescuers leaped onto Parker's back, rolling him off.

The officers slowly gained control of the situation. They finally silenced all of the dogs except for the five Parker battled. The cops gathered around with guns pointed.

"Hold your fire," Sheriff Warren yelled. "We don't want to hit Parker."

"The hell with that, Sheriff!" the officer Parker had pulled the trigger on shouted back. Didn't you see him? He was trying to kill me."

"I said, hold your fire! The boy's got rabies. He can't help it."

All the officers stared at the battle. The dogs ripped and tore at every part of Parker's body, but he still stood, knocking them left and right as they attacked.

Parker gave another roar.

"Don't just stand there, boys, get in there and help him out," the sheriff commanded.

There was no response as they watched.

"Well, shit, then!" Sheriff Warren said and stepped into the battle, pulling the dogs back and flinging them away.

The officers opened fire as their targets were slung off and away from the sheriff and Parker.

Parker still struggled with Dawg as the last of the attackers were killed. He finally got a good grip on the dog's head and twisted hard.

Dawg's vertebrae answered with a definite crack, and the large dog's body went limp.

Parker dropped the dead carcass to the road.

"You okay, Parker?" Warren asked as he shuffled to him, arms reaching.

Parker returned the gesture by leaping at the sheriff, knocking him to the ground, hard. He bit, tearing into the side of his neck.

"Ah, help!" the sheriff screamed.

Parker pulled back, taking a chunk of flesh from the sheriff's throat. He scampered to his feet and dashed between the cars blocking the road, leaving the sheriff with his hand pressed to his life-leaking throat.

"Shoot the son-of-a-bitch!" Sheriff Warren ordered, "What in God's name are you waiting for?"

Parker ran down the road, then ducked into a hedgerow on the side and out into the rain-soaked field toward Sand Creek.

The officers seemed too stunned to react immediately but soon ran after him.

After the first few steps, Parker lost his shoes as the rich black mud sucked them from his feet. He stayed close to the hedgerow, hoping it would provide at least some cover. Then, after fifty yards, the guns reported.

Bullets snapped by his head, some snipping off limbs. The officers were bogged down with their own mud-balled shoes. He had a good head start, but he knew they'd be on him soon.

After two hundred yards, the hedgerow ended, and Parker ran out and into the yard of the first house. He recognized the Bumfield's place ahead and ran to the front door.

It was unlocked, and he swung it wildly, then rushed into the front hall. A body caught his foot, and he stumbled to one knee and hand. There was no way of knowing for sure that it was Mrs. Bumfield's, but the shredded, bloody white blouse and ripped blue jeans clued him. The dogs had been savage. He stood and stepped over her body, then staggered into the living room.

Light from the streetlight outside left shadows in the room. In the dull glow, there was another body. Mr. Bumfield lay on his back near the kitchen doorway, his arm stretched out toward a gun rack on the wall.

Parker felt painful convulsions as he looked over the horror. His throat, his chest. It felt like a monster raved inside, trying to get out, like one of Nick's "ill-a-jitmut aliens" about to rip through his body. He couldn't control his saliva, and it drooled from his mouth.

He looked around the room with his hand clenched tightly on the front of his shirt, reacting to the pain in his chest. Behind him was the large tapestry. The dogs playing poker. Having a party. Having a good time.

Parker growled out, grabbing it by one side, and tore it from the tacks holding it to the wall. He threw it, picture first, over Mr. Bumfield's body and stared down at it.

What about the Bumfield's granddaughter, the cute little girl staying with them? Where was she? Could she have survived?

"Tricia!" Parker called, his voice now very hoarse as he ran frantically through the house, "Tricia!"

She wasn't downstairs. He looked at the stairway, then bounded up the steps. A doll lay at the top, and he picked it up slowly. It was familiar. It was the same doll Tricia had carried with her when he had been there before. It's head hung by a small piece of cloth. White cotton stuffing pushed out, and it felt wet and sticky from slobber and blood. Parker looked down at the doll as if it were the ravaged little girl. He moved its little arms gently and tried to put its head back into place.

"Tricia. Tricia," he said softly in a gravelly low tone as clear mucus flowed from his nostrils, tears streamed down his face and saliva frothed from his lips and dripped onto the doll.

He screamed out a deep guttural yell and yanked the doll's head from its body. His arms stretched out with its body in one hand and head in the other as he stood, reaching, looking to the ceiling. To heaven. To God.

The twisting convulsions inside his torso grew stronger. His lungs and heart were tying in knots inside his chest, and he cringed down into a ball. He coughed painfully.

A noise.

Parker stilled himself, no longer paying attention to the hurt. A whimpering came from down the hall. He stood slowly, but his neck and shoulders were too painful to straighten, and he moved in a stooped position toward the sound. It came from a bedroom at the end of the hall. He stumbled. His feet were lead weights as he stomped each clumsy step, the pieces of doll still gripped tightly in his hands.

The demon, rabies, was in him, now, trying to gain control. But he would not submit, not until he had done all he could.

He stopped at the door and saw that the bottom panel had been ripped apart as if attacked by a lunatic with a chainsaw. He opened the door and flipped the light switch. His bloodshot eyes shifted about the room, his lips parted, tongue protruding slightly, and saliva still dripping down the front of his shirt. He saw nothing that could be making the noise.

The whimpering started again. It came from the closet. The door was torn open, just as the first, with countless, deep groves in the wood. The dogs had gotten in there also. Parker stomped slowly to the door, wondering what he would find inside. Was it Tricia making the noise or an injured dog? If it was Tricia, would she look like Jack had in his last moments, life flowing from her in crimson streams? He turned the doorknob with the doll body hanging in the same hand.

CHAPTER 59

The light from the room swept the dark closet as the door opened.

Tricia's scream was like the frantic squeal of a rabbit being butchered. Parker thought of how repulsive his face must look. She huddled defensively against the back of the closet with her knees up to her cheeks and jabbed toward him with a blood-covered wire coat hanger in her injured right hand, breathing from her open mouth, jaw trembling. Her red and white gingham dress was shredded on one side and blood spotted her ankle-length white socks and white canvas sneakers.

Parker knelt. "Tricia," he said in his gruff, low voice as he reached for her.

She looked at the outstretched hands and her ripped apart doll, then looked up to Parker's eyes.

She squinted. The fear drained from her face, leaving it blank and emotionless. It looked as though she recognized a good friend dressed in a hideous Halloween costume. Her lips quivered into a familiar tight grin. She dropped her weapon and shot up and grabbed Parker around the neck, hugging him firmly. "I knew you'd come, I knew it!" she cried.

Parker dropped the doll and walked out of the room with her, holding her just as tightly. He walked down the steps and, taking care to shield her from the bloody scene in the living room, out the front door.

An ambulance pulled up across the road and another approached along with several highway patrol and sheriff's patrol cars, all with lights flashing. Parker walked swiftly. It seemed the monster trying to control him had been temporarily tranquilized by the relief he felt when finding Tricia. But he knew it would return soon. This time, the rabies would not release him. It had just been playing with him like a cat toying with a mouse. The last episode was so overpowering, so traumatic. The next time, he would not be able to fight it. He knew he would succumb. But there was still one thing he must do, one last thing he had to find out before he gave in to the raving disease inside.

"It's all right, now," Parker tried to assure Tricia as he handed her to the young man and woman attendants running up to meet them. They helped by prying her arms from around his neck, and the young woman took his place with her arms wrapped around the girl. "You'll be okay," he said.

A familiar sound came from behind. Parker stood still and listened, then looked up into the tree in the Bumfield's front yard. The tree was shadowed in stripes by its own limbs from the many bright lights of the gathering vehicles.

He heard the cry for help again, a faint mewing, then spotted the little gray kitten, looking down from a large branch.

"Someone take care of the kitten," he shouted in his gravelly voice to the EMTs, pointing with bent finger into the tree.

The officers were pulling up now, and they'd be after him. He had to escape. Parker ran behind the Bumfield's house, then around their neighbor's backyard fence and behind the hedge trees. He ran along the row and past the sheriff's car, still parked in the same spot on the road. Sheriff Warren leaned with his back against his patrol car, his hand still pressed to his neck. Two officers assisted him as an ambulance pulled up nearby, and an attendant rushed over. They couldn't see Parker in the darkness, and he passed by with only the trees separating them.

A highway-patrol chopper suddenly roared overhead, its search-light beam wagging along the ground. Parker hunkered down against a hedge tree, avoiding its brightness, and something caught his eye in the ditch just six feet away. It was Jack's gun. He crawled out quickly, snatched it up and ran up to the road to where his truck was parked. He slipped in quietly, easing the door shut.

With all the yelling and other noise, no one heard or noticed Parker's truck engine start. He drove slowly, with lights off. When he made it to the intersection an eighth of a mile down, he could speed away. Parker watched in the rearview mirror as he crept along. After only a few yards, the sheriff looked up and waved his free arm.

"There he goes! There he goes, get him," he ordered. Several officers appeared from the darkness, some ran to their cars, others ran down the road after Parker's truck with firearms drawn.

Parker put his foot in it and his truck fishtailed as he accelerated. But within a hundred feet from the intersection, he began to feel faint and suddenly blacked out, succumbing to the demon inside. His face smacked into the steering wheel. The truck slipped into the muddy ditch but swerved halfway out and stopped, perpendicular to the road.

Parker came to as the windshield shattered. Bullets struck the truck as the officers found their target. Cracks, snaps, and zips filled the air as the bullets flew around and through the truck. A bullet struck the rearview mirror, and it fell from the fractured windshield and into his lap. Another bullet glanced off the windshield wiper and ricocheted across Parker's left shoulder, laying his shirt open and leaving a bloody line three inches long.

Parker cranked the steering wheel and floored the accelerator. The truck swerved away, tires throwing gravel violently as he sped for safety.

The pain was back full force. The end was very near, and the tremendous hurt and confusion made him want to give in; after all, death was inevitable. Still, there was one thing he must do.

CHAPTER 60

The phone was a scream of terror, and Julie woke, startled, in Nick's small bed. She slipped out, taking care not to disturb the kids, and ran to the phone in the master bedroom. She caught it after the third ring and looked at the clock radio beside the waterbed. It was five thirty-five a.m.

"Hello."

"Is this Mrs. Parker?" the voice asked.

"Yes, who's this?" Julie asked, knowing the call would be concerning Tony.

"This is Tyrone, down at the dispatcher's office, Mrs. Parker. Sorry to bother you in the middle of the night."

"That's all right, Tyrone, what's wrong? Is it Tony?" Julie remembered Tony had talked to Tyrone just before leaving.

"Well, yes. So he must not be there, huh?"

"No, Tyrone. I haven't seen him since he left after talking to you."

"Everyone's looking for him. There's some people with anxious trigger fingers, too."

"What happened?"

"They claim that he's got—rabies."

Julie bit her knuckle. She knew it had to be true. It made sense. That was why he'd been acting so strangely. It was that skunk bite.

"According to the sheriff's office, he attacked several officers and drove away in his truck. You wouldn't happen to know where he is, or where he would go, would you?"

Julie thought a minute. Tyrone was silent.

"Maybe. Maybe, I do," she said.

"Where?"

"I don't think I should say. Tell everyone to back off. I'll bring Tony into the hospital, but everyone has to back off!"

"Okay, Mrs. Parker, but be careful. In the state they say he's in, he may not recognize you."

Julie hung up and slipped into some jeans and a shirt. She gathered up the kids and loaded them into the minivan without waking them. There was no place to take them at this hour. Surely, he wouldn't be violent. He would recognize his own children.

* * *

Only a handful of stars still sparkled above the riverbank, yet to be extinguished by the orange dome birthing on the eastern horizon.

A dark, filthy figure rested on its haunches among the spirea bushes, mulberry trees and sapling cottonwoods beneath the forty-four foot copper sculpture of an Indian. It was a human form, a man, or at least resembled what once had been. He breathed from his mouth, heavy and labored. His half-open eyes blinked, wincing from an occasional dewdrop that found its way through the thick branches. Clear, syrup-like mucus oozed from his nostrils down the whisker stubble of his top lip. His tongue, swollen and thick, stuck out past his lips. Saliva foamed from the corners of his mouth, then dripped in strings down his ragged blue shirt. His clothes were ripped and stained as if tie-died in dark crimson. A plastic badge hung from a torn piece of his shirt. It was scratched, chipped and spotted with blood. *T. PARKER*, it read in large white letters engraved on a black background.

The pitiful figure clenched his teeth hard. It felt as though his skull was cracking open, exploding as it throbbed. A large demonic rat nested inside. Its name was rabies. It raked its sharp, thin teeth across the tissue of his brain. With each gouging bite, he winced. The rabies monster tortured him—the disease, the demon. It would eat away at his brain until he would have none left. He would have no more thoughts. His skull would be empty, except for the rabies.

The pain subsided, leaving only a tingling numbness. He tried to remember what had taken place, but it made his brain throb with the intensity of a gong. Was it a dream, or was the terrible carnage that flashed through his mind real? Was he a murderer?

A boy played in his memory, a boy that called him daddy. With the boy was a woman with high cheekbones and a big smile. She held a baby with golden curls and large, happy, blue eyes.

The hurt returned, spears piercing his entire body. He drew his head to his chest, held his eyes closed tight and coughed out a pain-ridden groan.

Now, he remembered blood and ribbons of flesh—the woman's throat exploding with blood, flesh ripped away. Now, the boy's. And now, the baby's.

The pain subsided again, and his mind went blank. He opened his eyes part way and sat for a moment in a lethargic stupor. He focused on his bloodstained clothes. His mind reactivated, but he knew the pain would return soon. He saw the injury on his wrist: the deep punctures and torn skin. It meant nothing, as if it weren't a part of him. He picked at the wound with clumsy fingers, dried blood packed under his nails, until finally pulling away a four-inch strip of his own flesh. He raised it to his mouth. Blood raced into the gap left in his forearm and dripped to the ground, but no pain ensued. With his tongue too swollen to allow enough room, he soon fingered the unlikely morsel from his mouth.

The blood. He remembered blood, a lot of blood. Bodies soaking in it: men, women and children. Was he responsible?

The torture struck again, racking him.

There had been guns. He remembered pulling the trigger. Shooting. Policemen screaming in pain. Bullets snapping by his ears. An old Indian man, smiling. A round Indian woman. "Tony, oh Tony," she'd said, smiling wide. Now he remembered her severed head in his lap. It was a dream. *It must be!*

His mind blanked, and he fell back into the numbness. A few seconds passed, and his eyes focused once again. He stared down at his groin. He had an erection. The monster, rabies, did this. This was only one of the things it did when it took over a man's body. He pushed it down with his fingers, and it throbbed back in unimaginable pain.

An involuntary scream pushed out from his constricting throat, and his face wrenched with hurt.

He remembered a woman, young and beautiful. Blonde hair. Firm body. He had taken her. He had grabbed her breasts and bitten into her tender skin. She'd screamed. He remembered her lying before him, bloody, flesh ripped.

He groaned in response to the memory, then brought his fist down twice to the offending member in his blue jeans.

The expected pain didn't come, only numbness.

Shuffling came from the dirt path along the riverbank. It was a muffled, irritating noise echoing inside his head. Someone was out there. Were they looking for him? Had they come to hurt him?

T. Parker watched through heavy eyelids. A man stumbled and staggered—a drunken man, a wino. He wore a dirty red stocking cap and had a scraggly beard. The wino stopped and looked out at the river while fumbling with something in front of him. A tinkling, leaking, water-being-poured noise came. The annoying sound clawed at T. Parker's brain. He held his palms over his ears, pushing hard, but it did no good. The noise intensified inside his head. It seemed to go on and on. Would it ever end?

He could take no more. He rose to his feet, body throbbing, every joint stiff and aching. *This irritating noise causes my pain!*

T. Parker edged toward the drunkard, and the man turned, eyes widening.

"No! No, please, my God, no!" the wino pleaded.

Parker leaped.

He grabbed the man by his open fly and shirt collar, raised him without pause above his head as urine streamed down his arm, then screamed out in a hideous laugh.

"No, please, don't kill me," the drunk begged once again. "I ain't got no money. I ain't got nothin'!"

He didn't consider the man's plea. The words were only meaningless, abrasive sounds. He thought of how he had done this before; how he had raised a body over his head, then brought it down across his knee, breaking its backbone.

He looked out over the river, and it distracted him. The water bothered and frightened him. His throat convulsed. The pain was razor blades, honing out his neck. His thirst became unbearable and demanding, but he knew he couldn't drink. It would be impossible to swallow, torturous to try.

He brought the man down to his head, then heaved him at the river, the horrible, pain-inducing water.

"*Glaaau-hau-hauuu!*" he howled in a wild, raging keen as the wino splashed into the water and began swimming the seventy-five yards to the opposite bank.

T. Parker quickly turned away. He stood stooped over, panting hard and raspy. A noise mingled with the wino's splashes, and he stiffened, considering it.

Hurried footsteps on the sidewalk above the riverbank.

More people were coming. He must hide. He turned and ran, stiff legged, back to his haven in the clump of small trees and bushes.

He sat, trying to quiet his heaving body. The pain impaled him again, and he wanted to scream. He had to remember. It was the only way to make sense of this. He had to remember quickly, before the monster inside his head gained complete control—before they discovered and killed him—or he killed again.

He thought of a black man, tall and well built. The memory caused a warmth in the center of his chest, and tears pooled in his eyes, yet he recalled fighting with the man, fists flying as they rolled on the ground.

"Stupid, bastard nigger!" he barked out in distorted words as the pain shot through his brain.

He could remember the black man's face, filled with terror as he'd pleaded for his life.

"Stupid, bastard—*Jack*!" He beat his temples with the heels of his hands while tears streamed down his dirt-caked cheeks.

Now, he remembered the black man lying in front of him, blood oozing.

"Jack," he repeated, sounding as if his mouth were full of sand. "No, Jack. Sorry, Jack."

T. Parker continued beating his head in answer to every excruciating throb. Little time remained. Soon he would be unable to think. Soon he would be overcome. He had to fight it. He couldn't give up. The rabies would win as it always does, but he had to fight. The memories offended and threatened it. What had happened? What had he done?

He remembered being bitten on the neck, and he raised his hand to feel of it. The wound was older than the others, swollen and scabbed. He picked at it until the scab lifted, leaving a dime-sized hole deep into his neck that welled up with liquid.

Now, he remembered holding a doll in his hands, its bloodstained cloth body torn in two. "Raggedy A-yun," a little girl's squeaky voice had said. "Raggedy A-yun, A-yun, A-yun," it echoed in his skull.

Another man flashed through his memory. He was terribly disfigured. He wore a black patch over one eye. He blew a silver whistle.

The thought of it made T. Parker's ears ring. It rang louder and louder until it blared like a siren, a train whistle blasting in his ears. He cringed and beat his temples then shook his head to stop the terrible noise, but it did no good. The siren only became louder.

There had been dogs. Dogs everywhere. They had bitten at him and attacked others, tearing at their bodies, ripping flesh.

The ringing—louder.

He recalled one dog in particular. He had breathed life into its mouth. He had pumped life into its heart. The thing had stood huge and black. Tremendous fangs—*Jezebel!*

* * *

Julie drove the short six blocks down to the Mid-America All-Indian Center by the river and parked in the parking lot. She could see the top of the *Keeper of the Plains* statue over a hundred yards behind the building.

If Tony were to go anywhere besides home, it would probably be here, especially with Doc and Jack dead. Years ago when they all had more time, they used to picnic by the statue. Tony used to meet Doc there on an occasional Sunday afternoon to talk, fish and relax. They mostly talked. Tony and Doc talked a lot together. After all, Doc had been like a father to him after Tony's own father died. He was sure to be missing Doc, and this is where he would come if there was still a Tony left.

If Tony did have rabies, Julie knew it was a death sentence. He would die, and it would be soon. She began crying. She was frightened and worried. She couldn't lose Tony, she just couldn't. He was such a good husband and wonderful father. She knew this thing with Sarah was just a passing thing and whatever happened must have been magnified, if not brought on, by the rabies. It wasn't his fault. Sure, he had flaws, and they were numerous, but still, he was a good and caring man.

Julie sat with her window down, debating how to approach him if he was out there.

A roar, a kind of yell came from the river. A splash. Someone had fallen in. It might be Tony. He could be drowning. Julie sprang from the minivan and slammed the door shut behind her, not considering it might wake the kids. She ran down the concrete path around the building and toward the *Keeper of the Plains*.

Julie slowed as she approached the statue and looked out onto the river. She saw a man splashing frantically as he swam toward the opposite bank. It wasn't Tony. She wondered why this man would be swimming, and so insanely, in the middle of the night. He must have been frightened.

Julie looked around warily. She looked at the bushes that lined the riverbank. Nothing moved. She was alone. The sidewalk led to the statue and ended, then a small path led down the bush-filled, sloped banks eight feet to the river. No one there.

Julie walked past the statue, slowly scanning the area, tears rolling down her cheeks. She stumbled down the narrow trail. He wasn't there. She'd lost him. She might never see him alive again.

"Daddy, what are you doing in there? Are you playing monsters again? Silly Daddy!"

It was Nick's voice, behind her. Julie spun around, heart pounding. Nick reached into the bushes. He pulled out a hand, dirty and bloody. Something came out and stood up slowly.

Nick grinned at Julie, and she gaped back at him. This thing that came out and was now holding Nick's hand was *not* Tony. It was only an empty shell. There was no life in the almost closed eyes. She looked at it closely, preparing to run to it and take Nick away. Its blank face was filthy with dirt and blood, streaked from tears and mucus and drool. It breathed with a labored whistle, and slobber frothed up around its lips as each breath blew out more sudsy saliva. Its clothes were torn, and its exposed flesh was injured with bloody gashes and punctures.

Then, she recognized pieces of the uniform shirt. The injury on the thing's wrist where Yankee had bitten deep. The sore on its neck, now swollen a great deal more, red and weeping.

"Tony?" Julie called softly.

Nick led him to Julie. There was no response on Tony's face. The only movement was his slow, short steps. The terrible disease had taken him. It had taken her beloved husband, hollowed the soul out of his body, leaving the pathetic thing she saw before her.

"Oh, no, Tony!" she cried out as she ran the short distance to him and hugged him. "Tony, please come back to me. Oh, God, please!"

"It's okay, Mommy. Daddy's just playing monsters," Nick explained. "Now, you be a good daddy and quit playing monsters. If you're good, when we get home, we'll play your favorite game, *Dweebs, Geeks, and Weirdoooos*," he said with a chuckle.

CHAPTER 61

Julie sat at Tony's bedside in intensive care for four long days. His condition was grave, and they expected him to die at anytime. Only the monitors on the machines maintaining his life showed any signs of it, but even those were weak. A nurse came in as Julie sat holding his hand, staring out the window.

"Mrs. Parker, there's a lady downstairs in the cafeteria waiting to see you," the young nurse announced. "She said she has your children."

"Oh, yes, that would be Sadie. She's been taking care of the kids," Julie said, standing up. "Please call me if—there's any change, won't you? I won't be gone more than twenty or thirty minutes. I just wouldn't forgive myself if he would, uh—go and I wouldn't be here."

"Sure, Mrs. Parker. We'll let you know," the nurse said and left the room.

Julie turned and looked down at Tony, still holding his hand. His face was clean and shaven now. Too clean. Hospital clean and chalky white. A tube came from his mouth and two from his nose, all taped to his face. An IV needle protruded from one arm, and various leads were strung to his body. The heart monitor on the other side of the bed showed a very weak and slow pulse as the respirator beside it emitted a low, steady hum and gave a sort of suction-pump noise every other second.

"You hold on now, you hear me?" she said softly.

She looked down at his pale body. It was near time; she sensed it.

"Don't you leave without me here to say goodbye."

She stared for a moment longer, holding his hand and forearm.

"Damn it, Tony!" she suddenly blurted out and grabbed him by the top of his hospital gown, putting her face to within inches of his. "Don't you dare leave me! I love you! I need you! You—you—shithead!"

Julie turned quickly and ran out of the room, past astonished ICU nurses and to the elevators.

--*

Julie had left too soon to see Tony's finger begin to twitch. Then his hand. His arm moved, and his eyelids rolled back.

He gasped a deep breath as if it were his very first.

One of the nurses just outside the room saw him move and yelled to a doctor, then rushed in. Parker pulled the tubes out of his face and attempted to sit up in bed.

The nurse gently pushed him back down. "Everything's all right. Settle down. You've been through a terrible trauma, Mr. Parker. Please try to calm yourself."

The doctor stood in the doorway, his white coat open wide, glasses on his shiny, bare forehead. "My God, he's going to make it!" he exclaimed.

"Water—drink," Parker said in a raspy whisper, his throat dry and raw.

The nurse hustled to the adjoining restroom and poured half a cup and returned it to his bedside.

Parker gulped the water down with the nurse's assistance.

"Ah, what—happened?" Parker asked in gasps, laying his head back on the pillow.

"Nurse, would you leave us for a moment, please?" the doctor said to the smiling nurse.

The nurse left without a word, and the doctor closed the door behind her. He checked the monitors on the equipment surrounding Parker's bed and then bent down and began to give him the once over with a stethoscope.

"My name is Doctor Osgood, Tony. You've given us all quite a scare. But—it looks like you've made it out of danger," he said, standing up straight as he glanced back at the strong pulses on the heart monitor. He looked back down at Parker with a wide smile, then sat down in a chair next to the bed.

"What happened—the rabies?" Parker asked, "Julie, the kids?"

"Your family's fine, Tony. As for you, to tell you the honest to God's truth, I don't know what happened."

Parker looked at him puzzled.

"Well, you see, I'm not one hundred percent sure what your paralysis and comatose state were caused by."

Parker frowned and shook his head.

"Yeah, I know, the symptoms. Tony, I've been reading up on rabies over the last four days since you came to us. I've learned a lot. One thing I've learned is that rabies is very unpredictable. I'm not saying that you, positively, didn't have rabies. It's just that our tests show very little, if any, signs of it. Of course, with a disease like rabies, that doesn't mean much. You probably know more about what I'm going to tell you than I do, but I'll say it anyway since it's the reasoning for my diagnosis.

"First of all, from what I've read in the newspaper and from talking with your wife, you've been through some terrific, unimaginable stress and trauma, both emotional and physical, lately. Is that not true?"

Parker nodded, his eyes rolling and blinking.

"Well, your life really started getting complicated after the skunk bite, did it not?"

Parker nodded again.

"The terrible killings, the feelings of guilt, possibly some sexual tension, arguments with your wife, the probability of losing your job, then losing so many of your very good friends. Your numerous injuries—huh, we gave you so many stitches—I quit counting after three hundred."

Parker closed his eyes and held them tight. The memories came rushing back, all the pain and anguish, crowding back into his brain.

"You questioned yourself if you had been properly inoculated. You were concerned that you hadn't, yet before you had a chance to check, you seemed to start showing symptoms, which meant that you were certain to die. But before you did, you felt it paramount that you avenge your friends' deaths and stop the senseless slaughter that you thought you were somehow responsible for."

Doctor Osgood stood up and walked to the end of the bed. He pulled off a clipboard that hung there and sat back down in the chair. He flipped the first page up and began reading.

"Rabies virus not isolated in patient. Negligible rabies neutralizing antibody titers found. No other viral or bacterial agents found." Doctor Osgood quit reading but continued looking at the clipboard. "You know, in hundreds of thousands of reported cases of human rabies, there has only been one survivor—a young boy in Ohio, I think."

The doctor looked back at Parker. "I discovered something interesting about human rabies during my research that even you may not have known. Since man is the only animal that can realize he may have the disease and thus dread its symptoms, he is the only animal that may actually start showing symptoms before the virus actually takes hold, in some cases within twenty-four hours after being bitten by a rabid animal. I believe the phenomena is sometimes referred to as *faux rabies*."

"But, Doctor...."

"Now, don't think that what I'm saying is that you were not in serious condition and in grave danger of losing your life. Oh no, not at all. The trauma your mind put you through was every bit as deadly as the rabies virus. I'm guessing you were very near a nervous breakdown, and you actually may have had one, exhibiting itself in the form of what you may have dreaded most—rabies symptoms. You'd seen them many times before in animals, isn't that true?"

Parker nodded.

"That is why I was so surprised to see that you pulled through. Your physical condition was very weak, let alone your psychological condition."

Parker looked at the doctor, still skeptical.

"You need rest. I'll be back in an hour or so to check on you again, and we can talk some more if you like. In the meantime, I'll have the nurse change your sheets and make you more comfortable. Oh, and don't worry. My conclusions can't be substantiated or, for that matter, disproved, now. Because of that and the possible embarrassment you might experience, and since we have no definite evidence that it was or wasn't rabies, I'm calling it *probable*," he said smiling. He turned away and walked to the door. "By the way, you might feel comforted to know that Sheriff Warren is recovering fine down on the second floor. He should go home today."

Parker vaguely remembered his uncontrollable rage, biting into the sheriff's throat, and he frowned.

"Do me a favor," Parker said hoarsely. "Don't say anything—to him about me—not having rabies. Might not be—too understanding."

The doctor chuckled and left the room.

*_*_*

Julie had a nice visit with Nick and Audrey and with Sadie and the girls. She had lost track of time, concerned more about how Nick would deal with being without his dad. She told all of them she would come home soon, possibly even today. It made Nick happy, too young to understand what it would mean. Sadie had given her hand a knowing pat. She'd read between the lines. Tony would soon die.

Julie was anxious to get back to the ICU. She glanced at her watch as the elevator crept slowly to the fourth floor. She'd been away from the room for almost forty-five minutes. The elevator seemed to take longer than ever before. It was as slow as a funeral procession.

When the doors opened, she stepped quickly toward Tony's room. She saw activity inside, through the open doorway, and didn't understand it. A nurse she didn't recognize had just finished changing the bed.

Julie watched from outside the door. Tony wasn't there. She looked at the number on the door to make sure it was the right room, the same one she had lived in for the past four days. Surely, she had the correct floor. Yes, it was the right room, but Tony was gone.

The nurse said, "I'll be right back." She turned and smiled at Julie as she walked past. Julie stood in the door, looking, thinking.

"Tony?" she called softly to the empty room.

He was gone. They'd taken him out. The life-sustaining machines were unplugged. The room waited for its next victim. Tony was dead.

Julie didn't feel sorrow as much as anger now. She'd known Tony was about to die. She had waited beside him for four days, waiting for death to come. But it *had* come, and no one told her about it. No one came down or called the cafeteria to let her know. They had deprived her the opportunity of whispering last words into his ear. She had not been able to say goodbye, to say I love you one last time.

Julie spun around to the nurses' desk with teeth clenched, but before she had a chance to release the anger, she heard a sound, a whisper.

"Julie? Julie, that you?"

Julie turned back to the vacant room. She almost expected to see some sort of divine image, an apparition.

"Joo-lee?"

She heard the whisper again and frowned, still looking around the small room. It was Tony's voice. He spoke to her from the afterlife. His spirit communicated to her from heaven.

She stepped cautiously into the room, goose bumps raising on her arms.

"Damn it—Julie," the whisper was much louder this time, "Will—you—answer me?"

Something crashed behind her. She turned quickly and looked at the closed door to the toilet. She reached for the doorknob and pulled the door open. An IV stand fell out into the room.

"Well—don't just—stand there. Help me—out," Tony puffed, looking up from the toilet. "Some fool—left the damn—seat up!"

She'd never seen anyone stuck in a toilet before, although she'd come close a couple of times, herself. It seemed to be his just dessert.

"Oh—oh, Tony," Julie said, laughing and crying at the same time with both hands over her mouth.

He motioned her in with one hand as he struggled and she hurried in and pulled him up.

"Thought I—was going to be stuck—there all day. Was too damn—embarrassed to call for—nurse," he said, obviously not seeing any humor in the situation. He gazed at her, leaning frailly against her. "Guess you—finally got even."

Julie looked back into his eyes. It was Tony. He was back. Tears poured down her face. "Tony, you're alive. You're alive!" Julie said, crying loudly.

"Easy, honey. Easy," Tony said back. "Not like I was—going to drown."

CHAPTER 62

It had been over two months since the *Days of the Dog*. As Tony Parker drove the old white minivan home late one Saturday afternoon, the last day of October, Led Zeppelin's *Black Dog* came on the radio. He tapped his finger on the steering wheel and gave a half grin while reflecting on the many changes brought on by that terrible week in August. The sun beamed bright on the warm, clear fall afternoon that was windy, as usual. The breeze kicked up trash, dried leaves and other debris and swirled them in cavorting dances, celebrating life on such a lovely day.

Parker had just left the Dillons grocery store with a bag of groceries after taking in some target practice at the Wichita Police Department's pistol range. He kept Jack's old .357 within easy reach at all times, now. He didn't like having it, but he felt he might need it someday. He wasn't sure that there would be any more trouble—not for sure.

He'd been on medical leave since coming home and would be until he resigned as animal control director within the next month. Soon, he would be back in school for the spring semester to get his DVM degree.

Doc and Patsy had willed their entire estate to Parker, and he had planned to resume Doc's old practice and specialize in large animals after graduation, but things had changed. He had been having that strange feeling of being watched again. It started when he was told Truong's son had arrived a week after Truong's death to claim the body and to take it back to Vietnam. He'd assumed that all of Truong's children had been killed during the war. Evidently not.

The nightmares had returned. He'd been waking up in the middle of the night, his heart slamming inside his chest, but was unable to remember what he'd been dreaming.

He had decided to take one of his old instructors up on an offer she'd given him. After graduation, he would work at the Manhattan, Kansas Veterinary School second in charge of rabies research—after all, he was well versed on the subject.

The Parkers planned to move to Manhattan in December. From there, Julie would have a short ten-mile drive to one of the Junction City elementary schools where she'd be teaching the spring semester. Now, she was attending classes at Wichita State University in preparation. Julie didn't leave the house anymore without a can of mace. She had talked Tony into buying her a dependable car, a new Ford Escort, and she was happy.

Parker pulled up to a stoplight alongside a red Mercedes-Benz. It reminded him of Sylvia Taylor. He grinned, thinking of her. She had forgotten about suing him and sued her husband for divorce, instead, when she found out his time in Topeka was spent more in the client's secretary's briefs than with the client's.

So many changes for so many people. Parker thought of some of the others who were truly affected by the *Dog Days*.

MacGreggor's nephew had been $445,000 richer for a full twenty-four hours after being given his uncle's money. Not trusting anyone, even the local banks, he put the money in a handbag when it was turned over to him. During a two-hour layover in Denver on his flight to Las Vegas, he was mugged in the men's room, and the money was yet to be recovered. The IRS saw the episode as a little too convenient, thinking it was a scam to avoid paying thousands of dollars in taxes due and was investigating him for income tax evasion and fraud. Parker gave a crooked smile. He didn't care much for the jerk anyway.

There had been three others who got their comeuppances, also. He thought of them as the light turned green and he proceeded through the intersection.

Roary Rapids' band split up after the incident at the Epic Center, and his father had all but disowned him. He now worked at a record and tape store in an eastside shopping mall.

Henry Haskins was fired from Channel Two News. He recovered from his injuries, the most serious of which were a couple of puncture wounds on his right forearm that, according to the doctor who attended him, looked more like they were from a woman's high-heel pumps than a basset hound's teeth. He moved down to Ft. Worth and got a job as a DJ on a small country-and-western radio station.

Lt. Hardessy hadn't been as lucky. The Dobermans had ripped off the better part of his nose and torn into his left arm and right leg so badly that he'd never have full use of them again. After extensive therapy, though, he hoped to fill a spot as a county dispatcher on the swing shift, and Tyrone wasn't too thrilled.

For a long while, it looked as though it would take an act of God for Pastor Santini to recover. He did. But the throat wound left a terrible scar. He had become a sort of local celebrity due to the attack and the days following he'd spent hanging onto life in the hospital. The number of his flock grew enormously from the ensuing publicity, and well-wishers came to his room by the dozens. "Pastor Carl's Sunday Mission" now broadcast with his sermons on Channel Two every Sunday morning. For him, it was a prayer come true. He now wore his keys on a chain around his neck.

Tommy Chin had made out all right. He was filling in as acting Sedgwick County animal-control director and was expected to be assigned the position permanently after Parker resigned. But Chin had been pretty busy lately, the city manager insisting on tough enforcement of the city's leash law, and Alvarez constantly on his ass whenever a rabies test came back positive. The skunks had been real bad lately.

Parker's eyes welled up as he thought of Jack. He missed his longtime confidant. He missed Sadie and the kids, too. They moved to Oklahoma City in September to be near Sadie's folks so they could help with the kids. Just before moving, she found out she was pregnant—due in mid-May. Sadie was sure it would be a boy. The girls looked forward to little Jack Junior's arrival.

Parker took in a long breath and sighed. *Sarah.* She found a job with the San Diego Zoo and moved to California after recovering from her injuries. The last Parker knew from a post card she'd sent, she owned a white Persian cat and dated the zoo's director. He chuckled.

Tricia Carpenter seemed to have recovered fairly well from the trauma she'd been through. She and her kitten now lived with her mother in Colorado Springs and had been calling Parker every two weeks to tell him about pre-school and her new home. She'd renamed the cat Tony. Her mother repaired Raggedy *A-yun* as best she could, and Tricia was yet to be seen without it.

The kids were fine. Julie and Tony were having a hard time keeping Nick in shoes. It seemed like he either wore out or grew out of a pair a month. Audrey was getting bigger and stronger and even cuter every day. Her golden curls and big blue eyes made it hard to be upset with her even after she ransacked the house on one of her toddler rampages.

Yankee and all of the other dogs were back to their old selves again after some intensive deprogramming. All the other dogs, that is, except Jezebel.

Jezebel hadn't eaten or drank anything the night she was tranquilized. They contributed death to a heart attack, probably brought on by a combination of the tranquilizer, excitement, exhaustion, and lack of food and water. Only Parker knew it was more than that. Jezebel had died of a grief-shattered heart.

Parker slowed down as he passed a little old lady walking a large Irish setter. He thought of how wonderful it was for the old woman to have a companion like that. A loyal friend that would be by her side and could always be trusted.

Driving farther, he saw several children out in their Halloween costumes. They were mostly younger kids, too young to be out by themselves at night, and darkness would soon throw its ebony veil over the city.

Jezebel was apparently the costume of choice this year. After all, she had been such a terrible monster. It seemed one out of every three trick-or-treaters were dressed in black and wore a black dog mask, either homemade or whipped out by a local entrepreneur trying to take advantage of the opportunity to make a buck.

Parker thought back on the panic. There had been at least a hundred different incidents rumored involving Jezebel during those terrible days of August. She was the devil's own dog, appearing at night in the shadows behind bushes and between cars. There were several stories of people waking in the middle of the night to see the phantom-like hound staring at them in the darkness. She seemed to just materialize inside bedrooms, waking sweat-drenched sleepers from their own nightmares.

Few people knew the real story—that Jezebel was an innocent victim. Parker had tried to tell it, but no one wanted to hear. The tabloids had a field day. According to them, Jezebel was the dog from Hell that ripped its own master's throat open and killed dozens of people. She was the night-stalking demon that gobbled down small children in just a few large gulps. Her true master, Truong, was one of Satan's disciples, half dog himself, who had recruited other dogs to help in his diabolical plan of vengeance on the American people.

Not a soul seemed to understand that every living thing has a demon locked up inside. Some of them are small and let out only on occasion. Others have been fed by years of hurt and turmoil and have grown to enormous proportions. These demons, when allowed to roam free, cause horrific suffering. Truong's demon was vengeance, and it was gigantic. A terrible war had released it, although much less could have turned its jailer's key. It had hideous, seeping, pus-filled wounds that reeked with the putrid smell of overwhelming pain and suffering, and it licked them often in self-pity. It longed to heal its wounds, but the only sure poultice was revenge. Only by causing pain and suffering such as Truong had felt, to bring a war to the home of his unwary prey, could the demon inside Truong make the world understand his terrible distress and hurt.

Parker squinted as he drove, seeing something run behind a clump of lilac bushes near the next intersection a block down. It was large and black and moved gracefully as if floating. Surely, it was only a child wearing a black witch's costume or perhaps one of the Jezebel ones. But Parker seemed to be drawn toward it as he slowed and turned the corner to follow.

Again he saw the black apparition as it ducked around the next corner and out of sight. It moved quickly, very quickly. Perhaps it was just a child, but could a child run that fast?

Parker was surprised to see the neighborhood he had suddenly ended up in. He pulled to the curb and sat for a moment, staring out across the street.

The old MacGreggor house had been condemned, and its windows and doors were boarded. Tall weeds of various types had taken control of the yard, and even more paint had peeled from the lap siding, exposing the old gray wood underneath. It made a heavy, lonely feeling in Tony Parker's chest.

Mrs. Crane stood in her front yard, trimming her hedges. He couldn't resist going over to see how the old girl was getting along. After all, she was all by herself, now.

"Hi, Mrs. Crane. How have you been?" Parker asked, stepping onto the curb.

"Hello. Oh, Mr. Parker, I didn't recognize you," she apologized. "Won't you come in and have a cup of coffee?" She pulled off her white cotton gloves and laid them and the pruning shears on the porch.

"No, thank you, Mrs. Crane. I was just passing by and thought I'd say hello."

"Well, I'm so glad you did."

"How have you been getting along?"

"Just fine. I just try to stay busy. You know." She nodded to the bushes she had been trimming meticulously, and Parker acknowledged her with an understanding smile.

As if a magnet pulled their eyes, both looked to the MacGreggor house.

Mrs. Crane drew a deep breath and sighed. She looked as if she was about to tell him something she wouldn't tell anyone else. A secret she could only trust with him.

"I still put bowls of food and water out for her," she said, gazing at the old house. "I know it's silly, but I do it anyway. Some mornings, when I go out to check it, it'll be gone, all ate and drank up. Probably one of the neighbors' dogs or some stray cats."

She smiled at Parker and crossed her arms in front of her chest as if she felt a chill. Parker felt it, too.

The smile left her face. "I know it's my imagination, but sometimes around midnight when I can't sleep, and I'm lyin' in bed— well, that old north wind whips through the neighborhood and between the houses—and I hear it howl. Sounds kind of like Jezebel. I know it's just the wind whistling, blowing between the boards covering that broken window, but still, I get a funny feeling about it. You know?"

Parker looked at Mrs. Crane, then back at the house. "Yeah, I know."

"Now, you don't worry none about this old woman, Mr. Parker. I'll be fine, just fine."

Parker took the wallet out of his back pocket and pulled out two twenties and a ten. "Here. I'd like to help with the dog food. Keep putting it out, okay?"

Mrs. Crane took the money from Parker's hand and stuffed it into her apron. She nodded and gave a misty smile.

Parker turned and walked back toward the minivan. That strange and familiar feeling came over him again as he stepped into the street. Someone, *something*, was watching him.

He looked back at the house, at each of the windows and at the front door. For a brief moment, he thought he could hear whining—small yelps, like puppies perhaps. He knew it must be his imagination. But, when he glanced at Mrs. Crane, he saw a knowing sort of smile on her face.

The wind blew between the houses, and the torn page from a newspaper tumbled out. It danced on the ground, then bounced over to Parker and wrapped around his ankle.

He pulled it off. It was old and yellow, torn and dirty. *Old* news. Two months *old.* "*JEZEBEL IS DEAD!*" it seemed to remind him in big, bold letters.

The wind passed through the reed-like boards over the broken window. "*Vvv-foo-au-ooooh!*"

Parker and Mrs. Crane stared at the house. It was just the wind, he knew that and was sure she did, too. Jezebel *was* dead. Heart attack. Tommy Chin said it. She had quit breathing, he was sure. Her body was incinerated at the animal-control shelter that morning, two months ago. Her body and the other dogs' that had been put to sleep were all incinerated.

Scenes flashed inside Parker's head. He started remembering things he hadn't before. Were they memories of real events or of dreams? He couldn't tell.

He remembered leaving Sand Creek after the terrible carnage. He remembered driving recklessly. Had he driven to the animal-control shelter? He remembered running in through the back-bay door. Plastic body bags filled with dead animals were stacked on the floor near the incinerator, left there to be burned that morning. He remembered opening the largest one. He'd cupped his hands over the muzzle of a huge, black Great Dane. He'd breathed into its mouth. He'd pushed on its chest.

That's where the memories ended. There were no more. It must have been a dream, a dream he'd had when he was in ICU at the hospital. It must have been.

Parker turned and got into his minivan. He examined the house as he edged away from the curb.

A flash of light, a reflection.

The sun's light shone on something inside the house, and it sparkled from the darkness, shooting out light from between the boards and through the tear in the front window shade like a laser.

Tony Parker felt a burning in his neck as he drove away.

Your thoughts and comments are welcome.

You may contact the author at *www.jezebelthenovel.com*
by fax at 1-800-567-6797 or by mail at P.O. Box 1101, Newton, Kansas
67114

Thanks,

Gordon A. Kessler